The Penalty

"Yesterday," said Drum, "a white man took a woman of the Hunkpapa."

Lucia screamed and turned to run, but his hands were on her. She struggled as he threw her to the back of her horse. She was held on the animal's back by the two braves who had not mounted.

Numbly, she felt Drum tearing off her high shoes. She must not be able to slip from them. Then his hands were at her legs, pulling off her long cotton stockings. He shoved up her dress and petticoats. They must not interfere with her being fastened to the horse. Using one of the cotton stockings, Drum twisted it and bound her ankles under the horse's belly. He bound her wrists together in front of her.

Lucia knew that her body, though innocent, had been selected to pay for the crime that had been committed against one of his people. Drum had decided that the penalty was hers to pay. *He would make her pay it, dearly, a thousand times over.*

GHOST DANCE

John Norman

DAW BOOKS, INC.

DONALD A. WOLLHEIM, PUBLISHER

1633 Broadway
New York, N.Y. 10019

For Gilbert and Katherine Taylor,
who know and love
a hard land.

FIRST DAW PRINTING, NOVEMBER 1979

1 2 3 4 5 6 7 8 9

DAW TRADEMARK REGISTERED
U.S. PAT. OFF. MARCA
REGISTRADA. HECHO EN U.S.A.

PRINTED IN U.S.A.

GHOST
DANCE

Chapter One

Old Bear rode alone.

Not moving his hands on the nose rope of his pony he let the animal take his own pace, biting at the grass when it would, not hurrying.

He rode the north bank of the Grand River, keeping with it as it wound its muddy trail through the dried grass and brush of Standing Rock.

It was right that Old Bear should ride alone, for his ride, his quest, was holy, and its meaning lay between himself and Wakan-Tonka, the Mystery. And it was right that he should ride this Sunday morning, as he did each Sunday morning, for this was the medicine day of the white man, and Wakan-Tonka had favored the white man and on this day his ear might be open, did he care to listen any longer to the medicine song of one of his forgotten children.

Old Bear did not see well these days and the clouds of the blue sky blurred into a mist that was like the roiling of the blizzard when it is first seen over the prairie, and even the grasses seemed far away and vague and the cottonwoods by the banks of the Grand River with their slick leaves glistened like glass and beads in the sun.

He sang to himself, his medicine song, as he rode.

Perhaps today would be the day when he would find the sign of the white buffalo.

Last night, as was his custom, Old Bear had left his daughter, a girl by the name of Winona, his wooden cabin, his handful of chickens, and his cow, and had gone on foot to the tiny wickiup he had prepared on Medicine Ridge, which place overlooks the Grand River.

In the wickiup, the entrance to which faced east, he put away his bandana, his broad-brimmed hat, his cotton shirt and his denim trousers. He drew on a breechclout, deerskin leggings and moccasins. Then he put on his buckskin shirt,

5

stiff with grease, old, and cracked, from which he had never cut the hair with which it was fringed, not even when the white man in the black dress had told him to do so.

He built a small fire, took a coal from this fire, and lit his pipe, lifted it to the gods and winds, and smoked and smoked and let the fire die more than once, and in this time he ate nothing but prayed a great deal, and at last, being an old man, fell asleep over the ashes of his fire.

Old Bear was Hunkpapa Sioux.

Nothing could change that, not the Departments of the Dakota and the Platte, nor the Indian Office itself, which lay at the ends of the wires and rails, in the land where the soldiers came from.

Old Bear had been one of Sitting Bull's White Horse Riders, and in the year the white man called 1876, for they could not remember years without counting them like pigs or sheep that look alike, he had taken third coup against Long Hair himself, who killed women and children, greatest of the Long Knives. We killed them all, had said Sitting Bull, but there will be more, like the grass and the birds, always more.

Old Bear had ridden with Sitting Bull north to Canada, and, five hungry years later, had surrendered with him. He could remember the house on the water that smoked and the guards and the long trip to the stone lodges, where his woman had died. Crazy Horse had died rather than go to such a place, and Old Bear had sometimes nodded to himself and wondered if the Oglala had not been right.

In time Sitting Bull, and Old Bear, and the others were released and sent to Standing Rock, where they would learn planting, harvesting and citizenship, where they must forget the buffalo, the unfenced prairies and the medicines of their fathers.

In those days Old Bear was War Bear, but one night Old Bear had had a dream, and he had awakened in the wooden cabin in his blanket, and had known that he was no longer War Bear. In the morning he had told his daughter, Winona, and she had nodded her head.

So Old Bear fasted in the wickiup on Medicine Ridge, nodding and sleeping, dreaming of a hundred fires, faces and wars. Of the brave They-Fear-Even-His-Horses and Rain-in-the-Face, whose medicine was strong. Of the beauty of the Paha Sapa, where the white men killed one another to find pebbles in the streams. Of the Great Councils and the Sun

Dances, and always of the brown rivers of buffalo, humped and shambling, pawing the ground, shaking the earth so that even a pony might lose its footing, making the ground so tremble with gladness that a man might feel it from the soles of his moccasins to the scalp on the back of his neck.

One could still read the old trails by the bones.

Perhaps, Old Bear sometimes told himself, the white buffalo will come back, and the medicine of the Hunkpapa will be good again.

Perhaps someday, he thought, I shall find the sign of the white buffalo.

With the first light across the brown prairie Old Bear had awakened in the wickiup.

It was now Sunday morning.

He rekindled the fire, and put stones on the flames. When the stones were hot he poured water over them and stripped, rubbing the sweat and steam into his body. Then he took some grease from an elkhorn container and rubbed himself, making the worn flesh glisten. When his body was smooth and smelled good to him, he drew three white lines across his face and drew on his clothing, his Indian clothing.

He came out of the wickiup bearing his faded buffalo-hide shield. In his hair, for it was his right, he wore an eagle feather. His quiver was on his back and his right hand was gripped on his bow.

The Hunkpapa girl waiting outside the wickiup was his daughter, Winona, who being thin was not beautiful for a Sioux girl, but her face was gentle, the eyes sharp and clear, and the hands, in two or three years, would be large and strong. She wore beaded moccasins but her dress was calico. Her hair, in two braids, was bound with tiny cotton strings.

She held the nose rope of Old Bear's pony.

Old Bear looked on Winona, not with much emotion. It was true she was not beautiful.

He wondered why it was that the young men had come to his cabin bringing horses and rifles.

One had brought three horses, for he was a rich Indian. Old Bear could remember when the pony herds of the Hunkpapa were so huge that you could tell their presence from miles away, because of the clouds of blackbirds come to feed on the grasshoppers stirred by their hoofs.

When I was young, said Old Bear to himself, I would not have brought horses for such a girl.

He did not speak to her for this was the day of medicine, but he nodded his head twice.

He reached for the nose rope of the pony and Winona, not touching him, placed it in his hand.

Across the pony's shoulders, as she did every Sunday morning, Winona had drawn blue jagged lines, for the flash of lightning, which would be good medicine for the swiftness of the pony; and a red circle on the animal's right forequarter, which recalled a wound that Old Bear's pony, one that had died long ago, had received when War Bear and two braves had driven a party of Crows away from the hunting ground near Wounded Knee Creek.

It was not the best medicine that Winona had done this, for she was a woman, but Old Bear's eyes were weak now, and his hand shook. It was better in the eyes of Wakan-Tonka that the marks should be well made, than that they should be poorly made and the pony and its rider needlessly endangered. Old Bear had known of a warrior who had made paint medicine badly and his pony had been insulted and had failed him, and the warrior had died. And once a man had told a lie and his medicine shield for that reason did not turn the bullet from the rifle of a marauding Crow, being ashamed that it should be borne by one who spoke with a double tongue.

Old Bear fastened his hand in the mane of the pony and, with Winona's help, mounted, sitting straight but frail on the animal's back.

Winona was careful in helping him not to touch the shield, for a woman must not touch a warrior's shield.

Old Bear uttered a cry, kicking his heels into the pony's flanks, and rode down the slope of Medicine Ridge toward the Grand River.

Winona watched him ride down to the river, the blue calico of her dress swept in the wind that moved across the top of Medicine Ridge.

Then she turned and retraced her steps to the cabin.

And so it was that Old Bear, a gaunt and withered brave of the Hunkpapa, with an eagle feather in his hair, rode alone along the north bank of the Grand River, on the Standing Rock Indian Reservation.

He had ridden in this fashion many Sunday mornings, looking for the sign of the white buffalo.

But he felt that this morning—this medicine day—was different. When he had touched his shield he had felt that. The medicine in the shield had told him that this was not a morning like other mornings.

Perhaps this would be the morning in which he would find the sign of the white buffalo.

Slowly, along the muddy bank of the Grand River, Old Bear rode until the sun was overhead, to his dim eyes a storm of fire in the sky, and the shadow of himself and his mount was a small dark cloud under his pony's belly.

He was about to turn back when he heard something moving in the brush across the river.

Old Bear strained his eyes to make out what it might be that moved in the brush across that pocketed, muddy belt of water and sand that was the Grand River.

If it were a patrol of Long Knives from Fort Yates, it would not be good to be caught in the forbidden paint. Old Bear was not afraid for his body, but his spirit was afraid, for if they saw that he was old, they might laugh at him, and this would be hard for him.

One time no Long Knife would have laughed.

Perhaps it was only a young Indian and his woman wrestling in the bushes, or a young antelope come down to dip its black nose to the muddy water, with its quick, delicate tongue daintily slaking its thirst.

Then Old Bear's eyes saw the blurred image of a rider on a paint horse.

"Hou Kola!" cried a strong voice, from across the river, carrying the accent of one of the western dialects. Then the figure moved toward him.

It was a man on a paint horse, splashing across the river. Twice the rider cried out, urging his horse through the sluggish, turbid water.

Old Bear strained his eyes, the better to make out the figure on horseback. The horse had stepped from the water, dripping and shaking its head.

"Hou," said the man, an Indian, who now on horseback approached Old Bear. He had lifted his right hand which was open and bore no weapon.

"Hou," said Old Bear, who also lifted his weapon hand, empty.

Old Bear grunted in surprise.

The man, like Old Bear, was dressed in the full regalia of a Plains warrior. Four eagle feathers, tied together, dangled from his left braid over his left shoulder; he wore buckskin, and a colored vest wrought with dyed porcupine quills; about his neck was a necklace of puma claws. He carried a lance, some nine feet long, and worked with blue and white beads. It was tipped with a long point of bluish, chipped stone and tailed with the wing feather of a hawk. His buffalo-hide shield carried the design of a coming moon, and his face was painted with radiating yellow lines, proclaiming the beginning of a new day.

This is no simple warrior, said Old Bear, looking on the paint. This is a medicine man.

Most surprising to Old Bear was that the man was so much younger than he, not young as a boy is young, but much younger than Old Bear—and yet, though so young, this man did not look as though he had ever tugged at the wheel of a wagon, as if he had ever touched the handle of a plow or thrown seed to domestic fowl.

Old Bear wondered if the young man were from the spirit world, come to guide him over the 'trail of stars.

No.

There was a rifle across his saddle. It would fire seven times, metal cartridges, before reloading.

There would be no white man's weapons in the spirit world.

The saddle was made of wood, and Old Bear had not seen one like it in many years. The pommel rose more than a foot above the horse's mane. The design, though Old Bear did not know this, might have been traced to Spanish saddles of more than three centuries before, used by conquistadores who had come to seek cities of gold and had lost their lives and horses.

Old Bear looked into the eyes of the man. They were as sharp and black as the hawk's, as keen as the eagle's. My eyes were once so, said Old Bear to himself. And the man's head was held high, like one who rides over land that he owns, and his back was straight and proud. Yes, said Old Bear to himself, so young men used to ride, so did I too ride.

"I am Old Bear," said Old Bear, "of the Hunkpapa."

The younger man looked at him, and his eyes blazed between the bars of yellow paint on his face, blazed as though with victory. "It is good," he said in his strong, young voice. "Good!" He looked proudly on the old Hunkpapa. "It is a strong sign," he said, "for I am Kicking Bear—Kicking Bear of the Minneconjou from the Cheyenne River."

"I am looking for the white buffalo," said Old Bear, feeling that somehow he could tell this to the young man, and that he would understand.

Kicking Bear looked for a long time at the old man on the painted pony who sat across from him. Kicking Bear did not smile or laugh. Then he said, "The buffalo are coming back."

Old Bear said nothing, but sat unmoving on his pony's back, his heart pounding.

"The buffalo are dead," said Old Bear. He whispered this.

"The buffalo are coming back," said Kicking Bear, suddenly laughing and raising his shield and lance with a joyous upward movement of his arms. He repeated, even shouted happily, "The buffalo—are coming back!"

"They are dead," said Old Bear, his hands clutched suddenly in the mane of his pony.

Kicking Bear reached forth gently and touched the old man's arm, then grasped it. Old Bear could feel the strong grip on his frail arm, feel the tightness and the stirring tremble of those locked brown fingers on his old arm. "The buffalo are coming back," said Kicking Bear.

Then Kicking Bear released the old man's arm and laughed again, as a young warrior used to laugh, as if going to claim his bride or in showing scalps to his father, and saying nothing more, Kicking Bear turned the nose rope of his pony and rode away from Old Bear, beginning to sing a medicine song.

For a long time after Kicking Bear rode away, Old Bear sat still on his pony. He still felt the fingers of the young man tight on his arm, and still heard his words. Were the buffalo coming back? What did the young man mean? One should not lie—and most of all not lie about such things, not about the dead, or the buffalo.

Not far from the hoofs of his pony, lying in the sage by the river, Old Bear saw the white shards of a buffalo skull, broken, lying near a patch of cactus.

The buffalo were dead.

But the young man had said they were coming back.

And one should not lie of such matters.

On the back of his pony Old Bear, in spite of the fiery sun overhead, shivered, trembled, and the pony, startled, shifted his footing.

Old Bear's eyes stung with tears.

Had it been a vision?

Could it be that even now Old Bear had died, and was riding with ghosts in the spirit land?

But he looked about himself, at the slow, muddy river, at the brush and sage, the sand, the cottonwoods along the banks. At the cactus, and the shattered fragments of the skull of a buffalo that lay near it.

No, said Old Bear, I am not in the spirit land.

But perhaps the young man had come from the spirit land, in spite of the rifle, come to tell him about the buffalo? Old Bear looked after the distant figure, who had ridden away singing medicine as it had not been sung for twenty years.

And the young man was riding toward the camp of Sitting Bull. This was also the camp of Old Bear.

Old Bear turned his pony to ride after the young man, to question him, to find out what he had meant. This was, after all, Sunday, and was a medicine day, and who knew what could happen on such a day, or who the strange warrior might be, or from where he might have come.

And this morning when he had touched his shield, Old Bear had known that today was not as other days, that this day was different.

With a sudden cry Old Bear kicked his pony into a sudden gallop, racing after the figure in the distance.

Forgetting the white buffalo.

Chapter Two

With one long, yellow, thick nail, Lester Grawson picked his teeth, leaning back abainst the cane seat of the luxury passenger car, watching the thousands of gaslights in the great city of New York loom like candles in the black night, over the shining rails as the train entered the yards.

"No," he growled, moving his sleeve so that it would not be touched by the black porter with his handbroom.

The porter turned to the occupants of the seat across the aisle. "Station in five minutes," he said. "Station in five minutes."

Suh, thought Grawson to himself.

Grawson folded the greasy napkin on his lap around the chicken bones and wedged it between the cane seat and the side of the car. He spit on his fingers and pulled on the red mustache that hung over his lips, wiping the grease from the hair. He dried his fingers on his trousers and peered out at the gaslights.

Good, thought Grawson, good, I'm here, and Edward Chance is here.

The train's whistle came through the thin glass of the single window.

Sparks glowed along the roadbed scattered from the funnel-shaped smokestack on the engine.

He heard the grinding of brakes and the train began to slacken its speed, groaning and clanking the heavy couplings of the cars. Looking out the window Grawson saw briefly the white faces of two gandy dancers, watching the train come in.

Irish, thought Grawson.

Grawson was a large man, short of neck, thick of shoulder, with a square, flattish face. Large hands, red knuckles. His teeth were yellowed by tobacco. His left eye moved peculiarly at times, flinching. But it was a strong face, between a pig and a bear, a face with heavy teeth, a wide nose, eyes as flat and expressionless, as heavy and blunt, as the blade of a shovel.

Grawson looked at himself in the reflection in the window, from the small kerosene lamp above his head. He twisted the screw, extinguishing the lamp. He did not want to look at himself. He had few mannerisms, few things, unimportant things, he worried about, but one was looking into a mirror. Grawson chuckled to himself. It was foolish, he chuckled. He knew it. But he did not care to look into mirrors. He was not sure what might, someday, look back at him. Maybe it would not be him. Maybe it would be something else. His left eye flinched twice, and he squinted out at the lights.

The train was passing now between freight tracks, passing coal sheds, passing piles of ties, passing other cars, drawing into the station.

It was a hot night.

Grawson wiped a roll of sweat and dirt from the inside of his high, stiff collar. He twiddled it for a moment between his thumb and forefinger and then mashed it with his thumb into a crack in the cane seat.

It was a damn hot night.

Grawson stood up and pulled his wicker suitcase from the rack, and his coat and newspaper. He put the suitcase between his feet and the coat and newspaper on his lap.

He closed his eyes and listened to the rolling of the wheels on the steel track. Five minutes, he thought.

Yes, she had been pretty, thought Grawson.

Clare Henderson had been a damn fine figure of a woman, the bitch.

God how I loved her, said Grawson to himself.

Grawson opened his eyes and saw the couple in the seat across the way staring at him. When he scowled at them they turned away. His left eye blinked, and then he closed his eyes again.

Now the wind came across Barlow's meadow some eight miles north of Charleston, a chilly wind in that gray time of day. It had rained the night before, that five years ago.

He could make them out now, Edward Chance and someone, alighting from the carriage, making their way through the high wet grass toward him and his brother, Frank.

"He won't fire, Frank," Grawson had said.

"I know," said Frank.

In the cane seat Grawson shook as though twisted with pain and groaned.

He opened his eyes and saw that the couple across the aisle had gathered their baggage and pressed to the head of the car, joining with others. Grawson looked out. The train was in the station now, the platform crowded. Redcaps scurried here and there. Relatives, spouses stood on the cement lanes under the lights, here and there one waving and running beside the train.

Grawson closed his eyes again. There was time. There was plenty of time. He had his whole life and how long did it take to pull a trigger?

Not long, Grawson remembered.

He had watched the two men, gallant Frank and the moody Edward Chance, back to back, with their white shirts, open at the throat, the red sashes, the long-barreled single-shot weapons held before them.

Damn Clare Henderson, cursed Grawson, not opening his eyes, pressing his forehead against the cold of the window.

Chance was to die. That had been understood. What had Clare told Frank, who wanted her and her house, and her people, so bad he would kill for them? What had Chance done to her? Grawson rubbed his nose with one pawlike hand. Not a goddam thing, I'd guess, he said, but crazy Frank, he'd do anything for her. And I would too, said Grawson to himself. I would, too. Amusing, swift, graceful Frank—a rider, a sportsman, a marksman—my brother, my brother.

"He won't fire," Grawson had told Frank.

And Frank had agreed.

It was the thing to do, not to fire. That was Edward Chance's job. He could not kill the man Clare Henderson wanted. In honor he could not refuse to meet him. Had he not been engaged to Clare himself?

Chance had wanted medicine, a profession. It would mean waiting years. He had no feeling for the cotton, for the land, for the tradition.

Chance was no better than a Yankee.

So he wouldn't marry her. So he couldn't. So he had to wait. But she would not. And how would she understand him?

I wonder, mused Grawson, what she told Frank.

He could imagine her twisting that scented, lavender handkerchief, the white face, the long black hair—the wringing hands, the tears. No one would protect her. No one would stand up for her. Her fathers and brothers were dead, honorably. If they had been there Chance would have been horse-whipped.

And so Frank Grawson had begun to take target practice, walking a dozen paces, turning, waiting for the handkerchief to drop, lifting his weapon, firing a single shot at a playing card tacked to a tree now some twenty-four paces away.

Why not me? Grawson asked himself. Why not me? And Grawson's lips twisted. Him, with his face like a grizzly, his teeth, those hands like clubs!

"He won't fire," Grawson had told Frank.

"I know," Frank had said, and smiled.

Grawson had gone to Clare, had begged her. "My choice is Frank," she said.

"He won't fire!" said Grawson, sitting up on the cane seat.

"We're in the station, Sir," said the porter. The man made no move with his whisk broom.

Grawson looked out.

He reached into his pocket and took out a liberty quarter and turned it over. He looked at the eagle on the reverse, with arrows in his talons.

"Like an avenging eagle," said Grawson looking at the man, "I come like an avenging eagle with arrows in my claws."

"Sir?" asked the man.

"Here," said Grawson, holding out the quarter and dropping it into the black palm.

The man lifted the whisk broom.

"No," said Grawson. "Don't touch me." And he left the car.

He heard the quarter drop to the floor behind him, but he did not turn.

"Like an avenging eagle," muttered Grawson, bundling up the platform, carrying his coat, the newspaper under one arm, his wicker suitcase in his left hand. "With arrows," he added. "With arrows."

Edward Chance had black hair, gray eyes, a thin face, not handsome, an unhappy face. There was little noticeable, little remarkable about Edward Chance, saving perhaps that he had once shot and killed a man. Chance had a good memory, and the patience to think things out, and ambition, and something to make up for. And his craft, medicine, was more than a business with him, more than a professional skill. It was a way of healing for his own heart too, and his heart had need of its healing, for the single bullet that had torn through the heart of Frank Grawson with such swift, irreversible finality had left its second wound in the heart of Cain.

Somehow Chance had expected Lester Grawson to appear, and now, five years later, five years, long years, after Frank Grawson had fallen to his knees, his face looking more surprised than anything, the pistol dropping off his limp fingers, the splash of red on his silken shirt, his brother, the gigantic, improbable Lester Grawson, as implacable as the winter or hungry dogs, had found him.

Chance studied the man across from him, over the green felt of the pool table, in the gaming salon on the third floor of the Manhattan Athletic Club. Grawson leaned over the table, lining up his shot, and the cue moved as though on wires, cleanly, swiftly, and struck the colored, wooden sphere with a sharp click, driving it into a side pocket.

"How did you find me?" asked Chance.

Grawson was lighting a small cigar. It was his fourth in the game. He chewed them down as much as smoked them, his large jaws absently, complacently grinding and shredding the brown leaves, leaving wet, black scraps of tobacco on his chin and mustache.

Grawson looked at him and grinned.

The man's left eye flinched several times.

Chance had seen this twitching several times before in the evening. He had seen this type of thing before and wondered about it. Chronic, guessed Chance, origin obscure, a nuisance, perhaps not really aware of it. So much we don't know. So much.

Grawson reached into his wallet and pulled out a small, stained, carefully folded piece of yellowed paper. It was a clipping from the *New York Times*. Chance had seen it before. He had even had one. It was the graduation list of his class, 1889, Harvard Medical School.

"Where did you get it?" asked Chance.

Grawson smiled, and pulled a wet piece of tobacco from his chin with the nail on his right forefinger. "Washington postmark," he said.

"Clare," said Chance, not bitterly.

Clare Henderson had done well for herself. The ruined fortunes of her family had been well recouped by judicious marriage. She was now the wife of a congressman from Virginia.

Beautiful, pale, black-haired Clare.

"Most likely," said Grawson.

Chance watched the smoke from Grawson's cigar, and the massive movements of the heavy jaw.

Grawson leaned to the table again, and sent another ball gliding smoothly across the felt and into the darkness of the pocket.

Again and again he shot, not missing.

Chance admired skill. He himself had skilled hands. He admired the work of carpenters, of ironworkers, carvers, saloon painters, the men who could handle ten-horse teams, the men who could use a rifle or a handgun well, and he admired Grawson, and the game was slowly taken from him, shot by shot.

Grawson stood up.

He replaced his cue in the rack.

"You've lost," said Grawson.

Chance put his own cue back in the rack.

"You're taking me back to Charleston to stand trial?" said Chance.

Grawson's left eye trembled, and the lid flickered.

"Yes," he said.

"May I see the warrant for my arrest?" asked Chance.

"It's in the hotel," said Grawson. "The warrant is my business."

Grawson reached into his wallet again and placed a silver star on the green felt.

"This is warrant enough," said Grawson.

Chance looked at the badge, the silver detective's star, Charleston of the Sovereign State of South Carolina. Grawson replaced the star in his wallet.

"I don't mind if you make trouble," he said, smiling, dabbing the ashes from the cigar on the felt on the table, "but I would not advise it."

"I don't want any trouble," said Chance, and he had spoken truly, for he was tired and now overcome with the shock, numb with the shock of being found. And now medicine, and himself, everything was finished, everything but the ride on the train, the formalities that would satisfy justice and the last climb, thirteen steps to the scaffold.

Chance felt as he had when he had resolved to die like a gentleman, as Clare had wanted, as Frank and Lester Grawson had expected, as he himself had expected. But that was before the moment the handkerchief had fluttered to the grass, the moment before he had raised his weapon with a gesture that now seemed incomprehensible to him, a gesture that was incredibly swift and sure and that terminated with a crack of a shot and a moon of blood on the shirt of a man twenty-four paces away. It the last instant, moody Edward Chance, the gentleman, or something within him deeper than the gentleman, deeper than his training and the proprieties of his tradition, had decided that he would live. That he did not want to die, and that thusly he must, and would, kill.

He saw the body of Frank Grawson in the white silk shirt, the scarlet sash, face down in the wet grass of Barlow's meadow. He shook his head.

"You can get your coat and bag," said Grawson. "I'll wait."

Chance looked at him quickly.

"You won't run," said Grawson. "If you did, I'd find you again."

Those blunt eyes like shovels seemed to burn for a moment, With pleasure.

He would like that, thought Chance, he would like for me to run—to run once more—as I did from Charleston, after the killing, when I didn't want more, when I wanted to get away, when I had to leave, when I cried and ran because there was nothing else to do, nothing else.

"Wait here," said Chance.

"All right," said Grawson, starting to light another cigar. "Take your time."

Chance disappeared.

Grawson's hands trembled for a moment on the cigar, and then he managed to get the tiny sheet of flame to the tobacco.

Grawson walked over to the window and looked down to the corner of 45th Street and Madison Avenue, at the gas lamps and the people in the street. A cab clicked by, drawn by two horses.

So it was coming to an end, thought Grawson. Five years was a long time to wait, but I could have waited more, plenty more.

He took the badge out of his wallet and looked at it, small in the fat palm of his huge hand, and then put it back again.

His letter of resignation to the Charleston Force had been tendered the day he had received the envelope from Washington. He had taken his savings and boarded the train for New York. The death in Barlow's meadow had been a duel, in a sense self-defense. It would not be murder, at best. No formal charges had ever been filed, nor would they be. Grawson had not filed them, nor would he. His brother had had a pistol, had asked for the duel. And Clare, she would not file charges, for the scandal would be improper, and what was Frank Grawson, or indeed, Edward Chance, to her? And the state would not make charges. It was as Lester Grawson had wanted. It left him alone with Chance.

It was right, wasn't it, to kill the man who had killed your brother? Especially when the law wouldn't do it. There was a higher law wasn't there, blood-law? I am the law, thought Grawson, the law that you can't write down but you know, the law before the books, the right before there was the earth or people or animals or Adam or Abel or Cain.

Grawson looked down through the window and saw the men in the cold meadow, and saw Barlow's oak in the background, the two white shirts.

"He won't fire," Grawson had said.

And Frank had smiled and said, "I know," and didn't run from that field but stayed there, and was going to shoot a man that wouldn't fire!

Grawson pressed his forehead to the window. He blinked and all he saw below was the dark street, and the pools of light on the sidewalk, spilled by the burning lamps.

Chance made his way to the cloakroom, moving without feeling the floor, seeming to move through a dark corridor. The lamps seemed dim, the conversation of groups he passed as meaningless as the click of the cues and spheres of the room behind him.

He wondered idly if he should have spent the last years differently, and decided he should not have.

He was more now than he had been and he felt that it might have been somehow worth it, and wondered whether they used the black hood still in Charleston, and if the knot were tied so as to break the neck when one pitched to the end of the rope. Faster. More merciful. Or if it would be suffocation, twisting at the end of the rope, bound, his tongue inside the hood thrusting out of the mouth, the eyes moving from their sockets.

He hoped the knot would be thick and tied below the right ear.

He wondered if he could ask the hangman for that favor.

His coat and bag were placed on the counter before him, and pushed towards him.

He took his coat and drew it on, and lifted the bag,

heavier than a general practitioner's bag, from the weight of the pistol.

He placed a silver quarter in the shallow wooden bowl. He noticed the arrows in the claws of the eagle, and then the coin was gone.

"Good-night, Sir," he heard.

"Yes," said Chance. "Good-night."

Edward Chance, physician, returned to the gaming salon, where he was joined by a large, red-mustached man who accompanied him down the three flights of stairs until they emerged together on brick-paved Madison Avenue.

"Cigar?" asked Grawson.

"No," said Chance.

A cab clattered past, like a high black box on four wheels, the cabby sitting behind with a long whip, touching the flanks of his team.

Grawson made no move to light himself a cigar. Chance had expected that he would, and was surprised when he did not. Grawson folded his arms, holding each in the hand of the other. Chance noted that the fingers of his right hand had trembled a bit. Then Grawson was calm. Grawson unfolded his arms.

"You'll want to stop by your rooms, or whatever," said Grawson, "pick up some things—maybe settle the bill with your landlady."

"Yes," said Chance, absently. "Thank you."

Somewhere across the street a girl was laughing.

"Then," said Grawson, "we'll stop by the hotel for my things—and then go to the station."

"Tomorrow night at this time," said Chance, not really thinking about it, "I'll be in Charleston again."

Grawson said nothing. His left eye and the left side of his face moved once, uncontrollably.

"I'll hail a cab," said Chance.

"No," said Grawson. "We'll walk."

It would be a long walk, but not more than two or three miles. Chance did not care. Let that walk be as long as it could. Let it last as long as it might.

Grawson looked up and down the street, which was not crowded now, the hour being well past midnight. Yet there were couples here and there. And an occasional cab.

The left side of his face twitched again.

"This way," said Chance, turning left and crossing 45th Street.

They walked on in silence.

To Chance it seemed their footsteps were very loud.

Inadvertently he noticed that Grawson's hands moved against the sides of his trousers, wiping sweat from the palms.

"Hot," said Chance.

Grawson said nothing.

I am the law, Lester Grawson told himself, I am the law, and I do not swerve, I do not yield.

He looked at the slighter man beside him, the pale, rather homely face, the deep eyes, the shoulders that seemed somehow crushed with whatever weight it was they bore.

How could he, Grawson asked himself, have managed to fire before Frank?

Dashing, swift Frank, splendid figure on a horse, laughing, supple as a whip, booted, debonair, gallant Frank—my brother. Frank is my choice, had said Clare. I have always watched out for Frank, said Lester Grawson to himself. He was what I should have been. I loved Frank, said Grawson. I loved Frank. Grawson's fists clenched and unclenched. I love him! Grawson could feel the side of his face move. He didn't like that. His face did that sometimes. And I loved Clare, said Grawson. So I must do this. For Frank, who would have wanted it. For Clare, who wants it. For—and Grawson looked at the slender, solemn Edward Chance, young but old—and he wants it, said Grawson to himself. He wants it! He won't run. A lamb. Blood on the hoofs. This lamb who shot my brother dead. He wants it.

"Are you all right?"

The voice came from far away.

It was Chance's voice.

"It's damn hot tonight," said Grawson.

"Yes," said Chance.

They had walked for some time when Chance turned left again.

Halfway down the street, between two four-story brick buildings, Grawson saw the alley. The yellow light of a street lamp flickered like a moth's wing on the bricks.

There, said Grawson to himself, there.

Like an avenging eagle with arrows in its claws.

As they passed the alley Grawson's hands seized the collar of Chance's coat and hurled him into the darkness against the bricks, and Chance struck the wall and reeled along the wall, turning twice, kicking over a garbage can and sending a startled cat screeching down the dark corridor.

Grawson cursed at the noise.

Chance moaned, his hands going to his head, and slipped to the surface of the alley, and Grawson sent a kick into the stomach of the huddled coat slumped at his feet; then he jerked it to a sitting position and hand in its hair struck the head once against the bricks. Then again. Chance shook his head, his hands groping out.

"I am the law," whispered Grawson. "The law!"

Grawson's heavy hands closed on the throat of the stunned man. Chance's fingers tried to pry apart the massive hands that clutched his throat.

Chance tried to slip down, his hands grasping for a weapon, a brick, stone, piece of glass, and closed on the handle of his bag.

The light of the street lamp became only a pinpoint in surging blackness.

Chance's hand thrust into the bag and closed on the handle of the weapon.

Grawson, drunk with the kill as he might have been, heard the hammer click and felt the pressure of the steel barrel on his adam's apple.

Sweat sprang out of every pore on the large man's body and his hands released Chance's throat. Chance struggled to his feet, not moving the pistol. His eyes were wild, bewildered.

"There is no warrant for my arrest," said Chance.

Grawson held his hands out from his body, and backed away a step.

"No warrant," said Chance. "No arrest." Chance's voice was no more than a tight whisper. His neck could still feel the talons of Grawson locked on it. The hangman's noose, thought Chance. The hangman's noose. "No arrest," said Chance.

"You're under arrest for murder," said Grawson.

Chance shook his head. "No," he said. "No."

Grawson's shovel-steel eyes glowed with pleasure. "Shoot," he said.

Chance noticed that Grawson's face seemed strangely quiet. His gaze was level. The face did not move. The movement was gone.

Chance shook his head. The pistol wavered in his grasp. "I can't," he said.

Grawson's left eye suddenly jerked shut and opened and his face seemed contorted with rage.

"You're a murderer," he said. "Shoot." Grawson's fists clenched. "You killed once—you're a killer—shoot."

Chance backed away.

Grawson advanced a step.

"I can't," said Chance.

With a cry of rage, almost a berserk fury, the huge body of Lester Grawson lunged at Chance, those great hands opened like the clawed paws of the grizzly he was, but Chance shoved the barrel of the pistol sharply, deeply into the diaphragm of the lunging figure, and Grawson doubled up in agony, his hands moving out to clutch at nothing. With the butt of the pistol Chance struck Grawson across the back of the neck, and then, carefully, holding the dazed man by the collar, he struck the man again, a dangerous blow, but with a physician's skill, not to open nor injure the skull, and the body of Lester Grawson lay on the stones of the alley.

Chance stood over the man, his own head a terrifying whirl of images. Chance stood over the man, scared. He held the muzzle of the pistol to the back of the man's neck, where the bullet would sever the vertebrae, but he did not fire, he could not, nor did he want to.

Once before he had stood thus, on a field north of Charleston, and had known that he would run, and that somehow he would never escape.

Once again his hand moved, and his finger touched the trigger, but gently, and the weapon did not fire.

Chance replaced the weapon in his bag, and turned away.

Grawson would come after him.

Once before he had run.

His choice seemed to him, standing in the alley, that hot night in a New York summer, to kill or to flee, and he had known what he would do.

He looked down at Grawson. "Why did you want me to kill you?" he asked. But the mute form lay like a mound under its coat, inert on the bricks of the alley. Chance bent down and felt the man's pulse. Grawson was strong.

Chance stood up again. "I am not a killer," he told himself. And he said it to himself very simply, and was a little surprised, and found that he had no reason to disbelieve it. And for the first time in five years, Edward Chance, though he was ready to run, and would, stood as straight as a man can.

He saw a milk cart trundling by down the street, looking yellow in the light of the street lamp.

He turned away and walked down the alley.

It was Sunday morning.

Three hours later, Edward Chance, unshaven, hungry, his coat torn, a bit of blood matted in his hair on the left side of his head, crouched in the straw in the corner of a boxcar of the New York Central Railroad and watched New York slide past the open wooden door.

He heard church bells.

He knew little more than the fact that the train was heading west.

What does it matter, he thought. What does it matter?

Chapter Three

One month had passed since the Sunday morning when Kicking Bear had first come to Standing Rock, the same morning that Edward Chance, a physician of New York City, some half a continent away, had fled from an ex-lawman of South Carolina, a man named Lester Grawson who pursued him in connection with the killing of Frank Grawson, his brother.

Lucia Turner, a slender, blue-eyed birch of a woman, her pale face flaked red by the Dakota wind, her blondish hair faded in the prairie sun, trudged from her soddy to the one-room, plank school where she would begin another day's teaching.

She carried a broom handle and swept it through the grass in front of her where she could not see her step. That way the rattler, if any should lie in her path, would strike at the stick.

At least that was what someone had said. She had forgotten who. She hoped that he was right.

There were plenty of rattlers on Standing Rock, as elsewhere on the prairie. William Buckhorn, one of her students, a Hunkpapa boy, not much taller than her broom handle, perhaps nine years old, killed them and cut the rattles off for her. She had had a coffee mug filled with them, before Aunt Zita had discovered them and thrown them out into the prairie. She had spent an hour looking for them, in case young William might wonder where they had gone, and she had recovered many. She now kept them in an empty baking-powder can behind the soddy.

Lucia paused on the top of the long, sloping hill that lay between the soddy she shared with Aunt Zita and the school.

It was desolate, the land, and the sky was huge and gray, and the wind was always blowing.

She could see the school from where she stood, the broom-stick in her hand, the sandy wind cutting her face.

Two years ago it had been painted white, but now the

paint had chipped, and the wind had pitted the walls with sand, and the sun and the rain, and the winter and the heat of the summer, had buckled and warped the wood. Rags and mud had been wedged into the cracks. On the north side, an abandoned wagon box had been leaned against the wall for extra protection. The one window, on the south, had been broken by a rock, and tar paper covered the hole.

Lucia missed Saint Louis, and the stone house that her father had built, and the calls of the young men on Sunday afternoon.

The school was cold in the winter, and it would be winter soon. The grass was already high and brown, and the wind more sharp, and the day shorter.

The squat, secondhand stove in the building, which Lucia tended herself, did not furnish much heat. There was no coal for fuel, and very little wood. Some of the boys would twist grass for her or gather cow chips. When the stove was lit it smoked, and the cow chips, predictably, smelled. Still it was better than the cold, the simple cold.

In the winter Lucia would add petticoats, wrap a blanket around her high shoes, and knees, and tie a heavy scarf over her head.

At least in the winter one didn't have to worry about the rattlesnakes.

Lucia feared snakes, dreadfully.

But she thought it kind of young William Buckhorn to think of her, and the baking-powder can filled with rattles was one of the few things that she cared for on this forsaken prairie.

Lucia, sweeping the broomstick before her, started down the hill toward the building.

Yes, she said to herself, it has seen its better days. And, she said, I am only twenty-two, and I look like I was thirty, and the prairie does that to a girl, a woman, and there are no young men here, and I am lonely, so lonely.

In what was supposed to be the play yard of the school Lucia had arranged for two swings, but the timbers from which they should have hung were as lonely as Hunkpapa burial poles. The ropes of the swings had been stolen the first night, two years ago, presumably to be applied to some more utilitarian purpose.

It was morning, a few minutes before the time to ring the bell. The children would be waiting in the draw behind the school. They would come when the bell rang. They had no wish to jeopardize their family's share in the rations, distributed every second Saturday.

There was a single teeter-totter in the play yard, but it had not been popular with the students.

It had been pointed out to Lucia by several of them that it was poorly built, for there was a leg in the middle rather than one at both ends, and of a consequence it was unstable, and perhaps dangerous.

Nonsense, had said Lucia, and had attempted to demonstrate its use, which was not easy alone.

But then she had placed two of the younger boys on the other end and had bounced up and down several times, grimly. It is fun, had said Lucia, feeling very silly. But it does not go anywhere, had said William Buckhorn. It just stays where it is.

And then he jumped up and down for her.

Just the same, he said.

And Lucia and the two boys had climbed off the teeter-totter, and, to the best of her knowledge, no one had been on it since.

But she had firmly refused to permit it, or the swing frames, to be chopped into kindling for the stove. Not even on the coldest days. Some things, Lucia had told herself, are matters of principle. Besides, under the snow, there were plenty of cow chips. But perhaps this winter? It was, after all, not of much use. No, said Lucia. Someday—someday perhaps—the children will learn to use the teeter-totter—and someday I will buy some more rope and they will learn to swing. My children will learn how to play.

Of course, as Lucia was forced to admit to herself, the children—the younger ones—could and did play, with pieces of string and sticks, and tumbleweeds, and by throwing rocks, and running after one another—but it was not the same.

There will come a time for the swings and the teeter-totter, she told herself. If we don't burn them first, she added. But we could always build others.

Lucia was not a great deal older than some of her pupils. The oldest was Joseph Running Horse, who was nineteen. The youngest was William Buckhorn, who was probably about nine. There were twenty pupils in all, crowded indiscriminately onto the same tiny benches, regardless of their age or size. There was only one girl, who was seventeen, Winona, the daughter of a subchief named Old Bear, whom Lucia had never seen.

Lucia would have liked to have had more girls in the school. She was pleased that Winona was an apt and dutiful student. It would do her good, and the boys good, that she should study with them, and show them that girls were quite as good at schoolwork as they. The Sioux had too little respect for women. Unfortunately the fact that Winona was quite as good at schoolwork as the boys had convinced some of the boys that schoolwork must be unfit for men, as must be anything a woman could do as well as a man.

Aunt Zita—God's crowbar, as Lucia called her, in her own thoughts—was a missionary, one of several whom God had appointed to illuminate the heathen with diverse and contradictory messages. It was because of Aunt Zita that Lucia had come to Standing Rock. Lucia had taught school in the East, in Saint Louis, in a large stone building with three floors and four high windows, with shades, in each classroom. Thus she was a woman of prestige at Standing Rock. The reservation needed teachers. The pay was eight dollars a month. But Lucia had had a small inheritance from her parents, and Aunt Zita had had the call. Without Lucia, Aunt Zita would not have been permitted on the reservation. The spiritual needs of the Indians were already amply supplied. But a teacher, a real teacher, that was something different.

Lucia reached the door of the schoolhouse. She leaned her broomstick against the side of the school. She took a heavy metal key from the pocket of her cotton dress and opened the door. Inside she went to her heavy oak desk and from the bottom left-hand drawer took out a wooden-handled brass school bell.

The room was cool, but Lucia decided it was too early in the year to light the stove. She glared at the stove. There would be time enough later to fight those battles.

Carrying the bell, Lucia then went outside, and stood looking down toward the draw where the children would be waiting.

She didn't want to ring the bell yet.

Aunt Zita had been the one with the call, she told herself, not me.

Aunt Zita—who would never even let the Indians inside the soddy.

Once Joseph Running Horse had been invited in by Lucia, and Aunt Zita, seizing a broom, had ordered him from the room. Afterwards, Aunt Zita had spent fifteen minutes sprinkling Sanitas into every nook and corner of the soddy. I am

interested only in his soul, had said Aunt Zita, which—thank
God—does not smell. If it did, she added, God help me, I do
not know what I should do. Lucia wondered if Joseph Running Horse truly smelled, and granted that he probably did,
though she had never noticed. She did know that she could,
upon occasion, particularly in July and August, smell Aunt
Zita, who continually wore the same, high-collared black
dress, with the long sleeves and the four blue buttons on each
cuff, and the petticoats over petticoats, sometimes as many as
five. I suppose I smell, too, thought Lucia. There isn't enough
water, or soap. To her disappointment, Joseph Running
Horse never approached the soddy again—nor did any of her
pupils—with the exception of young William Buckhorn, who,
when Aunt Zita was absent, would occasionally come to the
door, drop his head shyly and put up his hand to drop a pair
of rattles into her hand, and then she would give him a piece
of brown sugar, and he would turn and run away as fast as
he could.

Lucia lifted the school bell and swung it up and down at
arm's length.

Her pupils emerged from the draw, wearing their hats, in
their overalls and cotton shirts.

Last to emerge, following the boys, as she always did, was
slim Winona.

How lovely she is, thought Lucia.

The first one to the school was Joseph Running Horse, because he was the oldest and strongest of the students, and
thus by right their leader and first.

Joseph Running Horse—or "Little Joe" Running Horse, as
some of the horse soldiers from Fort Yates called him—was
small for his age, but his frame was supple and wiry, and his
face old beyond his nineteen years.

He, like the others, was Hunkpapa Sioux. His father had
had him baptized by a white man who had worn a black
dress and had given two handfuls of bullets and a quart of
sugar for each head on which he was permitted to pour water
while mumbling words that many white men themselves did
not understand, medicine words. This had occurred several
years ago, and the bullets had then been needed very badly,
and the squaws liked sugar.

As the pupils filed past, it occurred to Lucia that the only
religion not represented officially on the reservation, except
for some of the minor Christian organizations, was the tradi-
tional Sioux faith. Lucia smiled a heretical smile to herself

The old ways, she knew, had not been forgotten. Water on the head and two handfuls of bullets and a quart of sugar and words did not change a man's heart. The old faith was not forgotten and the tiny crosses handed out usually ended up in the skin medicine bags which hung in the cabins, or in the summer, from the poles of the skin lodges. If the medicine of the white men was strong medicine, it would do no harm to let it work too for the Sioux.

Lucia entered the school last and checked to see that all the boys had removed their hats, and then went to the front of the room, and rapped sharply on the desk with her knuckles. The gesture was, she recognized, unnecessary, for no one was not paying attention, but somehow it reassured her, making her seem more prim and teacherly, making this handful of planks on the windy prairie seem more of a school.

"Joseph Running Horse," she said, "come to the board and write your name."

This was a morning ritual for the entire class.

The first thing the Indians were to be taught was the marks for their own name. There would be papers for them to sign. After this one could teach them to read, and later to write the words they read. Finally they might be taught to do simple sums.

Lucia usually managed to avoid the geography lesson, particularly since the time the class thought she had lied to them. Probably they had never forgotten it. She had said the earth was round and that there was water in great seas on the other side of the earth. But, they had reasoned, even a white woman should know that the water would fall out if that were the case, and besides, they had listened to warriors who had ridden for more than three moons and these old warriors assured them that the earth was still flat, even so far away.

Running Horse had scrawled his name on the board, taking care not to do it too well. After his name he drew a stick figure of a galloping pony, that to let Lucia know what his name really was.

"Winona," said Lucia, "please come to the board."

The slim brown girl bashfully left the bench. She sat in the rear of the room, and none of the boys would sit close to her. She was barefoot, to save her moccasins for more important times, when the weather would be cold.

When she reached the board she dropped her head shyly.

Joseph Running Horse was still there.

"You may return to your seat, Joseph," said Lucia.

Winona drew from memory, rather than wrote, her name on the board, forming the letters of the white man as carefully as she might draw a diagram in the sand. Then she added the sign for first daughter, which in Sioux is the word Winona. Lucia had known that there were no other daughters, or sons. Winona was the only child of Old Bear, her father. Her mother had died somewhere away from the reservation.

Joseph Running Horse, who had not left the board, stood watching Winona.

He's wondering how many horses she'd cost, thought Lucia, who was promptly ashamed of herself.

Joseph Running Horse, still holding a piece of chalk, then drew a circle on the board, which included his stick figure of a galloping pony and the sign of the first daughter.

Winona's eyes flashed in anger, and she hissed a word at him in Sioux. It meant "Short Hair," or an Indian who cuts his hair to be like a white man. Her back straight, she returned in pride to her bench.

One or two of the boys in the room laughed.

Tears of shame burned in the eyes of Running Horse, the chalk snapped in his hands.

"Go to your seat, Joseph," insisted Lucia.

Running Horse turned to the board and angrily drew a head, a circle surmounted with a stick feather. Through the throat of the head he scraped a horizontal line, and added the sign of the galloping pony.

He was Indian—Sioux—he, Running Horse!

The cutthroat tribe, thought Lucia to herself, and was troubled.

"Go to your seat, Joseph," said Lucia softly.

Joseph Running Horse stood angrily for a moment, and then abruptly returned to his bench, sat down with his knees hunched up, and stared at the floor.

Outside the wind began to rise, and through the window Lucia could see the high brown grass flowing toward the south. The strip of tar paper in one corner of the window snapped as the wind tugged at it.

Winter, thought Lucia, another winter.

I won't stay, she thought.

She rapped again on the desk for attention, as if by this action to restore the small world of that single room once more to the past, to begin the morning once again.

But it would not be the same, she thought, for she realized that tomorrow either Winona or Running Horse, probably both, would not return to school, nor the day after, nor the day after. Winona was, as Lucia recognized, a woman, and Running Horse, a young man, had in his way spoken for her, and had been refused. No longer were they her children, no longer could they be her children.

Winona had said "short hair" to Joseph Running Horse, and in that instant, for the first time, really, Lucia understood the depth of that insult. How even the gentle, quiet Winona, who worked with such care and scarcely moved in class, hated the white man, how she had spat out that epithet, how stung had been Joseph Running Horse that she had said this thing to him.

How they must hate us, thought Lucia. We have taken their land, exterminated them, taught them whiskey and seeds, plows and disease.

We have taken everything, she thought, and we have given nothing.

And here she stood before them, white, to teach them to sign their names and read the words of white men, whom they hated.

For a moment Lucia wanted to touch them, to speak to them of more than letters and words, but she could not.

But she told herself that what she wanted, really wanted, more than anything, was simply to leave this place—this terrible place—as they could not. She wanted to return to a city, to Saint Louis, to a brick school, libraries and music, to leave the prairie, to see carriages again and hear the iron-rimmed wheels roll on the cobblestones, and see street lamps, and yards with grass in them, to sew on Sunday afternoons and wait for the young men to call.

I will leave, said Lucia to herself, I will leave. Aunt Zita may stay if she can, but I will leave.

Lucia was about to summon the next pupil to the board when she looked back, past the unlit stove, over the heads of the pupils, to the open door of the little frame building.

In the threshold stood Drum.

He was the son of Kills-His-Horse, now a legend among the Hunkpapa. Kills-His-Horse had taken many scalps and counted coup more than a hundred times. He had owned seventy ponies and could kill five buffalo with five arrows in the time a man's heart could beat a dozen times. Twelve years ago, in the winter, not far from the frozen Powder River,

Kills-His-Horse, attacked by a Crow war party, wounded, had cut the throat of his pony and fallen behind it, and managed to kill six of his enemies. Out of ammunition he had limped forward, knife in hand, to charge the war party. It had circled him, moving away from him as he charged, keeping him always in the center of the circle. Then he had sat crosslegged on the frozen grass in the snow and waited for them, and one of the Crows had shot him through the back of the head. Kills-His-Horse had had six sons, and five had died, two at the Little Big Horn. His remaining son, Drum, had now come into his manhood, and had not yet earned the eagle feather of the warrior, nor would he, thought Lucia, for the days of the eagle feathers are gone.

Drum regarded her and she dropped her head, unaccountably confused, blushing.

Drum must have been in his mid-twenties, and had known women, and she felt this as he looked at her, sensing his dispassionate gaze cut away the cotton of her clothing, seeing her not as a teacher, but as hated, as white, as female.

The Sioux had too little respect for women.

Lucia had been called a good woman by an old Indian once, and he had said it as he might have said good horse, or good rifle. To the Sioux the purpose of woman was clear. She was for the use of man, like his horse, his weapons, his blankets, his robes. Like the antelope and the vanished buffalo. For his use.

Foolishly the thought crossed her mind that women could now vote in Wyoming, and that in Boston they might elect members to the school board. But of course not the Indian women. Nor Indian men.

"Have you come to school?" asked Lucia, raising her head and looking directly into Drum's eyes.

Drum's eyes were shrewd, sharp, deep, unfriendly. His straight, hard lips wrinkled in a small sign of distaste.

Lucia knew that he understood little English.

"Have you come to school?" she repeated, more slowly, enunciating each word.

Winona, eyes sparkling, translated the words for Drum.

His expression did not change.

He and Lucia looked at one another over the benches. None of the boys stirred. Lucia became acutely aware of the sound of the wind outside.

His arms folded, the young Indian continued to stand motionless in the doorway, the wind from outside moving the long, rawhide-bound braids of his hair. He wore moccasins and a breechclout, leggings and an unusual buckskin shirt. It was dyed scarlet, and on the chest, in bright yellow, was the rim of a rising sun. Buckling in the shirt was a beaded belt, from which hung a long-handled steel hatchet. Lucia hadn't seen the Indians dress like that except twice a year at the dances.

"Ghost Shirt," whispered William Buckhorn to the fat, stolid-faced little boy who sat next to him, pointing to Drum's bright scarlet buckskin with its flaring rim of a morning sun.

Lucia was grateful to William Buckhorn. He had spoken in English, undoubtedly for her benefit, not for that of his companion.

She had heard of the Ghost Shirts, whose wearers could not be slain, of the Ghost Dancing, where men and women danced with Crazy Horse and Red Cloud, but they had been dead for many years.

"I'm glad you've come to school," said Lucia. "I have heard much about you, and your very brave father, of course."

Winona translated this quickly for Drum.

The smallest sign of displeasure passed over Drum's young, handsome, very cruel face.

Then, looking past Lucia, to the board, Drum saw Running Horse's circle, that line of chalk that had enclosed his name with that of Winona.

Drum looked at Winona sharply, but she shook her head in denial, her eyes wide, and then he looked at Running Horse, who dropped his head and stared at the planks of the floor.

Drum's hand slipped the long-handled hatchet from his belt and swung it far behind his shoulder and with a swift, free overhand motion, hurled the hatchet toward the board. Lucia screamed as the steelish blue blur and the whirling white handle flew past her, striking the board, shattering it and sinking deep into the wall behind it.

It had split apart the name signs of Running Horse and Winona.

In an instant Drum had retrieved the hatchet.

He seized terrified Lucia by the arm and threw her violently to the side of the room.

Lucia struck the wall with considerable force, and before, stunned, she could turn, she became aware that Drum, hatchet in hand, had followed her, and was standing behind her. Not turning, terrified, unaccountably she felt her knees giving way and she half knelt, half crouched against the wall, shrinking against it, and when she turned her head she saw Drum's hatchet lifted. Whimpering, Lucia fell to her knees and covered her head with her hands. She suddenly felt as though the top of her head were torn away as Drum's hand reached into her long blond hair and yanked her head savagely up and twisted it so that the pupils might see fear on her face.

"Teacher," said Drum, using the English word. "Teacher!"

Drum released her, and Lucia, unable to move, knelt against the wall, leaning against it, shrinking against it, her hands before her mouth.

Drum looked down on her and she shivered.

Drum laughed and turned away.

Lucia did not try to rise. She did not know if the young Indian would have permitted it. She did not feel that she could stand if she had wanted. She knew only that she was afraid, terribly afraid.

Drum was speaking to the class, swiftly, harshly in the Hunkpapa Sioux that sounded so gutteral to her ears. His eyes shone and his hands moved rapidly. He had forgotten her.

As Drum spoke, the eyes of the pupils became wide and his words were greeted with grunts of astonishment, gasps. And as he spoke, one after another of the boys left the schoolroom. Lucia could see them through the open door, running across the prairie toward various settlement districts and camps.

When Drum had finished speaking only Lucia, Winona and Joseph Running Horse were left in the room.

Drum now turned and looked again at Lucia.

Lucia's eyes met his, briefly, before she dropped her head, unable to meet his gaze, daring only to stare at the boards on which she knelt.

Never before had a man so looked upon her.

She shuddered, involuntarily, her entire body trembling under the cotton dress.

This pleased Drum.

He had looked upon her as he might have looked on a horse he might someday own, looked upon her as though he might remember her at some more auspicious hour.

Then Drum strode to the door. He paused in the threshold for an instant and wheeled to face Joseph Running Horse. "Short Hair," he said in Sioux. Joseph Running Horse did not look up, but the muscles of his face tightened like twisted cable about the bone of his jaws.

Winona pattered after Drum in her bare feet, to hold the nose rope of his pony.

Lucia numbly heard the sudden sound of pony hoofs, rapid, diminishing.

Joseph Running Horse went to the door and looked out, after Drum.

Then he turned and slowly, his leather work-shoes heavy on the planks, went to Lucia's side, and extended his hand, helping her to her feet.

Lucia arose and smoothed her dress, and with her two hands thrust the hair that had fallen across her face behind her head.

"Thank you, Joseph," she said.

"You are welcome," said Joseph Running Horse.

Lucia went to the open door of the empty school and looked out across the prairie, the brown prairie.

There was no sign of Drum, nor of Winona.

"What did he say to them?" asked Lucia.

"Much," said Joseph Running Horse, "and many things not good for you to hear—but most he came to tell us that the dancing will begin at dusk, on the banks of the river, in the camp of Sitting Bull."

"The Ghost Dance," said Lucia.

"Yes," said Joseph Running Horse.

Lucia looked out again across the prairie. "What else did he say?" she asked.

But Joseph Running Horse did not answer her.

Lucia turned to him. "Please, Joseph," she begged.

Joseph Running Horse suddenly looked at her. "You do not like Standing Rock," he said. "You do not like us."

Lucia was startled.

"You go away," he said. "You come from Saint Louis—you go back."

"I—I do like you," Lucia faltered.

Running Horse looked at her for a long time. Then he said, "It is better you go away—there is going to be trouble— much trouble here."

"I don't understand," said Lucia. She shook her head. The Indians were tamed now, broken, civilized. She had seen them, the old men in their cotton shirts, the squaws in calico. The wooden cabins, the chickens, the cattle. The Indians had been educated to the plow, taught to drive mules, just like white farmers. Keep the Sioux off horseback, she had heard, keep the devils off horseback.

"They say," said Joseph Running Horse, not looking at her, "that the buffalo are coming back."

"You surely don't believe that?" said Lucia.

"I do not know," said Joseph Running Horse. "I do not know what to believe."

"When do they say the buffalo are coming back?" asked Lucia.

"In the spring," said Joseph Running Horse, turning to face her, "—when the white people are dead."

Lucia said nothing. She felt empty and sick.

Joseph Running Horse stepped outside the school building, but he did not put on his hat.

He dropped it into the dust, and turned to leave.

"Joseph," called Lucia, "where are you going?"

The young Indian turned to face her. "To grow my hair," said Joseph Running Horse.

"No," said Lucia. "Tell me!"

"I am going to seek a vision," he said. "I must dance."

"Not you," said Lucia, "not the Ghost Dance."

"No," said Running Horse, "not the Ghost Dance."

Lucia looked puzzled.

"An old dance," said Joseph Running Horse, "a dance they do not dance any longer."

Lucia stood in the doorway of the school, not understanding Joseph Running Horse, who no longer seemed a boy to her.

"I must learn the truth," said Joseph Running Horse.

"What truth?" asked Lucia.

"About the buffalo, about the Hunkpapa—about Joseph Running Horse," he said.

Lucia said nothing.

"I will dance," said Joseph Running Horse, "until I know the truth."

Then he was gone.

Lucia stepped from the school, and called after him, but only the wind answered her.

The door of the school banged shut behind her, caught in the rising Dakota wind, and she jumped.

I'm behaving like a little girl, she thought. And how abominably I acted in the schoolroom. I shall not allow myself to be frightened again. That rude Mr. Drum must be reported to the agent.

Then she cried out with fear. "Joseph!" she cried. "Joseph, come back!"

But Joseph Running Horse had disappeared, and Lucia was alone, and the wind suddenly seemed not only swift, but cold, very cold.

Winter, she thought.

"Joseph," she called again.

But again only the wind responded.

I will dance, he had said, until I know the truth.

I will not stay another winter, said Lucia to herself, I will leave now.

Calmly she re-entered the school, arranged the benches in proper order, took the heavy metal key from the desk, and closed the desk, making sure each of the drawers was shut.

She left the school, and turned the key in the lock, and dropped it into the pocket of her dress.

She picked up Joseph Running Horse's hat from the dust where he had dropped it.

She dusted off the hat and placed it on the small bench near the door of the school.

She saw the broomstick that she had carried that morning, to sweep the grass for rattlers.

She turned and looked out over the bleak prairie, over the brown grass bending under the huge, gray sky, and looked toward the Grand River, and listened for a long time to the desolate, persistent wind.

Then not fully understanding why Lucia Turner turned and began to run, her broomstick leaning forgotten against the wall of the school, began to run stumbling and falling under the windy, gray sky of Standing Rock toward the soddy, afraid, more afraid than she had ever been in her life.

Chapter Four

Corporal Jake Totter was goddam mad.

He leaned on the bar in the one saloon in Good Promise, South Dakota, his heavy face in his stubby fingered hands, and glared into the bottom of the small, heavy glass that sat before him.

He cheated me, said Totter to himself. He had to of.

The squat glass, the inch of muddy amber fluid, the puddled rings on the mahogany bar from Chicago, all blurred and snapped back into focus with a fierce snort and shake of Totter's yellow-haired, close-cropped head.

His heavy fist, yellow hairs bristling from the vague, freckled patches, closed on the small glass, hiding it, and he chucked down the last of the drink, bourbon from the bottle's label, though what-in-hell it might really be he hadn't figured out, and didn't much care, not any more.

Totter squinted over the bar into the mirror across from him, studying his image over and among the bottles stacked against the glass. He was pretty much satisfied with what he saw. Not perfect, of course, but pretty damn good.

Totter's blunt, heavy nose had once been broken to the left and never set. His face as a whole was squarish and freckled. The eyes were gray and narrow, the mouth big and loose. Two of his tobacco-stained teeth were missing on the left side of his face. That from the same barrack-room fight that had broken his nose, and cost him his sergeant's stripes, for the third time.

Not perfect, Totter admitted, but pretty damn good. And nobody could deny he had a way with women. Nancy upstairs had admitted that.

It wasn't right that a man like him should be done wrong to.

Goddam Southerner, he was, thought Totter.

Should've beat the hell outa him.

Will beat the hell outa him, thought Totter, the living tar.

Totter wiped his mouth with his sleeve, the blue of the army jacket scratching across the unshaven face, and turned to put his back to the bar, and look to the third table to his left, about ten yards from where he stood.

He cheated me, said Totter to himself.

He had to of, he thought.

The bland, nondescript gentleman in his wide-brimmed hat, string tie and white suit, sitting at the table, dealing the cards, happened to look up about the time Totter turned to face him. The gentleman's noncommittal, smooth face read the signs aright, perhaps from long experience of such matters.

Payday, said Totter to himself, already broke, cheated me, had to of.

The gentleman signaled the bartender expertly, and Totter heard liquid sloshing into his glass behind him.

Totter wavered at the bar, and took one step toward the table, and stopped, and shook his head, and unbuttoned his holster, and took another step, and then turned back to the bar to seize the glass again.

I'll beat the living tar outa him, said Totter to himself, the living tar.

He chucked the drink down, wiped his mouth again and turned to the table.

He squinted, and waited for the room to come back to something that looked possible.

The gentleman in the broad-brimmed hat was gone.

Totter fumbled his way across the sawdust on the boards of the floor and leaned on the table, spilling chips, planting his hands in cards, spilling a drink.

The gentleman's chair was empty, clearly.

"He cheated me," yelled Totter, and slammed both fists on the table.

Chips jumped and glasses shook, and nobody at the table said anything.

Payday, said Totter to himself, and it's all gone, all gone.

Totter could've cried, but he was too goddam mad to cry.

He kicked a brass spittoon halfway across the room, a long swirl of brown water flying out of it, leaving a trail of puddles and spots across the floor.

"Take it easy, Soldier," said the bartender.

Totter knew there was a shotgun under the bar, but he didn't see it yet, and so he knew he didn't have to pull out, not yet at any rate.

"He cheated me," said Totter.

"Have another drink, Corporal," said the bartender. "On the house."

Totter, being a man of principle, did not immediately take the drink, but waited an amount of time appropriate to a man of principle, and then stomped to the bar and took the drink.

Goddam Southerner, he was, said Corporal Jake Totter to himself. Goddam soft-talking Southerner. We whipped 'em, we whipped 'em good. Whipped 'em.

Should of beat the living tar outa him.

Should of.

Beat the hell outa him.

Should of.

Should of.

Should of.

It had been another hot, dry summer, that summer of 1890.

Homesteaders claimed that the rain graphs prepared in Washington were forgeries, to dupe people into settling desert lands.

The maps of General Fremont had been honest.

He called it the Great American Desert, from the Rockies to the Missouri Basin.

And now it was fall again, and once more the crops had burned and the grasshoppers had come, and the trains and wagon trails were filled with the predictable exodus of homesteaders and settlers, broken and impoverished, their dreams vanished in the dust and rainless skies.

Thousands upon thousands, this year like last, and the year before, picked up their stakes and moved out.

You could ride through the land, for hours, without seeing a human being, though the abandoned sites of their habitations might be in evidence, the soddies with their fallen roofs, the furrowed, barren fields, the dry, cracked boards of empty corncribs, the miles of sagging wire, swaying in the dusty wind.

The town of Good Promise, South Dakota, population 407, no railroad, lay pretty well within a network of Indian reservations, of which Standing Rock was only one.

There were more than thirty thousand Indians in the Department of the Dakotas.

The Ghost Dance had swept through the reservations, an Indian Pentecost carried by seers and prophets, men like the Minneconjou, Kicking Bear. The powerful medicine of these men, shirts that could turn bullets, chunks of meat brought fresh and hot from the spirit world, their signs and miracles, breathed into the plains nations, mostly Cheyenne and Sioux, the vision of the apocalyptic destruction of the white race, the return of the buffalo, the restoration of the days of the eagle feather. Once more the grass would grow waist high, and green, and the brown humps of the buffalo would bend northward again in the now almost forgotten flowing rivers of hide and meat. The Son of Wakan-Tonka, the Christ, rejected by the white man, would return to His true children, and they would accept Him, and give Him robes and ponies, and meat and beads, and smoke with Him the pipe of friendship and of peace.

The town of Good Promise, never much as it was, now seemed very small, with its few boarded stores and shacks on the prairie. Outside the town lay dozens of abandoned homesteads, and farther out a handful of isolated ranches, where stubborn men nursed their small herds on prairie browse, and beyond that lay the Indians, some thousands of them, and the Ghost Dance.

A lone rider came up the unpaved main street of Good Promise, the dust of the street hanging fetlock high about the hoofs of his rangy sorrel stallion.

He was a stranger and so was marked by the people of Good Promise. No one came to Good Promise in these days. Plank bars lay near the doors. Many of the windows had been shuttered, except for the cracks you could shove a rifle barrel through. At each end of town there were men on the roofs of buildings. Wagons were bunched at each end of the street, so they could be drawn by men across the street, making a barricade, closing the town, making it into a fort. No children played in the street. There were no women in sight. Not many men. Those there were carried weapons, and they watched the rider as he approached.

The stranger had a beard some six or seven days heavy on his face, and it was a tired face, not old, but worn and lined. His eyes were half closed, and he slumped in the saddle, and the boots in the stirrups moved with the horse's pace, and you had to look to make sure he wasn't asleep, but he wasn't. You could tell that from the eyes. They weren't much open, but they were, and he was looking.

Back of the saddle, fastened with the blanket roll over the

saddlebags, was a small black bag, something like those physicians carry around in their buggies.

This man wore a dark shirt, plaid, cotton, and over this shirt, like a jacket, he wore another shirt, this one of brown corduroy, with the sleeves cut off at the elbows. His pants were blue denim but pretty much white now, from the sun and the rain, and washing. He wore a broad-brimmed hat, white and low-crowned, something like those once favored by Southern gentlemen.

He also wore a Colt, and when he dismounted in front of the saloon, the natural fall of his hand was at the handle of the weapon.

Edward Chance tied his sorrel to the hitching post and entered the saloon.

Edward Chance was tired, and he wanted to cut the prairie dust with a drink, and find some place to wash, and eat and sleep.

Mostly he wanted to be left alone.

When Chance shoved open the swinging doors and entered the saloon he was surprised at the number of men inside. The street outside had been mostly empty.

Of course in the days of the Ghost Dance it was good to have a place to gather together, and talk and drink, and tell each other there was nothing to worry about, and see plenty of men and guns in the same place.

Hadn't troops been ordered into the area? Hadn't they taken target practice near the ration points on Saturday? There was nothing to worry about, but the saloon was a good place to listen for news, to meet friends, to forget the dust and the wind outside.

Chance noted that there were about nine tables in the saloon, and each was full; at most of them men were playing cards, nursing their drinks, making them last a long time from the looks of it, almost all the glasses about half full.

The bar, too, was crowded, and there Chance saw the blue uniforms of two or three soldiers, contrasting with the vests and jackets of the civilians.

There must have been townspeople there, homesteaders, too, probably, some ranchers, and the soldiers.

These people suddenly seemed to have one thing in common, their interest in Edward Chance.

The cards had stopped clicking and slapping.

It's because they don't see many strangers, said Chance to himself.

It could have been that, but what Chance didn't know was that no one came to Good Promise in these days, because of the Ghost Dance, the Indians. A man would have to have plenty good reason to come to Good Promise this dusty, dry fall. And the men in the saloon, looking at Chance's bearded face and haggard features, decided that he must have had that plenty good reason.

And so it was that most people, for the wrong reasons, figured Edward Chance right that afternoon in Good Promise —that here was a man running from something, and they figured him wrong only in figuring he was running from the law.

He was running from Lester Grawson, whom he would not kill, who would kill him.

Chance was running because he wanted to stay alive.

The resources of the law though, Chance had told himself a dozen times, a hundred times, could always be tapped by Grawson, with his badge, his credentials, with documents from Charleston, forged or otherwise, to which he would have had access.

Thus the people of the town, supposing him to be fleeing from the law, were not as mistaken as one might have supposed.

For most practical purposes Edward Chance was indeed running from the law, and knew it, that law that might, with a shuffling of papers, benignly surrender him into the hands of Lester Grawson, Charleston detective, for return to the scene of some hypothetical crime, a return that once had stopped short in an alley in New York City, and next time might terminate in some grove of cottonwoods, or perhaps on the open prairie, or perhaps in some homesteader's abandoned shack, wherever Grawson, at his pleasure, would decide to perform the execution.

Chance went to the bar. "Bourbon," he said.

The bartender set a small heavy glass before Chance, turned, took a squarish bottle from in front of the mirror and filled the glass.

The bartender hadn't said anything, nor had anyone else.

Irritated, Chance threw the drink down, not looking the way it tasted. The swallow of amber fire burned its way down his gullet and hit his empty stomach like dropping a torch into a barrel of oil.

Chance put down a silver three-cent piece on the bar, which the bartender retrieved.

Chance became aware of a burly figure in an unfastened blue jacket next to him.

Chance put down another three-cent piece. The bartender picked up the second coin, then refilled the glass.

"Where you from, Stranger?" asked the voice of the man next to him, the man in the blue jacket. Chance noted the two wide, yellow chevrons on the sleeve. The speaker was drunk. The voice was not pleasant.

Chance turned to look at Corporal Jake Totter. He saw the heavy face, its lines loose from alcohol, the unfriendly gray eyes red and prominently veined. Mostly Chance noted that the nose had been broken and had not been set properly, or had never been set.

"East," said Chance.

Chance returned to the drink. He picked up the glass.

"I said where you from, Stranger?" repeated the voice. A wide hand, heavy as a wrench, held down his arm.

Chance turned again to regard the man in the unbuttoned blue jacket. He saw long white underwear under the jacket, black around the collar. The man wore suspenders. On the back of his head was a cavalry hat, with crossed sabers on the turned-up brim. Around the man's neck there was a yellow neckerchief.

"You're out of uniform, Soldier," said Chance.

"You ain't from the East," said the voice. The words had been slow, measured, slurred with drink, hostile.

"I am," said Chance.

"You're a liar," said the man.

"Take your hand off my arm," said Chance.

"I know that South-talk," said the man. "You're from the South."

"Once," said Chance.

"We whipped you," said the man.

He removed his hand from Chance's arm and pulled off his jacket, put it on the bar, and put his hat on top of it. Chance noticed that the men in the bar had gathered around, but leaving an open circle near where they stood. Chance thought that someone might as well come up now and draw a scratch line on the floor. How drunk is he, Chance asked himself. Damn drunk, Chance answered his own question.

"We whipped you once," said Totter, wiping his underwear-clad arm across his face, "and by God we can do it again."

"Forget it, Corporal," said Chance.

Chance had been four years old when the war had ended. He doubted if Totter had been much older. Maybe six or seven.

Chance tried to take the drink calmly, but when he lifted it to his mouth, Totter's arm lashed out and splashed it in his face. The rim of the glass stung his cheek.

It was quiet in the saloon.

Chance put the empty glass down on the bar, with a small click. His face was expressionless. He did not look at Totter directly, though he watched him in the mirror. "You owe me for that drink, Corporal," said Chance.

Totter, in the mirror, spat in his hands and wiped them on the sides of his trousers, across the yellow stripe that ran to his boots. Then he balled up his fists and hunched over.

Chance noted that Totter was standing with his left side turned a bit toward him. Judging from Totter's fists this was not a boxing stance, but a natural precaution, protecting himself from a kick. Chance suddenly realized that Totter would not be a particularly pleasant man to fight, particularly not in a saloon. Totter knew what he was up to, and what he guarded against he presumably would not be above doing. If there was a fight it would not be a good one to lose. Therefore, Chance told himself, there must be no risk of losing it.

But Chance did not want to fight.

He had enough trouble.

There would be a sheriff in this town, undoubtedly, and if he were picked up in a brawl, there would be questions, difficulties.

But Totter owed him for a drink.

"I'll forget this," said Chance, still not facing Totter, "if you buy me that drink."

When Totter charged, Chance was not at the bar. He had moved to one side and Totter plunged into the wood. As he did so Chance's hand seemed to brush at his throat and, choking, Totter sank to the floor, his hands at his neck, his face turning black.

No, said Chance to himself, there would not be a risk of losing it.

What Chance had done could have caused death, if done by an amateur hand, with too much force, too clumsily, not properly, but Chance, a skilled physician, had not broken the cartilage that would have closed the windpipe, that might have closed the life of a drunken soldier in the dusty town of Good Promise, South Dakota.

Chance hauled Totter to his feet and half threw him over the bar, taking the man's wallet from his hip pocket, and gouging about in it until he found a liberty nickel which he tossed to the bartender, who filled his bourbon glass for him and shoved it back to him, along with two Indian-head pennies in change. Chance returned the pennies to Totter's wallet and shoved it back in the man's hip pocket; then he sat Totter down on the brass rail at the foot of the bar, and Totter slid from it to the sawdust floor, sitting there, holding his throat.

"He didn't even hit him," said one of the men watching.

"Get up, Jake," said a soldier standing nearby.

"Get him, Jake!" urged another.

But Jake Totter sat in the sawdust, holding his throat, trying to get oxygen into his lungs.

Chance chucked down the drink.

He looked down at Jake, who was breathing better now, but with difficulty. The burly figure sitting on the floor was now, it seemed, sober, sick, enraged. He rolled over on his side and threw up against the bar.

As Chance watched him, Totter struggled to his knees, fumbling at the holster at his side.

"Don't, Jake!" yelled one of the soldiers.

The service revolver in Jake's unsteady hand jerked out of the holster.

Edward Chance's Colt had slipped from its holster and before Jake could bring his gun up Chance fired once into the body of Jake Totter, who yelped and grunted and was spun back against the bar, rolling along the floor, hugging his right shoulder.

Chance put the weapon back into the holster.

"Get a doctor," yelled somebody.

"No doctor closer than Fort Yates," said one of the soldiers.

A couple of soldiers had turned Jake over.

They pulled his hands from the wound. There was a large, irregular scarlet stain on the white underwear and a powder burn.

One of the soldiers looked up at Chance. "The army will get you for this, Mister," he said.

"Jake was gonna plug him," said a man in overalls, peering in between a couple of ranchers.

"Get a doctor," said somebody else.

"I ain't gonna ride to Fort Yates," said one of the towns-people. "Not these days I ain't."

Chance wondered what was wrong about riding to Fort Yates, wherever that was, these days. There were a number of things he didn't understand about this town, the people. They seemed to be afraid, jumpy. He was out of touch.

"There ain't no time to go to Fort Yates anyway," said a rancher.

"Jake's a goner," said one of the soldiers.

"No," said Chance. "It's a simple wound, no complicating fracture."

"How do you know?" asked someone.

"Because I planned it that way," said Chance.

He moved one of the soldiers away and knelt beside Jake, unbuttoning the long underwear and shoving it away from the wound.

He touched Jake expertly, who looked at him vaguely through half-closed eyes, his head lolling to one side.

"Get a doctor," said somebody.

Chance stood up, wearily. There was a bitter smile on his face, a tired, bitter smile.

"I'm a doctor," he said. "Put him on a table."

Chapter Five

After treating Totter, Edward Chance lost little time in riding from Good Promise, and as he rode he often turned his head, looking for any distant dust that might be rising from behind him, but there was only his own dust, and it settled undisturbed on the prairie in that late October afternoon.

So he was running again.

But where could he go this time?

Corporal Jake Totter, the man he had shot, would live. The wound would be painful, but was not dangerous.

It had been clearly self-defense.

Still Chance had little doubt that the army, if not the sheriff of Good Promise, would wish to apprehend him, perhaps for purposes of an inquiry, and so he rode, not pushing his horse, but steadily.

As he crossed the open prairie, staying away from the occasional roads that rutted its endless sage and buffalo grass, he paid no special attention to where he was going, or the direction. For one thing he didn't know the country. For another he was motivated to do little more than put miles between himself and Good Promise, and to stay away from towns and farms in doing so.

Suddenly Chance reined in his horse.

Looking down, he saw a small cottonwood wand, not much more than a foot high. Tied to the tip of this wand, moving a little in the prairie wind, was a small, cloth bag.

Chance dismounted.

He jerked the small bag from the stick wand and opened it. It was filled with brown, dry flakes, and when Chance lifted it to his nose and smelled it, his guess was confirmed. Tobacco. Or at least partly tobacco.

He tied the small bag back on the cottonwood wand.

Chance got to his feet and looked out over the prairie. Of course the prairie here looked no different than it did for a hundred miles in any direction. Chance wondered how far he had ridden. How far he had come.

He wondered if the little marker, if that was what it was, had been put up by a drunken cowboy, or perhaps by a child or farmer. But what for? If someone had left extra tobacco for the next traveler, there might well have been a note, or something. At least the tobacco should have been more clearly marked.

Someone might have ridden past and not even noticed.

Vaguely, for no particular reason that he could determine, Chance thought of the mariners of ancient Greece, pouring oil and salt into the sea before a voyage—and of the Romans, giving the first drops from their goblet to the gods, the pouring of the libation.

Chance wondered why he should have thought of these things.

Then, suddenly, Edward Chance felt cold on the prairie.

I am now in another country, he said to himself. I have passed a boundary.

He looked at the little bag of tobacco.

An offering, undoubtedly.

But an offering of whom, to what gods?

Where am I, wondered Edward Chance.

You are in a country, said his own voice to him, whose gods are not your gods, whose gods you do not know, whose gods are not friendly to you.

I'll camp, said Edward Chance to himself, and move on after dark. There'll be a moon tonight. In a few hours I'll be away from this place.

About a hundred yards to his right Chance saw a clump of cottonwoods, fringing a low, sloping valley between the rounded hills of the prairie. Probably a creek, he thought. Water, and a place to camp till dark. Then I'll move on.

Chance led his sorrel toward the trees, and in them found a small leg of a creek, not more than a yard or so wide. He let the horse drink, but not too much. He wanted to move on, and soon, as soon as it was dark.

Among the trees, grateful for the cover, and suddenly feeling weary, as well as hungry, Edward Chance unsaddled his horse and tethered him to a tree. He then put some rocks together and built a small fire between them and opened and heated a can of pork and beans, using the same can later for coffee.

After finishing, Chance lit a small briar pipe which he had

purchased in Saint Louis, the fourth day after he had fled from Lester Grawson.

Chance had not smoked much in the East but now, somehow in the solitude and loneliness of his westward journey, the small wooden pipe, giving him something to fumble with, something warm, something with slow, unhurried smoke, had seemed to be welcome to him, and so he had smoked.

Chance, pipe between his teeth, spread a blanket under a tree, not far from where his horse was tethered. Then, using his saddle for a pillow, he pulled off his boots, and lay down, looking up at the sky.

The sky was peaceful, blue, untroubled.

Chance watched the smoke from the little briar curl upward, slowly, softly.

Going nowhere, thought Chance, and not minding.

Suddenly Chance sat upright.

The noise.

Where had it come from? A noise, a human noise, something like a soft cry, an ugly almost inaudible cry, from somewhere through the trees.

Chance rolled on his belly and drew the Colt.

It was quiet, and he waited for some minutes, not hearing the noise again.

The leaves of the cottonwoods above him rustled. He heard the soft splashing of the creek as it moved over and around rocks.

Then Chance heard the noise again, the noise of a human being, in pain, suffering.

Without holstering the Colt, Chance laid it next to his face and put out his pipe, shoving it in the pocket of his corduroy shirt. Then, staying as low as he could, he pulled on his boots. He then picked up the Colt and, moving on his elbows, crawled toward the sound. The grass tickled his neck and the Colt, after a minute or so, seemed heavy in his hand. His palm was sweating and his grip on the weapon was less sure. He put the weapon down, dried his hand on the grass, picked it up again and inched forward.

Taking advantage of bushes to his left he continued for several minutes to move slowly forward. He felt the bushes scratching at the back of his shirt. At last he worked his way over a tufted hump of ground, and could look down into a small grassy clearing beyond. It was well hidden, and lay not more than sixty yards from where he had thrown his blanket and saddle.

There was no movement in the clearing, and for an instant Chance had simply assumed it was empty, and that the sound came from elsewhere.

Then he saw it.

Not more than twenty yards away.

In the center of the clearing there was planted a cottonwood pole, green and springy, about eighteen feet high.

Around this pole, in a circle, the grass had been beaten away, torn from the ground by the footsteps of a human being.

In the late afternoon light Chance squinted, trying to make out more clearly what he saw.

In a fork in the pole was a bundle of branches wrapped in bark. Hanging from the pole were several objects: a tiny bundle of sticks, from which dangled little bags, perhaps of tobacco; a piece of meat, judging from the insects that swarmed on it, tied in the shape of an animal; what appeared to be a rawhide doll; and what was unmistakably a human being.

Chance sucked in his breath.

A young Indian was fastened to the pole by two long, taut strips of braided rawhide. These rawhide strips were fastened to pegs of wood which had been forced under the lateral muscles of the Indian's chest. His chest had been cut open. Then the pegs had been thrust in, behind the muscles, and fastened at both ends to the two rawhide strips that ran like twin carnival streamers to the tip of the greenwood pole.

The young man was hanging back, his weight dragging against the pegs under his flesh.

His naked chest and belly were covered with blood, some of it fresh and red, much of it dry and caked. Hanging backward, the Indian had his hands extended like stone toward the lowering sun. His eyes, half closed, seemed to stare blindly at the sun, not blinking.

He wore a breechclout, which, like the rest of his body from the chest down, was stained with blood. From his back, adding to the weight against the pegs under his chest muscles, hung a buffalo-hide shield. On his sweating head, the man wore a porcupine quill headdress and each of his wrists was circled with a bracelet of twisted sagebrush.

Chance shoved the Colt back in his holster. He must cut

the man down. He knew that, even if he were interrupting
some form of primitive execution.

Drawing out the knife he wore at his belt, Chance rose
cautiously to his feet, but did not go immediately into the
clearing. Rather, quietly, he circled the clearing, establishing
to his satisfaction that only he and the young Indian were in
the vicinity. Only then Chance approached the young Indian,
who seemed more dead than alive.

Then Chance was at the Indian's side. He was a young
man indeed, probably less than twenty. Slowly the head of
the young man turned toward him. If he saw Chance he gave
little sign of it. But when Chance lifted the knife to cut the
rawhide strips the Indian's hands gently pushed him away.

"Good God," thought Chance, "he doesn't want to be cut
down."

Chance tried once more and once again the Indian's hands
pushed away Chance's hand.

Chance inspected the man's chest, and even his table-
hardened stomach, familiar with ugly, hazardous facts of surgery, retracted for an instant, making him briefly nauseous.

The pectoral muscles were nearly torn through.

Chance cleared his head and took a deep breath, and was
once again the physician.

But was he?

For he had resheathed his knife.

Chance had sworn an oath, but looking on this man, he
understood, swiftly and incomprehensibly, that this man had
a right to the cruelty and the pole, and that Chance must not
deprive him of this right.

Chance did not understand what was taking place, but he
sensed that he must not interfere.

It seemed the young Indian's eyes shone on him for an instant, bright.

Then the young man gave a great cry, which startled
Chance, and he backed dancing away from Chance, the two
strips holding him in his bloody circle. The pole bent after
him, cruelly tensing the twin strips of rawhide. Drops of
blood fell into the beaten circle beneath the Indian's moccasins, mixing with the dust. Now the young man was shouting
in some guttural tongue that Chance could not begin to understand. It sounded like no language that he had ever heard.

Lord, thought Chance, backing out of the circle, he's trying
to tear himself loose.

He didn't really want to watch, but he felt he had to. It

wasn't just curiosity, nor was it the nobler motives which might have been associated with Chance's humane calling. It was something else, and Chance didn't really understand it. He knew only that he must watch.

He went back to his saddle, got his matches and tobacco and returned. Then he lit his pipe again, hunkered down about five yards from the bloody circle and watched the young man dance.

He'll be dead in an hour at this rate, thought Chance. It will be hard to bury the body. I have no tools.

The young Indian continued to dance around the pole, now singing as he danced, a guttural chant, repetitious, punctuated by sudden shouts.

As Chance, smoking, grew more accustomed to the torture that was taking place before him, he took his eyes from the young Indian.

The streamers, fastened at the top of the pole, had been notched in, to permit turning.

Around the foot of the pole, here and there, thrust into the dirt, were some slender, wooden wands, like that he had found on the prairie. Each carried its tiny cloth bag, presumably filled with tobacco.

About three paces to the west of the pole there was a buffalo skull, lying on a cushion of sagebrush. It faced east. Behind the skull, on two forked sticks, lay a long Indian pipe. The stem of this pipe, like the buffalo skull, faced east.

Chance returned his attention to the young Indian.

Obviously it had a meaning, to someone if not to Chance. As he continued to watch, somewhat to his uneasiness, his feelings of fascination, of horror, became gradually replaced with a certain, if not awe, respect.

It was a ceremony.

This place was holy.

The pole and the cruelty and the blood were holy.

What do I believe in, Chance asked himself, for which I could dance like this, and he answered his question simply, nothing.

No bear would do this, said Chance to himself, no wolf, no bird, no animal.

Only man.

And Chance, seeing this man suffer, doing nothing to relieve his pain, smoking quietly in a cottonwood grove in South Dakota in the year 1890, thought he understood more than he had found in the books of anatomy, more than he had found in the dissected cadavers in Cambridge, more than his professors had known, or than he had ever thought that he himself would know. Something here had given him, he felt, perhaps mistakenly, perhaps not, a short, terrible glimpse of something deep and possible in the race of which he was a member, something perhaps long buried and generally forgotten, something that might be akin to the meaning and the essence of man, in all its ugly, splendid keenness.

"Hea!" cried the young Indian, a shout in no language, more an animal cry than anything, something between victory and laughter.

As the hair climbed on the back of Chance's neck, he heard the beginning of a faint, ugly tearing sound. The sound became louder. "Hea!" cried the boy again, laughing and hurling himself backward.

There was a sudden, sickening rip and the young man had fallen backward to the grass. He was sprawled unconscious on the grass, free at last, lying outside the dusty, bloody circle.

He's loose, said Chance to himself, getting up. Chance's legs were stiff. He had watched a long time.

The two pegs on their rawhide strips dangled against the pole, making a little knocking noise in the wind.

Chance went to the boy, whose chest was open and thick with new blood. It was coming through the flesh, rising like red spring water through sand. Chance took off his brown corduroy shirt and shoved it against the wounds, anything to stanch the flow, which must be done immediately.

A quarter of an hour later, Chance gave the boy a sip of water from his canteen.

Joseph Running Horse looked up at Chance. "I have watched the sun," he said. "For three days I have watched the sun." Chance nodded, understanding nothing. Joseph Running Horse lapsed back into unconsciousness.

Chance didn't ride on that night, but stayed in the grove of cottonwoods, near the tiny creek.

He wrapped Running Horse in his blankets to prevent shock, and built a fire which he tended during the night.

The chest wounds, unsanitarily clotted against the material of Chance's shirt, would close in their own fashion. The Indian would not allow Chance to use the curved needle and the catgut thread to close the wounds.

"There must be scars," Running Horse had said.

He would not even allow the physician to dress the wounds with clean bandages.

The next day, to Chance's surprise, Running Horse was eating, and could walk about the grove. He seemed weak, but that was all.

The young Indian gathered together the paraphernalia of the dance.

The soldiers must not find it.

He built a fire, throwing into it the branches wrapped in bark which he had fitted into the fork of the cottonwood pole. They were the branches which he had cut from the cottonwood to make the pole. It was only right that the whole of the little cottonwood should have participated in the holiness of the dance. Chance noticed that the meat, before Running Horse threw it into the flames, was tied into the humped shape of a small buffalo. Next to be given to the flames was the small rawhide doll, which was the figure of a warrior, and which, Running Horse told him, would give him victory over his enemies. Then Running Horse burned the tobacco and twigs, and the tobacco bags and wands which he had planted around the pole and elsewhere as offerings to Wakan-Tonka, the Mystery. Lastly he burned the pole itself, with its pegs and rawhide strips. The buffalo skull he placed in the bushes. This left only the long Indian pipe, which lay on its forked sticks with its stem pointing east.

But Running Horse did not touch the pipe.

He left it resting on the forked sticks in the small clearing, inside the dusty stained ring that marked the path of his dance. He looked at the pipe, and then at Chance, but did not touch the pipe, nor did he speak to Chance.

That night, Chance made coffee over their small fire and, on a sharpened stick, cooked pieces of a prairie chicken which Running Horse had struck down with a rock.

"You have seen me look at the sun," said Running Horse. "Let that be good medicine for both of us."

"All right," said Chance, not understanding.

After the two men had finished the prairie chicken, Chance swigged some of the coffee which he had boiled in the pork-and-bean can, and then handed the can to Running Horse.

Running Horse took a swallow of the coffee, a large swallow which must have burned his mouth, but he said nothing. He swirled the black, hot fluid about in his mouth, holding it for a time, and then gulped it down.

Chance winced.

Running Horse grinned. "Perjuta sapa," he said.

"Purjuta sapa," repeated Chance, hesitantly. "That is coffee?"

"Yes," said Running Horse. "Sioux for coffee." Then the young Indian grinned again. "It really means black medicine."

Chance laughed.

He had also learned his first word of Sioux.

The two men had eaten together, and shared the coffee. Chance felt that this meant something important to Running Horse, but he didn't know what.

Chance asked for some other Sioux words, for the common articles about them.

Surprised, Running Horse had told him.

Chance was the first white man he had known who was interested in learning to speak his language. Not even the schoolteacher at Standing Rock, the pale white woman with blond hair, had done this.

Chance took out his briar, and after he had lit it, Running Horse took it from him and lifted it to the stars, and to the winds, and then to the earth.

Running Horse took a long puff, and then another, and handed the little briar back to Chance, who took it and smoked it.

"I have smoked your tobacco," said Running Horse.

"Yes, you have," said Chance, wondering what was going on.

"I have smoked your tobacco," repeated Running Horse, looking at Chance.

Without really knowing why, Chance, followed by Running Horse, stood up and went over the small hill to the clearing where the long Indian pipe still lay on its forks, inside what had been the circle of the dance.

Chance looked at Running Horse, and the young Indian nodded.

Chance took the pipe carefully from the forked sticks. It was beaded, white with blue beads, and it seemed very old, very fragile.

He handed the pipe to Running Horse, who walked before him and carried the pipe back to their campfire. There Running Horse filled the pipe with some of his own tobacco.

The Indian lit the old pipe and drew on it until a steady swirl of smoke curled from the high, narrow bowl. Then he handed the pipe to Chance.

Trying to remember things as well as he could, Chance lifted the pipe to the sky, and then to the four directions, and lastly lowered it near the ground and lifted it up again.

He then smoked.

The smoke was hot and strong, and it stung his tongue. It was a combination of white man's tobacco and some other taste, which Chance didn't recognize.

He handed the pipe back to Running Horse.

"I have smoked your tobacco," said Chance.

"Yes," said Running Horse.

Chance then relit his own pipe and each of the men smoked together, not speaking for some time.

"I am your friend," said Running Horse.

"I am your friend," said Chance.

"Good," said Running Horse.

Chance was startled by the young Indian's next words. "Why are you running from other white men?" asked Running Horse.

For a moment Chance was confused, but then, simply, he remembered that such a question might now be asked, for they were friends, and a friend might ask such a thing.

And so Chance, not hurrying, explained as well as he could who he was, what he had done, and how it was that he had come to the small grove of cottonwoods and discovered the dance of Joseph Running Horse.

He told everything, about Grawson, about Totter, even the duel and Clare Henderson.

Running Horse listened gravely, and at the end he said, "My lodge is your lodge. My fire is your fire."

Chance thought it over. One place Grawson, or the law, or even the army would never look for him would be here, with the people of Running Horse.

He needed a place to stay, to hide, if only for a time, perhaps a few weeks.

"I am grateful to share your lodge," said Chance. "I am happy to share your fire."

"Good," said Running Horse.

He puffed on the long blue-and-white beaded pipe.

"What place is this?" asked Chance.

"Standing Rock," said Running Horse.

"A reservation?" asked Chance.

Running Horse smiled. "Yes," he said.

"There aren't many who come here?" asked Chance.

"No," said Running Horse, "never many." And then he added, "Now almost nobody."

"Why not?" asked Chance.

"They are afraid," said Running Horse.

"Why?" asked Chance.

"It is the time of the Ghosts," said Running Horse simply.

"I don't understand," said Chance.

Running Horse looked at him in puzzlement. Could it be that anyone was so ignorant as not to know of the Ghost Dance and the Ghost Dancers?

"This is the time when the Sioux dance the Ghost Dance," he said.

"Were you dancing the Ghost Dance?" asked Chance.

Running Horse looked at him with offended pride, and straightened his body, sitting cross-legged across the fire from Chance, holding the pipe across his body. "No," said Joseph Running Horse. "I looked at the sun."

Chance said nothing.

Running Horse took another puff on the pipe and then looked at Chance. "Do you wish to know the name of the dance that Joseph Running Horse danced?"

"Yes," said Chance.

He found himself staring in the firelight at the savage wounds on the chest of his companion.

"The Sun Dance," said Joseph Running Horse.

Chance nodded.

Chance stared into the fire and poked it with a stick, watching the sparks fly up, like needles of fire against the darkness in the grove of cottonwoods.

"Why?" asked Chance.

"To learn," said Joseph Running Horse, "if the Ghost Dance is a true dance."

"I don't understand," said Chance.

"Tomorrow," said Joseph Running Horse, "you will understand."

Running Horse put out his pipe, and so did Chance, and Chance pulled off his boots, and the two men tugged their blankets about them and with the dying fire between them lay down.

"Tomorrow," said Joseph Running Horse, speaking in the red darkness, "I will show you the Ghost Dance."

Chance lay still for a while, then spoke. "Is it all right to see the dance?" he asked.

He heard Running Horse speak in the darkness. "You may die," he said.

"Oh," said Chance.

"But I do not think so," said Running Horse.

There was a long time of darkness between them.

"Why not?" asked Chance.

"You have seen the Sun Dance," said Joseph Running Horse. "That is strong medicine. It will protect you."

Chance thought about this for a time. Then he said, "I hope you're right."

"Yes," said Running Horse, after a bit. "It is also my hope."

Chance pulled the blankets up under his chin. The ground seemed hard. The saddle was not the softest of pillows. The sweat in his socks began to feel as though it might freeze, and so he pulled off his socks, rubbing one foot against the other.

So tomorrow he might see the Ghost Dance, and might die, all in one day, he mused.

And Chance laughed in the darkness.

"White men are crazy," said Joseph Running Horse.

"All men are crazy," said Chance.

"Maybe," said Joseph Running Horse, and turned over to go to sleep.

Later, after he could no longer see the black of the cottonwoods against the black of the sky, and had counted more than a thousand stars in that glistening, frosty October night on the Dakota prairie, Edward Chance, physician from New York City, spoke again.

"Running Horse," he said.

The young Indian, to Chance's surprise, was not asleep.

"Yes," he said.

"When you danced to Sun Dance," asked Chance, "—did you learn what you wanted?"

"Yes," said Running Horse. His voice was sad in the darkness.

"Is the Ghost Dance a true dance?" asked Chance.

"No," said Joseph Running Horse.

Chapter Six

———— ••━━━•• ————

Chance ached, each muscle stiff, each bone not wanting to bend at the joints.

He was wet through, from a few minutes of rain shortly before dawn, that and the dew that covered the grass with cold, glistening drops.

He wished he had slept naked.

He sat up in the wet blankets and shivered. He stretched his legs and arms, painfully. Everything was gray, and quiet and wet.

A snap of twigs to his left startled him.

A tiny flame, the size of a hand, was biting its hot, bright way through some shavings Running Horse had cut the night before and wrapped in leather.

Running Horse was kneeling before the tiny fire, snapping his fingers over it, as if by this sound to encourage it to grow.

The world seemed less gray then, warmed by that spark of fire and the crouching body of Joseph Running Horse, who was his friend.

Running Horse looked at Chance, and drew his knife.

"I dreamed," said Running Horse.

Chance had not.

Running Horse lifted the knife and approached Chance, who watched him, but did not move.

Running Horse held the knife poised.

"Be my Brother," said Running Horse.

The young Indian took Chance's arm, pulling the sleeve back.

Chance felt the warm sting of the blade enter his arm.

"I am proud to be your Brother," said Chance.

Chance took the knife and slowly, with a surgeon's firmness, drew its blade across the forearm of Running Horse.

The two men then held their cuts together, that the blood might mingle and be the same, as the blood of brothers.

62

"It was so in my dream," said Running Horse.

"I am glad," said Chance.

"Now," said Running Horse, "I will take you to see the Ghost Dance."

About noon Chance and Running Horse kicked the flanks of their horses, moving them through the leisurely eddies of the Grand River, and climbed the low, wet sloping bank on the other side to the buffalo grass of the rolling prairie above.

Across the river the men dismounted and shared some strips of dried beef which Running Horse extracted from a beaded, leather bag he had tied in the mane of his pony.

Mounting again the men continued their journey.

By now the sun and the wind had dried the broad patches of prairie grass from the early morning's rain, and the hoofs of their horses, Chance's shod, raised dust with each print, which clung in the tangled, matted hair of the fetlocks, wet from the crossing of the river.

For a long time they rode, following the slow run of the bending river, making their way through clusters of cottonwoods where they occurred, and by now the sun was behind them and it was late afternoon.

Once they passed four horses grazing.

Pintos, said Chance to himself, Indian ponies.

But they saw no one.

Running Horse, pulling on the nose rope of his pony, stopped and lifted his hand.

Chance drew back on the reins, checking his mount.

They listened, and as Chance listened, a shiver struck like a snake the length of his backbone, and lifted the hair on the back of his head.

Carried on the wind from perhaps half a mile away was the sound of the Ghost Dance.

It was not in itself a frightening sound, but it could frighten people, and it did, white people, those who understood it and those who sensed what it might mean. Chance was one of those who sensed it.

The song itself was not frightening.

It was rather slow, rather monotonous, mournful perhaps, sad, but not frightening.

Unless one knew what it meant, or sensed it.

The sound came to Chance in fitful puffs, brought on the wind. Hearing it was like seeing something through fog, where you see it and then it disappears, and then it is seen again.

Looking ahead in the direction of the sound Chance could see a hazy pool of dust in the sky, a lake of floating dryness marking the place beneath which the moccasins of hundreds of human beings pounded the earth in a ritual alien to anything he knew, performing the prayer of the Ghost Dance.

This is a holy place and a sacred time, said Chance to himself. I do not belong here.

But when Running Horse kicked his pony ahead, Chance followed.

There didn't seem to be any place to go back to.

They had not ridden fifty yards when a single rifle shot whined over their heads.

They hauled their mounts up short.

"Wait here," said Running Horse, and, lifting his right hand high with the palm open, kicked his pony ahead, toward the direction from which the rifle shot had come.

By the time Chance had loosened the Colt in his holster and dried his hands on his shirt, for about the fifth time, he saw Running Horse, about two hundred yards away, waving him ahead.

Chance rode to join the young Indian, riding upright in the saddle, not bothering to look right or left. He knew he was now well within the range of the unseen rifleman and that the order of the moment might as well be the appearance of confidence, if not the reality.

He joined Running Horse at the top of a small rise, where they both dismounted.

Chance had not seen the rifleman who had fired at him, and this made him nervous.

He glanced around and finally spotted the man, two men actually, separated by about forty yards, each dug in. both a bit below the crest of the hill, behind rocks, under the tangled roots of a large sage.

Neither of them were looking at him now.

"Look," said Running Horse, pointing downward from the rise.

Below them, in a dusty trampled area about as large as a square city block in Charleston, Chance saw the Ghost Dance.

From a distance, in the dust, it looked like a giant wheel, with no hub, only a rim, turning slowly, to the left, on an invisible axis, wailing and crying as it turned.

There was no sound but the chant and the soft drum of moccasins in the dust.

Chance saw that the dancers were alternately men and women, which surprised him. The dance, he knew, for the Plains Indian was a proud masculine discipline, for warriors, and the squaws could only stand in the background, stamping their feet, keeping time, but here the squaws danced with their men.

This is the dance of a nation, thought Chance to himself. For the first time the Sioux nation, as a nation, dances.

Chance and Running Horse made their way downward, walking their horses.

To his surprise Chance was scarcely noticed.

The dancers did not seem to see him at all, and other Indians, mostly resting from the dance, or watching, paid him no attention.

Most of the dancers danced with their eyes half closed, their bodies lost in the monotonous, hypnotic rhythm of the turning wheel, moving always to the left, the leather of their moccasins pounding in the dust.

"See the Ghost Shirts," said Running Horse, pointing to the shirts worn by the dancers, some of which were white, some scarlet. There was a sun, a rising sun, on the chest of these shirts, a representation of a buffalo on the back.

Chance nodded, wondering what it all meant, not wanting to ask Running Horse at the time, expecting him to tell him when he wished.

Suddenly Chance's hair rose on the back of his neck.

There was a weird, shrill scream and an incredibly old woman, buckskin skirt flapping about her brown sticks of legs, stumbled backward from the circle, her white braids flying, and took two or three steps backwards and then fell unconscious into the dust.

Her place in the circle immediately closed, and the wheel continued to turn implacably, at the same slow pace as before, to the same unbroken, repetitious chant. Not the beat of a moccasin in the dust was lost nor a single note of that wailing litany.

Chance made as though to go to the side of the old woman.

Running Horse held his arm. "No," he said.

Chance saw three Indians approaching the old woman. Each of them carried a small flag, one blue, one yellow, and one white.

Their leader, a tall robust man with large, fierce eyes, squatted down beside the old white-haired squaw who lay unconscious in the dust. He thrust his yellow flag in his belt and leaned over the old woman.

"It is Kicking Bear," said Running Horse, and his tone of voice suggested that Chance would of course know the name. Chance didn't.

"See," said Running Horse. "He carries the yellow flag. That is the color of the light of the spirit world. White is the color of the light of earth. Blue is the color of the sky world."

Chance was watching Kicking Bear.

Suddenly with a shriek Kicking Bear had sprung to his feet, leaving the old woman lying in the dust. Over his head he clutched a huge chunk of fresh, steaming meat.

Chance assumed he must have taken the meat from the old woman.

Kicking Bear began to sing and dance, carrying the meat over his head in both hands. His eyes not seeming to see this world, he danced into the circle, facing and stirring the numbed dancers.

"What is he doing?" asked Chance.

"He is singing," said Running Horse, "that the old woman has been to the spirit world, where the Indians and the buffalo and horses still live. He sings that is true, for he sings he has in his hands fresh buffalo meat, brought by the old woman to prove that she has been in the spirit world."

Kicking Bear, inside the circle, holding the meat over his head, danced in place and the great wheel continued to turn, carrying its rim of dancers past him one by one.

It seemed to Chance that as the dancers passed him, that strange, slow, vast dance somehow changed, perhaps becoming more profound or keen or intense, something almost intangible taking place, something subtle but significant, suggested in little more than the way a hand or head might move, or a moccasin strike the earth. Then it seemed to Chance that the wailing of the dance was rising and falling like a howling wind.

The circle seemed alive now, eternal, no beginning or end. The ring of eternity, thought Chance, moving through the dust of an Indian reservation, turning, unchanging at a place called Standing Rock, and I am here.

"Running Horse," said Chance.

"Yes," said Running Horse.

"Where did he get the meat?" asked Chance.

"Maybe from the spirit world," said Running Horse.

"Do you believe that?" asked Chance.

"My eyes tell me it is true," said Running Horse, "but the Sun Dance tells me that it is not so, that it is not true."

"What do you believe?" asked Chance.

"The Sun Dance," said Joseph Running Horse.

The two Indians who had been with Kicking Bear, putting their flags in their belts, picked up the old woman who lay in the dust and carried her away from the turning circle of the dance, toward a log cabin in the background.

Running Horse motioned to Chance to follow them, and together they did.

At the door of the cabin, smoking, wrapped in a heavy blanket, cross-legged, sat an old Indian, a stocky, heavy man, with a wide mouth, a leathery face, rather deeply lined, a large nose, and an expression as calm as burnt, wrinkled wood. He sat wrapped in his blanket, smoking, calm as a rock.

Before this man in the blanket the two Indians placed the old white-haired squaw, who had fallen out of the Ghost Dance.

Seeing Chance and Running Horse, the man gestured for them to sit down on the ground across from him.

Then, putting aside his pipe, the man leaned forward and lifted the old woman gently in his arms.

She opened her eyes, and looked at the man, and Chance saw pleasure transfigure the dried, wrinkled apple of her face, and through toothless gums she began to mumble disjointedly in Sioux, half to the man, half to herself.

"What does she say?" Chance asked Running Horse.

"She says," said Running Horse, "she has been with her husband and her children, and has cooked berries and meat for her grandson, who has not been feeling well. He likes berries and meat."

"Where is her family?" asked Chance.

"They have been dead for many years," said Running Horse.

The stocky man in the blanket began to speak to the old woman, and his voice, deep and strong for an old man, seemed to Chance surprisingly gentle.

The old woman smiled and lay in his arms, nodding her head.

"What does he say?" asked Chance.

"He says," said Running Horse, "that he will soon ask to ride with her husband on the hunt, for there is no greater hunter among all the Sioux than her husband."

The old woman happily closed her eyes, and the stocky man, with a look, summoned the two Indians who had brought her to him, and they gently picked her up and carried her from the vicinity of the cabin, crooning softly to herself, a lullaby, Chance surmised, the sort of thing one might sing to quiet a child.

The man had now retrieved his pipe and was once more placidly smoking.

He didn't look at Chance or Running Horse.

"Who is he?" asked Chance.

Running Horse said nothing.

The man looked at Chance. "I am Sitting Bull," he said.

Before Chance had an opportunity to respond he became aware of a man standing near them, or rather of a shadow that was suddenly there that had not been there before, then two shadows, long shadows in the late afternoon sun.

Chance looked up and saw Kicking Bear, scowling down at him, so sweating from the dance that even the dust on his leggings was black with water.

He no longer held the meat which he had shown to the Ghost Dancers, but he carried a Winchester rifle.

Behind him there stood, in a scarlet Ghost Shirt, a young Indian, very strong and, in a cruel fashion, handsome, at whose belt there hung a long-handled hatchet.

Chance did not know this second man but Running Horse knew him.

He was Drum, the son of Kills-His-Horse.

Kicking Bear looked down at Chance, and then he looked to Sitting Bull and said something swiftly in Sioux.

Sitting Bull continued to smoke, his expression not changing.

"What did he say?" asked Chance.

"He said you must die," said Running Horse.

Chapter Seven

Running Horse uncrossed his legs and rose lightly to his feet, standing to face Kicking Bear, who scowled at him in anger.

"No," said Running Horse.

"Short hair," said Kicking Bear, speaking in Sioux.

This time Running Horse did not flinch, and his eyes did not drop before those of his accuser. There was not even a tremor in his prominently boned face, not even a shadow that moved for an instant through his dark, clear eyes.

Never again would the epithet of Short Hair disconcert the boy, the young man, named Running Horse, for he had learned three days ago, at the stake of the Sun Dance, who he was, and now knew himself in his own eyes, honestly, not through the words that others might try to fasten upon him.

"I am Hunkpapa," said Running Horse, speaking in Sioux.

"You are not Hunkpapa. You are Minneconjou. Why are you here?"

Kicking Bear stepped back, angered. He turned to look at Sitting Bull, but the chief was smoking imperturbably, staring at the ground a few feet from him, seemingly lost in thought.

Kicking Bear turned to face Running Horse. "I bring the Ghost Dance," he said. "I bring the word of Wakan-Tonka. I am a prophet, big medicine."

Running Horse did not respond.

"Why do you not dance the Ghost Dance?" challenged Kicking Bear.

"How do I know you bring the word of Wakan-Tonka?" asked Running Horse.

Behind Kicking Bear, Drum tensed. He loosened the long-handled hatchet from his belt.

"Because," said Kicking Bear, simply, "the Son of the Mystery, the Christ, the Messiah, told me so Himself."

"How do I know you speak the truth?" asked Running Horse.

"You have seen buffalo meat from the spirit world," said

69

Kicking Bear. "You have seen shirts that will turn bullets."
He snarled at Running Horse, "What signs will satisfy you
that I speak the truth? I show you miracles to prove the truth
of my sayings."

"Like white men," said Running Horse.

For a moment Kicking Bear seemed paralyzed in the rigid-
ity of his anger.

"My miracles," he said at last, "are true miracles."

"How do I know this?" asked Running Horse.

"You have seen them," said Kicking Bear.

"I know what I have seen," said Running Horse, "but I do
not know if what I have seen are miracles."

Kicking Bear, infuriated, turned again to Sitting Bull, but
still the old chief seemed oblivious of what was passing.

The drift of this conversation, partly theological, was at the
time lost on Chance, for it was conducted largely in Sioux,
but the practical matter involved was nonetheless quite clear
to him. There were two men present who wished him to die,
and there was a confrontation taking place between them and
Running Horse.

In his mind, not moving a muscle, Chance rehearsed the
swift movement of his right hand to the butt of the Colt in
his holster.

Suddenly Chance was aware that Kicking Bear was speaking in English, undoubtedly for his benefit.

The large Indian, in his Ghost Shirt, carrying the Winchester, turned to the young Indian with the hatchet who stood
behind him. "Drum," he said, "Running Horse brings a white
man to watch the dance."

Drum's eyes clouded for a minute as he tried to make out
Kicking Bear's English.

Irritably Kicking Bear repeated what he had said in Sioux,
and a look of pleasure crossed Drum's face. Then, haltingly,
the English sounds unfamiliar and not coming easily to him,
Drum said, Chance thought with creditable pronunciation
and grammar, "I will kill him."

An instant after he had spoken, the handle of the hatchet
had been turned in his hand and the hatchet, underhanded,
was swinging backward, reached the tip of its backward arc,
and then, blade foremost, began to swing smoothly forward.

The head of the hatchet would catch Chance under the
chin as he sat cross-legged on the ground.

It would split his skull from the jaw to the hairline.

Chance threw himself backward, pushing against the dirt

with the heels of his boots, at the same time moving the Colt from the greased, black leather of its holster. Before Chance had hit the ground on his back the weapon was in position and his finger had nearly closed on the trigger, but Chance did not press the trigger.

Running Horse had leaped between Chance and Drum and had seized the hatchet on the upswing and now the two young Indians, locked in struggle, rocked back and forth, almost over the spot where Chance had been sitting.

Chance scrambled to his feet.

Sitting Bull continued to smoke.

Chance stood with the Colt ready.

He saw Kicking Bear raise the Winchester and put the muzzle behind Running Horse's ear.

Chance's Colt chopped once and Kicking Bear's trigger hand, blown open, smashed against the splattered trigger housing of the Winchester. The weapon leaped from his hands as though it were hot and he had thrown it from him. Kicking Bear, howling, reeled about, thrusting his injured hand in his mouth.

The sound of the gunshot and the howls of Kicking Bear brought several Indians running, those who had been watching the Ghost Dance, or resting.

The wheel of the Ghost Dance itself, incredibly, continued to turn to the left, as always, with the same unbroken rhythm of foot and chant.

Chance, looking about himself, uneasily, but feeling it the safest thing to do, holstered the Colt.

Drum and Running Horse still grappled before Sitting Bull's cabin, grunting, their feet slipping and scraping in the dust.

Chance noticed that Kicking Bear, to his surprise, was now sitting down quietly, cross-legged, not far from Sitting Bull, philosophically wrapping a strip of scarlet cloth with his left hand and his teeth about his injured hand.

He did not seem particularly disturbed.

Chance saw that Sitting Bull, still smoking, was watching the young Indians fight before the cabin, no expression in his broad, wrinkled face.

Going to the chief's side Chance hunkered down.

"Can you stop this?" asked Chance.

"Yes," said Sitting Bull, puffing on his pipe.

"Why don't you stop it?" asked Chance.

"It would shame the young men to stop them," said Sitting Bull.

"Somebody can get killed," said Chance.

"Yes," said Sitting Bull.

Drum, natively, being a larger man, was undoubtedly stronger than the younger, more slightly built Running Horse, but the latter's desperation and tenacity had made the match seem fairly even.

Then Drum, at last, managed to twist free from Running Horse's grip and Chance leaped to his feet but before he could interfere the long-handled steel hatchet rose, flashed once in the cold, autumn sun, and slashed downward.

Running Horse twisted backward but the blade of the hatchet tore through his shirt from the neck to the belt, leaving a sharp, broken bright line of blood where it grazed the body in two or three places.

Running Horse's shirt fell open.

The hatchet fell from Drum's hand, to lie unnoticed in the dust, and the young Indian, only a moment before so intent upon war, slipped stumbling, shaken, back into the Indians who crowded about, leaving the circle of conflict uncontested beneath the moccasins of Running Horse.

Running Horse tore the useless shirt from his shoulders and threw it to the dust.

On his chest were the twin wounds of the Sun Dance.

Kicking Bear said it, from the side of the cabin. "He has looked at the sun."

Sitting Bull now stood.

All eyes turned toward the chief, and as he stood, not speaking, he let his heavy, dark blanket, thick with smoke and grease, slip from his shoulders.

Large on the broad chest of the old chief, but white and old, were the twin scars of the Sun Dance.

He went to Running Horse and put his arm about the shoulders of the young man. Standing in this way he faced the Indians, and Drum and Kicking Bear.

"He has looked at the sun," said Sitting Bull. "I am proud."

The face of Running Horse in this moment seemed the most magnificent thing that Chance had ever seen.

"The white man must die," said Kicking Bear, sitting on the ground, finishing the knot of scarlet cloth that bound his hand. "He has seen the dance."

Running Horse spoke to Sitting Bull. "The white man is my friend," he said.

"Then," said Sitting Bull, "he will not die—because he is your friend."

Sitting Bull took his arm from Running Horse's shoulders and stood before Chance.

He put his right hand on Chance's shoulder, holding the pipe cradled in his left hand.

"The lodge of the Hunkpapa is your lodge," he said. "The fire of the Hunkpapa is your fire. The kettle of the Hunkpapa is your kettle."

"Thank you," said Chance.

Sitting Bull looked at him. "Let us go inside," he said. "Let us smoke."

"I would like that," said Chance.

The chief turned and gathering his banket about his waist, and holding the pipe, led the way into the cabin, Chance and Running Horse following him.

At the sound of the gunshot, when Chance had wounded Kicking Bear, Winona, the first and only daughter of the subchief Old Bear, had run with many other Indians to the cabin of Sitting Bull.

There she had stood in the midst of the Indians who had watched Running Horse and Drum struggle, and had seen the hatchet of Drum inadvertently reveal the wounds of the Sun Dance on the chest of Joseph Running Horse.

Now the Indians had returned to watch the dance, and Chance, Running Horse and Sitting Bull having gone into the cabin, Winona and Drum stood before the cabin.

She looked at him, her large, dark eyes questioning. Why had he attacked Running Horse? Had he seen the wounds of the Sun Dance? What did it mean? Were they not both of the Hunkpapa?

"Pick up my hatchet," said Drum.

Winona obediently knelt down to the dust and picked up the fallen hatchet, handing it to Drum so he would not have to stoop.

"Running Horse thinks to shame me," said Drum. "But he will not do so."

"He has danced the Sun Dance," whispered Winona, looking toward the closed door of the cabin.

"It means nothing," said Drum.

Drum slipped the hatchet back in his belt.

"You would have killed him," she said.

Drum looked at her closely.

Winona dropped her eyes. "He is of the Hunkpapa," she said, confused.

"No," said Drum, "he is only a Short Hair, doing what the white men want."

"No," said Winona, lifting her head. "He is Hunkpapa." And she added, "And he has danced the Sun Dance."

"Do you care for him?" asked Drum.

"No," said Winona, dropping her head.

Drum grunted his satisfaction.

"I am lonely in the lodge of my father," said Winona, not raising her head.

"I will bring him horses," said Drum.

"What if he does not take your horses?" she asked.

"Then," said Drum, "I will take you to the Bad Lands and we will live in the old way, and later when he is ready to take my horses I will bring you back."

"When will you bring horses to the lodge of my father?" asked Winona.

"When my honor is strong," said Drum.

Winona looked at him, puzzled.

"By dancing the Sun Dance, Running Horse has sought to shame me," he said, "but instead I shall shame him."

"Please," said Winona, "do not think of Running Horse." Hesitantly she put her hand to the buckskin sleeve of Drum's shirt, daring to touch him. "Think of the girl," she said, "whose name is Winona."

A scowl from Drum made her withdraw her hand.

"They will laugh at us if they see you do that," he said. Then he added, bitterly, "You show your love where people can see. You must have pride. You are too much like a white woman."

Tears crowded Winona's dark eyes, and she dropped her head before this rebuke.

Drum contemptuously fingered the calico of her blue dress.

"Like a white woman," he said, scornfully.

Winona trembled. "I have very little," she said.

"Why should I bring horses for such a woman?" asked Drum. "I, the son of Kills-His-Horse?"

Winona could not answer his quesiton, nor did she dare to try. It was incomprehensible to her that a brave such as Drum, the son of the great Kills-His-Horse, might want her. Often enough had her father lamented her lack of flesh, the want of skills that a woman should know, her diligence with the words and ways of the white man.

"I am unworthy of Drum, the son of Kills-His-Horse," she said.

"I will come for you," said Drum, "when I have made my honor strong."

Winona flushed with happiness.

Lifting her eyes to his, unconsciously her arms, the fists closed, crossed themselves over her breast, as might have a woman's who kept a man's lodge in greeting him as he returned from the hunt or war.

This time Drum did not scowl.

"Good," he said.

"What must you do to make your honor strong?" asked Winona.

"Shame Running Horse," said Drum.

"But how?" asked the girl, the blue calico blowing about her ankles.

"I will wait," said Drum, "and when the white man who is the friend of Running Horse leaves the Hunkpapa, I will kill him."

Winona was startled.

"He has watched the Ghost Dance," said Drum, "and I said that I would kill him."

"He is not important," said Winona.

"Drum, the son of Kills-His-Horse, has said that he will kill him," said Drum, "and Drum, the son of Kills-His-Horse, does not lie."

Winona shook her head. "Let him go," she said. "He is not worthy to count coup upon."

Drum seemed to consider this for a moment. Then he said, "Then I shall not count coup on him, but shall only kill him."

"Let him go," said Winona.

"Do you care for Running Horse?" asked Drum, sharply.

"No," said Winona.

"When you see the scalp of the white man hanging from the poles of my lodge," said Drum, "you will know that my honor is strong again."

Winona looked away.

In her thinking there was little of the old way that was not dead. She did not like the white men nor the reservation but she knew, though only a woman, more of the meaning of guns and numbers and supplies than he, a warrior, who thought with his bravery and his medicine to turn the bullets of foes and would think nothing of pitting himself, his rifle and a paint pony against whatever odds he might find arrayed against him.

Drum was not wise, thought Winona to herself, but he was brave, and in her eyes he was beautiful.

For herself Winona did not want killing, for there had been enough of that. and in the end she knew it would be the Indians, her people, who would suffer most, for this was the true, undeniable meaning of the arithmetic of guns and horse and soldiers and wagons of ammunition—and too she did not want the white woman who taught in the school to die, for the woman had been kind to her, nor did she want the strange white man with Joseph Running Horse to die, for he had done nothing to hurt her or her people, and he was the friend of Joseph Running Horse, who was of the Hunkpapa, and had once drawn a circle on a blackboard which had enclosed his name with hers.

But she knew that Drum would do as he wanted, for he always did.

The thought crossed her mind that she might be able to save the white man, if she could warn him, and he could run away before Drum came to kill him.

But Drum must never find out.

"I must go," said Drum.

Awkwardly it seemed that he would reach out to touch her arm, but he did not do so, but turned and saying nothing more left Winona standing outside the cabin.

How fine is Drum, she thought, and how fortunate am I that he would think of bringing horses to the lodge of my father.

She could hear the Ghost Dance, the stamping of the feet, the rise and fall of the wailing chant.

But Joseph Running Horse, she thought to herself, he has danced the Sun Dance.

He has not ridden his pony in the high grass and painted his face. He has not stolen horses nor taken a scalp, nor counted coup nor burned the lodges of his enemies, nor led their women bound behind his pony, but he has done more than all these things—more than all—he has been alone, and he has danced the Sun Dance.

Kicking Bear gingerly fished a piece of beef from the kettle with his left hand and began, his head thrown back, to feed it into his mouth.

Chance, with his knife, pinned a piece of beef to the bottom of the kettle and then pulled it out.

Sitting Bull, having satisfied himself, was smoking his pipe.

Running Horse, who had eaten rapidly and heavily, sat to one side. He did not speak much, as befitted a young man in the presence of older men.

In another part of the room Sitting Bull's wives and children ate from another kettle, one long since removed from the fire.

The kettle before Chance rested on a platform of rocks, and bubbled over a small fire, set in a hole in the middle of the dirt floor. Chance's eyes stung from the smoke. Not enough smoke, from Chance's point of view, found its way out the smoke hole in the roof.

Chance looked at Kicking Bear.

"I would like to learn about the Ghost Dance," said Chance to Kicking Bear.

Kicking Bear dropped the last of the beef down his throat and swallowed it.

Kicking Bear seemed to hold no particular grudge against Chance for the wound of his hand, about which there was wrapped a long strip of scarlet flannel.

Chance had offered to treat the wound but Kicking Bear had assured him loftily that he himself, Kicking Bear, was a great medicine man and would handle the matter, so Chance had not insisted, and then Kicking Bear had let him look at the hand anyway.

After he had done what he thought he should, Chance carefully bandaged the hand, and told Kicking Bear that he would not be likely to close the first and second fingers of his right hand from that time on.

He had then watched Kicking Bear, with his teeth and left hand, carefully undo the bandage he had placed on the wound, take something from his own medicine bag, which contained among other things, a small, dead bird, place this something—Chance saw now it was a leaf—on the wound, drop the white bandage in the bag, and then, patiently, with difficulty, rewrap the wound with the original strip of red flannel.

"Why?" asked Chance.

"Make it get well," had said Kicking Bear.

Chance thought maybe that was supposed to explain the leaf. Then he pointed to the flannel wrapping.

"Why this?" he asked. "Why not the white bandage?"

"More pretty," had said Kicking Bear.

Chance had begun to explain the theory of infection, but Kicking Bear would have no nonsense of this sort, and so he had desisted.

Yet from this time Kicking Bear had tended to regard Chance as a practitioner in his own trade, and worthy of respect in that regard, if not in any other.

It was well known that white men, though evil and untrustworthy, were shrewd and cunning, and knew many secrets.

It was undeniable their medicine had great power.

In particular Kicking Bear had been impressed with the stinging, brownish liquid Chance had poured on the wound from the tiny glass vial in his mysterious black leather bag, for the liquid had burned horribly and that had convinced Kicking Bear that it must be extremely efficacious.

For that liquid, in fact, Kicking Bear, not to be outdone, had given Chance in return two small leaves, from a plant Chance did not recognize, and six narrow bark-peelings, each about three inches long, from what was probably an aspen. These Chance had gravely wrapped in paper and put in his bag.

It was thus, all this done, that Chance felt it might now, following the meal, be permissible to question Kicking Bear on the theological complexities of the Ghost Dance.

"So tell me about the Ghost Dance," said Chance.

Kicking Bear looked at him, glaring, but not a glare of anger, rather one of righteous impatience with Chance's obvious lack of information.

"You can read it in your own Holy Books," said Kicking Bear.

"I don't understand," said Chance.

"Many, many years ago," said Kicking Bear, wiping his mouth with the flannel cloth wrapped about his wounded hand, "the Great Spirit so loved the white men that He sent His only Son to live among them and teach them the good trails and the true medicine, but the white men were white men, and they took the Son of the Great Spirit and foolishly nailed Him to a big wooden cross and killed Him."

"This is true," said Running Horse. "The woman who lives with the teacher at the school has told us these things, and so have many others, like the men in the black dresses."

"But," Kicking Bear went on, "the Great Spirit did not like this, which is easy to understand, and He is not so easily shamed by the white men, not Him, and He has appointed a time for the ending of the world and the great judgment. At this time the Son of the Great Spirit, the same One who was nailed to a cross and would not stay dead for the white man, will come to judge the white men and destroy them."

"Yes," said Chance, "I have read these things, or at least something like them."

"Well," said Kicking Bear, "the time of the judgment is spring. When the grass comes again and the trees are fresh with leaves, the Messiah is coming—the Second Coming, it is called—but this time He is coming to the Indians."

"I see," said Chance.

"The Indians," said Kicking Bear, "will not take the Son of the Great Spirit and nail Him to a tree. They will be happy to have the Son of the Great Spirit come and live among them, and teach them the good trails and the true medicine. They will give Him a fine buffalo-skin lodge, and good wives and good horses. They will treat Him as a chief."

"Where are the white men all this time?" inquired Chance innocently.

"Dead," said Kicking Bear. "In the spring the Messiah will come and the earth will roll up and cover the white men and their railroads and soldiers and big brick buildings. But the Indians who dance the Ghost Dance, only those, will dance on the top of the rolling earth and by the mystery of their dance be saved, and when the earth has covered the white men and their stone cities the earth will once more be new and beautiful. On the prairies the grass will grow waist high, and be green, and the streams will be swift and clear, and the antelope and the buffalo will come back to their country and with them will come all the dead Indians, and their horses and dogs, and there will be much singing and the making of medicine and much feasting and talking and hunting and being friends, and no white men."

Chance was prepared to suppose that there might be more between heaven and earth than was dreamed of in his philosophy, but he was reasonably sure that most of these things were not among them.

"Do you really believe that?" asked Chance.

Kicking Bear looked at him. "Yes," he said.

"Why?" asked Chance.

"Because I have talked with the Messiah," said Kicking Bear simply, "and He has told me it is true."

Chance felt a shiver move along his spine.

"You talked with the Messiah?" asked Chance.

"Yes," said Kicking Bear, "in the country of the Yellow Stones, where the water is like steam and the rivers burn, the Messiah came to me in a vision and He taught me the Ghost Dance and the Ghost Songs, and told me to teach these things to His children."

"How do you know what He said was true?" asked Chance.

"Does the Son of the Great Spirit lie?" asked Kicking Bear.

"I suppose not," said Chance.

"Look," said Kicking Bear. "I will show you." He got up and went to the corner of the cabin where he had leaned his Winchester. Carrying the weapon in his left hand he returned to the fire. "The Messiah," he said, "taught me to make the Ghost Shirts and I have taught this to the Hunkpapas." To Chance's surprise, Kicking Bear handed him the weapon. The Indian then went to a bundle of his belongings, containing his medicine bag, which lay near the door of the cabin. With his left hand Kicking Bear rummaged about through a blanket of items and drew forth a large buckskin shirt, dyed scarlet. He shook the shirt out and held it up for Chance to look at. There was a half-moon on the chest and the image of a buffalo on the back. It was a Ghost Shirt.

"When I wear this shirt," said Kicking Bear, "no bullet or knife can hurt me. The medicine of this shirt is strong."

"You should have worn the shirt this afternoon," said Sitting Bull, between puffs on the pipe. Chance thought he detected the faint glimmer of a smile in the chief's eyes, but he could not be sure, for the expression of Sitting Bull was now as apparently imperturbable, as impassive, as expressionless as before.

"Yes," agreed Kicking Bear. "I should have."

Then Kicking Bear held the shirt before his body. "I will show you," said Kicking Bear to Chance, and motioned for Chance to pick up the weapon and fire at him.

"I don't want to shoot you," said Chance. No sixteenth of an inch of deerhide was going to stop a Winchester bullet, and Chance had enough troubles without worrying about shooting down Kicking Bear, prophet of the Ghost Dance. Grawson was enough to have after him. There was no point in having the entire enraged Sioux nation on his trail as well. Chance smiled to himself. "No thank you," he said to Kicking Bear.

"Shoot!" demanded Kicking Bear.

All Chance could think about was the dead bird in the medicine man's medicine bag, the leaves Kicking Bear had given him, the peelings of aspen. "No," said Chance, very firmly, "no thank you."

"I will do it," said Running Horse, and before Chance could stop him, Running Horse had pulled the rifle from his lap and discharged it point-blank at the chest of Kicking Bear.

"God!" yelled Chance, springing to his feet. The cabin was still ringing with the report of the Winchester and the smoke from the expended cartridge burned Chance's eyes and nostrils.

He expected to rush to the side of Kicking Bear but the Indian was still on his feet.

Running Horse could not have missed at that range, but there seemed to be no mark on the shirt, or Kicking Bear.

"I have seen this before," said Running Horse, handing the Winchester to Chance, who took it numbly.

"Now you see," said Kicking Bear, folding the Ghost Shirt on his knee with his left hand, "the Ghost Shirt is Big Medicine."

There was not even a powder stain on the shirt.

"In the spring," said Kicking Bear, "when the Messiah comes, the white men may try to stop Him, or try to kill Him again. That will be bad for the white men because then the true children of the Messiah, the Indians, will have to fight. They will have to take to the warpath to protect the Messiah." Kicking Bear now had the shirt half folded, half wadded up. "In the fight the Ghost Shirts will protect the Indians, but the soldiers will die, because they have no Ghost Shirts."

On an impulse Chance cocked the Winchester and, firing from the hip at the porcelain mug on a shelf across the room, pulled the trigger.

The bullet burst the mug into a thousand gleaming white porcelain fragments and sank two inches into the beam log behind the shelf.

Chance handed the weapon back to Kicking Bear and sat down, wanting to think things out.

Then Sitting Bull spoke. "The soldiers," he said, "may try to stop the Ghost Dance. That will be trouble. That will be war. My people will fight."

"Do you want that?" asked Chance.

Sitting Bull looked at him stolidly. "No," he said. "But my people will not stop the Ghost Dance."

"Why not?" asked Chance.

"Because they believe it is the will of the Great Spirit," said Sitting Bull.

"Do you believe it?" asked Chance.

"I do not know," said Sitting Bull. "Maybe it is true. I think it is hard to know the will of the Great Spirit."

"What will you do if soldiers come to take you away?" asked Kicking Bear.

"I will go with them," said Sitting Bull, taking a tiny twig and pushing it into the fire under the kettle.

"The Hunkpapa will not let their chief be taken away," said Running Horse.

Sitting Bull took the twig, now burning, and put it in the bowl of his pipe, relighting it, and then threw the twig away. He puffed once or twice on the long-stemmed pipe. "That is bad," he said, "for then many men will die." He puffed some more and then looked at Chance. "Then there will be war," he said.

Chapter Eight

———————

It was the twelfth of December, 1890.

Winter, though its signs occasionally made themselves felt, was still holding off. On the whole it had been a strange, warm dusty fall. There had been no snow as yet.

When winter comes, thought Chance, it will come fast and hard.

For more than a month Chance had shared the quarters of Running Horse, a small one-room cabin which Running Horse had occupied alone since the death of his mother, two years earlier. There had also been a younger sister and two brothers, one younger and one older, all of whom had died of smallpox in 1866. Running Horse himself, Chance had observed, in tiny, scarcely noticeable pitted scars on his face and neck, bore the marks of the disease.

It takes a people time, thought Chance to himself, to build a resistance to disease, time for the disease to weed the stocks, leaving behind the surviving, the hardy. The fair resistance of the whites to this disease, still not adequate, had been purchased cruelly over centuries, generation by embattled generation.

Chance wondered if wool blankets from smallpox wards still found their way as gifts and trade goods to Indian encampments. Probably not, he thought, the Indians are no longer dangerous. And that was in the East, he told himself, when we were more barbarous, or more frightened.

And maybe it's not true, he said to himself, maybe it's not even true.

It's time I left, Chance told himself, I've stayed too long.

That night, as they shared their kettle, Chance decided to speak to Running Horse.

He wanted to give Running Horse something to thank him for the hospitality he had been shown, but he didn't know what. He knew Running Horse well enough to know that he would not accept white man's money, and Chance had noth-

ing much else of value. Perhaps his watch, he thought. He
could buy another.

But then Running Horse would want to give him something else, of comparable value, and what did Running Horse
have of suitable value that he could really afford to spare?
And if the gifts were not of somewhat equivalent value Running Horse would be shamed. Perhaps my shaving mirror,
thought Chance, but that didn't seem right. This requires
thinking, said Chance to himself. The whole problem is preposterous perhaps, but not here in this cabin at this time.
This matter will be important to Running Horse, said Chance
to himself, and thus it is important to me.

While he was ruminating these matters, the affairs of the
world, in the figure of Joseph Running Horse, impinged on
his meditations.

Running Horse, having finished the meal, was smoking
across from him.

"Today," said Running Horse, "Sitting Bull gave me this.
It was brought to him from the agency."

From inside his shirt Running Horse produced a paper, it
was *Harper's Weekly*, and a handbill.

Chance took them quickly.

"There is your picture," said Running Horse, pointing to
the handbill.

For an instant Chance's hand felt like shaking, but did not,
and he was glad it did not.

Rather, saying nothing, he looked over the materials. After
he had read them, he said, "You must thank Sitting Bull for
me. It was good of him to see that I got these things."

Chance would be moving out in the morning.

In *Harper's*, there was a feature story, picked up from an
Omaha newspaper, which had perhaps received it from a
weekly in Good Promise, or perhaps the story had drifted in,
carried by a homesteader, moving eastward, sold for fifty
cents or so. It told of an outlaw surgeon, who had shot a
soldier in Good Promise, South Dakota, and then treated his
wound and disappeared. There was no picture but the de-
scription was not bad. Chance realized he must wrap the medicine kit inside the blanket roll from now on. The other item,
the handbill, was a wanted poster, with his picture, a descrip-
tion, and the information that he was wanted for murder
and that there was a reward of one thousand dollars, not for
capturing or killing him, but simply for information leading
to his arrest.

Grawson, thought Chance, he's saving me for himself.

The address to which the information was to be sent was an office number in a government building in Washington, D.C.

Why doesn't it just say Lester Grawson, Chance asked himself.

Chance clenched his fists, wadding the handbill in his right hand.

He was damn sure he was not wanted for murder, and if he was, there was no thousand-dollar reward. That was a fantastic sum of money—for anything—let alone for information.

There would be no reward.

Grawson might say so, but the reward would never be forthcoming, never. Still its promise might get him for Grawson. The promise would be sufficient. Chance could bitterly imagine the meaningless check drawn on the State of South Carolina which Grawson might, taking his prisoner into custody, bestow on some duped, grinning homesteader or bounty hunter, a custody that would end probably with a bullet in the back of Chance's head.

The resources of the law belong to Grawson, thought Chance, infuriated. Grawson, with his badge, his credentials, his forged warrant for arrest.

Even the handbill might have been, on Grawson's authority, printed in Washington and forwarded through standard channels. Chance wondered if anyone would have bothered to check on the matter. Why should they, he asked himself. Grawson has the official papers. Who would expect that Grawson, with his badge, his credentials, his warrant, his letters, was not employed in the work of the law but serving the ends of his personal vendetta?

He's a killer, thought Chance, and good people will bless his guns.

Chance considered surrendering himself to the authorities, informing them of Grawson's pursuit, but that would mean involvement at Standing Rock, trouble with the army in the Totter shooting, and at best the law could only tell him that Grawson must first attack, and then they would have a case, in short, that they were helpless until, in effect, Grawson caught and killed him.

So Chance would run again.

"I was told more by Sitting Bull," said Running Horse.

"What?" asked Chance.

"Today a policeman from the land of the Great White Father, at the end of the wires and rails, came to Standing Rock."

"Grawson?" asked Chance.

"I do not know," said Running Horse, "but he is looking for you."

Chance's heart stopped.

"How?" asked Chance. "How?"

"I do not know," said Running Horse.

Chance tried to think, clearly. The handbill, the fight in Good Promise, the army, the authorities.

"I think," said Running Horse, "that at the agency it is known a white man who heals is staying at the lodges of the Hunkpapa."

Chance nodded. Word of his being on the reservation might have drifted back to the agency, perhaps from talk of women at the ration points.

He had done what he could in the weeks with Running Horse to practice his craft, examining the sick, setting bones, treating sores, trying to get the Indians, if nothing else, to boil water and wash bandages. A number of Indians, learning of his presence, had made the trip to Running Horse's cabin to profit from his skills, some from as far away as forty miles. Yes, Chance said to himself, the word that a white doctor was on the reservation might well have made the rounds, and in this circuit might easily have been picked up by the Indian Police, who would then as a matter of course have reported it to the agent. Probably no one had been out to investigate already simply because of the Ghost Dancing. The entire reservation was a powder keg and the authorities were not eager to risk setting it off. The agent, or the army at Fort Yates, or even the sheriff in tiny Good Promise, might have put these things together, and sent the telegrams eastward.

Chance had little doubt that the sum of it was that Grawson was at Standing Rock, and would be looking for him. Grawson—whom he had left so far behind.

"Do you want me to kill him when he comes?" asked Running Horse.

"No," said Chance, "no."

"Then you will kill him," said Running Horse, taking a puff on his pipe.

"No," said Chance, "no."

Running Horse put down the pipe. "Why not?" he asked.

"I don't want to hurt anyone," said Chance. "I did once—I killed a man—I don't want to hurt anyone else."

The next morning, before dawn, Chance saddled the sorrel and mounted, intent on a quiet departure from the Standing Rock Reservation.

"Do not forget," said Running Horse, who watched him preparing to go, "you are my Brother and one of the Hunkpapa."

Chance smiled, remembering the knife in the grove of cottonwoods.

"I will not forget," he said, "my Brother."

In the saddle, Chance turned and unbuckled one of the saddlebags, drew out the briar pipe he had smoked with Running Horse in the cottonwoods, and handed it to him.

"I am grateful to my Brother," he said.

Running Horse accepted the pipe, simply. "Wait," he said.

Chance watched as the young Indian went back into the cabin and returned, carrying his own pipe, the beaded, long-stemmed, fragile clay pipe with the high bowl.

"No," said Chance.

Running Horse handed the pipe to Chance.

Chance, sensing he must take it, did so.

Carefully Chance tied the pipe across the blanket roll behind his saddle.

Then he lifted the reins, pulled the sorrel's head west and touched his boots to the horse's flanks.

As he rode from the cabin he turned in the saddle and lifted his hand in farewell to Running Horse, who also raised his hand, the palm open and facing Chance.

The physician from New York rode alone down the street between cabins.

He was running again.

Chance looked around him, at the squatty cabins and the scattered tepees in the background. This morning, in the quiet, he could hear the Grand River slushing between its banks.

A dog barked in the distance, and Chance, turning, saw to his surprise five mounted Indians, young men all of them, leaving the camp and riding gently into the back prairie. They carried rifles. Among their number was Drum, whom Chance recalled had once fought Running Horse before the cabin of Sitting Bull. He dismissed them from his mind, and rode on.

Then Chance reined up.

Standing near the door of a cabin, under the eaves, he saw a girl, a lovely Sioux girl in blue calico, who lifted her hand as though she might speak to him. Her eyes, for some reason, seemed frightened.

He walked the horse to the side of the cabin.

She looked up at him, and then her eyes fell as though she could not speak.

Chance made to move the horse away but her small brown hands held the horse's mane.

"What do you want?" asked Chance.

"Sing your death song, White Man," she said, not lifting her eyes.

Chance did not understand.

The death song was sung by warriors who go into battle.

"I am not on the warpath," he said, smiling at her.

"Sing your death song," she said, and loosed her grip on the horse's mane, and turned and ran into the cabin.

"Wait!" called Chance.

The cabin door shut, and Chance could hear the wooden latch snap into place. The door could not be opened from the outside unless the latch string were, from the inside, thrust through the tiny latch hole in the wood.

Chance puzzled for a time and then pulled his horse to the center of the street between the cabins and continued his journey.

Inside the cabin, Winona, the daughter of Old Bear, leaned against the door, her back pressed against it, her head thrown back, the latch string knotted in her left hand.

She was sick with what she had done.

She had jeopardized the lives of one or more of her own people, perhaps even that of Drum, who was to be her husband. But she could not let the white man ride foolishly to his death, not knowing. Why she could not do this she did not know.

To herself she said, "Good-bye, White Man. Good-bye, Friend of Running Horse."

Lucia Turner shut her eyes to close out the mud walls of her soddy. She ground her fingernails into the cracked palms of her hands. She felt so dirty, always so dirty.

Lucia sat on a wooden kitchen chair on the dusty floor of the mud soddy she shared with Aunt Zita.

Aunt Zita had been called by the Almighty to bring salvation to the heathen.

God bless the heathen, thought Lucia to herself.

In front of Lucia was an unpainted plank table. This morning she had run a splinter into her finger and had dug it out with a needle sterilized in the chip fire in the range against the north wall. Putting her hand on the table it wobbled. On the table there was a cracked coffee cup, turned upside down so as not to catch the dirt that seemed to drop from the ceiling when the wind blew.

Lucia looked about herself.

The sod bricks of the house were flaking, and a thin line of dust lay along the base of the walls, where spiders chased game among the particles.

In one corner, incongruously, there loomed a high walnut china cabinet filled with porcelain from Saint Louis.

It had stood in the dining room of her father's house on a thick blue and red rug, now sold, which had come from China on a clipper ship more than forty years before.

The only other large memento of the house, that beautiful quiet stone house in Saint Louis, was the huge brass bedstead with its eiderdown mattress, against one wall, on which Aunt Zita slept.

Lucia slept across the room on a military cot, supplied by the agent, the Irishman McLaughlin, and probably obtained from the quartermaster at Fort Yates.

It was not particularly comfortable but it was as far away as possible from Aunt Zita.

Lucia liked that.

Moreover Aunt Zita prayed aloud at irregular hours and occupied not infrequently the intervals between her devotions with noises of righteous, stentorian slumber.

Lucia listened to the wind outside.

It never seemed to stop blowing.

A bit of dust slipped from the ceiling and filtered its way to the planks of the kitchen table. Lucia brushed some of it from her hair.

Lucia's fists clenched on the table.

She would leave.

She knew she would.

She would win yet.

Aunt Zita, of course, had simply refused to leave, and had ordered Lucia to dismiss the subject from her mind, and rapidly.

It is here that God has placed us, Aunt Zita had said, and it is here that we belong.

He may have placed you here, Lucia thought, but He didn't place me here, and I'm leaving.

Leaving!

But how could she leave?

Could she simply pack and hitch up the buckboard and drive away?

That didn't seem possible.

What of Aunt Zita?

My work, had said Aunt Zita, in this forsaken place is not yet done, and you will stay with me until I have finished.

I want to go home, said Lucia to herself. I want to go home.

Chance was riding toward the western borders of Standing Rock but he hadn't been much out of the settlement on the banks of the Grand River when a small white building, with chipped paint and a wagon box leaning against its north side, caught his eye.

Curious, he rode up and looked at the school.

There was a padlock on the door, some tumbleweeds caught against the building, and under a bench which stood near the door.

He moved his horse away, over a rise, and happened to see a small boy, Indian, about nine years old, digging with a sharpened stick among some rocks and cactus.

The boy did not pay him attention, but he knew the boy had seem him almost immediately, and then had applied himself again to his digging.

Chance rode up to see what he was doing, and looked, but didn't see. What was the point of it?

The young Indian had torn up the ground in a hole about two feet deep and as much wide, digging well past the frost line.

"What are you doing?" asked Chance.

The boy did not reply.

"What are you doing?" asked Chance again, this time, as well as he could, putting his question in Sioux.

Immediately the boy looked up and the small brown face broke apart in a wide happy grin.

Chance saw plenty of teeth in the broad little face.

The boy said something in Sioux, probably that he was digging or hunting. Chance made out the word "rattlesnake."

"Go slowly," said Chance in Sioux. He wanted something like "Be careful," but he didn't know the expression.

The concern on his face was read by the boy, who laughed.

"I watch," said the boy, and he had spoken in English.

It was not yet winter, but it was late fall. The snakes, Chance supposed, would be hibernating, somewhere in nests under the frost line.

"You speak English," said Chance.

"If I want to," said the boy.

"Good boy," said Chance in Sioux.

The boy laughed.

Chance asked to see the stick and the boy handed it up to him. Chance sharpened it with the bowie knife at his belt and handed it back to him, wiping the knife on the side of his pants, then sliding it back into his sheath.

"What's your name?" asked Chance.

The boy told him and Chance didn't understand.

"In English," asked Chance.

"William Buckhorn," said the boy.

Chance knew he hadn't said "William" before.

Chance wondered why he was digging for snakes. It was a foolish and dangerous thing to do. He supposed the boy's parents might have sent him off to kill snakes, and bring the skins home. He shuddered. It was a stupid, foolish thing to do. Dangerous.

Chance, in both English and his smattering of Sioux, tried to convey his objections to the lad who listened intently.

The boy thanked him and then returned to his digging.

As Chance turned to go, the boy, not looking up, said, "You are the man they are looking for."

Chance stiffened in the saddle. "Who?" he asked.

"At the agency," said the boy. "Two men. One from far away with red hair, very big, very strong. And a soldier from Fort Yates, two yellow stripes."

It would be Grawson, thought Chance, and someone to help him, to guide him through the reservation, to furnish another gun. Two stripes. A corporal. Maybe Totter. "What does the soldier look like?" asked Chance.

"Like all white men," said the boy.

"That's not much help," said Chance.

"He has a crooked nose," said the boy, looking up and smiling, making a gesture across his face, as though his nose were being bent to one side.

It would be Totter, thought Chance. Both of them. Grawson and Totter. I've got to get out of here. Still there's no immediate hurry. They won't come this far out, not with the Ghost Dancing. I'll have time. "Thanks," said Chance to the boy, and then, in Sioux, told him that his heart was light that he had spoken with him, that he was happy to hear what had been told him.

Then Chance bid the boy farewell, mistakenly addressing him as a man, which mistake did not displease the boy, and rode away.

Before Chance had left, the boy had said, first in Sioux, then in English. "I am William Buckhorn. Let the snakes watch out."

Then he had gone back to his digging.

Lucia Turner was alone in the soddy.

Aunt Zita, more than an hour ago, had put on her black carriage gown, taken the buckboard, her box of Bibles and pamphlets, and departed for the ration point, an area marked on the prairie not far from the administration buildings of the agency.

There she could preach to the Indians.

"It's Saturday morning, ration day," had said Aunt Zita that morning.

"Yes," Lucia had said.

"They'll have to come in for their handouts," had said Aunt Zita, pulling on her black gloves.

"Then you can preach to them," observed Lucia.

"Man lives not by bread alone," had said Aunt Zita.

"You are kind to think of the Indians."

"My duty," had said Zita.

"Blessed are the merciful," Lucia had said.

"For theirs is the Kingdom of God," Aunt Zita had added.

"For they shall obtain mercy," Lucia had corrected.

"Not unless they repent their heathen ways," had said Aunt Zita, and turned curtly and left the soddy.

A moment or two later Lucia had heard the buckboard rattle away.

Aunt Zita, staying overnight at the agency, would not be returning until the next day, perhaps about evening.

As yet Aunt Zita had not been given permission to use the building set aside as a Protestant meetinghouse, primarily because her credentials, perhaps in order in heaven, had not seemed sufficiently impressive to the agent at Standing Rock,

a most prejudiced decision in Aunt Zita's mind, undoubtedly
motivated by ulterior considerations. His name was, after all,
McLaughlin, and he would be Irish, and was undoubtedly a
secret and sinister instrument of papism, diabolically attempting to propagate Romish superstitions among the innocent
heathen of Standing Rock.

He had even had the gall to point out to Aunt Zita that
her presence on the agency was lawful only by virtue of her
kindred relationship to the schoolteacher, Miss Lucia Turner.

You shall not foil the work of God, Aunt Zita had told
him.

I hope that I shall not, he said.

My work, Aunt Zita had told him, is that work.

What work, he had asked.

The work of God, she had said, and left him without a further word, left him to his conscience.

For they shall obtain mercy, Lucia thought to herself.

At least it would be safe for Aunt Zita at the ration point,
used every second Saturday.

There would be soldiers there.

Of late, because of the Ghost Dancing, Aunt Zita had not
visited the settlements and encampments themselves. She had
been turned back more than once, at rifle point, by strangely
clad Indians.

Aunt Zita had thought the better of martyrdom, and had
turned the buckboard about and driven away.

Martyrdom would interfere with my work, Aunt Zita had
pointed out to Lucia.

Lucia had agreed.

With God's work, Aunt Zita had added.

Lucia had said, oh. Once, in a careless and unwise moment,
Lucia had asked Aunt Zita the grounds of her assurance of
her call, her vocation. It came to me in prayer, Aunt Zita had
said.

Lucia had thought about this for a while, and then had decided to stop thinking about it.

Lucia's father, now dead, had given her books to read
which were not available at the finishing school. Though she
was a girl, he had taken her for walks, and spoken of the
trees and the stars, of insects and the changes of animals, and
the mysterious world of which all she knew occupied but the
corner of a particle. They had spoken gravely of many
things, and Lucia had learned how much that men did not,
and perhaps could not, know. She had learned not simply the

records of empires, the tracks of the bones of time, but tried to see if they spoke the stories that she had been told, and found that they did not. Though she was a girl, and destined for the home, for sewing, the work of a house and the raising of children, he had wanted her to sense the depth of the puzzles about her, and the flatulence of the common formulas that would trivialize the depth of mysteries, humiliating and domesticating them into the comforting, cardboard truths that men, terrified of the dark, would sell their lives by rather than renounce.

Sometimes Lucia wished that she had the faith, the untroubled, uncomplicated mind, the ironclad serenity of Aunt Zita, who held the universe, its inhabitants and its purpose in the pocket of her apron. Then, thinking about it, Lucia decided that this was not her wish at all. She recalled her father and loved him, and rejoiced in his gift to her, that gift of question and wonder that so often hurt her, that refused to let her have rest, that would bring her not simple happiness perhaps, but the torment and awe that somehow, in rare moments, were beyond such happiness, becoming inexplicably something nobler and more priceless, becoming something that in the wind and under the stars gave her keen, unutterable joy.

Yet Lucia was a woman, and it was lonely and cold in the dark spaces between the stars, lonely and forsaken at the ends of time, and the mysteries of an alien universe were no more marvelous to her, nor should they have been, than the growth of a blade of grass or a kitten's fur or the imagined touch of a man's gentle, loving hand.

Lucia looked at the range against the wall of the soddy, smelled the fumes of the chip fire, and the iron of the range seemed warm and beautiful to her, and even the smell of the burning cow chips seemed somehow individual and sharp, and pleasurable and welcome.

Lucia got up.

She took the cover from a wooden bucket in one corner, tapped with the chipped iron dipper through the plate of ice frozen over the water, put some four dippers of water into a heavy metal pot, blue with black flecks, recovered the bucket, measured coffee, and set the pot on the range.

Lucia was very pleased that Aunt Zita would be gone for several hours.

She wasn't worried about Aunt Zita, for the woman would be riding to the agency, in the full daylight, and would return the next day, probably in the early evening, well before dark.

It did not occur to Lucia, whose school had been closed for nine days, due to lack of attendance, that she herself would be in greater danger than Aunt Zita. She was alone, unarmed, and not far from the Grand River encampment of Sitting Bull, who was generally regarded as a ringleader of the Ghost Dancing.

Major McLaughlin, the agent at Standing Rock, who had been very kind to her, had assured her that the Ghost Dancing would stop soon and that she could resume her duties. In the meantime, her pay, more than a dollar and a half a week, would be continued without interruption. Vaguely, when the major had spoken of the ending of the Ghost Dancing, Lucia had gathered that Sitting Bull was to be taken into custody, or somehow dissuaded from encouraging the Ghost Dancers. The major had not gone into detail and Lucia had not pressed him. He had apparently not wished to speak to her at any length about it.

Lucia thought of Sitting Bull, now an old man and almost a legend with his people, a medicine chief of the fighting Sioux in their days of greatness, one of the coup-counters at the Little Big Horn, a symbol in his way of his people's vanished glories, with which the Ghost Dancing itself seemed to have some pathetic, obscure connection. Lucia wondered what would happen if someone, most likely the Indian police acting on orders from the agent, were to attempt to arrest or capture Sitting Bull.

Nothing would happen, said Lucia to herself, but the Indians would not like it. No, she said to herself, they would surely not like it.

But there was nothing to worry about.

The day of the eagle feathers was gone.

Lucia could smell the coffee on the range now, and all was well with her, and her world.

Let the wind blow, she said to herself.

Lucia turned over the coffee cup on the table so that it was rightside up.

She poured the cup until it almost brimmed over on the table.

Satisfied, she went to a large, ironbound trunk, against the wall of the soddy where her cot stood.

Fishing about in this trunk, beneath linen, sheets, blankets, clothes, assorted boxes and packages, bags of hairpins, spoons wrapped in tissue paper, and such, Lucia extracted, from amidst several books near the bottom, an inexpensively bound novel, written in French.

She was rather pleased that she had learned French at the finishing school.

She placed this novel squarely on the plank table by the coffee, found her place and, sipping coffee, slipped from the soddy at Standing Rock to the marbled floors and mirrored walls of the palace of Versailles in the time of Louis the Fifteenth.

Brazen was she indeed, Madame de Pompadour, making her entrance at court on the arm of his majesty himself, the king, that woman so bold and proud under the scornful but frightened glances of the scandalized noblewomen.

The little soddy filled with the gay rustle of silk and the click of high, hard heels on the marbled floor.

Listening closely one could remark the minuet, something by Mozart perhaps.

The coffee popped and bubbled on the range.

Lucia leaped up once more and this time from the trunk, from the secret depths of a fur muff, she drew forth a wire and cloth contraption, bright and flouncy with red and yellow ribbons, from New Orleans.

It was deliciously vulgar and had been purchased secretly before she left Saint Louis—why Lucia was never sure.

Lucia threw back her head and laughed as she tied on the bustle.

Swinging her hips she flounced from one end of the soddy to the other.

Her father would certainly have been surprised, but then fathers never understood these things, and Aunt Zita would have been horrified, and would have thought that she understood them only too well.

It is sinfully attractive, thought Lucia, rather.

And I am pretty, thought Lucia, I think.

I wonder, she asked herself, if a man would desire me, if he would want me—want—yes, she said—want me.

Why not, she asked herself.

She laughed again.

Then, with a certain provocative regality, a certain aristocratic insolence, Madame de Pompadour, favored mistress of his majesty, on his very arm itself, entered the court, bold and proud under the scornful but frightened glances of the scandalized noblewomen.

Lucia curtsied to them.

"Who am I, did you ask?" she demanded, turning and fastening her insolent gaze on one unfortunate, cringing imaginary grand lady. "Why I am Madame de Pompadour," she replied, in stately tones. "You know," she added, giving her a wicked wink and jerking her thumb behind her, "the mistress of his majesty."

"Pardon me," said Edward Chance, who was leaning in the window of the soddy.

"Oh!" cried Lucia.

"I'm sorry," said Chance, removing his hat.

"Go away!" said Lucia. She tried to untie the bustle, but her angry fingers knotted the ribbon. She began to cry. "Go away!" she said.

"I smelled the coffee," said Chance.

"Go away!" said Lucia.

"All right," said Chance.

His head disappeared from the window.

Lucia stood in the center of the soddy, jerking at the ribbon on her side. She heard the leather sound of Chance's saddle as he put the weight in its stirrup, heard the brief snort of the horse, its movement.

Lucia jerked once more at the bustle, which now hung like a dead, gaudy bird at her hip. Then she laughed. She went to the window and thrust her head out.

"I'm sorry," she called.

Chance, in the saddle, looked at her.

"There's coffee," said Lucia Turner.

Chance sipped the coffee. It was hot and fresh, and black and bitter the way he liked it.

The girl was across the table from him, working her fingers in the knot of the bustle.

"You startled me," she was saying. "I didn't mean to be impolite."

"That's all right," said Chance. He wondered if she were wise, inviting a stranger into the soddy. He supposed she believed him to be working with the agency people. Certainly strangers seldom moved through the reservation.

"May I help?" asked Chance, awkwardly, watching her work the bustle knot free.

She dropped her head shyly, and blushed, as he had hoped she would. "I think not," she said, but then she looked at him and smiled, "thank you."

Then she had the ribbon undone and smoothed out the bustle and returned it to the muff in the trunk.

It seemed to Chance a strange place to keep a bustle.

The girl returned to the table and sat across from him, her hands folded in her lap.

It had been a long, long time since Edward Chance had been this close to a woman. She was plain to him, but not really. At least not objectionably so. There was a fragile thinness to her face, rather high cheekbones, soft, pale eyes, blue. The hair was burned shades lighter than it should have been. She should have worn a bonnet more. Her complexion was rough, chapped by the wind and washing with cold water. But she held her head well, and there was a fresh, honest look in her. She was obviously curious about him, but was too well-bred to inquire pointedly. Her speech was midwestern, except there was a trace of a refined, genteel accent, acquired probably in the Northeast, perhaps at some school. Chance decided, looking at her, that she was not really unattractive. No, Chance decided, not at all. If her hair were brushed and her clothes were better, and if it wasn't for the soddy and the plank table, and if she had been pouring him tea, instead of coffee, at a table with a tablecloth, and in a house with wallpaper, she might even have been pretty. Chance decided, speculatively, that he might even have liked her. He supposed it was lonely on the prairie. He wondered why she was alone. She made good coffee, he thought. She was pretty. Yes. Not beautiful like Clare, but pretty. Prettier even than the woman he had paid for in Chicago, with the scarlet sheets and the black ribbon choker in the two-story yellow house on State Street. It would not do, of course, to tell her that she was prettier than that woman.

Lucia, her hands folded in her lap, was pleased that the stranger liked her coffee, pleased the way a woman is pleased when a man likes something she does.

He was a rather ugly man, Lucia admitted to herself, but he did not look unintelligent, nor did he look particularly coarse. His accent informed her that he was from somewhere in the South, but his attire and his presence on the reservation were ample evidence that his background could not be gentlemanly. His hands were rather clean, to Lucia's surprise, and the nails were clipped short. They were long-fingered, nervous hands, not rough from handling rope or tools. He liked her coffee. He was asking her about herself and the school, and she was telling him. His eyes were gray, the hair

black. He was fairly tall, but not overly so. He seemed polite.
It made her a bit nervous how he looked at her. She wondered if he found her pretty. He looks lonely, she thought.
I'm lonely, she thought. Then she was asking him about himself, to make conversation. He didn't say he was married. He
didn't say he worked on the reservation. He was moving
through. She wouldn't see him again. He wore a pistol, low.
Many men did. Especially now. He had liked her coffee, and
she would not see him again. His name, she had learned, was
Edward Smith. A plain name, for a plain man, but a nice
man, well-spoken, courteous. Rape me, she thought, rape me.

"Would you like any more coffee, Mr. Smith?" she asked.

"No," said Edward Chance. "I'm riding out now, but
thanks very much."

He would go through the door and she would not see him
again.

"It has been nice meeting you, Mr. Smith," said Lucia Turner. "If you pass this way again, please drop in."

"Thank you," said Edward Chance.

There was a slight noise at the door and Lucia's half
scream was stifled in her throat as Chance slipped behind her,
his left hand covering her mouth, his right arm locked about
her waist holding her helpless. "Don't make noise," whispered
Chance. Lucia was too startled, after her first fright, to even
whisper. She shook her head, yes. Who was this? What was
he afraid of? He released her and she saw that the pistol had
moved from his holster. She hadn't seen it drawn but it was
in his hand. "I'm sorry," said Chance, softly. Then, curtly, he
gestured toward the door. "See who it is," he said, his lips
more forming the words than his mouth spoke them.

Lucia, shaken, stared at Chance.

"You're a criminal," she said.

The barrel of the pistol gestured to the door.

Lucia went to the door. "Who is it?" she asked.

A boy's voice answered. "They are coming," he said.

"Go away, William," said Lucia. "Go away."

Then to her surprise the man in the room with her moved
past her, dropped the gun into his holster and opened the
door. He spoke to the boy briefly in Sioux.

God, thought Chance, already they're here. The two men.
How far?

Not far.

The boy seemed sick. He was leaning against the plank
doorjamb of the soddy.

I've got to get out, thought Chance, now.

"What's wrong, William?" the blond woman was asking.

Chance moved through the door and, shading his eyes, stared into the distance.

A tiny drift of dust perhaps a mile or so away could be seen. They weren't coming fast. He'd have maybe fifteen minutes' start.

The boy had seen them from the top of the rise, and had apparently run to the soddy to warn him. He was covered with sweat, breathing heavily. And probably only because he had spoken a few words of the boy's language, something that set him apart from all the white others.

Chance swung into the saddle.

"Mr. Smith!" called the blond woman.

He looked back. The boy had fallen across the threshold. She was trying to pick him up.

"He's ill," she said. "Something's wrong."

"I'm going," said Chance, pulling the head of the sorrel away.

He had not even thanked the boy.

He turned back, briefly, calling in Sioux. "I am grateful," he said. "It is a good thing you have done for me."

But the boy did not reply.

"Something is wrong with him," screamed the woman.

Chance kicked the pony in the flanks and the startled animal had leaped into a gallop and then, fifty yards away, was jerked up short, rearing and snorting on its hind legs.

It had happened. Of course it had. Chance cried out in rage.

The bit twisted cruelly in the horse's mouth and Chance kicked him savagely toward the soddy. With a shrill snort the animal was jerked back on its haunches before the soddy, and Chance was out of the saddle, jerking his kit from the saddle roll.

He shoved Lucia away and picked up William Buckhorn and placed him on the kitchen table. From the boy's hand, as it unclasped, four rattlesnake rattles fell to the floor of the soddy.

Sweat poured down Chance's face. The inside of his shirt was drenched. The needle punctures, two sets of them, were on the calf of the left leg.

"He shouldn't have run," said Chance, talking to himself. "He shouldn't have run."

Chance improvised a tourniquet from bandages and the handle of a wooden spoon Lucia found for him.

He took a scalpel from his bag, wiped the blade with a cloth patch, passed it through the flame of the chip fire and then dipped it in a bottle of alcohol.

He cut crosses on the punctures and pressing his mouth against the boy's leg began to press and suck out what poison he could, spitting it on the floor of the soddy.

He worked without speaking for several minutes, gathering in the blood and poison and spitting it out.

William Buckhorn stirred, and his glazed eyes opened, and regarded Chance.

"They are coming," he said.

"I know," said Chance.

Chance lifted his face to Lucia. It seemed pale and haggard, desperate, angry. "How close are they?" he said, and the way he said it made her afraid.

She ran to the door.

"Two men," she said. Then she turned. "They're here," she said.

There was no hurry now.

Chance bandaged the boy's leg. He explained to Lucia about the tourniquet. "Get him to the agency as soon as you can," said Chance. "Find a doctor."

"There's a doctor at Fort Yates," said Lucia.

"Send for him," said Chance.

The men did not approach the door. Chance heard a shout from outside, perhaps from some seventy-five yards away.

It was Grawson, telling him to come out.

"Thank you for staying," said Lucia.

Chance had opened his revolver, was checking the cartridges. He spun the cylinder and closed the weapon.

"He would have died," said Lucia.

"Maybe," said Chance.

"Who are they?" asked Lucia. "The men outside?"

Chance smiled. "The law," he said.

"What did you do?" asked Lucia.

"I killed a man," said Chance.

Lucia's face went white.

"Come out, Chance!" called Grawson.

"Your name is not Smith," said Lucia.

"No," said Chance, smiling.

Before Chance could stop her, Lucia Turner had squared

her shoulders and gone to the door. She threw it open and stepped out into the sunlight.

"Who are you and what do you want?" she called.

She was told.

Chance, from inside the soddy, could hear her clearly. "There's no one here by that name," she was saying.

"Come out, Chance," Grawson called.

"I'm alone," Lucia was saying. "Go away."

Chance wondered why she was doing this. Because of the boy, because he had stayed.

It was foolish. His horse was outside, saddled, the saddle-bags packed.

"There's no one here," Lucia said. "It's my horse," she said.

Chance tensed as he heard a shot.

Lucia screamed.

"Your horse is dead, Chance," called Grawson. "Come out."

"Get back in here," hissed Chance to Lucia.

She obeyed him.

She was inside the soddy.

William Buckhorn lifted himself on one elbow on the table. "I will fight, too," he said.

"Keep the boy quiet," said Chance.

"You ain't got a chance," called a voice. That was Totter's voice. Not smart of him to reveal his position. He was on the other side of the soddy, away from the door. Covering the window.

Chance slid the bar behind the door, and, on his hands and knees, crawled over to the window. He stood up then, inside the window, and moved about an inch of his head from the frame, to get an eye on the outside.

Two shots smashed into the soddy, the first splintering the board that framed the window on the left, the second splashing a long, thin stream, almost like water, of dust into the center of the room.

So that was where Totter was.

Chance's cheek stung with splinters. His eyes were blinded from the shower of dust.

Lucia had screamed.

"Come out," Grawson called.

Chance tried to clear his eyes and cut his face with the sight of his Colt.

Lucia was beside him. She had dipped the him of her skirt in the water bucket and was wiping his face and eyes.

"Thanks," said Chance. Then, "You've got to get out of here."

"Are you all right?" she asked.

"Yes," said Chance.

"I brought you some rattles," said William Buckhorn, peering over the edge of the table, looking for them.

"Yes, William, yes," said Lucia and crawled over to the table.

"There they are," he said, pointing to the ground.

"Yes, thank you, William," she said, and took them in her hand.

"Big ones," said William Buckhorn.

Just then Totter's carbine thrust through the window, poking down to find its target. Chance, under the window, grabbed the barrel with one hand and jerked the gun toward him. The weapon discharged, the bullet ripping through his shirt, creasing his wrist, the sudden burn making him drop the Colt. Trotter struggled to hold the carbine, too frightened and desperate to let go. Chance jerked him halfway through the window. The broken nose, the distorted squarish face, cursing, was almost against his. Chance twisted the carbine out of Totter's hands, swinging the barrel against the side of his head. A line of blood as straight as the barrel creased the corporal's head. He fell backward, off balance, and scrambled around the outside corner of the soddy. Chance foolishly stood in the window and snapped off a wild shot. Totter had already rounded the corner of the soddy. Two pistol shots whined past Chance, knocking a double handful of dust to the floor across the room. Chance leaped back. Grawson had changed his position, covering Totter at the window. Standing well back in the room, partly shielded by the frame, Chance fired once at Grawson, who had risen to one knee. He saw some fur leap away from the collar of Grawson's coat, and then Grawson was prone again, firing at the window, once, twice. Chance supposed Totter would be around somewhere in front now, covering the door. He would still have his service revolver. Chance leaned the carbine against the wall and picked up his Colt from under the window. He rubbed his wrist. The numbness was going away. The fingers were unbroken, not sprained. Only a burn.

Now it was quiet outside.

They would not rush the soddy, or at least it would not be

wise to do so. Chance didn't figure Grawson would try that, not until dark at any rate. He was surprised that Totter had come as close as he had. He probably hadn't known any better. It was not a mistake Grawson would have made. Then Chance smiled to himself. Grawson had had a good shot at him, when he was near the window. Maybe Grawson had encouraged Totter to make his play at the window, to draw Chance into view. Grawson was smart, Chance decided, and then he smiled, and Totter was probably not so smart. Grawson would have been ready to expend Totter. Nice fellow, Grawson. I'll cover you, he could imagine Grawson saying to Totter, and Totter saying, all right.

Chance sat on the floor for about fifteen minutes, mostly listening. He looked out the window twice. Nothing much to see. The grass, the prairie, his dead horse.

"I'd better get you out of here," said Chance to Lucia. "And the boy needs a doctor."

He stood up near the window, out of sight.

"Grawson," he called out.

"Come out," he heard.

"There's a woman and a sick child here," he said. "A boy. He needs help."

"Come out," called Grawson.

"Let them go," said Chance. "I'm not coming out, and they may get hurt."

There was a long pause, and then he heard Grawson call. "All right. Send them out."

Lucia was wrapping William Buckhorn in two blankets.

"I'm not going," he said.

"Yes you are," said Chance.

"All right," said the boy.

"I'll take him to the Grand River Camp," said Lucia. "I can carry him there. Then we'll get horses and take him to Fort Yates. There's a doctor at Fort Yates."

"I killed four of them," said William Buckhorn, being bundled in the blankets.

"Why do you kill rattlesnakes?" asked Chance.

The boy looked at the schoolteacher and dropped his eyes. He mumbled, and spoke in Sioux. "For her," he said, "she is afraid of rattlesnakes. I kill them so she will not be afraid, and will stay with us."

"I know the answer to that question, Mr. —Smith," said Lucia. "I made the mistake of giving him some brown sugar once when he killed a snake, and then he kept killing them. I tried to stop giving him the sugar, but he kept killing them anyway. Outside I have a whole baking-powder can filled with rattles. Then I started giving him sugar again, not for the snakes, but to have him come here. So few of the Indians do. I told him not to hunt any more of them but he never listens. I scold him but it doesn't do any good."

"You don't speak Sioux," said Chance.

"No," said Lucia.

"You think he kills the snakes so you will give him sugar?"

"Of course," said Lucia.

Chance smiled and gave the boy's head a rough shake. "I think," he said to Lucia, "that you then owe this young man four lumps of brown sugar."

"I don't want to encourage that sort of thing," said Lucia.

"Four," said Chance. "Not one more nor one less, but exactly four."

"This is no time to speak of brown sugar," said Lucia.

"Four," said Chance.

Lucia went to a box on a shelf near the range and picked out four lumps, large ones, of brown sugar. She gave them to Chance and he placed them, counting them out, into the palm of William Buckhorn, who then solemnly swallowed them, one after the other.

After the last one Lucia could have sworn that William Buckhorn, in a manner surprisingly like that of a white child, winked, more of a careful squint than anything else. This squint, or signal, was clearly directed to Mr. Smith, who then returned it in kind.

"She's coming out," called Chance out the window.

William Buckhorn in her arms, a heavy burden for her, Lucia stopped at the door. "There's food in the locker by the range," she said, "some bread, bacon, flour, beans. Take what you want."

"Thanks," said Chance.

"After dark," said Lucia, "dig out the back."

Chance smiled. "I thought about it," he said. "What if they burn the roof first?"

"They'd better not," said Lucia. "This house is government property."

"Yes," said Chance, "I guess they'd better not." He smiled.

He had considered this matter with some care. The walls wouldn't burn. Only the roof. He could stay under the table, along the wall. It wouldn't make too much sense to burn the roof. At least he didn't think so.

If it came to that Grawson would do it, but hardly in the first hours.

Grawson might even enjoy the siege, the patient waiting. He would.

Chance wondered how they were fixed for rations.

Probably not badly. They wouldn't have known how soon they would catch up with him.

There seemed to be ample food in the soddy.

But Chance had already decided to dig out, this first night.

Covering the window and the door, they might not even realize, perhaps for hours, he had made his escape.

He could make it to the Grand River Camp.

Running Horse would help him get a horse.

He would be gone.

With luck, if things worked out, he would be gone.

Lucia smiled, too.

"If I'm in the neighborhood again," said Chance, "I might want to stop in for another cup of coffee."

He unbarred the door for her.

"I would be pleased if you did so, Mr. Smith," said Lucia.

"How is that?" he asked.

"You never killed anyone," she said. "Not murdered anyway."

"How do you know?" he said.

"Because you stayed to help William," said Lucia.

Then, quickly, she turned and, as Chance swung the door open, stepped outside, carrying the boy. His head looked out of the blankets over her shoulder.

"Good-bye, Warrior," said he, speaking in Sioux.

"Good-bye, Warrior," said Chance, also speaking in Sioux.

Then they were gone.

Chance swung the door shut and barred it, and would wait until dark.

A coyote yelped somewhere, maybe a quarter mile from the Turner soddy.

The moon was very white and the prairie dust shone as though it had snowed silver.

Corporal Jake Totter, his service revolver clutched in his right hand, lay on his belly back of the soddy.

He grinned.

He could hear a scratching from the inside.

Totter pointed the barrel of the pistol at the wall of the soddy.

He could fire now if he wanted, through the wall, now, and smash open Chance's mouth and forehead with a half dozen shots. He decided to wait. It might be worth it, seeing the look on Chance's face, just before he pulled the trigger six times.

Then Chance stopped digging.

Totter waited, not minding. He licked his lips. They were dry. He put his left fist under the barrel of the pistol to support it.

Then Totter saw the tip of a knife blade poke through the wall, and then there was a hole about the size of a coffee cup, and then about the size of a lard pail, and then an arm poked through and he saw the side of Chance's head.

So intent was Totter on his quarry that he failed to hear the sound of a pair of horses not more than a handful of yards away.

Totter's finger had begun to close on the steel trigger of his weapon when suddenly the bright silvery night shattered apart almost in his ear and God he cried out scared his own sound mingling with the shriek of the Hunkpapa war cry.

The horses came around the side of the soddy and Totter's finger closed wild on the trigger of his weapon and the fire jumped out of the barrel high and wide of Chance and Totter was covering his head with his hands and rolling away and one of the hoofs of the running animals caught him in the face like a pumpkin and he spit blood and teeth through the hole in his face.

"What the hell!" yelled Grawson from somewhere in front of the soddy.

Chance's arm disappeared from the hole and he leaped across the soddy and jumped headfirst out of the window, hitting the dust, rolling and getting up and running.

Two shots were fired but Chance didn't know whether they were fired at him or the Indians.

He ran along the bottom of the hill between the soddy and the school on the other side.

Another shot was fired.

There was no mistaking that one. It kicked a rock from the side of the hill, a few feet to his right.

It had been a pistol shot.

The range was too far now for clean shooting with a small weapon.

If Grawson had fired, Chance wondered why he hadn't used his carbine.

Another shot splashed dust behind him.

There was a cut in the hill, that led up behind the school. The school was high. He headed for the school. He ran up the cut, up toward the school, and the hair stood up on the back of his head as he heard a pair of horses behind him.

He turned to fire.

A voice cried "Brother!" in Sioux.

"Brother!" cried Chance in the same tongue.

Joseph Running Horse, astride one of the horses, the other with an empty saddle, had his hand lifted in greeting. Chance took the reins of the second horse, put his boot in the stirrup and hoisted himself to the saddle.

There was a carbine in the saddle boot of his horse, and he knew why Grawson hadn't used the weapon.

"Come," said Running Horse, urging his horse up the cut.

Chance followed and he saw the white boarded school on the top of the hill. They rode past two mounts for swings on which there was no rope. Past a lonely teeter-totter in the silvery schoolyard.

Running Horse pulled up behind the school.

Chance saw a woman near the wagon box against the north side of the building.

She came to his horse. "You must hurry," said Lucia.

Chance looked at Running Horse.

Running Horse simply said, "We have their horses."

Chance dismounted and faced the girl, saw the strain of her fear, saw how her hair could be beautiful when the wind moved it in the moonlight.

"Thank you," said Chance.

She dropped her head. She had one of the blankets she had carried William Buckhorn in, wrapped about her shoulders like a shawl. The girl seemed confused. Then she lifted her head. "You were kind to William," she said. "I didn't want you to die because of me."

"I wanted to kill them," said Running Horse. "With the knife. It would have been easy. They were apart, not watching behind. She did not wish it."

Lucia looked at Running Horse as though she could not believe what she had heard. "Joseph," she said.

Running Horse was speaking to Chance, and he paid the woman no attention. "Shall we go back and kill them now?" he asked.

"No," said Chance, "but my heart is filled with gratitude to my brother."

"They will follow you," said Running Horse. "It will be better to kill them now."

"No," said Chance, "I don't want to hurt them. I just want to go away."

"Someday you must fight," said Running Horse.

"I just want to go away," said Chance.

"Your Brother will fight with you," said Running Horse.

"Thank you," said Chance, "but I just want to go away."

"All right," said Running Horse, "do what you want."

"Mr. Smith," said Lucia, "I sent William to Fort Yates, in a wagon. His parents are taking him."

"Good," said Chance, "I think he will be all right."

Lucia smiled. "You'd better be leaving now, I think," she said.

Chance grunted. Yes, he would have to be leaving now. There would be no place where he would be staying too long. There never would be.

He looked at the girl and her face, thin and delicate in the moonlight, seemed very lovely to him.

There would never be a place he could stay too long.

Chance felt bitter, and very sad.

"Someday," said Chance, "if it's all right with you, I would like to come by again."

She looked up at him, and to Chance's surprise he thought her eyes were moist. "That would be nice, Mr. Smith," the girl was saying.

"Chance," said Chance, "the name is Chance."

"So I understood from the gentlemen outside the soddy," said Lucia.

Chance smiled. "They were right," he said.

"You have a long ride," said Running Horse to Chance.

"I know," said Chance.

Lucia started briefly. It was true, what Running Horse said. This man was running. This man who had spoken gently with her, whom she had told about herself, whom she found somehow strong and aware of her, and of whom she had found herself aware, as she had never been before—of a man. She had feared the stirrings that coursed through her at his nearness, how she might shiver at his touch, feel faint, and she had not wanted to come with Running Horse but she had known that she would, and she did. She would say good-bye, and he would be gone, and she would remember him, more so than the young men in Saint Louis, perhaps more so than any other.

He was an outlaw, Lucia reminded herself, a criminal, a man who must run, an animal that must prowl at night and hide in the day, away from honest men.

But he had been kind to her and he was strong, and he had stayed to help William, to work with an injured boy while men came with weapons to shoot and kill him.

"Yes," said Lucia, "it would be nice if you would come by again."

His hand reached out and held hers, so swiftly, so suddenly, it frightened her.

"I will," he said. "I will."

She had seemed so beautiful to him in that instant that he had wanted to cry out.

He must leave her.

Never could there be such a woman for him. Only the others. The painted, empty others, the strangers whose last names he would never know, selling themselves to him or any other, not caring.

Maybe it was only his loneliness, but that he did not believe.

The others had not changed the loneliness.

With this woman, unlike the others, he was no longer alone.

What a fool she would think him.

He cared for her.

"Please," she was saying, and Chance said, "I'm sorry," and withdrew his hand.

Lucia stepped back and shivered inside the blanket.

"It's cold," he said.

"Yes," she said, "it is."

Touch me again, she thought, please touch me again.

"Good-bye," said Lucia Turner.

"Good-bye," said Chance.

His hands reached out, not really much of a gesture, and somehow her hands had seemed gently to meet his, and then his hands were on her shoulders and they had stepped toward one another and their lips touched and Lucia cried out and clutched Edward Chance to her and then she felt him taking her into his arms, felt his iron, tightening arms choking her body, and could not breathe so hard did his arms hold her.

"I'm sorry," he said, and when by an act of will he thrust her from him, she could see the heat still in his eyes, hear the heaviness, the deepness of his breathing, and she could feel the mark of his kiss on her mouth.

"I'm not the kind of girl you seem to think I am," she was saying, and hating herself for it.

"Please forgive me," he said.

Lucia pulled the blanket about her shoulders. "Good-bye, Mr. Chance," she said.

"I'm sorry," he said. "Truly."

"I quite understand," she said, and turned to leave.

Joseph Running Horse said something that sounded like, "Huh!"

Lucia stopped.

"Take her with you," said Running Horse to Chance.

Lucia, not facing them, could not believe her ears.

"Take her with you," Joseph Running Horse was saying.

Lucia suddenly felt like running, but instead she turned abruptly about, reddening, to face them.

"What are you talking about, Joseph?" asked Lucia.

Running Horse looked at her. "Do not talk now," he said. Then he faced Chance. "You can let her go at the end of the reservation."

"I—I don't understand," stammered Lucia.

Running Horse looked at her. "You could gather wood and cook for him and keep him warm in the blanket."

"Joseph!" said Lucia.

"It's not done," said Chance.

Lucia blushed furiously, a change of complexion that was evident even in the moonlight.

"You mind your manners, Joseph Running Horse," said Lucia.

"Tie her to your horse," said Running Horse to Chance.

"I won't stay here and listen to this," said Lucia. And then she said, "Oh!" as she suddenly felt a rawhide coil of a braided lariat dropped about her shoulders and drawn tight, pinning her arms to her sides. The other end Joseph Running Horse had already looped about the saddle horn of Chance's horse.

"Joseph!" said Lucia, as primly as she could manage.

"You are only a white woman," said Joseph Running Horse. "We are Hunkpapa."

"I thought you liked me," said Lucia accusingly.

"I do," said Running Horse. "You will like my brother, and it will be good for you."

"No!" said Lucia, growing frightened.

Chance, more bewildered than anything, had stood by this conversation.

"And he will like you," said Running Horse, "for you are a good woman."

Good woman, good rifle, good horse, thought Lucia. She squirmed in the rawhide loop. "Please explain to him, Mr. Smith," she said, she begged.

"Yes, yes," said Chance quickly. "No, Running Horse, it wouldn't be right. She has been very kind. Has helped us."

"It is for her own good," said Running Horse.

"It is simply not done," said Chance firmly.

"No," said Lucia, even more firmly.

"All right," said Running Horse. "I thought it was a good idea."

Chance thought to himself, yes, it is an excellent idea, but it is just not done.

"I go watch," said Running Horse. Before he left he turned to Chance and said, rather sadly, "Good-bye, my Brother," and Chance knew that the young Indian did not expect to see him again, and Chance thought it was probably true, too, and said to him, "Yes, my Brother, Good-bye."

"Farewell," said Joseph Running Horse in Sioux.

"Farewell," said Chance, in Sioux.

Running Horse disappeared, and Chance knew that he would not have to worry about Grawson or Totter for the time being. Running Horse would "watch" and he would have the start he needed, probably until morning.

"Please," said Lucia.

Chance removed the lariat from her body. "I'm sorry," he said, but he seemed to be smiling, and Lucia was not sure that he really meant it.

"I don't know what got into Joseph Running Horse," she said.

Chance thought to himself that Running Horse had been very practical in his Sioux fashion.

"He thinks differently," said Chance. "He's Sioux." And Chance thought to himself it was not so much that he thought differently, as that he was willing, for one reason or another, to act as he thought. He had seen Chance had wanted this woman, and had understood, somehow, or thought he had, that she had wanted him, and so he had proposed that Chance see that it came about. But Running Horse, naturally, did not understand white women, nor, Chance told himself, did he himself.

"The very idea," said Lucia, and Chance was pleased that she laughed.

She looked up at him. "It seems I am fortunate that you are a gentleman, Mr. Chance."

Chance smiled. "I suppose so—Miss—Turner."

Lucia looked in the direction Running Horse had disappeared. She shivered. "He seems to think a girl would enjoy being dragged across the prairie," she paused, and looked at Chance, her eyes mischievous, "—on an out-law's rope."

"Not so much that part of it," said Chance.

"Oh," said Lucia, and looked down.

They stood together quietly for a time, neither of them speaking.

"You are very beautiful," said Chance.

Lucia did not look up, but in that instant like a fire running through her body she understood fully and for the first time in her life how it is that a woman can give herself completely to a man—though she knew she could not and would not do so—understood how it is that a woman could be shameless, rawly and utterly female. Knowing this thing she stood trembling at his saddle, aching, wanting him to touch her, to claim her weakness by his strength. Bind me, she thought, I desire to be yours. I will follow your horse like a captive squaw. But I must be made to do so. Must I ask you to tie your rope on my throat, to be tethered and led away, a woman?

"Good-bye," said Chance.

I don't want him to go yet, she cried out to herself, he can't go yet. He must not go yet.

She is a good woman, Chance said to himself, a gentle and tender and beautiful woman and there is no place in her life for an outlaw, a man who runs from the law, and though he be tempted to be cruel and love her he must not yield to this cruelty; if he cares for her, he must care enough to go; if he wants to love her, he must love her enough to say "Good-bye," to leave her standing here alone, as he will always remember her.

"Good-bye," said Chance.

"Running Horse called you his Brother," said Lucia, quickly, desperately.

"It's true," said Chance, explaining nothing.

"I don't understand," said Lucia.

"You don't even speak Sioux," said Chance. He must leave. He must be hard with her.

"No," said Lucia, hurt, "I don't."

He turned from her and, slowly, recoiled the rawhide lariat and tied it to the saddle.

"I'm sorry I don't speak Sioux," she said.

Chance turned to face her. "I'm glad," he said.

"But I don't want to stay here," she said. "I'm going to leave."

Chance hoisted himself into the saddle.

He looked down at her, the blanket wrapped about her shoulders, her face lifted to his.

"Do you know why Buckhorn, the little boy, kills snakes?"

"For sugar," she said.

"No," said Chance, "because someone whom he likes very much is afraid of them—he is afraid they will make her go away."

Chance turned the horse, kicked it in the flanks, and rode from the white-boarded school, leaving behind him a young, blue-eyed woman who stared after him.

"Good-bye, Mr. Chance," she whispered.

Chapter Nine

It was a dark, bitter rider who left the white school on the hill, his horse moving easily, the shadows in the silver light moving like spiders beside him.

Through the cactus and the sage in the December night on Standing Rock he rode, not noticing much of anything, keeping the horse always west.

They were long, cruel hours, and Chance would not make them easier.

He cursed himself for running, but knew that it was what he must do.

He was not a killer and he would not go back and kill.

He must leave Grawson to pursue, and he must forget the girl.

She had been brave, that girl, to have risked a hand in the games of men, and simply because he had been kind to a child, because he had stopped long enough to care for an injured boy.

Did she know the danger in which she had placed herself? Could she really understand a man like Grawson, understand that, cheated of his prey and knowing it, he might kill her as easily as the paw of a puma can fall across the neck of a fawn? But Grawson would never know her part in this. It was Indians, simply Indians. Running Horse had seen to that.

My Brother, Running Horse.

The girl had been in her way beautiful, and she had been lonely, so lonely, lonely as Chance was lonely.

They had listened to one another, not just looking and nodding, but hearing and understanding, and caring.

And, Chance told himself, she had held him, no matter what she said. She had cried out and kissed and touched, though she might deny it for a hundred years.

We might have loved one another, thought Chance, in a different time and place.

Chance stood up in the stirrups under the moon.

"I don't want to run!" he cried aloud to the prairie. And all the hatred and frustration that had built its slow fires in his heart over the weeks burst ugly bright in his body and he wheeled the horse to face the backtrail and his boots tensed to hurtle the animal into a gallop back to the school, back to the soddy, to fight to the death those that followed him and would kill him, to kill them or die, and if he lived, to go to the soddy and say to the girl, "My name is Chance. I've come back."

But Chance turned the horse again, west, enraged, weeping. Run, run, run.

The horse snorted.

Startled, Chance looked up. There was a ridge not more than fifty yards from him.

On the top of this ridge, clear and black against the moon, was a rider, an Indian, who carried a lance, winged with feathers; on his left arm was a buffalo-hide shield, from which hung five streamers of leather. With him were five braves.

The man lifted his arms, with shield and lance. He called out, "I am Drum, the son of Kills-His-Horse."

Chance remembered the Indian girl in the camp of Sitting Bull. She had spoken to him. "Sing your death song," she had said.

Chance threw back his head and not knowing why laughed like a madman.

"You bastards," yelled Chance, "I love you, you dirty bastards!"

It was the end of it. No more running. The end of it. It was over.

With a wild shout Chance kicked his horse up the ridge toward the Indians.

They were waiting for him to turn and run.

He didn't.

Chance was in the midst of rearing, snorting horses, sprawling bodies, screams of surprise.

At point-blank range Chance jerked twice on the trigger of the heavy Colt.

One brave fell backward blindly, pawing at his face, not reaching it.

Another, grabbing his gut, rolled over the neck of his pony and fell under the hoofs of the animals.

Chance jerked the trigger of the Colt again but the hammer struck on the rim of a bad cartridge and Drum's lance thrust through his shirt and Chance could feel blood inside but the lance ripped through and came free and another brave was behind and Chance swept the barrel of the Colt back and caught him in the throat and he dropped off the rump of his pony with a noise like gargling.

They were scattered.

Two were dead; another was dragging himself into the sagebrush.

About thirty yards off, the other two braves and Drum were gathering together, to come at him, and Chance yelled again, insanely, jerked his horse around and charged them. This time the knot of Indians broke with startled yelps and each rider separated, and they melted into the prairie, each one taking a different direction.

Chance found himself alone on the top of the ridge.

He had won.

Chance walked his horse down the other side of the ridge.

There was no point in being targeted against the sky.

It would be stupid to chase the Indians, and Chance wasn't stupid. But he had been lucky, he knew, damn lucky.

Not being afraid of dying he had done pretty well.

He knew that if he had run he would have been dead by now.

It hadn't even occurred to the Indians that he would attack them. They had wanted the hunt, the chase, making it last, then cutting him down when they pleased.

Drum hadn't even taken his rifle out of the buckskin sheath across his pony's back.

He had wanted to use the lance.

Drum would not make that mistake again.

It occurred to Chance, incredibly, that he was hungry. He pawed through the saddlebags on Grawson's horse, but there was no food there. Chance wondered idly if there had been. Perhaps Grawson had taken it with him, to eat while he watched. Chance recalled Lucia's offer of food. Pinned down in the soddy, tense, waiting, he hadn't eaten. He wished he had. Even a piece of bacon would be all right now. He wouldn't build a fire, too dangerous. He could eat it in the saddle, raw.

The various digestive juices, the names of which Chance recounted dismally to himself, were working on his stomach.

A jack rabbit lit out of the brush almost at his horse's feet and took its long bounding trajectory across the prairie.

Chance urged the horse after it and thought of taking a shot at it, and then thought the better of it. The shot would mark his position if there were any of the braves about. At last the rabbit entered some brush and seemed to stay there. Chance dismounted, picked up a rock and approached the brush. There didn't seem to be a rabbit and, poking around, Chance found the hole. He threw the rock away disgustedly. Then he lay on his belly and reached his arm down the hole. It was a damn sight deeper than the reach of his arm. Chance stood up and disgustedly slapped the prairie dust from his clothes.

His horse was browsing about ten yards off and Chance walked over to get it and the horse moved ahead of him, and Chance moved after it and the horse found something else to eat, always about ten yards further away than Chance happened to be at the time.

Then Chance said a few things to the horse which he would not have said in the presence of Lucia Turner, or for that matter in the presence of the woman in Chicago.

He stumbled after the horse, his feet shuffling in the dust, muttering.

Once he got to within about four or five yards of it and then it shied away and stood looking at him, as though it might never have seen him before.

Chance whistled softly and coaxed and wheedled but the animal had better things to do.

Nibbling here and there out of reach.

Then Chance, not thinking, angrily, hungry, began to run after the animal, and it moved easily away again, effortlessly maintaining that same maddening, delicate interval.

Then he stopped and began to cajole it once more, and wished he had the rope that was on the saddle, and felt like putting a bullet behind its ear.

Then Chance said, "Ah," for he had seen to the left, about a hundred yards away, a small grove of trees, and Chance circled so as to drive the horse into the trees.

"Yah!" he yelled, rushing forward.

The horse turned and cantered into the trees. There, after a minute or two, Chance ran the animal into a mass of brush and as it was backing out snorting he grabbed the bridle.

Instantly the horse became calm and obedient, infuriatingly domesticated.

"Goddam you," said Chance, giving its neck a couple of

happy slaps. "Yes," said Chance, "double goddam you." The horse rubbed its nose against his shoulder.

Chance heard a tiny noise.

It sounded like dried peas or pebbles in a wooden bowl, and it was over his head.

He looked up.

In the moonlight above him, hanging from a branch of the cottonwood beneath which he was standing, he saw a gourd rattle swaying softly, gently, in the wind. It was from this that the sound came.

He looked up past the rattle and was startled.

In the branches of the tree, a few feet above the rattle, there was a wooden scaffold, and on the scaffold there was a large bundle, wrapped in leather and tied tightly.

In other trees Chance saw similar scaffolds, each with a similar burden.

From the scaffolds, here and there, hung other rattles, and bone whistles and pieces of colored cloth. From some of the scaffolds there hung, like dark disks in the moonlight, leather shields.

He knew what place this was, and that there would be food here, offerings of corn and dried meat, but he also knew that he would not eat it.

The eastern sky was gray now, the moon a pale disk in a robe of fading stars.

The first definite light of the sun, flung from its rim's edge, lay over the prairie now like a cold, golden blade, a saber gleaming at the bottom of the horizon, bleak and glinting in the east.

Chance stooped down and tore up a handful of grass and sucked the moisture from it.

The wind cut through the grove of cottonwoods, stirring the rattles and the streamers of colored cloth, faded now, hanging from the branches. Over his head the buffalo-hide shields turned and swayed, moving with the wind.

Chance shivered.

It had taken him longer to catch the horse than it should have, and he had stayed perhaps a bit too long in this place, looking about.

Had he not been as hungry as he was he might have stayed in the grove until dark, and then moved out at night.

He could eat the offerings on the graves, and he supposed it was the thing to do, in spite of the repulsion. He asked himself why he should not do so. He told himself he was not yet that hungry. Also, he told himself, I am the brother of Running Horse, and he would not want that.

Swinging up into the saddle Chance moved the horse out of the trees.

They had broken cover only a pace or two when Chance flung himself out of the saddle, the rifle shot cracking over his head, two others splattering into the damp ground under his horse's hoofs.

Running he dragged the protesting animal back into the shelter of the trees.

Of course they had followed him, Drum and the others. They had been waiting for him to come out of the trees.

They should have waited longer.

They had been eager, too eager, as young men are eager.

Chance tied the horse well back in the grove, where it could not be seen, trying to shelter it back of a knot of cottonwoods.

He slipped Grawson's carbine from the saddle boot, checked the weapon quickly, scooped a handful of cartridges from the saddlebag into his pocket.

Why hadn't they come into the grove to get him?

Chance ducked back through the trees and getting to the edge of the grove, crawled forward on his stomach, inching with the carbine up a tiny, bush-covered rise that would give him a view of the prairie.

Water from the bush he crawled under slid down his neck, and Chance cussed to himself and lifted his head over the rise, just enough to bring his eyes over the grass.

There were three of them.

They had withdrawn apparently, more than a hundred yards from where their shots had been fired.

Chance estimated the distance and the wind. He decided not to try a shot. There would be little more than a random chance of getting a bullet within yards of them.

He watched them, astride their ponies.

They made no move to approach more closely. They had returned their rifles to the buckskin sheaths carried across their thighs.

For a minute Chance angrily regretted losing his horse and spending the time necessary to recapture it, and for not leaving the grove immediately, but as he lay there on the damp grass, watching the young men in the distance, he realized that he would be dead now if the horse hadn't escaped, if he hadn't taken shelter in the grove.

He had scattered them, but they would have regrouped almost immediately, picked up his trail in the moonlight, followed him and brought him down on the open prairie, apart from cover, where their three carbines to his one would have made the difference.

He might have survived, but it was not likely, especially after they had learned that he was dangerous.

Unaccountably, to Chance's mind, they had not feared him to begin with. He was not an Indian.

But now, judging from the distance, they feared him, but would not give him up.

Chance was puzzled why they did not fire into the trees, trying to draw his fire.

Perhaps their ammunition was severely limited.

Sometimes Indians went into battle with only a handful of bullets, sometimes only three or four.

The Indians could not make their own bullets, as could the white man.

Chance wondered if the white man would have held his land if he had only two or three bullets per man and a handful of stone- or metal-tipped arrows, and his wits and his courage. Probably not, thought Chance, especially after the buffalo were gone. What if the enemy could take the white man's beef and wheat and corn from him, as they had taken the buffalo from the Indian?

Chance carefully backed from the tiny, grass-covered rise and slipped back among the trees. Then, under cover, changing his position, he emerged from the grove, standing at the edge of the grove in full view. If any of the Indians reached for their carbines, he would have time to retreat into the trees. He wanted to see if they would fire. And he did not want to betray the position on the small rise. It was too good to reveal until he was reasonably sure of a hit.

Chance was now out of the grove about fifteen yards. The young men watched him. When he was about thirty yards out, they began to separate and move their ponies toward him, walking.

As they approached, he turned and, slowly, walked back into the trees. He had judged this matter fairly carefully, taking into consideration the time it would take to withdraw the carbines from the buckskin sheaths, the difficulties of firing from a moving platform at the distance and in the wind, and the time it would take to dismount and fire. Even so he knew they would have time for at least one shot apiece. And, as he walked away, and neared the grove, three shots rang out, cracks and whines in the air, passing through the trees, but he did not hurry. Then he was back among the trees and turned to face them, and they fired no more, though he was clearly visible—and they were moving back again, out of the range of a reliable shot. So Chance learned that they had ammunition, that they would fire only on him when he was out of the grove—probably because they did not wish him to die in the place of the scaffolds, did not want him to die in a place holy to the Sioux. And he had taught them, as Running Horse would have liked—that he did not fear them, that his medicine was so strong that he could walk slowly and alone before them, not fearing their bullets. That would give them much to think about. Also it might anger them, and that would be good. It had been a risk, but Chance hoped, not as great as it had seemed, and the advantages to be accrued were considerable.

Among the trees Chance saw that one of the young Indians, Drum, no longer carrying his carbine, had advanced several yards. There, at the edge of carbine range, he sat down cross-legged, and took out a pipe and tobacco. Chance smiled as he watched the young Indian deliberately light the pipe, and begin to smoke. The other two braves remained at least fifty yards farther back. It was Drum's answer to his own act of courage. He let the young Indian finish his pipe, and did not fire. It was doubtful that he could have struck him at that range, and it would be a loss of face to have attempted to hit him and miss.

Drum, after a time, stood up and, carrying the pipe, returned to his pony, and his two companions.

Then the four of them, the Indians and Chance, sat down to wait.

Chance knew that he did not feel like waiting too long. He was hungry.

But he would wait until after dark. That would be the best time. In spite of the moon.

Chance might have stayed for some time in the place of scaffolds, living off the offerings on the platforms, but he did not care to do this, and more importantly, Grawson and Totter would be somewhere, and they would, presumably, eventually, find him if he remained here.

He would move out at night and see what happened.

An hour went by and then another hour and Chance sat in the grove, keeping his eyes on the distant trio of Indians, waiting for dark.

He was hungry, damn hungry.

He supposed they were, too. Why not? Maybe they had the practical sense to bring something with them. But most likely not. They had expected to be finished yesterday. They would learn war, as Chance was. He should have stuffed bread in his pocket in the Turner soddy, should have eaten at any rate.

Chance noted, with begrudging approval, that the Indians had taken up a good position several hundred yards away. They were sitting on the slope of a rise that bulged up out of the rolling prairie about them like a bear's shoulder. They were out of carbine range, of course. Most importantly, they were high enough to see the cottonwood grove as an isolated feature of the landscape. They could see if he left the grove, without splitting their forces, without getting out of earshot of one another. He would be spotted by all of them, together, within half a mile of leaving the trees, no matter what direction he took.

They might be young but that sort of thing was in their bones. They were Sioux.

Next time they would know enough to bring more food.

They had tobacco at any rate.

Chance didn't.

For Chance there might not be a next time.

Chance shifted his position and sat with his back against the trunk of a cottonwood, some yards back from the edge of the trees.

Tobacco.

He wished he had the clay pipe now that Running Horse had given him, and a handful of his own weed. It made him angry to think of the young men on that bear's shoulder of ground, talking and smoking, mostly smoking.

He wished Grawson hadn't killed his horse. He'd liked the animal.

He wondered what had happened to the medicine kit tied behind the saddle, and wondered if young Buckhorn was doing all right, and if the blond schoolteacher thought of him, if she might wonder what had happened to him.

He guessed Buckhorn would be all right; that was a tough youngster.

Probably the schoolteacher would give the medicine kit to

Running Horse; and he would tie it to the rafters of his cabin, with his own medicine pouch and the hawk feathers, knotted together with twine, that hung there, so Chance could get it if he ever came back.

And the schoolteacher—she—she would, presumably, think no more of him, at least after giving Running Horse the medicine kit; he had been there and he had left; he was nothing, and was gone; he had drifted in and out of her life, a human weed not too unlike those rolling tumbleweeds that blew across the prairie ending up somewhere at the wind's end; he would not see her again; perhaps she had forgotten him already; he would not forget her; he would remember; he would not forget. Never.

Chance lifted his head sharply.

Carried on the wind, from a distance, he heard a man's voice, thin and frail, singing.

In the shadow of the trees, his carbine ready, Chance saw the man, an Indian, wearing the forgotten regalia of a Plains warrior, riding slowly toward the grove.

It was not Drum, nor either of his two braves.

It was an old man, unafraid, riding directly toward him. None of the young braves in the distance had tried to stop him.

Did they want him to be killed?

The old man wore a flimsy, ceremonial breastplate of dyed porcupine quills. Besides this, he wore only a breechclout, moccasins and a single eagle feather, which stood high in his white hair. He carried a bow and three long buffalo arrows.

Chance leveled the carbine, set for extra steadiness in the crotch of a tree, directly at the center of the old man's flimsy breastplate of porcupine quills.

But he did not pull the trigger.

Rather he let the old man ride almost to the muzzle of his weapon, and then withdrew it from the crotch of the tree.

Hearing the sound, Old Bear, the father of the girl Winona, stopped and listened, and leaning forward, made out the figure of Chance, one shadow among others, but one unmistakable, one bearing a weapon.

Chance lifted his arm in the sign of peace. "Hou," he said.

Old Bear sat still on the pony's back for a time, and then he, too, lifted his arm. "Hou," he said.

"You are a white man," said Old Bear.

"Yes," said Chance.

"Why are you here?" asked Old Bear.

"My horse strayed," said Chance.

"Go from this place," said Old Bear.

"If I go from this place," said Chance, "three braves will kill me."

"I saw no braves," said Old Bear, puzzled.

"They let you ride through them to come here," said Chance.

"Are they Crows?" asked Old Bear sternly.

"No," said Chance. "They are Hunkpapa Sioux, and their leader is named Drum."

Old Bear seemed to stiffen. "He wants my daughter for his lodge," said Old Bear.

"I won't hurt you," said Chance.

"He is bad," said Old Bear. "Bad." And the old Indian made a gesture as if throwing something from him into the dirt, and disgust showed on the wrinkled face. "He wants me to die," said Old Bear. "He wants you to kill me."

"I won't hurt you," said Chance.

"Who are you?" asked Old Bear.

Chance looked to make sure that the young Indians were still where he had seen them last. "I am called Chance," he said, "and among my own people I am a doctor."

"You were at the camp of Sitting Bull," said Old Bear.

"Yes," said Chance.

"The medicine of the white man is strong," said Old Bear. "It is their strong medicine which has defeated my people, not their bullets or their soldiers."

Chance stood by the old man's pony, not knowing what to answer, not completely understanding what he had meant.

"How long have you been here?" asked Old Bear.

"Since last night," said Chance.

"Have you food?" asked Old Bear.

"No," said Chance.

"Did you take food from the graves?" asked Old Bear.

"No," said Chance.

Old Bear reached to a sack that was tied in the mane of his pony. Out of this he drew a handful of corn which he placed in Chance's hands, which Chance gobbled down, and then two grease cakes, of which Chance made similarly short work.

"I will give no offering today," said Old Bear.

"Thank you," said Chance.

Old Bear turned on the pony's back, squinting toward the

hill in the distance, probably seeing little, but knowing, or sensing, where the young men would be.

"Once," said Old Bear, "the Hunkpapa would not kill a white man because it would shame them."

"Yesterday," said Chance, "I killed two of them, maybe three."

"Your medicine is strong," said Old Bear.

"I was lucky," said Chance.

"Strong medicine makes good luck," said Old Bear.

Old Bear turned again to face Chance. "It is said you are the brother of Joseph Running Horse."

"I am," said Chance.

"Then you are Hunkpapa," said Old Bear. "You are a white man but Hunkpapa. That is why you are strong. You have the medicine of two peoples."

He looked back to the jutting break in the prairie on which Drum and his braves waited.

"Yet," said Old Bear, "they would let me ride to your gun."

"It's my fight," said Chance. "Not yours."

"I was not always Old Bear," said the old man, not looking at Chance.

Chance said nothing.

The Indian turned to face Chance. "I was once War Bear," he said.

Chance was silent.

Old Bear sat astride his pony for a long time, not moving. Watching Chance.

His hands, with their thin, worn fingers, stiff and swollen at the knuckles, held the nose rope of his pony, and, lying across the pony's mane, his ash bow and three buffalo arrows. His body, Chance noted, had been smeared with grease. The white hair of his braids had been tied with leather strings, deerskin Chance guessed. In the mane of the pony, opposite where the sack of corn and grease cakes had hung, there was tied a medicine bag, formed from the skin of a beaver, still retaining the head of the animal.

"You did not kill me," said Old Bear, speaking as if noting something about the weather, or what day of the week it was.

"No," said Chance.

"When you leave," said Old Bear, "I will go with you."

Chance said nothing.

He watched the old Indian dismount. It was hard for the

old man but Chance knew that he must do nothing to help, that he must not even appear to notice.

When the old man was afoot he turned to face Chance.

"Before I hunt the white buffalo," said Old Bear, "I sometimes come here to pray with the spirits of my people."

Again Chance said nothing.

Hearing of a white buffalo puzzled Chance. He had never seen one, certainly, but for that matter had seen only a handful of buffalo of any sort, thin, scraggy creatures, unsteady and afflicted by parasites, remnants of the great herds that had once covered territories, now curiosities in traveling circuses. A white buffalo, Chance supposed, would be an albino. But why should an old man hunt an albino buffalo?

But now the old man had forgotten about Chance and was lost among the cottonwoods of the place of scaffolds. Chance could hear him singing his prayers to the Mystery. Once Chance saw him with his hands against the trunk of a tree in whose branches there was fixed one of the oblong, dark, burdened platforms, leaning against the tree, his head down.

At last the old man returned to his pony.

"We will now leave," said Old Bear.

Chance did not help the old man mount.

He untied his own horse, slipped the carbine into the saddle boot, loosened the Colt in its holster.

At the edge of the grove, both mounted, Old Bear turned to Chance.

"Once," he said, "I was War Bear." His dim eyes seemed to blaze fiercely for a moment. "Do you believe that?" he asked.

"Yes," said Chance, speaking in Sioux, "your tongue is straight."

Suddenly the old man smiled, and then laughed, throwing back his head.

He leaned over his pony's neck, speaking in Sioux. "Once no young man of the Hunkpapa would do what Drum has done. They would not let me ride under the guns of an enemy. Do you understand what I am saying?"

"Yes," said Chance, also speaking in Sioux. "I hear the words of a father of the Hunkpapa."

Old Bear laughed again and he lifted his bow happily. "Come!" he shouted in Sioux, "Let us ride together!"

And so together Chance, a physician from New York, and Old Bear, once of Sitting Bull's White Horse Riders, left the place of scaffolds, on the Standing Rock Indian Reservation in South Dakota, in the late afternoon of a Sunday in 1890, and rode together into the open prairie, toward Drum, the son of Kills-His-Horse, and two braves, who rode slowly to meet them.

Chapter Ten

━━━◆━◆━◆━━━

Winona, the daughter of Old Bear, was making her way back to the Grand River encampment.

Head down, leading her pony by the nose rope, she was in no hurry to return home. The two travois poles dragging behind the pony left a double track in the prairie dust, but not a deep one, for the travois was empty.

No rations had been distributed at the ration point.

Yet it had been, yesterday, the second Saturday, and every second Saturday was ration day.

Like several of the other women, Winona had even stayed the night at the ration point, but it had been to no avail. This morning they had been told to go away.

There had been rations, but the soldiers and the Indian police had not permitted them to be distributed.

Winona recalled the abundance of sides of beef, lying in the dirt, spotted, stinking, but meat; and the piles of bulging flour sacks, and the bolts of cloth; some blankets; but nothing had been given to them, though they were the children of the Great White Father, and he had promised them these things made holy by being written on paper and signed by men in white collars and black coats, who were subchiefs of the Great White Father himself.

Winona wished she could speak to the Great White Father. She would tell him what his people had done, and he would be angry.

But he was far away, like Wakan-Tonka, the Great Mystery, and Winona wondered if there was a Great White Father, or if the white men were only lying again.

Perhaps there was a Great White Father and he was like the other white men, and would laugh at her and not give her the rations.

No rations unless your men come! That had been what the half-breed interpreters in their plaid shirts and white-man hats had said, with their hair cut short.

This was to stop the Ghost Dancing.

Near the ration point the soldiers from Fort Yates had been practicing with their big guns, running about them, and shouting, but not shooting them. If the men had come the soldiers would have shot the big guns, off into the prairie, so the men would remember that they had the big guns. But the men had not forgotten, and did not need to be reminded. But only the women, with their ponies and travois, came to the ration point, so the soldiers only ran about the guns, and shouted and pretended to shoot them.

The soldiers were to protect the Indians, she had been told. Suppose bad Indians came to kill them and steal their rations and take their scalps. Then the soldiers would drive the bad Indians away.

The pony Winona was leading snorted uneasily, but Winona did not notice.

Warriors should not come to gather rations.

That was woman's work.

If you had to hunt something, that was different. But why should a warrior come to the ration point, just to pick up a piece of meat and put it on a travois? A squaw could do that. But you will not get your rations, had said the half-breeds, unless your men come.

The men would be angry when the squaws came back without rations. They might beat them with sticks or they might bring out the little clay bowls hidden in the cabins, with paint, and their hidden feathers, and come for the rations themselves, on their ponies with knives and guns.

Maybe that was what the soldiers wanted.

In the past few months, in an effort to make the Sioux more independent, the amount of rations distributed to them had been steadily decreased; now there were no rations distributed at all; and supplies were low in the Standing Rock camps. Although the decrease in the supplies distributed was apparently a violation of treaty arrangements, the rationale of the action was apparently to make the Sioux more independent.

The Sioux themselves, of course, took the words of treaties seriously, and furthermore regarded the diminishment of supplies as a deliberate attempt on the part of the white men responsible to starve them into submission, to make them be what the white men wanted them to be, for example, to be good Indians and stop the Ghost Dancing, but the Ghost Dancing was the wish of Wakan-Tonka, Who was greater by

far even than the Great White Father himself, who was only
as dust beneath the feet of Wakan-Tonka, or little noises in
the trees when the wind blew. The dancing was holy, and
must not stop. White men did not know the prayer of the
dance. What would they do if the Indians told them to take
down their churches and stop singing their own holy songs?
They would not like it. They would be angry.

One Indian woman at the ration point had tried to steal a
piece of meat and one of the soldiers had thrust a bayonet
into her hand. She had stood in the dirt, her feet planted
wide, sucking her hand, making obscene gestures at the soldier with her other hand.

How could the Sioux grow their crops when the white
farmers could not do so themselves, and that was their way
of life, as buffalo had been to the Indians?

The Sioux had asked for their own cattle and horses, like
the white ranchers, but this had been refused. Indian cattle
would overload the market and white men, for some reason,
were unwilling to give the Sioux horses.

How could the Sioux be farmers?

They were hunters, and warriors, not farmers.

And it did not rain, nothing grew. The white farmers could
leave the land, get on wagons and iron trains, and go away.
But the Indians could not leave.

They must stay, and now there were no rations.

Did the Great White Father wish his children to die?

Maybe the buffalo will come back in the spring, thought
Winona to herself, as Kicking Bear has said, if the dancing
does not stop.

Seek ye first the Kingdom of God, had said the woman
with a nose and head like a chicken at the ration point, with
bright eyes and scrawny hands, bear your crosses, blessed are
the poor in spirit, live not by bread alone. And then the
woman, with her black hat wrapped about her face, in her
black dress, had pressed a little book into her hands, telling
her to love all men.

I am hungry, thought Winona.

She had dropped the little book at the ration point, leaving
it behind in the dust under the hoofs of the ponies, the poles
of the travois, the milling feet of the angry squaws.

The pony snorted, and shied a bit, this time lifting his head
and looking about, jerking on the nose rope, but Winona paid
the animal no attention.

I am hungry, she thought.

Then she was angry. How could she have Old Bear come to the ration point? How could she ask him to stand beside the travois, an old man, scarcely able to see, a warrior, while she dragged the white man's beef, meat from the spotted buffalo, to the travois?

Winona was in no hurry to reach home.

She was alone on the prairie. The other women, even those who had stayed overnight at the ration point, had by now hurried on ahead to tell their men that the white men and the bad Indians at the ration point would not give them their rations.

How could she tell Old Bear? What would she say to him?

He might take up his bow and call for his pony, and ride away, saying only, "I will hunt buffalo," and she might never see him again.

Winona wondered if the men would come in war to claim their supplies. It would not be good. The Sioux no longer told their children that courage was enough, and medicine. In these days Wakan-Tonka seemed to decide the fortunes of war like a common merchant, adding the weight of guns and men and giving victory to the heaviest side.

It was strange that Wakan-Tonka should act so. Perhaps He was testing His children and, in the spring, as Kicking Bear and the others said, His Son would come to slay the white men and live among them, bringing back the old Indians and the antelope and the buffalo as His gifts.

But, Winona asked herself, how will the Hunkpapa live through the winter?

This time the pony stopped, shook its head, and snorted explosively, and nearly pulled the nose rope from Winona's hand. She cried out angrily in Sioux, jerking back on the nose rope and then, startled, cried out as Corporal Jack Totter's hand closed on her arm.

"She's got a horse," Totter told Grawson.

Already Grawson was cutting the quilted rope of the travois from the pony's body.

"My horse!" cried Winona.

"You stole it," said Grawson.

Winona struggled but could not pull away from his grip, and Totter now held her by both arms, facing him, looking into her face with pleasure.

"My horse," said Winona.

Totter's face was thrust close to hers and she saw the rough yellow stubble on the heavy jaw, the pale blue eyes, the swollen, cut bruise that was the right side of his face. He had been kicked by a horse or struck in the face by a gun butt. He was grinning at her, holding her tight.

"Where's your man?" asked Totter.

Grawson slipped his knife back in his belt. The travois poles lay in the dust. His hand tore the nose rope from Winona's hand.

"She's alone," said Grawson.

He leaped to the back of the pony and it reared, and he retained his seat on the animal's back without a saddle, and jerked savagely back on the nose rope, and then rode the animal back to its haunches, and tore its head from one side to the other until it bled and stood still, trembling beneath him.

"What camp you from?" asked Totter.

Winona said nothing, her arms numb, her fingers numb. She shook her head.

"What camp?" repeated Totter.

"No comprendo," said Winona, using the common Spanish phrase. There had been a time when many Indians had been familiar with Spanish, more so than English. She had heard the phrase from some of the old Indians. Old Bear had used it sometimes when he did not wish to speak with a white man.

"Girl," said Grawson, from the pony's back, "did a white man come this way?"

"No comprendo," said Winona.

"When did you see a white man last?" asked Grawson.

Winona shook her head. "No comprendo," she said.

Totter shook her savagely, and her head flew back and forth on her shoulders and her teeth struck together and the world seemed to jerk back and forth and the sky turned red and then black.

"No comprendo," she said.

Totter's arms let her go and she fell at his feet, her hands reaching out for the ground, stumbling like drunken feet, and she found the ground and then her hands would not hold her and she fell between Totter's boots, lying on her side, her eyes closed, sick.

With one boot Totter turned her over on her back.

She tried to rise, but Totter put his boot on her stomach and pressed her back, and she lay still, keeping her eyes closed, her head back with her glistening braids in the dust, trying to come to her senses, sick, knowing she could not

move until the white man would be pleased to permit her to
do so.

"From out here now," Totter was saying to the other man,
"most likely she's from Sitting Bull's camp on the Grand
River."

"Let's go there," said Grawson. "Maybe he went that
way."

"There's trouble there," said Totter. "Our best bet is to
light out for Fort Yates, get some men, then go there."

"Take too much time," said the other man.

"You'd better take that time," said Totter. "You'll get shot
up at Grand River."

"Hell," said Grawson.

"They got the Ghost Dance there now," said Totter.

"I'm not going to lose him," said Grawson.

"He probably ain't even there," said Totter.

"He was," said Grawson. "We heard plenty about the
white medicine man—and that's him."

"He probably ain't there now," Totter said.

"You scared, Corporal?" asked Grawson.

"I don't aim to get myself killed being stupid," said Totter.

"I'll go alone," said Grawson.

"Tomorrow is plenty of time," said Totter, and he winked
at Grawson. "Take my word for it, tomorrow is plenty of
time."

"How's that?" asked Grawson.

"The Indian police got some business tomorrow in certain
places," said Totter.

Grawson was silent for a while. Then he said, "All right,
I'm going to Fort Yates now, and tomorrow Grand River."

"That's smart," said Totter.

Sick, frightened, in pain, Winona heard only blurred
snatches of this conversation, not following the English as
well as she might have, if it had mattered to her to listen. It
seemed only noise to her. She was clearly aware only of her
misery, her fear, the ground beneath her back, Totter standing over her.

She heard the hoofs of the horse and Totter yelled and
stepped over her, running after the horse.

"What the hell!" Totter was yelling.

The horse stopped.

"Wait up!" yelled Totter. "Let me ride behind you!"

The man on the horse, heavy in a fur-collared civilian's

mackinaw coat, wearing a fur cap, his gloved hands cruel on the nose rope, made a noise, almost like a bear might laugh.

"Report to me at Fort Yates, Corporal," said Grawson, and then the pony snorted in pain and the hoofbeats took their way into the distance, and several yards away Totter stood cursing, shaking his fist after the retreating Grawson.

Winona rolled to her stomach, and climbed to her hands and knees, shaking her head, then struggled unsteadily to her feet.

The horse was gone, the travois poles lay nearby in the dust with the cut quilted ropes of the harness still tied to them. She was alone. Totter's back was to her.

Winona, stumbling, began to run across the prairie, toward the Grand River camp.

She had not gone more than a dozen steps when she heard Totter's yell behind her, ordering her to stop.

Then she heard him laugh.

And heard the sound of running boots and the breaking of brush behind her.

Blindly, no place to hide, nowhere to go, Winona ran, stumbling, fighting for breath, scrambling between cactus and sage, her feet slipping in the dust, a wild thing, hunted.

She could hear the breathing of Totter behind her, the heavy fall of his boots, the long stride.

More swiftly she ran than ever she had but the sounds of Totter's relentless pursuit, the thunder of his boots, the rasping of his breath, grew even nearer.

She cried out as she sensed him lunge for her and leaped to one side and Totter sprawled in the dust and her heart leaped and she cried out in terror as she fell, her right ankle locked in the manacle of his heavy grip and together they rolled in the dust, she biting and striking at him, screaming, and then with his fist he struck her on the side of the head and night and its stars exploded in her head and her arms and legs could not move, and then, taking his time, he hit her again, hard, this time in the stomach, and she threw up and lay still, wanting only to be able to breathe, and was only dimly aware of him rolling her onto her stomach, taking off his yellow neckerchief and tying her hands behind her back.

"I won't hurt you," he said.

He rolled her over again, on her back, and looked her over. She was breathing heavily, covered with dust. She struggled a bit, twisting, trying to pull her wrists apart, but could not. She could see that Totter was pleased with her. He liked the look of her. And she was his now.

She put her head back, looking at the great, wide blue sky.

Totter lifted her by the shoulders into a half-sitting position.

"I won't hurt you, Nancy," he said.

Winona did not understand.

Her eyes fastened on his unshaven mouth, his thick, hard lips, the vicious bruise and cut on his cheek, on his eyes, wanting her.

He tried to press his mouth on hers and she turned her head savagely, drew back and like a striking snake spit in his face.

Totter laughed good-naturedly and pressed her back to the dust, then with his left thumb and forefinger opened her mouth, holding it open, and with his other hand scooped up a handful of prairie dust, pouring it into her mouth slowly, gagging and choking her.

"Now you ain't got so much spit to spare," said Totter.

Then it occurred to him that an Indian girl had spit on him and he slapped her twice, open handed then back handed, and then spit in her open face.

Tears burned in Winona's eyes and she struggled for breath, trying to cough the dirt out of her mouth.

Totter wiped his face with her hair and then, grinning, forcing her mouth open again, he scooped up another handful of dirt.

Winona shook her head, no. Please, no.

"You be a good girl and be quiet?" asked Totter.

Defeated, Winona nodded.

"Nice Nancy," said Totter. "That's a good Nancy."

Her hands tied behind her back, Winona suddenly shuddered and her shoulders left the ground but Totter pressed her back, and she twisted, but could not free herself from his grip, and her young brown body, now resisting by instinct, but unable to do so successfully, bound, shuddering, twisting in the dust, acknowledged its womanhood.

Clutched in the sweating palm of one of her brown hands, tied behind her, was a pair of yellow chevrons, which she had torn from Totter's sleeve in their struggle.

Chapter Eleven

His face black with rage Drum, carrying his lance and carbine, rode his pony to within a few feet of Old Bear's horse, suddenly reining in.

With his right hand he thrust his lance, feathered and tipped with the blade of a bowie knife, butt down in the soil beside his pony, like a flag.

Old Bear did not move.

The other two braves circled to cover Chance with their rifles, from both sides.

Chance licked his lips. It felt like running his tongue over dry rock. His eyes were narrow, sharp in their focus on Drum, watching mostly the young Indian's hands.

But Drum's carbine, though not in its buckskin sheath, was held on its side crossways over the pony's back. His right hand rested over the stock, his left, holding the nose rope of his pony, lay over the side of the barrel. Drum himself apparently had no immediate intention of firing in Old Bear's presence. But Chance wondered about the braves flanking him. Perhaps Drum would signal them, by a gesture, or a word he would speak like any other word. But perhaps the braves would fire only if Chance did. Perhaps none of them wished to fire in Old Bear's presence. Certainly Old Bear himself did not act as though he supposed anyone were going to fire.

Chance's grip was light on the Colt handle, but his arm was racing with blood, making his fingers tingle.

He wasn't sure what was going on, and there would be no time lost clearing leather.

A dozen times in his imagination he imagined the gun leaping from its holster.

He struggled, sensing a swift, possible victory, and freedom, against the temptation to throw himself from the horse jerking the Colt free and, from under the animal's belly, and shielded on the other side by Old Bear's pony, start firing, first, to the left, then the right, then Drum.

Then, deliberately, painfully, Chance took his hand from the butt of the pistol, letting its palm ride the pommel of his saddle.

This was Old Bear's game. He would play it his way.

"Ride away," said Drum to Old Bear, with an angry gesture. "Go! Leave the white man to us!"

Old Bear did not reply immediately, but waited until it was understood by everyone, even Chance, that Drum had not waited for the older man to speak first.

Drum scowled, and the two braves shifted uneasily on their ponies.

"Who is the owner of the loud tongue?" asked Old Bear.

Drum struck himself on the chest with his fist. "Drum!" he said, almost shouting. "The son of Kills-His-Horse!"

Old Bear regarded Drum calmly.

"Is this how the son of Kills-His-Horse speaks to a chief of the Hunkpapa?" asked Old Bear.

The old man's voice had been quiet, as soft as the rolled leather of a rawhide whip.

Drum choked, and scowled at Chance, and the young Indian's hands clenched on the carbine.

But he could not now look at Old Bear, meet the silent question of those proud, dim eyes.

Drum stared at the dust beneath his pony's hoofs, at the brown grass, the stones, the dust.

When he lifted his head Chance saw tears of shame and rage in his eyes.

"Forgive me," said Drum.

"It is done," said Old Bear.

"My heart is angry," said Drum, "that the white man should live. He has killed two braves, and he has hurt another."

Old Bear looked at Chance.

"They were trying to kill me," said Chance.

"Why?" asked Old Bear.

"I don't know," said Chance.

Old Bear turned to Drum.

"Why?" he asked.

Drum was silent.

Old Bear repeated his question to the flanking braves, but, like Drum, they said nothing, and refused to meet his eyes.

Then Drum said, "I would wear the feather of an eagle."

Old Bear grunted.

"The white man is the brother of Running Horse," he said. "That is why you want him to die."

"No," said Drum, "to wear the feather of an eagle."

"You want to shame Running Horse," said Old Bear, "and take my daughter to your lodge."

"Running Horse is a short hair," said Drum.

"He has danced the Sun Dance," said Old Bear.

"I want only," said Drum, "to wear the feather of an eagle."

"Speak to me with a straight tongue," said Old Bear.

Drum looked down. "I want many things," he said.

"Now," said Old Bear, "you speak with a straight tongue."

Drum looked up at the old man, who sat so straight, gaunt and frail on his pony.

"But most," said Drum, "I want to wear the feather of the eagle."

For a long time Old Bear said nothing.

Chance thought that a look of great sadness touched the face of Old Bear, and in that moment for the first time, Chance began to understand the meaning of that single white, black-tipped feather that stood in the old man's hair.

At last Old Bear said, "The eagles are dead."

"No!" shouted Drum.

"They are dead," said the old Indian.

"I," said Drum, jerking the thumb of his closed fist to his chest, "will wear the feather."

"Then you will die," said Old Bear.

"I am not afraid," said Drum.

He snatched up the feathered lance from the dirt beside his pony and shook it.

"So, too, was Kills-His-Horse," said Old Bear.

"I am the son of Kills-His-Horse," said Drum.

"Yes," said Old Bear, "I see in you the son of Kills-His-Horse, with whom I rode the warpath many times, and I see that it is true that you will wear the feather of the eagle, and that you will die."

During this time, Chance had said nothing, though he had followed what was said.

Old Bear turned to him. "Do you understand these things?"

"I think so," said Chance.

"All men die," said Old Bear, "but few men die with the feather of an eagle in their hair."

Chance nodded. "I understand."

Old Bear pointed to Drum. "He is young," he said, "but he is such a man."

"Yes," said Chance. "He is such a man."

Old Bear turned to Drum. "It would be better to let this man go."

"I will not," said Drum.

"Then you must fight," said Old Bear.

A look of pleasure suffused Drum's face. "Yes," he said.

The two braves flanking Chance grunted their approval.

"It is sad," said Old Bear, "that two of the Hunkpapa must fight."

"He is a white man," said Drum.

"He is the brother of Running Horse," said Old Bear.

"He does not even have a name," said Drum.

Chance puzzled about that, for a moment, and then understood.

Old Bear was looking at him steadily. Then Old Bear looked at Drum and the two braves. "He killed two braves, and hurt one other," he said.

"Yes," said Drum.

"He has strong medicine," said Old Bear. "The medicine of two peoples."

"My medicine is stronger," said Drum.

"And he is a warrior," said Old Bear.

"I am a greater warrior," said Drum.

"His name," said Old Bear, "is Medicine Gun." The old man pointed his finger at Chance. "Medicine Gun!"

And it was as simple as this that Chance received the name by which he would be known from that day forward among the Hunkpapa, with the exception of Joseph Running Horse, who always spoke of him as "My Brother."

Without looking at Drum or the braves, Old Bear turned his pony back toward the Grand River settlement, and Chance followed him, and Drum, and the two braves.

As Chance rode with the Indians back to the settlement on the river he told himself how mad this was. He had run from Grawson—from the law—had not stood and fought, and now he must fight—for no reason that he understood—and kill or die.

There had been another duel, long ago, but with clean silken shirts, red sashes, seconds, a doctor in attendance, a measured set of rules to which gentlemen might be expected to adhere.

This time his opponent would be a young Indian man, swift, half-naked, fighting before his people, following what rituals or traditions Chance couldn't guess, and whose honor would not be satisfied with a wound, or a touch, but only by death and Chance's hair at his belt.

Chance wondered what the weapons would be.

They had seen him use his pistol.

Knives, Chance guessed, knives.

Behind the cabin of Sitting Bull there was a council fire, and about the fire, sitting in circles, were the hunched figures of Indian men, wrapped in blankets, some of them smoking.

Outside the rings of seated men there stood squaws and children.

Beyond them, when he came around the corner of Sitting Bull's cabin, accompanied by the chief himself, the subchief Old Bear, and Running Horse, his brother, Chance saw, vaguely in the darkness, the shadows of several ponies, picketed, at hand.

There had been tales of soldiers coming to the camp, to stop the Ghost Dancing, to capture Sitting Bull and return him to the stone houses of the days after the death of Long Hair.

Here and there, in the flickering light, Chance could see loaded travois, lodge skins and provisions bundled across the poles.

Chance sensed that many of the men seated about the fire carried their medicine bags tied to their belts.

Chance could see that some of them had rifles under their blankets.

At the fire itself Kicking Bear stood, and behind him Drum, and the two braves.

"I will fight for you," said Running Horse.

"No," said Chance.

"Drum is very fast," said Running Horse.

Chance had little doubt of it. "Thanks," he said.

"You must be very fast," said Running Horse.

Chance didn't quite follow why Running Horse was saying this. They both knew that Drum was dangerous, and that he would move swiftly. "All right," he said, "I'll try."

Chance did not feel, and was grateful, that there was particular hostility towards him in the camp, in spite of the fact that he was white, and that the women, as he had learned, had returned from the ration point empty-handed.

He had helped many of these same Indians in his stay in the camp.

And they knew that in some strange way he, too, was a stranger to the white world outside the boundaries of the reservation.

The Indians were bitter this night, but not towards him.

Chance found himself standing across the large fire from Kicking Bear, Drum, and the two braves.

Sitting Bull, Old Bear and Joseph Running Horse had all taken their seats, sitting cross-legged, in the forefront of the circle of men about the fire, some ten or twelve feet from the fire.

Without a word the two braves behind Drum took their places, seated, across the fire from Chance, they too leaving open the circle of earth about the fire, that track on which whatever was to take place would soon take place.

Kicking Bear wore a white muslin Ghost Shirt, deerskin leggings and beaded moccasins. There were three yellow lines drawn vertically on his face, one on each cheek, the other running from his upper lip over the nose to his hairline, like the rays of a rising sun. In his belt there were two wooden-handled, long, steel butcher knives.

Chance studied Drum carefully. Other than moccasins he wore only a breechclout and leggings. His hair had been greased and freshly braided, and was tied with two strips of red cloth. His chest and face had been painted with white, black and red lines, painted for war. He did not move but stood with his arms folded, watching Chance. At his belt there hung the steel hatchet Chance had seen him use when he had fought Running Horse.

Kicking Bear, saying nothing, jerked the hatchet from Drum's belt, who seemed not to notice. Then Kicking Bear circled the fire and paused before Chance; then his hand quickly reached for the handle of the Colt, and Chance's hand closed on his, and Kicking Bear looked at him. Chance released his hand and, quickly, Kicking Bear removed the Colt from its holster.

Kicking Bear then went to Sitting Bull and placed both weapons in the dust before the chief.

Then Kicking Bear went to the side of the fire away from Sitting Bull, and stood to Chances' left and to Drum's right, and stood there, it seemed for minutes, not moving.

Chance looked across the fire, to his antagonist.

Drum, painted, standing very straight, was watching him, his arms still folded, his face for most purposes inscrutable, only his eyes betraying him, revealing suppressed eagerness, the intention to kill.

The hair on the back of Chance's neck lifted.

He swallowed, hard.

He recalled the words of Running Horse, you must be very fast.

He would try.

With ceremonial solemnity, Kicking Bear, looking neither to the right nor left, removed the two steel butcher knives from his belt, and then he held them, one in each hand, high over his head.

Thus he stood for perhaps a minute.

Suddenly with a cry Kicking Bear flung the two knives into the dirt, one on each side of the fire.

Drum snatched the knife at his feet and leaped across the wide fire. His other hand swooped down and jerked the second knife out of the dirt.

Chance saw Drum standing opposite him, the fire at his back, lifting the two knives in triumph.

Drum's body, the fire bright at his back, was black, a demonic silhouette edged with flames, in each fist a steel claw nine inches long, that caught and flashed the firelight. And then Drum, exultant, began to chant and back dancing away from Chance around the fire, and Chance could see him, his young, strong body ugly and wild with the grotesque paint of war, red, white and black, and Drum seemed to be studying the ground, and dancing, as if looking for a sign, the spoor, the ashes, the traces of an enemy.

Chance had been too slow.

The other knife had been his.

Now Drum straightened and pointed to the ground.

He began to chant again, "I have found him. I have found my enemy. Now I will kill him."

Come ahead, you bastard, thought Chance.

Drum looked across the fire at Chance.

Uttering a wild cry, the war cry of the Hunkpapa, Drum charged through the fire, hurtling himself toward Chance.

For an instant the sudden cry had so startled Chance that he could not move and stood as though tied to a stake, numb, as the twin knives of the young Indian struck down at him, but at the last instant he managed to twist to one side, and

Drum, in the fierce momentum of his charge, plunged past him.

Chance, off balance, twisting, struggling to get rightly on his feet, not taking his eyes off Drum, stumbled blindly backwards through the fire, kicking its kindling to the left and right.

Then, hunched over, but ready, on the other side of the broken stars of the fire, in the half-darkness, Chance waited for Drum.

This time the young Indian would approach slowly.

Chance crouched down and picked up a flaming brand from the scattered fire.

Drum came about the right edge of the scattered fire now, both knives held low, below his belt, blades up.

It would be a visceral stroke, difficult to block, not the foolish overhand blow that he had first struck.

Chance wanted to get the fire of the brand in Drum's hair, heavy with grease.

Suddenly Drum's moccasined foot swept through the ashes of the fire lifting a curtain of ash and sparks toward Chance, to blind him, but Chance, as soon as Drum's foot had moved, had himself charged and came through the hot veil of ash with its tiny, drifting points of fire, his eyes shut for the instant against the hot ash, the sparks stinging his face, and then was through it, blinking away the hot ash that clung about his eyes, swinging the limb of kindling like a flaming club and struck Drum across the forehead and the wood, half burned, broke and Drum's head snapped back and before he could react Chance had leaped on him, pinning his arms to his sides, knocking him over backwards, but it was like trying to hold a puma and Drum's half-naked body, slick with sweat and glistening with paint and grease began to slip from him, and Chance desperately caught his wrists, each of Drum's hands still with its knife, and together they rolled in the dust in the circle, sometimes to the very knees of the Indians, watching and smoking, sometimes into the charred embers of the fire itself, first Chance on top, then Drum.

Drum bit the side of Chance's face and then sank his teeth deep into Chance's arm, again and again, biting as innocently and viciously as any wild animal, but Chance could not release him, dared not, and he, Chance, the gentleman, tried to inch the young Indian's hair, glistening thick with its ceremonial grease, against one of the glowing scraps of kindling in the circle.

Drum's face, a grimace of sweat and paint, was inches from Chance's, unshaven, the muscles in the jaw taut.

There was a long, lateral welt across Drum's forehead, black from the soot of the wood that Chance had used to strike him, smearing the paint.

The side of Chance's face bled from the marks of Drum's teeth.

The only sound was the breathing of the men, the scuffling of dirt, the tiny crack of the flames in the scattered embers of the fire.

Then as Drum tried to move his left hand away and Chance seemed to resist, Chance suddenly released Drum's left wrist, freeing his own right hand, and Drum's hand, with its knife, of its own muscular tension flew wildly to the side and at the same time Chance's hand, with all the power of a suddenly released spring, simultaneously doubled into a fist and flew toward Drum's head, catching him on the side of the jaw with a blow that might have broken a board but only staggered Drum for a moment, did not cause him to lose consciousness.

Chance had not supposed he could knock Drum out. As a physician he knew enough physiology to understand that when men fight for their lives consciousness is not easily surrendered. It is many times easier to knock a man out when life is not at stake than when it is. To cause Drum to lose consciousness he might have had to hit him with an ax handle, or a dozen times with the blow he had, but he had not counted on knocking Drum out, but only stunning him for the moment he needed.

Chance, in the instant when Drum tried to shake the pain and exploding light from his head, let his hands go and grabbed Drum by the hair dragging him and moving him with his boot in the midst of a pile of brands from the council fire and then with the flat of his hand shoved his head back into the embers, and shuddered at Drum's cry as his long black hair, thick with its grease, took the fire.

Drum leaped up twisting away from Chance screaming and, suddenly, hair flaming, charged again, unwarily, and Chance's boot caught him in the solar plexus and Drum, grunting, scarcely able to move, hurled the two knives high and away over the circle of Indians, and they flew over the heads of the watching squaws and children and disappeared in the darkness.

And then he threw himself on the ground rolling and knelt down to scoop dust over his head.

Now there were no weapons. Drum had seen to that, knowing he could not fight, knowing he must prevent Chance from getting a knife, knowing he must put out the fire that tore at his head.

Chance stood back, breathing heavily, not knowing if the fight were over or not.

He knew that warriors did not fight with their hands, but with weapons. It was not seemly to be unarmed. Yet in such a situation, having only one's hands, feet and teeth, Chance supposed, they might still fight. He didn't know.

Chance looked at Running Horse, but Running Horse said nothing. Chance didn't know, now, what was to be done. Was the fight over? Or was he to try and finish Drum, strangle him?

Drum was on his feet now, sucking in the air in gouts, covered with dust, the paint smeared, his hair loose and thick with grease and dirt.

His eyes regarded Chance with hatred, with the inflamed savagery of a mad wolf, not a human being.

He snatched his hatchet, the long-handled hatchet, from the dust before Sitting Bull.

Chance stepped back. He was more afraid of the hatchet than the knives. He could lose an arm even blocking a blow, and bleed to death in minutes.

But Drum, struggling with himself, threw down the hatchet, angrily into the dust before his chief.

It was not permitted him.

Then, unarmed, with a cry, he rushed at Chance and Chance met him and they grappled, grunting in the circle.

"Stop," said Sitting Bull.

Drum and Chance disengaged themselves and stepped back, breathing heavily, looking at the chief.

"It is enough," said Sitting Bull.

Old Bear, by his side, grunted his approval.

"You are Hunkpapa," said Sitting Bull. "Do not fight like drunken white men."

"Give us weapons," said Drum.

"Where are your weapons?" asked Sitting Bull.

Drum was silent.

"It is enough," said Sitting Bull.

Drum looked at Chance. "There is enmity between us," he said.

"All right," said Chance, relieved that the business was over, at least for the time.

He knew that Drum had not fared as well in this battle as he had intended, when he began it, with his paint and proud dancing, when he had intended to kill Chance swiftly and skillfully.

He had been, in effect, disarmed, and he himself, to save his life, had thrown the weapons from the circle.

He had been forced to grovel in the dirt to end the flames that had burned in his hair.

It would not be soon that Drum would forget the encounter of the night.

The night had not been worthy of Drum, and there would have to be, Chance understood, another meeting.

There was only one thing to be grateful for, as Chance saw it. They had met as warriors of the Hunkpapa, and that meant that Drum would no longer kill him as he might a white man, or a Crow, silently, without warning, from ambush, for that would have been murder, the unlawful slaying of a member of one's own people. By meeting Chance in the circle of the council fire, Drum had acknowledged him as a warrior of the Hunkpapa.

Kicking Bear had come to Drum and placed his blanket about his shoulders.

Without another look at Chance, or at anyone, Drum straightened and left the circle, followed by Kicking Bear and one of the two braves who had accompanied him.

The other brave stopped to retrieve Drum's hatchet from the dust before Sitting Bull.

When he had the hatchet he said something to Sitting Bull, angrily, about using the fists in fighting, as well as Chance could make it out. He began to expostulate with the chief, shamed that his companion had not been victorious.

Indians might wrestle, particularly boys, for sport, but the folding of the hand into a fist and using it as a striking weapon was something that never seemed natural, or acceptable, to them.

The doubled fist, Chance then realized for the first time, is undoubtedly a learned use of the body, like swimming. It is undoubtedly relative to a culture, as unusual to those unaccustomed to it as the oriental practice he had once heard a sailor speak of in a bar, that of using the side of the hand to strike a blow.

At any rate the young Indian was protesting, seemingly on

the grounds of Chance having used an unfair method of combat.

Nothing was said about Drum's biting or his attempt to blind Chance, or for that matter about Chance's kicking Drum in the stomach.

Chance decided he would like a smoke.

At last Sitting Bull, after listening patiently, shrugged under his blanket and grunted, meaning nothing, and the young Indian, dismissed, gave the matter up and, with a last look at Chance, and holding Drum's hatchet, left the circle.

Running Horse picked up Chance's revolver and handed it to him. Chance wiped the weapon as well as he could with his sleeve. He would take it apart, clean and oil it before morning. He slipped it in his belt rather than in the holster. There would be time to put it in the holster when the weapon was clean.

Chance noted that now, lighted by a twig from the fire, which the squaws had now built up again, a single pipe was being passed about the circle of men.

It was the council pipe.

"I'd better go," said Chance to Running Horse.

"No," said Running Horse. "Stay, and take council with us."

And so Chance sat down between Running Horse and Old Bear, near Sitting Bull, and when the pipe came to him, smoked, and passed it to his left, to Running Horse. The full ceremony of the pipe was performed only by Sitting Bull, Old Bear and certain of the older men in the circle. Chance did what he saw most of the others do, simply take a puff or two, acknowledging the council and their role in it, and passing the pipe on.

The smoking and the waiting took time, and Chance saw that few decisions would be likely to be reached in a state of anger or emotion. One had time to think, to settle oneself, to consider matters at some length before beginning to speak of them.

But before the talk began, an Indian, only a boy, came to the side of Old Bear. He said to him, very softly. "Come to your lodge."

"There is council," said Old Bear, angrily. Had the young no understanding, no manners in these days?

"Come to your lodge," repeated the boy.

Grunting, Old Bear stood up and made his way back

through the hunched figures of the Indians sitting in their blankets about the fire.

Vaguely Chance wondered what the matter was. He saw Running Horse apprehensively look after Old Bear.

The council, at last, the first smoking done, began, and Chance, with his sparse knowledge of Sioux, struggled to follow the proceedings.

Chapter Twelve

Chance and Running Horse, after the council, made their way in silence back toward Running Horse's cabin.

There had been anger at the rations not having been distributed, and some of the Indians had feared that this meant the soldiers would soon attack, to fill them, an inference which Sitting Bull, with his remarkable and unruffled common sense, tried to discourage. He could not, of course, foresee the events of the following morning.

The Indians themselves, on the whole, though they stood ready to fight if necessary, defending themselves, their chief and their families, were not yet inclined, to Chance's relief, to put the matter of the rations on rifle muzzle terms.

There was a general suspicion that the white men had simply made another of their mistakes, or perhaps better, had done something stupid again, and might perhaps still be patiently reasoned with. There was, after all, the matter of the treaty, and treaties, now that the Indians were on reservations, seemed to be taken more seriously by the white people, more seriously at any rate than when the Indians had still held land the white people wanted.

Besides, how could the men come to collect the rations, even if men were to do this squaw's work, when there was the Ghost Dance to be danced?

No, it could simply not be done. The agent in the administration building and the colonel at Fort Yates perhaps simply did not understand these things.

The Ghost Dance was holy.

Moreover, why should there be fighting now, when the Messiah was going to come in the spring and the ground was going to roll over the white men anyway, and over their stone lodges and their railroads and cannon, leaving not even their bones to puzzle the trampling, returning buffalo?

It would be foolish to fight now.

War, in any case, particularly after smoking, was a serious

matter, not to be lightly decided upon, particularly in the winter, and with the buffalo gone.

And so it had been decided to send some braves to see the agent, and in the meantime to dance the Ghost Dance, keep the ponies at hand and the weapons loaded.

If the food did not come soon, of course, then the Indians must leave the reservation. Indian wives and children, like white wives and children, required food. There were many white ranchers within a day or two's ride from the reservation, who raised thin herds of the white man's spotted buffalo, and these white man's buffalo would have to serve. No Hunkpapa family would starve while its man had an arrow for his bow or a bullet for his gun.

At Running Horse's cabin an Indian, one of the two braves who had accompanied Drum, was waiting for them.

Chance's hand went to the revolver in his belt.

"Come to the cabin of Old Bear," said the man, and turned, leading the way.

Not understanding, Chance followed Running Horse and the other Indian.

Suddenly Running Horse broke into a run, not waiting, and ran to the door of Old Bear's cabin. Chance, surprised, jogging behind, leaving the other Indian back.

At the door Running Horse did not knock but stood outside and called his name, to be given permission to enter. One does not beat on the side of a lodge.

There was a grunt from the inside and Running Horse, followed by Chance, and a few seconds later by the other Indian, entered the cabin.

Behind the fire, his back to the far wall, facing the door, in the position of the master of the lodge, sat Old Bear, his face utterly impassive.

He did not smoke.

Running Horse, visibly apprehensive, was sitting down, cross-legged, across the fire from Old Bear. He would not, of course, speak first. Chance, bewildered, sat down beside Running Horse. The other Indian sat down against the wall, by the door.

Looking about, Chance saw, in a corner of the cabin, among the goods and boxes, the sacks and robes and articles of Old Bear, a large, bulky shadow, an object wrapped in a blanket, and suddenly, with a start, he saw that it was the bent figure of a human being, motionless yet alive, the figure of a girl, kneeling on her heels, her arms folded under her, her head fallen forward, almost touching her knees.

No sound came from the concealed figure.

Outside he heard a voice. "I am Drum, the son of Kills-His-Horse."

"Enter my lodge," said Old Bear.

Drum scarcely looked at Chance, but seemed to be as puzzled as he himself was. Only Running Horse seemed visibly disturbed.

Drum's hair now hung loose and wet over the back of a buckskin shirt. It had been cleaned with sand and water. The paint had been washed from his face, and undoubtedly the rest of his body. He still carried a long welt across his forehead from the encounter with Chance hours before. The young Indian wore buckskin leggings and a breechclout, and had wrapped about his waist a blanket, which he drew about his shoulders when he sat down opposite Old Bear. He had been accompanied by the other brave, the one who had protested to Sitting Bull about the fight between Drum and Chance, and this brave sat down next to his fellow near the door.

Kicking Bear was nowhere in sight, and Chance gathered that he had not been summoned.

Whatever was to take place was not a matter for medicine men. He himself was there merely by virtue of having been with Running Horse when Running Horse was called to the cabin. No one had told him to go away. Perhaps that would not have been courteous. Perhaps he should go away. But he was here now. He gathered that what was to transpire was really between Old Bear and the two young Indians, Drum and Running Horse.

Chance wondered why Old Bear had not lit a pipe and passed it around.

Neither Drum nor Running Horse, both of whom must have been aware of the figure in the corner of the cabin, gave any sign of having seen it.

For a long time Old Bear said nothing, and then he looked at Drum, and said, "You, Drum, wanted the white man to kill me at the place of scaffolds, so you could take my daughter to your lodge."

Drum said nothing, but stared into the fire.

"You, Running Horse," said Old Bear, "have worn your hair short. You have become too much like the white man."

Running Horse dropped his head.

"But," said Old Bear, "you have danced the Sun Dance."

Running Horse looked up, gratefully.

"And you, Drum," said Old Bear, "though you are young and sometimes you are bad and you do not understand many things, you are yet strong and brave, and it is not your fault that in you is the memory of the eagle feather you have never seen and should not hope to wear."

Drum's eyes blazed at this.

"And," continued Old Bear, "you are the son of Kills-His-Horse, who was my friend."

Drum looked as though he might speak, but he did not do so, for Old Bear was not yet finished.

"There was a chief of the Hunkpapa," said Old Bear, "who once had many horses and had taken many coup and fought at the river with Sitting Bull and Crazy Horse against the warrior Long Hair, and this chief became old and the days of the eagle feather passed like the sight of his eyes and he then lived on the beef of the white man, his enemy, and had one daughter to cook in his lodge and care for him, and this daughter, though she was not beautiful nor skillful, was dear to him, and he did not wish to let her go from his lodge."

Old Bear was quiet for a time, staring down at the fire, and then he began to speak again.

"But it seemed that two young men wanted to bring horses for this woman, though she was neither comely to look upon nor could she work skins and do the beadwork of her people, and that there was bad blood between these two young men, though they were both of the Hunkpapa. One was willing even to see the old chief die to have the daughter come to his lodge, and would kill the brother of the other, to shame him."

"So," continued Old Bear, "the old man thought about these things and one day, in a place of peace, when he had prayed to the Mystery, he understood that he was old, and that his daughter was young, and that there should not be bad blood between the Hunkpapa, and that she must leave his lodge."

"I will bring you many horses," said Drum.

"But," said Old Bear, continuing, "although the old man's heart was good his head was not wise and he had waited too long."

Drum looked puzzled.

"And the old man is no longer young and the lance is heavy for his arm and it is hard to draw the bowstrong."

No one spoke for a time. At last Drum asked, "Is it the

words of a father of the Hunkpapa that his daughter may now leave his lodge?"

"She may do what she wishes," said Old Bear.

"I will bring many horses," said Drum.

Old Bear looked at Running Horse, sadly.

Running Horse hung his head. "I have only one horse," he said.

"I do not need horses," said Old Bear.

"Your daughter is worth horses," said Drum, "and I will give them."

"I want my daughter to go to the lodge she wishes," said Old Bear.

Drum laughed aloud and struck his knee with the palm of his hand. "The daughter," said he, "has promised to come to the lodge of Drum, who is the son of Kills-His-Horse."

Running Horse reacted as if struck.

"Is it truly the wish of Drum the son of Kills-His-Horse to take my daughter to his lodge?" asked Old Bear.

"It is my wish," said Drum.

"And what is the wish of Running Horse?" asked Old Bear.

Running Horse looked down for a time, and then looked up, meeting the old man's eyes. "My wish is the wish of her father," he said, "that she go to the lodge she wants."

"In the morning," said Drum triumphantly, "I will bring horses."

Old Bear looked steadily at Drum and then, stiffly, rose to his feet. He went to the corner of the cabin and took the girl by an arm, pulling her into the light of the fire. When she stood before them, Old Bear tore away the blanket.

"I will bring no horses for this woman," said Drum.

Winona did not raise her eyes.

Her hair was loose and filled with dirt, and her face was stained with dirt and tears. The left side of her face was discolored where Totter had struck her. Her blue cotton dress was half torn from her body, and she held it to her by her left hand. Her right hand was clutched into a small fist, clenched beside her exposed, bruised right thigh.

Old Bear seized the fist and with his two hands lifted it and pried open the fingers, revealing inside the pair of yellow chevrons torn from Totter's sleeve.

"I am an old man," he said.

Drum took the chevrons.

"I am your eyes," he said, "and I am your arm."

"I, too," said Running Horse.

"In the morning," said Drum, looking at Running Horse, "we will meet to make medicine."

"Yes," said Running Horse.

Winona, who had not spoken, now lifted her head, and looked at Drum.

He regarded her with contempt. "You will not now come to my lodge," he said. "I do not want you now."

Old Bear put the blanket about her shoulders and she drew it close about her, once more lowering her head.

Drum turned and left the cabin, and was followed by his two braves.

"You may stay in my lodge," said Old Bear to the girl, "as before."

"It would shame you," she said.

"No," said Old Bear. "I would not be shamed."

"I will go away," said the girl.

"Stay with me," said the old man.

Winona suddenly cried out and lunged toward the door, and Old Bear tried to restrain her but she pulled away and fled into the winter night, leaving only the blanket in the hands of Old Bear.

Old Bear dropped the blanket to the floor and sat down behind his fire, in the place of the master of the lodge. "Leave me," he said.

Chance and Running Horse left the cabin.

Outside Chance turned to Running Horse. "What are you going to do?" he asked.

Running Horse looked at him, his expression unreadable. "I am going back to my cabin," he said.

Chance shrugged, and accompanied the young Indian back to his cabin.

Winona, cold, huddled by the slow-flowing, chill waters of the Grand River, south of the camp of Sitting Bull.

Alone with no one before whom to be shamed she had wept, and poured dirt over her head, and with a sharp stone she had cut her long black hair, rubbing and sawing the strands, until it hung no further than the back of her neck, and then with the stone she had struck herself, again and again, in the thighs and arms, bruising herself, hurting herself.

Now she was quiet and cold, and sat huddled by the

waters, watching them move their slow winter way between the frozen mud of the banks.

She cried out, startled, as she heard a twig snap near her, and looked up.

Running Horse, a broken twig in his hands, stood near her. About his shoulders he wore a blanket, which he had brought from his cabin. He threw the two pieces of the twig he had snapped into the water.

"Go away!" cried Winona.

But Running Horse did not move, but stood looking at her.

"Short hair!" she cried viciously, wanting to hurt him. "Short hair! Short hair!"

He looked on her, yet without showing pity, on her bruised and now bleeding body, the dirt with which she had covered herself, the jagged remnants of her once long, beautiful hair.

"Go away!" cried the girl.

But Running Horse would not leave.

She sprang to her feet in rage, seizing up the sharp stone with which she had cut her hair, and her body.

She took the stone and slashed at Running Horse's face and the stone gashed him on the left cheek leaving a wide wound and a sudden mark of blood, like a streak of paint. He did not move.

She dropped the stone, and with her hand almost touched his face. "I am sorry," she said.

The girl turned away and dropped to her knees, rocking and sobbing, her head to the ground.

"Go away," she wept. "Go away."

Running Horse sat down, cross-legged, on the ground near her.

"I am Running Horse of the Hunkpapa," he said. "I have a good horse. I can shoot with a rifle. I can hunt meat."

"Go away," said the girl.

"I have some white man's money," said Running Horse. "My brother is Medicine Gun, who knows the medicine of the white man. I saved my brother from men who would kill him. I fought with Drum and he did not kill me."

"Leave me," begged Winona.

"I am brave," said Running Horse. "I am strong. Even the spotted sickness of the white man could not kill me. I have a steel knife. I have a white man's pipe given to me by my brother. I have blankets and corn and beef and a fire in my lodge which needs tending."

Winona raised her head and turned slowly to face Running

Horse, her eyes glazed with tears, her body miserable with pain.

"What are you saying to me?" she asked.

Running Horse dropped his head.

Suddenly without warning she hissed at him. "You are a fool and a short hair. I am only a white man's woman."

"The fire in my lodge," said Running Horse, "burns low."

"I would shame you," she cried.

"No," said Running Horse. "I am not ashamed."

"That is because you are only a short hair," said the girl, contemptuously.

"I have danced the Sun Dance," said Running Horse.

Winona huddled even closer to the ground, rocking in her misery, her arms folded around her.

"On the other hand," said Running Horse, speaking as he did because he had no male relative to do this in his stead, "you are not very much, and are probably not worth many horses."

Winona looked up. "I am the daughter of a chief," she said.

"That is true," said Running Horse, "but he is old and has only one horse."

"He was a great warrior," said Winona.

"That is true," said Running Horse, "but it is not he who would tend my fire."

Winona looked at him angrily.

"He has a daughter," said Running Horse, "who should feel grateful if a man would look at her."

Winona bit her lip.

"She is a stupid girl," he said, "who does not know how to sew or dress skins, and she cannot bead moccasins or make belts."

"But she is very beautiful," said Winona.

"No," said Running Horse, "she is like a stick, like a she-coyote, not like a buffalo cow, fat and strong."

"A man would be a fool to want such a girl," said Winona.

"Yes," said Running Horse, "I suppose so."

For a long time neither of them spoke, and then Winona laughed.

"I have heard," said Running Horse, "that Running Horse is a fool."

"That is not true," said Winona.

"He is no good," said Running Horse. "He is only a short hair."

Winona looked at him shyly. "I have heard," she said, "that he has danced the Sun Dance."

"Maybe," said Joseph Running Horse, "I do not know."

"A girl," said Winona, "would be honored if such a man might think of her."

"That is true," said Running Horse.

Winona looked down. "Could the heart of such a man be pleased with a girl who is stupid and ugly?"

"Maybe," said Joseph Running Horse, "I do not know."

He looked at her.

"Could the heart of the daughter of a chief be pleased with a fool who is only a short hair?" asked Running Horse.

Winona looked down, not meeting his eyes. "Maybe," she said, "I do not know."

"Well," said Running Horse, getting to his feet, "when you find out, you will let me know."

Winona, too, rose to her feet, and knotted the dress over her left shoulder.

Running Horse began to climb up the bank, slipping a bit, and then he was on the level.

He waited for Winona to climb up after him, not helping her.

"I am going to my lodge," he said.

She stood near him, her head lowered. "Your fire will need tending," she said.

Running Horse tenderly took the blanket from his own shoulders and holding it about himself, opened it to the girl, and she stepped against him, and put her head to his shoulder, and he folded the blanket about her.

"One blanket," he said.

"Yes," said the girl, "one blanket."

Chapter Thirteen

It was December 15, 1890.

On Medicine Ridge, above the camp of Sitting Bull on the Grand River, Drum and Running Horse met. It wasn't long before dawn. Exchanging no sign of greeting or recognition, they sat facing one another, saying nothing.

Between them lay two golden chevrons, which Winona had torn yesterday afternoon from the sleeve of Corporal Jake Totter.

Drum, with his teeth and fingers, carefully, losing not even a raveling, separated the chevrons. He gave one to Running Horse and kept one for himself. Both of the young men put a chevron in their medicine bags.

Kicking Bear now made his way slowly up the side of Medicine Ridge. He was wrapped in his blanket and hunched against the cold. It was barely light in the east now.

The medicine man squatted beside the two young men and drew a small, dead animal from under his blanket. It was a badger, that had been caught in a string noose. It was still warm.

Kicking Bear took out his knife and slit open the animal's belly. With an oval cut, not removing the knife from the animal, he loosened most of its organs and intestines from the furred skin, and then, wiping his knife on his leggings and putting it back in his belt, he took his hands and scooped out the organs and viscera.

The now-hollowed cup of the badger's skin slowly filled with blood, the level rising in the cavity. Kicking Bear then took the heart and liver and kidneys of the animal and squeezed them between his hands, adding what blood and fluids they contained to the cup of fur.

The first clean streak of dawn made the cold prairie glisten like the blade of a steel knife.

The young men watched Kicking Bear, who was intent on the blood in the animal's hollowed belly. He would not look

on the blood directly, but only from the side. This medicine
he made for others, not for himself.

The death smell of the badger was keen in the nostrils of
the two, silent young men. They must wait to see if the
badger would speak to them.

Kicking Bear had told them he knew how to do this thing,
and he had prayed, and he had had no difficulty in snaring
an animal. The signs were good. The badger had come
promptly to the snare. Both Drum and Running Horse were
grateful to the badger.

"He is ready," said Kicking Bear.

Running Horse went to the badger and looked deeply into
the shallow cup of blood.

He looked for a long time at his face, mirrored in the
blood. His reflection stared up at him, and it seemed to Running Horse that it was gray and solemn.

Running Horse staightened and looked at Kicking Bear
and Drum. "I have seen myself old," he said.

Kicking Bear grunted with satisfaction.

Drum looked into the bowl of blood, into that tiny mirror,
seeking for his image, and suddenly he had found it and his
face jerked at what he saw and his lip trembled for an instant,
and then he looked again, for a long time, into the blood, as
though there must be no mistake in the sign he read.

"What do you see?" demanded Kicking Bear.

But Drum did not respond to him. It seemed he could not
tear his eyes from the small image in the red mirror, that
small image, red and terrible staring up at him from the
secret of the badger's blood.

"What do you see?" repeated Kicking Bear.

Drum, at last, lifted his head, and looked at both of the
men, at Kicking Bear, prophet of the Ghost Dance, and at
Running Horse, like himself a brave of the Hunkpapa.

"I will die as the son of Kills-His-Horse," said Drum.

Once more Kicking Bear grunted, but this time his re-
sponse was not of satisfaction, nor of fear, nor of commisera-
tion, rather a noise that betokened only the acknowledgement
of Drum's words, and that he had not been surprised.

Drum was shaken, but he did not seem frightened. He sat
back, cross-legged, breathed deeply.

"The medicine has been made," said Kicking Bear. "It is
over."

Kicking Bear slowly poured the blood from the badger out
onto the ground and with his hands and fingernails scooped a

small hole in the scarlet mud, into which he placed the organs and viscera of the animal. Then he scooped dirt over the place and put some stones on it. The carcass of the animal itself he thrust in his belt.

Running Horse hesitantly put forth his hand and touched Drum's arm.

Drum looked into his eyes.

"I will not forget again," said Drum, "that we are both of the Hunkpapa."

"I am glad," said Running Horse.

Kicking Bear now stood up, his blanket wrapped about his waist, and raised his arms to the east, where the rim of the sun now burned over the prairie.

"Wakan-Tonka!" cried Kicking Bear. "Drum, the son of Kills-His-Horse, has made medicine. His death will be the death of a brave of the Hunkpapa. Until his death he will be strong, fortunate and victorious! There will be no medicine that can prevail against him!"

Kicking Bear lowered his arms and turned to Drum. "Let your heart be strong," he said. "You cannot escape death, so live without fear."

Drum rose to his feet, and Running Horse, too, got up.

Kicking Bear came to Drum and placed his hands on his shoulders. "What is there now to fear?" asked Kicking Bear.

Drum looked at him for a long time. Then he said, slowly, forming the words carefully, "Nothing. There is nothing left to fear."

"The fearing is done," said Kicking Bear. "It is finished!"

"Yes," said Drum, slowly, "it is finished." He looked at Running Horse. "I feel strong," he said. "Strong."

"I am glad," said Running Horse.

Drum did not take his eyes from Running Horse. "So you will grow old, Little Warrior?" he said. "And you will have children and grandchildren?"

Running Horse looked down.

"Tell them of Drum," said the young Indian.

A dog began to bark in the distance, down in the camp of Sitting Bull.

"Look!" cried Kicking Bear, pointing to the camp.

Drum and Running Bear stood numb for that second with astonishment, for filing into the camp, on horseback, was a contingent of blue-coated Indian police, about thirty of them. They were coming in quietly, purposefully.

They reined up outside the cabin of Sitting Bull.

With a cry of rage Drum scrambled down the side of Medicine Ridge, half falling, half stumbling, running headlong toward the camp. Running Horse raced behind him, shouting at the top of his voice, trying to rouse the camp.

The Indian policeman, burly, with his short hair, in his ill-fitting blue uniform, guts cold, hands trembling, with his white man's orders, hesitated before the calm wood of the door to Sitting Bull's cabin.

Then he drew his pistol from the cavalry holster at his belt.

This was the cabin of the troublemaker, the hated Sitting Bull, who would not smoke with him, and his kind, and who as long as he lived would not do so, Sitting Bull who stood in the hearts of the people as a symbol of the old life that had gone with the departing buffalo, who as long as he lived would remind the people of the pipes of stone, the days of many horses and the feathers of eagles.

The Indians who were wise would understand that these were the days of the white man, and would be good Indians, and live as the holy teachers of the white men cautioned them, being meek, and bearing their crosses and loving all men, even Crows. And when the Indians were good they would receive gifts from the Great White Father, and maybe even a badge and a gun, and a blue suit that would make them more than a chief, almost as much as a white man himself.

The Indian policeman had no great love for the white man, but he knew that the wars were over, and he knew who had won them. Sitting Bull did not know that. Sitting Bull would not smoke with him. Sitting Bull called him a short hair.

The policeman threw his weight against the cabin door bursting it open.

He stumbled into the cabin, followed by several of his men, clutching their weapons.

Sitting Bull, on one side of his lodge, sat up, wrapped in his blankets. "What do you want?" he asked.

The Indian policeman pointed his pistol at the chief. "Come with me," he said. His voice was loud, like a white man who talks to an Indian. Then he remembered the formula given to him by the white men. "You are under arrest," he said.

Sitting Bull sat quiet for a minute. Then he said, "Very well, I will go with you."

The Indian policeman gestured with his pistol, impatiently, for the chief to rise and dress.

Already there were four or five dogs barking outside and he could hear the noises of the camp.

Outside, two of the Indian police were fumbling to put the high wooden saddle of Spanish design on Sitting Bull's white horse.

Some of the Indians of the camp, now roused by the clamor of the dogs, stumbled out of their cabins and tepees, forming a puzzled, hostile ring about the Indian policemen outside the entrance to Sitting Bull's cabin.

The police pointed their weapons at the Indians and ordered them to draw back.

Several of the police looked anxiously in the direction from which they had come.

Old Bear, standing in the door of his cabin, observed this and he too looked down their backtrail. He could see nothing, but his war sense told him that there would be soldiers, white soldiers, not far distant. Indian police for diplomatic reasons, not soldiers, had been sent to the cabin of Sitting Bull, presumably to seize him and take him away to the iron and stone houses.

But there would be soldiers.

The white man would not trust this thing altogether to short hairs.

There would be soldiers.

Old Bear went back into his cabin and removed his rifle from a cracked, beaded, buckskin sheath.

Edward Chance was awakened by the barking of dogs. He was in Running Horse's cabin.

Winona, who had accompanied Running Horse back to the cabin the night before, and who had accepted and given love in the very room in which Chance had pretended to sleep, breathing heavily, wrapped in his blankets, smiling, facing the wall, was already up.

The fire was started.

Chance sat upright, blinking the grit of sleep out of his eyes, puzzled, wondering about the dogs.

He looked at the girl. She now wore moccasins and a fringed, deerskin dress, having visited Old Bear's cabin last night to gather her belongings. Her face had been washed and her hair, cut short to the back of her neck, had been combed. She was piling articles in the cabin which might be of use in a journey, particularly food, clothing and ammuni-

tion, into the center of a striped cotton blanket on the dirt
floor.

Outside Chance could now hear cries, angry shouts.

"What's wrong?" he asked Winona.

Winona stopped for a moment to face him. Her face was
ashen. "A bad thing," she said, "a bad thing, Brother of my
Husband."

"Where is my brother?" asked Chance.

"I do not know," said the girl.

She turned to her work.

Chance reached for the Colt, which he kept next to him,
and shook the holster and belt from the weapon.

Swiftly he went to the door, the weapon in his hand. It
smelled clean and ready. He had cleaned and oiled it last
night.

Chance saw Winona take down the hawk feathers from the
rafter and his own medicine kit, and put them in the striped
blanket. He noted that the medicine bag of Joseph Running
Horse, like the young Indian, was gone.

Yesterday morning Joseph Running Horse, borrowing a
white man's hat, had ridden casually to the Turner soddy, re-
quested and had been given the kit. He had brought it back
to the cabin, in case Chance might return. Neither he nor
Chance had expected him to return as soon as he had, or in
the company of Old Bear, Drum and the two braves.

Yesterday morning now seemed a long time ago.

Chance edged the door open.

There was an angry, milling crowd of Sioux outside Sitting
Bull's cabin. And Chance could see the blue uniforms of Indian police.

He put the weapon in his belt and, unobtrusively, left the
cabin, to see what was going on.

He saw Sitting Bull, half dressed, shoved from the cabin by
a large Indian policeman.

At the sight of the chief the crowd cried out.

"Go away!" cried the Indian policeman. "Go away!" He
waved his pistol at the crowd. He held Sitting Bull by the
right arm.

The crowd surged closer, against the rifle muzzles of the
police.

Sitting Bull lifted his hand. "No!" he cried. "I will go with
them. Do not fight!"

The Indians hesitated.

Chance slipped closer. He saw the Indian policeman suddenly thrust his large revolver in the old chief's side. "Go away," said the man, "he is coming with us." The man's voice had been fierce, loud, but it had almost broken.

Chance edged into the crowd deeper.

Sitting Bull looked at the man, speaking calmly. "Yes," he said, "I am going with you. Do not shoot."

Someone near Chance cried out, "Do not go with them!"

The Indians among whom Chance stood pressed in ever closer, pushing against the rifle muzzles, and the rifle muzzles tried to hold them back, but they still came forward, some shoved by those behind, and the muzzles of those thirty odd rifles, brown fingers on the triggers of each, were pushed back like a fence of sticks by the movements of soil and rock and the Indian policemen, some of them, felt the logs of the chief's cabin terminating their retreat, holding them and the blue uniforms where they were, penned in, encircled by their brethren, the free Sioux, muttering, many of them armed.

Many of the Indian police kept looking, almost frantically, down the backtrail.

It puzzled Chance.

Old Bear, who stood with his rifle in the doorway of his cabin, watched. There would not yet be the sight of a cavalry pennon. There was not yet the peal of the distant bugle. The soldiers were too far away. They would not come until they heard gunfire.

Old Bear, calmly, loaded his weapon.

The soldiers would come.

Voices in the crowd shouted encouragement to Sitting Bull, threats against the policemen. Chance's Sioux was adequate to follow most of what was said, and there could be no mistaking, in any language, the mood of the throng—fury.

"Do not go with them, Sitting Bull," someone shouted. "They will put you in the stone houses!" shouted another. "They will kill you on the prairie!" cried out another man. One man brandished his rifle and called out to his fellows, "Let us kill the Short Hair Dogs!" Another cried out, "Sitting Bull, if you go with them, you are afraid of the white men!"

Sitting Bull, to Chance's surprise, seemed calm.

He scarcely seemed to pay that much attention to the cries, or to the push of the pistol muzzle in his side.

Rather he seemed to Chance to look over the heads of the policemen and the crowd, to the height of Medicine Ridge, across the Grand River, perhaps across the prairies which his people had once ruled as nomadic kings, a people whom he had once led on horseback, rifle in hand, feathers in his hair, across green prairies shaking to the hoofbeat of the bison.

No one knows what was in Sitting Bull's mind, nor why he said what he did, but he looked at the Indian policeman, the burly, short-haired policeman, so much the master with his white man's gun, and said, "I will not go with you."

The revolver shot was abrupt, decisive, point-blank, half muffled in the flesh and blanket of the chief.

The body of Sitting Bull, dead, had not fallen to the ground when through the circle of stunned Sioux, past Chance, there hurtled a shrieking, dark shape that leaped on the Indian policeman, bearing him to the dirt.

It was Drum, unarmed.

A policeman turned to fire, and a shot exploded in his ear and he spun backwards, the blue circle broken. The other policemen opened fire at the range of inches into the bodies that pressed against them, and other weapons, those of the Hunkpapa, fired into the segments of that shattered cordon.

Drum had wrested the policeman's pistol away and knelt on him, screaming, firing the last five shots into the man's face.

Suddenly Chance saw Running Horse grappling to his right with an Indian policeman. Running Horse, like Drum, carried no arms.

One of the Indian police shouted to his fellows, "Inside!" and turned to enter the cabin of the dead chief, but now Old Bear raised his rifle and fired once, and the man jerked and clutched at the door of the cabin, trying to get in, and then in the time it takes to try to breathe his hands froze on the sides of the door barring the entrance.

There were more shots, both from the police and the Hunkpapa.

The man in the doorway was torn from the opening and pitched aside by the other Indian policemen, who swarmed in the door. Chance heard a shot from inside the cabin. He learned later that one of Sitting Bull's sons had been shot by the police.

The door closed and rifle barrels poked out the windows firing at the crowd that now scattered, Chance running with them, getting back to the shelter of Running Horse's cabin. Running Horse himself was nowhere in sight. The policeman with whom he had been grappling was dead, though whether Running Horse had killed him, or someone else, Chance did not know.

An Indian to the left of Chance stumbled, caught in the back by a bullet, his hands flying back over his head, and pitched into the dirt.

Then Chance was at the cabin entrance, and inside. He swung the door open, and knelt inside the opening, his weapon drawn. He would not kill with it, but he was willing to fire on the cabin, to keep the police penned inside, to keep them away from the windows, to save as many lives as he could.

Chance squeezed off a shot at the cabin wall, chipping some bark from the wall, about a foot from the right side of the window.

To his amazement he saw Drum, still in the line of fire, not more than ten yards from the cabin, kneeling over the body of the Indian policeman. He had taken a knife from the man and Chance did not care to watch what he was doing.

But the young fool was mad. He would be killed.

Drum worked calmly, the bullets flying about him, bullets from both sides.

Drum was on his feet now, the scalp, wet and red with blood in his hand, held over his head, and Chance, from where he knelt inside the cabin door, could see the blood running down Drum's arm, staining the sleeve which had fallen ripped to his shoulder.

Drum walked slowly away from the cabin, holding his trophy high.

The rest of the Indians had drawn back. Chance could see them here and there, firing from cabin windows, from around the edges of cabins, from behind boxes and a wagon, firing on Sitting Bull's cabin.

And from inside the cabin rifles thrust forth from the windows, and the Indian police, crowded in the cabin, besieged, fired as they could, where they could, trying to answer the ring of encircling snipers, trying to answer the sharp, sporadic cracks of the miscellany of weapons beneath whose sights they found themselves.

And through this cross fire, unscathed, walked Drum, the scalp held high over his head, looking neither to the left nor right.

"Get down," yelled Chance to Drum as he passed the cabin.

Drum turned and looked at him.

"I wear the feather of an eagle," said Drum, quietly.

"Get under cover," yelled Chance.

Drum turned to face the cabin of Sitting Bull. Still the bullets tore about him. The rifle muzzles in the windows of Sitting Bull's cabin jerked and discharged their fire, and more bullets pelted the cabin from the fire of the Hunkpapa.

It was as though Drum lived a charmed life.

The young Indian, facing the cabin of Sitting Bull, lifted the scalp even higher over his head and shook it. He called out to the police in the cabin, "It is I who have done this, Drum, the son of Kills-His-Horse, your enemy."

The scalp was wet in Drum's angry fist, the blood appearing between the clenched fingers of his fist, moving down the wrist.

"It is I," he cried, "Drum, the son of Kills-His-Horse, one who wears the feather of an eagle, one who is your enemy, one whose feet are set upon the warpath."

Then, angrily, Drum thrust the scalp in his belt and turned and walked from the line of fire, going behind the cabin, perhaps heading for his own lodge, to gather his weapons.

Running Horse moved swiftly along the side of the cabin and pressed inside, past Chance.

"My brother," said he.

"My brother," said Chance.

Winona handed Running Horse his weapon, and he worked the bolt, seeing that the girl had loaded it, slid the bolt forward, locked it. Then she gave him a handful of bullets. Most he put in his medicine bag; five he held between his teeth. Then he slipped out of the cabin, moving behind it, to take up some position out of Chance's view.

Chance thought of following him, but supposed it didn't much matter.

He was aware of activity behind the cabins, the neighing of horses, the sharp cries of women.

With the first shots the squaws had unpicketed the animals and where skin lodges stood, they had been struck.

Already the poles of travois, loaded, were being lashed to the sides of ponies.

There were more shots.

Across the way he could see Old Bear firing from his cabin door.

There were some Indians on the roofs of some of the cabins, firing.

Suddenly through the sporadic shots and the sudden splintering and chipping of wood about him Chance heard, thin, but clear, in the distance, the notes of a bugle.

This was the first it had occurred to him that there would be soldiers.

They had been waiting in support of the Indian police, had heard the firing, and were now riding in.

Old Bear, terrible in his enraged frailty, leaped into the dirt street, even in the line of fire, calling for the Hunkpapa to withdraw.

It might have been planned.

For all Chance knew it had been, at least in its general outlines.

While a handful of Indians kept the cabin under fire the rest faded back, running to their lodges and cabins.

Their horses and their goods were ready.

Winona, the bundle of goods in the striped blanket on her back, slipped from the cabin and scurried along its side and behind it.

Running Horse's pony was at hand, picketed behind the cabin. He did not own a saddle.

Chance went to the corner of the cabin and picked up his saddle and saddlebags. He saw that Winona had rolled and bound his blankets across the back of the saddle.

Chance slipped from the cabin, carrying his saddle and gear. No longer were the police in the cabin firing, though he could see a rifle muzzle projecting from one of the windows. He supposed they were finished fighting. They had heard the bugle. They would stay where they were. Perhaps even the rifle in the window was simply propped up. They would stay in the cabin until the soldiers came.

The notes of the bugle sounded again, this time much closer.

Now even the firing of the Hunkpapa was done, and Chance supposed that the rear guard had fallen back, to cover the retreat which must now be underway.

The camp seemed fairly quiet now; even the dogs were gone. There would be some fires in the cooking holes, here and there, that would burn down to ashes in time. Near the wagon in the street behind which some men had earlier been firing, there was a sack of spilled corn, and a handful of sparrows had fluttered down to peck at it. It seemed very quiet. There were, of course, a number of Indian police, maybe twenty or more, hiding in the dead chief's cabin, too frightened or too wise to come out, probably both.

Before the cabin there were a number of bodies, mostly Indian police, clearly recognizable by the short hair and the blue uniforms, and other Indians. One body Chance would never forget, a heavy body, stocky, old, with long black hair that had not yet been braided that morning, hair streaked with white, hair that had never been cut. It lay wrapped half in a blanket, stained with red about the size of a saucer on the side facing Chance, twisted in the dust not far from the door of the cabin, the body of a man who had been kind to Chance, that of a proud man, a calm man, resourceful and wise, who had loved his people and their land, and council fires and antelope, and the giving of gifts and the hunting of buffalo, and the blue sky and the prairie and the feathers of eagles.

Chance turned away and went behind the cabin.

Running Horse and Winona were waiting for him.

Running Horse helped him saddle his horse and then the three of them, Winona with her bundle riding behind Running Horse, joined the orderly retreat of the Hunkpapa, who by now had mostly disappeared in the brush along the Grand River.

They would head for the ancestral retreat, called by the white men the Bad Lands, where the sudden arroyos and rugged hills might defy regiments of long knives.

At the head of the long, ragged string of Indians, and ponies and travois and dogs, rode Old Bear, his eyes fierce and hard, the chief of the Hunkpapa.

When the cavalry from Fort Yates, flag and pennon fluttering, thundered into the camp of Sitting Bull, shouting, brandishing their sabers, brave in the sound of their bugle, they found nothing, only the empty camp and, of course, some Indian policemen in one of the cabins.

Needless to say, they also did not find Edward Chance, which proved to be a particular disappointment to two men who rode with them, Lester Grawson and Corporal Jacob Totter.

Above the camp, on Medicine Ridge, watching, not moving, stood the solitary figure of Kicking Bear, medicine man, he who had brought the Ghost Dance to Standing Rock.

The death of Sitting Bull would enkindle the Sioux and the Cheyenne.

The news would spread like the sweep of a wind-driven burning prairie from Standing Rock to Pine Ridge, to Cherry Creek and throughout the departments of the Platte and Dakotas.

The messenger would say, "Sitting Bull is dead." And the

warriors would gather their ponies and take up their weapons.

For the first time in years, the feet of the Sioux and their brethren, the Cheyenne, would be on the warpath. This would be the Holy War, the war of the Ghost Dance.

It was wrong, for spring was the time, not winter, with the coming snows and the ice and wind, and the barren prairie and the lack of food.

Kicking Bear stood on Medicine Ridge.

He watched the soldiers and the Indian policemen milling about the cabin of Sitting Bull, hitching up a wagon for a body.

When the soldiers and policemen had ridden away, when the wagon too was gone, Kicking Bear turned his back on the camp of Sitting Bull.

There was nothing more to be done.

Strange was the will of Wakan-Tonka.

It had begun here, the Holy War, here on the muddy banks of the Grand River.

Chapter Fourteen

———•◦———————◦•———

Lucia Turner was up and about the soddy.

She lifted off one of the range lids and stirred the fire. This morning she was using kindling in the range, rather than cow chips or twisted grass. Perhaps it would put Aunt Zita in a better mood.

Lucia had been awakened that morning early, around dawn, by gunfire in the distance, coming from the direction of Sitting Bull's camp. She had hurriedly dressed and climbed to the top of the hill, on which the school stood, but she had seen nothing. Then, after a time, she had returned to the soddy, puzzled, a bit frightened, hoping there was nothing wrong. She had heard firing before, and usually it had been due, as it happened, to drunken Indians. But usually that sort of firing took place late at night, not at dawn.

The pile of kindling behind the soddy had been diminishing rapidly. All that was left of it now was a coal bucket filled with it, sitting beside the range.

Lucia, too, of course, preferred a meal prepared over a wood fire.

Several weeks ago Lucia had purchased a cord of fuel for one dollar from a man in a wagon who did business with the agency, but he no longer came as far into the reservation as the soddy.

If worse came to worse Lucia might hitch up the buckboard and drive down to the Grand River. There she might find a fallen cottonwood and get some of the dried branches. Perhaps she could hire Joseph Running Horse to cut the wood for her.

He had come by the soddy yesterday to ask for Mr. Chance's medicine kit.

She had given it to him.

"I hope he is all right," she had said, pretending not to be too much interested.

"Yes," had said Running Horse, "I hope so," and then he had taken the kit and left, leaving her.

She would have liked to have kept the kit. He might have come back for it. She might then have seen him again, once more, to see him, to speak to him.

She had only said, "I hope he is all right," and Running Horse had said, "Yes, I hope so," and then Running Horse had gone, taking the kit. It had been too quick, too simple, for the hours of remembering, for the not forgetting.

Yes, Mr. Chance, she said to herself, I might have some coffee on. You've shaved, I see. You know, I never expected to see you again. Naturally I'm pleased that you dropped by. William is fine. What brings you back to the reservation?

I'll never see him again, never, said Lucia Turner to herself, hurting in the saying of it, the empty knowing of it to be true.

Never.

Never.

Never.

"Where is my breakfast?" asked Aunt Zita.

Lucia shook herself and puttered noisily about with the coffee pot, not answering.

Aunt Zita had been in a vicious mood since yesterday evening, when she had returned with the buckboard from the agency to find a dead horse only a few yards from the soddy and the soddy itself flaked with bullets.

Lucia had told her nothing.

Yesterday Lucia had taken the saddle and gear from Chance's dead horse. She had then heaped dust over the animal. Today, hopefully, she would see some Indians and get them to take it away and bury it. If Joseph Running Horse passed by, he would help. Yesterday, when he had called for Chance's medicine kit, she had forgotten to ask him. She also supposed she should give the saddle and the rest of the gear to him. But the entire matter had, yesterday, slipped her mind. If William Buckhorn's father had returned from Fort Yates, he could probably be counted on to help Running Horse. The two of them could rig a travois. There probably wouldn't be too much work, except maybe for the digging.

"You'll have to get that horse out of here," Aunt Zita had said.

"I know," had said Lucia. "I'll get some of the Indians to help."

"They'll probably eat it," Aunt Zita had said.

"No," Lucia had said, rather firmly, "they will not."

Actually, Lucia had thought to herself, if the horse had been fresh killed, they might. She had learned from Aunt Zita how the rations had not been distributed Saturday and she had supposed, rightly, that supplies might well be scarce in the Standing Rock camps. And one could eat horse meat. She had heard that. At any rate Indians could. She herself, of course, could not do so. The thought of it, for no reason that she could clearly understand, turned her stomach.

"Indians will eat anything," had said Aunt Zita.

Lucia grimaced. She had heard, and knew, that Indians would eat dog, too. She supposed they might indeed eat anything, or about anything. Of course they would have preferred buffalo. Or beef. Or mutton. Some of the younger Indians had never tasted buffalo. Lucia had had it only once, on a dining car on the way to Standing Rock. A rancher had shot it and given a shoulder to the conductor, and the conductor had given the steward a cut for the schoolmarm. Its taste was difficult to describe. Not like beef. Not just like beef. She had liked it. Aunt Zita would not touch it.

"Did you hear gunfire this morning?" asked Lucia.

"No," said Aunt Zita.

"I did," said Lucia.

"From Grand River, I imagine," said Aunt Zita.

"Yes," said Lucia, "it was."

"I think I know what it's all about," said Aunt Zita.

"Tell me," said Lucia.

"I want to know what happened here when I was gone," snapped Zita.

Lucia looked down, and continued busying herself with the breakfast. With a fork she turned a piece of bread on the wire toast rack sitting on the black iron top of the range. She used a wooden spatula to loosen Aunt Zita's eggs in the skillet.

"Well?" said Aunt Zita.

"All right," said Lucia, "a man came by when you were gone, and two men were after him, and wanted to kill him, and I helped him get away, with the help of a friend of mine."

Lucia had said all this in one breath and stiffened inside her cotton dress bending over the range, waiting.

"I want to hear a great deal about this," said Aunt Zita,

and the words might have been spoken by the head of a stone angel.

Lucia scooped the eggs on a plate with the spatula and quickly picked up the toast with two fingers and darted it onto the plate, not altogether displeased that she had left it too long on the wire rack.

She put the plate on the kitchen table in front of Aunt Zita.

"The toast is burned," said Aunt Zita.

"I'll make you some more," said Lucia.

"I want my coffee now," said Aunt Zita.

"I'll get it," said Lucia, and, using her apron as a potholder, picked up the coffee pot with two hands and poured Aunt Zita a large cup of the fragrant, black liquid. She then poured some milk from a jug which she had brought up earlier on its string from the well into the coffee, and put in two heaping tablespoons of white sugar, the way Aunt Zita liked it, and then gave her the cup.

"My toast," said Aunt Zita.

Lucia cut a slice of bread from the loaf and put it on the toast rack.

"Why was there shooting at Grand River?" asked Lucia.

"Take this away," said Aunt Zita, pointing a long white finger at the dark toast on her plate.

Lucia took it. She might have eaten it herself but instead she used the lid iron to move one of the flat circular lids on the range and drop the bread into the flames, and then she replaced the lid. She would later remember that she had thrown away a piece of bread.

Lucia turned around and faced Aunt Zita. "Please," she said.

"My toast," said Aunt Zita.

Lucia turned the toast and waited a minute until it had browned, and then served Aunt Zita.

Lucia sat down opposite her, and watched her knife press butter onto the toast.

"Please," said Lucia.

"I heard yesterday," said Aunt Zita, chopping at the eggs with the side of her fork, "from one of the men who drives one of the beef wagons who heard from a lieutenant at Fort Yates that the Ghost Dancing is about over." Aunt Zita looked at her wisely, a flap of egg on her fork halfway to her mouth. Then the fork moved and the bit of egg disappeared between her thin lips.

"I don't understand," said Lucia.

"What's behind the Ghost Dancing?" asked Aunt Zita.

"I don't know," said Lucia.

"Sitting Bull," said Aunt Lucia.

"There's Ghost Dancing on all the reservations," said Lucia.

"Sitting Bull is behind it," said Aunt Zita. "Get him and you stop the dancing."

Lucia went pale.

The gunfire this morning, at the Grand River Camp.

"Get him," said Aunt Zita, chewing, the side of her mouth bulging with buttered toast, "and you stop the Ghost Dancing."

Lucia felt sick.

"There was trouble," said Lucia, weakly. "I heard shots."

"Well," said Aunt Zita, shoving back her plate, "the trouble's over now."

Lucia picked up the plate and put it in the dishpan near the range. She would heat water and wash it later. Lucia herself was not hungry. Somehow she did not even, now, feel like coffee.

"Now," said Aunt Zita, "tell me—and tell me honestly, mind you—what happened here when I was gone, exactly what happened here when I was gone."

Then Lucia, numbly, pretty accurately, filled in the details of what had occurred during Aunt Zita's absence from the soddy. She left out very little, except perhaps that Edward Chance had held her in his arms, and that she in that moment had not objected, that her lips had touched his, and his hers, and that she had lived over that moment in the hours that separated her from him a thousand times, that she would never forget that moment, an instant at midnight on a moonlit hill at Standing Rock when two human beings, each lonely, had cared for and touched one another, she and a fugitive, a stranger.

"What was the man like who was here?" asked Aunt Zita.

"He was a nice man," said Lucia.

"A criminal fleeing from justice," said Aunt Zita.

"I don't know much about it," said Lucia.

"And you thought he was a nice man," said Aunt Zita.

"Yes," said Lucia, "he seemed to be a nice man. I thought so."

Aunt Zita looked at her. Her eyes sparkled like a cat's. Her voice was measured, and the words came out one at a time, like individual drops of cold syrup pouring from a bottle.

"The prairie," said Aunt Zita, "is a lonely place for a young girl."

Lucia looked at her and flushed.

"Did you tell him to go away?" asked Aunt Zita.

"No," said Lucia.

"Why didn't you tell him to go away?" asked Aunt Zita.

"He only wanted a cup of coffee," said Lucia.

Aunt Zita regarded her coldly.

"It would have been impolite to send him away," said Lucia.

"Why didn't you send him away?" asked Aunt Zita.

"I told you," said Lucia.

"It would have been impolite—"

"Yes," said Lucia.

"Is that the only reason?" asked Aunt Zita, her voice as pointed as a sewing needle.

"I don't know," said Lucia. "I don't know."

"I see," said Aunt Zita. "I see."

Outside, the prairie wind, unhurried, rustled through the sage.

Lucia looked at the older woman. "I don't like you," she said.

The girl arose from the kitchen table and went to the door of the soddy, opening it and looked out. She looked at the gradual, sloping hill that lay between the soddy and the school, on another hill beyond; she looked away toward Grand River; she looked at the sky, huge and gray that Monday morning of the 15th of December, 1890. She noticed, from the direction of Grand River, a bit of dust hanging in the air, horsemen, but did not think anything of it.

She could hear Aunt Zita's words behind her. "Thou shalt honor thy father and thy mother," said Aunt Zita.

Lucia turned to face the older woman. "I did better than that," she said. "I loved them."

"I," said Aunt Zita, "stand now in their place."

"No," said Lucia, "you are not in their place." She felt her breath quicken. "You took their house," she said, "you sat in their chairs, you ate from their plates, you slept in their bed, but you were not—ever—in their place." Lucia suddenly realized her fists were clenched. She closed her eyes, and when she opened them she had regained control of herself. "Never say that again," she said.

The girl turned away, bitterly. The bit of dust on the horizon was larger now.

"A good woman," said Aunt Zita, "takes no pleasure in the presence of men, save perhaps an interest in the salvation of their souls."

Lucia was watching the dust on the horizon.

"I myself," Aunt Zita continued, "have saved the souls of many a man, whom I brought to repentance, for which they will be grateful at the time of judgment."

"I have never saved a man's soul," said Lucia.

"Perhaps in time you will receive an opportunity," said Aunt Zita, "perhaps in time you can even marry for marriage can be the lesser of various evils and in marriage you can make of your bed a school for the soul of your husband."

Lucia watched the dust on the horizon. It was getting nearer.

Aunt Zita's words drifted to her, as if from a distance. They sounded like something she had read, something Aunt Zita had given her to read.

Lucia wished that the approaching dust might have been lifted by the rapid hoofs of the horse of Edward Chance, that he might be riding back, even now, riding back for coffee as he had asked, that he might be coming even now to fetch her, to claim her for his own, to tell her that he wanted her, that he loved her, she and she alone.

She smiled bitterly.

Never, never would she see him again. She had little to remember him by, only the memory of a single kiss which she would never forget, and the sound of the hoofs of his horse as he vanished in the night.

It could not be the dust from the hoofs of his horse, not if he were coming alone. It was the dust of several horses.

"I myself," Aunt Zita was saying, "have never allowed myself the weakness of the flesh."

Several horses, several.

"Nor must you," said Aunt Zita.

Suddenly Lucia turned to face the older woman, her face crimson.

"What do you mean?" she demanded.

Lucia forgot about the dust, the horses.

"Did you place your lips on him?" asked Aunt Zita.

Tears suddenly burned in Lucia's eyes.

"Did you allow him to put his mouth on you?" asked Aunt Zita.

Lucia burst into tears and ran to the cot on which she slept, throwing herself on it, pushing her face into the folded blanket that covered the pillow, the dust in the distance forgotten.

Aunt Zita rose from the table, her spine as straight as an angel's sword, her eyes as hard as the points of nails.

She stood over Lucia.

"Did you put your mouth on him?" demanded the older woman. "Did you allow him to put his mouth on you?"

Lucia lifted her head, her eyes filled with tears. "I would have let him do anything he wanted," she said.

Aunt Zita's black-sleeved arm whipped forward and her thin, bony hand struck Lucia fully across the mouth, viciously, jerking her head back.

"Shameless," said Aunt Zita.

Lucia put her fingers to her mouth, which felt numb. Her lips, she could tell with her fingers, were wet. She tasted blood.

"Anything he wanted to," repeated Lucia, scarcely hearing the words.

Once again Aunt Zita's bony hand lashed her mouth.

"Anything," said Lucia, "anything."

Aunt Zita stepped back and Lucia, in tears, mouth bleeding, struggled to her feet, stood up on the dirt floor beside the cot, bent over, facing her, her fists clenched. "Anything!" she screamed at the older woman. "Anything!" Then she turned awkwardly back to the cot, and fell on it again, weeping.

Aunt Zita's face was white and hard.

"We are going back to Saint Louis," said Aunt Zita.

Lucia began to laugh, crying, the sounds muffled in the blanket, laughter, hysterical, preposterous, tears, not controlled, wild, laughing, crying.

Aunt Zita looked on the distraught figure of the girl as though she might have been demented.

"We are going to leave this place," said Aunt Zita.

Lucia sat up on the cot, wiping the sleeve of her dress across her eyes.

"No," said Lucia. "I'm going to stay here. I'm going to wait for him." Then she put her head down and held her sides, laughing.

"You are mad," said Aunt Zita.

Lucia looked up. "He may come back for a cup of coffee,"

she said. "Don't you understand?" And then she laughed again.

"Mad," said Aunt Zita. "You are mad." Then the older woman turned away and walked to the center of the room, and then sat down at the kitchen table, not facing Lucia. "This is a Godforsaken place filled with heathen," said Aunt Zita. "They're even the color of the devil that possesses them." Aunt Zita stared at the wall of the soddy. "In this place, Lucia Turner," she said, "you have been lured into listening to the call of the flesh." Aunt Zita turned and faced Lucia. Her eyes were stern. Her voice was cold. "On your knees, Lucia Turner," she said, "and together we will beg God's forgiveness."

"No," said Lucia.

"Together we will beg God's forgiveness," said Aunt Zita.

"If God must forgive me for how I feel," said Lucia, "then you must beg Him, for I will not."

"You are shameless," said Aunt Zita.

"I'm in love," said Lucia.

Aunt Zita stared at Lucia. The silence in the soddy was as tangible and inflexible as the blade of a knife.

"I'm in love," said Lucia, quietly, herself amazed at the words she had spoken, words that she had not known to be true until she had heard them said, words that made her happy and yet hurt her more than she could tell, because Chance, the man, was gone, and would not return. "Yes," said Lucia, quietly, now calm, not crying, wanting to hear the words said again, as if she had not trusted herself to have spoken them, as if she did not trust herself to speak them again, "I am—I am in love."

Suddenly outside there was a shout and the sound of several horses, a cry in Sioux, the snorting of animals.

Lucia ran to the door of the soddy, throwing it open.

About fifteen yards from the soddy, on stamping, bare-backed ponies, were seven riders, their mounts white with the lather of sweat. Feathers were twisted into the manes of the ponies. Four of the riders wore a feather, a single white, black-tipped feather, among them their leader, whom Lucia recognized as Drum. The braves wore no paint but their blankets were loose around their waists, leaving their hands and arms free for using their weapons.

Drum, mounted, speaking rapidly in Sioux, gestured over the hill and toward the soddy.

Then Drum, and four riders, kicked their ponies in the direction of the school, while two young men leaped from their ponies and rushed to the soddy.

Lucia stood, bewildered, in the doorway of the soddy.

One of the braves seized her by the arm.

"Guns!" he said. "Guns!"

"No," said Lucia. "No guns. We have no guns."

The brave thrust her aside and entered the soddy, followed by his companion.

"Get out of here!" cried Aunt Zita. "What do you think you're doing?"

The two braves began to ransack the soddy, upturning chests, throwing over boxes, tearing the bedclothes, hunting for weapons or bullets. They picked up kitchen knives and one of them took a bolt of yellow cloth. Lucia saw, with a sinking heart, the walnut china cabinet crash to the dirt floor of the soddy, the glass panels breaking, the dishes inside shattering.

Aunt Zita pounded on the back of one of the braves.

With a cry of rage he turned and seized her by the arms and forced her toward the range.

His companion with a kitchen knife forced open one of the circular lids, revealing the burning kindling inside.

The Indian who held Aunt Zita then held her by the arm and with his hand in her hair forced her head toward the circular opening and she screamed the wailing, unutterably horrifying scream of a terrified old woman.

Lucia seized up a piece of wood from beside the range and stood between the Indian and Aunt Zita and the range.

"Stop!" she cried.

The other Indian easily took the piece of wood from her, and held her about the waist, struggling.

Lucia screamed as the red fist thrust the head of the old woman into the flames and the soddy and the sky itself was rent by the old woman's agonized shriek.

Lucia broke away from the brave who held her and seized Aunt Zita's shoulders and with a strength she never knew she possessed tore her literally from the range and the man who held her and led the screaming woman to the wall of the soddy, holding her hands that she might not with her fingernails tear the burned flesh from her face.

Lucia heard the two braves laugh, returning to their work.

One was taking a pillowcase and putting all the food in the soddy into it.

The other was delicately picking a piece of burning kindling from the range.

Lucia took a handful of butter from a stone bowl and rubbed it onto the face of the old woman. Her gray hair had not caught fire. The old woman's shoulders shook and she shrieked, her entire body trembling, knotted up, its knees under its chin by the dirt wall of the soddy. Lucia seized up her coat and put it about her shoulders.

The brave who had the piece of burning kindling was now applying it to the plank roof of the soddy, to the beds, to the furniture.

Lucia, half dragging, half carrying Aunt Zita, got her out of the soddy.

They had scarcely left the soddy when she saw Drum and his four braves returning from the direction of the school. She could see smoke, and knew that the school was burning. It was gone, the white-planked school with its chipped paint, the swings without rope, the foolish teeter-totter, the walls, the roof, the benches, the slates, the books, what all that had stood for.

Lucia knelt beside Aunt Zita in the dust beside the burning soddy, weeping, holding the older woman by the shoulders, trying to console her.

She looked up to see Drum standing over her.

"Sitting Bull is dead," said Drum to her.

He looked on the piteous old woman, his face expressionless. He loosened the hatchet he wore at his belt.

He took the old woman's hair in his left hand and swung the hatchet back.

Aunt Zita, whimpering and moaning, understood nothing. Lucia, holding Aunt Zita, put her own head across that of the older woman.

She looked at Drum fiercely, half blinded with tears.

"No!" she said.

Drum said something in Sioux and one of the other braves pulled Lucia's hands from about Aunt Zita's neck. "Lucia!" cried the old woman, reaching out for her.

She opened her eyes, the lids seared by the flames, and saw Drum's hatchet, and shook her head, "Please no, don't hurt me, please."

Drum's face was expressionless as the bluish steel of the hatchet blade, red in the flames of the burning soddy, stood as still as a poised hawk at the back of its arc, before its descent, its fall, to the forehead of the old woman.

"She is a Holy Woman!" screamed Lucia.

Drum's arm did not fall. He turned to look at Lucia.

"Holy Woman!" screamed Lucia. "Bad Medicine kill Holy Woman! Bad Medicine!"

A shadow crossed Drum's eyes, and he lowered the hatchet. "Holy woman?" he asked.

Lucia shook her head vigorously. "Yes," she said, "Holy Woman! Holy Woman!"

Drum shrugged. It did not matter to him one way or another whether he killed the old woman.

He released Aunt Zita and with the hatchet in his hand gestured across the prairie.

"Run, Holy Woman," he said. "Run!"

Aunt Zita struggled to her feet and, terrified, her face opened and blistering even under the butter, fled across the prairie.

She did not look back.

Stumbling and screaming she ran from the small group by the burning soddy.

She did not look back.

Drum regarded Lucia, who was staring numbly after the fleeing figure of Aunt Zita.

Drum spoke rapidly in Sioux to his men. They brought Lucia's horse, the horse which Lucia and Aunt Zita used with the buckboard.

The roof of the soddy, with an angry roar, fell between the dirt walls.

Drum now looked again at Lucia, who was still held tightly by the arms by the brave who had torn her from Aunt Zita.

Drum spoke in Sioux to the brave and he released her, and Lucia stood alone, among the Indians. They mounted, except for Drum and two braves.

He looked at Lucia.

"Are you a Holy Woman?" he asked.

Lucia looked up at him, calmly. "No," she said, "I am not a Holy Woman."

Lucia watched Drum's hatchet. It was fastened to his right wrist with a leather thong. He held it in his hand lightly, the blade swinging a bit a few inches above his ankle.

Then she saw him replace the hatchet in his belt, and she felt as if she might faint with relief.

She hardly heard for a moment what he had said as he had

replaced the hatchet. Then, she seemed to hear it after he had
said it, not when he had actually spoken the words. "Yesterday," had said Drum, "a white man took a woman of the
Hunkpapa."

Suddenly Lucia screamed and turned to run, but his hands
were on her.

She struggled as he took her and threw her to the back of
her horse. It wore no saddle. She was held on the animal's
back by the two braves who had not mounted.

Numbly, she felt Drum tearing off her high shoes. She
must not be able to slip from them. Then his hands were at
her legs, pulling off her long cotton stockings. He shoved up
her dress and petticoats. They must not interfere with her
being fastened to the horse. Using one of the cotton stockings, Drum twisted it and bound her ankles under the horse's
belly. He twisted the other stocking and bound her wrists together in front of her. Precarious on the unsaddled horse, Lucia's bound hands, when the braves released her, clutched
desperately in the animal's mane.

She looked at Drum, frightened, but would ask for nothing.

The two braves mounted their ponies.

She was proud, Lucia Turner.

But, too, the girl knew that begging would make no difference, that her pleading or cries, or tears, would have been
unavailing.

This young man, now at war, had not made her his captive
to release her if she might weep or whine.

He had said that a woman of the Hunkpapa had been
taken by a white man.

Lucia knew nothing of this but did know that her body,
though innocent, had been selected by Drum to expiate the
crime that had been committed against one of his people.

Drum had decided that the penalty was hers to pay. He
would make her pay it, dearly, a thousand times over.

But why she?

Was it simply because she was at hand? Might it as well
have been another?

Lucia felt sick to her stomach; she knew that it could not
as well, in Drum's eyes, have been another.

She closed her eyes, holding the mane of the horse.

She knew then he would have come for her in any case.

This was a man in whose eyes she had seen, long ago, that
she had been wanted, coveted as a possession, like a rifle or a

horse; this she had known as long ago as that terrifying morning at the school; this was the man who had not forgotten the terrified girl who had so abjectly, unworthily, cringed from him; this was a man who remembered her well, and scorned her, and who in accord with ugly permissions of war as he understood it, had chosen to return for her, claiming her by warrior's right because it pleased him to do so, claiming her by the right of the warrior to choose among the undefended, desirable females of the enemy, to slay them, or if he cares, to spare them for his pleasure.

Sick, Lucia knew that it was no accident that Drum and his braves had come to the soddy. It had not been just guns, or food, or the urge to kill and burn; it had been, as much or more than all these things, for her. They had come to fetch her, to bind her and take her away with them.

She opened her eyes and lifted her head.

She would not beg.

And had she done so, what might it have accomplished? It might have amused Drum, or irritated him, and if he were irritated, or when he ceased to be amused, she would be punished, beaten by his own hand or given to Indian women to be taught discipline. A white squaw, Lucia knew, learned obedience quickly at the hands of Indian masters.

Already she felt her fingers growing numb from the stocking that bound her wrists. She moved her ankles, trying to pull free. The knots tightened. She could feel on the interior of her legs the warmth of the horse, the oil of its hair, the scrub of its winter coat.

Drum placed his hand on her thigh, and she shivered, looking down at him.

He looked up into her face. "White teacher," said Drum, "you belong to the Hunkpapa now."

Drum mounted easily and, with his six warriors, and his captive, rode from the burned soddy.

They rode first to the school, which was still flaming, the smoke rising and staining the gray sky.

They waited there until the roof had fallen, and the north wall, where the flames were most fierce, collapsed, even the wagon box which had been leaning against it tumbling into the flaming timbers and planks.

It was there only that Lucia, for no reason she clearly understood, wept.

Drum's hand, holding a rope attached to the halter of her

horse, jerked the animal's head away from the building, and he kicked his mount in the flanks and took his way from the hill, followed perforce by his captive, then six braves.

They rode southwest, toward the Bad Lands.

Chapter Fifteen

It was Christmas Eve, in the Bad Lands of South Dakota as well as elsewhere.

Chance blew on his numb fingers, and fumbled with the stone pipe, fearing that he might drop and break it. He thumbed his last pinch of tobacco into the bowl, giving himself the small present he had saved until this night. He struck a match on the bottom of his boot and lit the pipe, and sucked the welcome fire through the dry tobacco, deeply until his tongue burned and he remembered there was such a thing as heat in the world.

Chance couldn't remember being as cold ever as he had been in the last few days, and the closely guarded cooking fires of Old Bear's band had scarcely seemed to heat the meat, let alone warm the air. On the way to the Bad Lands two cattle had been killed. These "spotted buffalo" as Old Bear called them, even in English, had been cut into strips and on the march, these strips of meat hung from the necks of the ponies.

Chance took a sweet puff.

Some homesteader, or rancher, he supposed, would send a bill for a herd of cattle to the U.S. Government.

Chance pulled the blanket more closely about his shoulders. He had no coat and the blanket was his only wrap, and that he owed to Running Horse and Winona. He'd even lost his hat somewhere—where he didn't know—maybe at the Turner soddy, maybe in the run to the school. The teacher hadn't given it to Running Horse with the medicine kit.

He thought of Lucia, then cruelly, hating himself, to avoid a longer cruelty, forced the thought of her from his mind. He had thought of her too much, remembered her too much, had not forgotten her, could not forget her. He must not—must not—think of her. There had been nothing between them, he reminded himself harshly, only a cup of black coffee and a kiss, a single swift meaningless kiss, which the girl had unhesitantly repudiated.

Chance put back his head and stared up at the gray sky yielding to dusk with the slow turning of the earth.

The mild fall of 1890 had retreated, almost in a night. Now the knife of winter was cold in the air. Still there had not yet been snow.

Chance lowered his eyes to the jagged terrain, sharp, jumbled, twisted, without water, most of it chalky, the grayish white of limestone, here and there reddish clays, volcanic dust, sand left by streams that hadn't flowed in thousands of years.

Nothing much could live here for very long, he said to himself.

In some of the draws an alkaline dust lay, smoking to the fetlocks of the horses. When it rained here, and it must sometime, Chance told himself, it must be like a hundred white rivers running loose, water white as bones running down the maze of arroyos in the limestone ridges.

The arroyos.

The ridges.

The rocks, the natural cover.

It would take an army to fight the Hunkpapa out of this country.

But how long could they stay here?

How long would the meat they had brought in with them last, and the dogs?

Old Bear had said this afternoon that in the sky there was snow.

They didn't want to kill the horses.

When they came out of the Bad Lands they wanted to be on horseback.

Chance leaned back against a limestone boulder, the dust of which covered the back of the blanket he had wrapped about his shoulders.

The tobacco was too dry perhaps, smoked too hot, but Chance did not object.

Something in the dust caught his eye, a few feet from him. He sat there smoking looking at it for a while.

He got up, went to the object, picked it up and returned to the boulder to sit down.

It was about the size of his hand, and an odd shape. Not exactly a rock.

Chance, curious, set aside the stone pipe and, because the

sky was now pretty dark, fumbled in his pocket for the penny box of wooden matches he kept there. He had about seven or eight left, seven to be exact, as he had counted them before lighting his pipe.

He lit one of the matches and looked at the object.

It was the fragment of a jaw, a fossil, with one tooth protruding like a knife. It had belonged to some kind of big cat, probably like a puma.

He dropped it into the dust beside him.

He picked up the pipe again, leaned back once more against the boulder and resumed smoking.

Once this country had been younger, if not gentler. Once it had been green; it had had water, trees, grass; once in this place the large soft-footed cat had followed the delicate antelope; once here long ago, before the eyes of man were here to see, there had trembled in this place the stirring of seeds, the opening of flowers, the lifting of the leaves of trees to the sun and the rain, and here too had occurred the inevitable rhythms of flight and feeding; here had been enacted, as a matter of course, the swift, remorseless rituals of the prey and his predator; here in this place had occurred innumerable events, patient, abrupt, sometimes brutal, sometimes beautiful, concealed, unwitnessed remote events, the traces of some of which, in virtue of the exchange of chemicals, were recalled in a fortuitous scattering of whitish stones, some of which more clearly than others remembered the shape of teeth, the curve of a shard of skull, the form of bones.

And now among the bones of this dead country had come the Hunkpapa, and Chance among them.

He glanced down at the fragment of the jaw lying near him in the dust.

The carnivore is dead, he thought.

And then he thought of Grawson, and the weapons of men, and smiled to himself, thinking that a new king had arisen to occupy the throne of the tooth, and wondered if this advent of the predator, seeking him or another, might not be as axiomatic in nature as water, flesh and salt, the flower and the claw. No, said Chance. It cannot be. Men are more. Men must be more. Here in man nature has made something that is more. Grawson is wrong. He is not innocent as the tiger and the cobra are innocent, condemned by their hunger and instinct to kill, sentenced by nature to inflict for no reason they understand tragedy on the uncomprehending and guiltless. Grawson is wrong. What he does is unjust. It is not beyond justice or apart from justice like the strike of the shark, the multiplication of the bacillus.

But Chance wondered, in his heart, if the predator who stalked him in the name of the laws of man, the name of justice, was indeed responsible, or if he were, like the stars and the protozoa, moved by forces beyond their reflection or control, forces that might be inherent in their nature and those of their environment, forces germinated by the systems in which they formed their part.

No, said Chance, this is too simple for man. Man is more.

There are the bones, the flesh, the vessels, the tissues, the organs, the exchange of gases, the processes of circulation and oxidation, but there is too the knowing, the recognition, the reflection, the being able to be other than one has been. Man is more. He must be more. I will have it, thought Chance, that man is more. That, thought Chance, until I know that it is false, or until I have evidence that it is false, I will believe.

Grawson is wrong.

I can face him, thought Chance, as a man who is in the right can face a man who is in the wrong. I can face him. I can say, I have weapons, and I resist you.

Chance smiled, and glanced down again at the fragment of jaw that lay near him.

In the end the hunter and the hunted lie down in the same dust, and it does not seem to matter. Yet, to Chance it did matter, and though it might never be recorded, even in the traces of bones, though it might vanish completely from the annals of time, he thought it well that the hunted might, once, turn and face the predator. No one would know; the story would be lost; but it would have been done, and it was worth doing.

I will resist him, thought Chance. I have run enough. I am tired of running. Now I will fight.

"Medicine Gun," said Old Bear.

Chance started.

"Ride with me," said the old man.

Not speaking, Chance put out the pipe and got to his feet, folding the blanket and laying it over a shoulder.

Old Bear led the way to the horses, and Chance and the old Indian unpicketed their animals and mounted.

Chance looked at the small, huddled camp of Old Bear. In the dusk, against the chalky limestone, he could see blankets propped on sticks and the openings of small dugouts covered with brush. Here and there, dark against the cliffs, stood a tepee, brought from Grand River. Few of the families present had such a luxury. Horses, closely picketed, shifted in the near darkness. The dim glow of the tiny cooking fires touched the darkness with an incongruous flicker. Wrapped in blankets, the families of the band were bunched together, waiting around the little fires, for the meat to cook and for the soldiers, sooner or later, to come for them.

Chance left the reins loose on his animal, and it followed Old Bear's down an arroyo leading vaguely northeast.

As he rode he wondered, the thought aimlessly crossing his mind, where Drum and his braves were. He had seen them fade from the band shortly after leaving the camp on the Grand River. They had left to find revenge for their murdered chief, to fight, to kill, to scalp, to mutilate. Then somewhere between Standing Rock and the Bad Lands, they must inevitably have died, falling under the guns of soldiers, or ranchers or homesteaders. They must be dead. They were days overdue.

Chance wondered where Old Bear was leading him, and why. For a long time they rode.

Chance's mind seemed to drift as had the smoke of the pipe.

In spite of himself, he found himself thinking again of Lucia Turner, of the softness of her hair, the gentleness of her eyes, of the delicacy of a wrist, of the sudden, unexpected smile, so shy and quick, then the sudden looking down, her laughing.

He was pleased to know that on this night, Christmas Eve, far from the cold, the hunger and the danger of the Bad Lands, she would be warm and safe, and happy, inside the thick walls of the soddy. The range would be hot and there would be coffee, maybe even a tiny evergreen in one corner decorated with ribbon and strings of popped corn, with its clip-on candles on the branches and a pail of water standing ready. He smiled to himself. He wondered what she would cook. Turkey, of course, if it were available. With dressing, and corn, and sliced apples, and biscuits and butter. He imagined her preparing the meal, setting the table, somehow for him. He imagined how she might look, wearing perhaps something dark, a dark blue, with a white collar, the dress protected by the white apron. Perhaps she might even wear yellow. He recalled having seen a few yards of yellow cloth in the soddy, and supposed she had intended to make something from it. Perhaps for spring, perhaps for her return to Saint Louis. Perhaps she had already left Standing Rock, perhaps already she had returned to the brick houses, the paved streets, the gas lamps of Saint Louis, a city. He wondered if, in the soddy, or in the comforts of distant, civilized Missouri, she would ever think of him, as he did of her, and then, angry, telling himself he was a fool, he put the thought of her from his mind.

At last Old Bear and Chance, emerging from a limestone draw, urged their mounts up a small white ridge, and surmounting this ridge, which lay at the edge of the Bad Lands, looked out across the prairie, which like a frosted ocean washed against the rocks of the Hunkpapa's retreat.

Chance looked from the Bad Lands to the prairies beyond.

Old Bear, not lifting his finger above his head, nor looking up, pointed to the sky.

"There will soon be snow," he said.

Chance nodded.

"There will be no food," he said. "There is not enough shelter. The people will die."

Chance said nothing.

"All this," said Old Bear, opening his frail arms as if to embrace the prairie and the directions and the stars over his head, "from the great forests of the north to the Father of Rivers was once the land of the people." The old man then rested his hands on the mane of his pony, but he still did not look at Chance, but rather continued to survey what had once been his domain, the domain of the Dakota, the people of the seven council fires, of the Sioux.

"The white man came," said Old Bear, "and with the knives pulled by horses cut our land open, turning the high, sweet grass to dust. He made the streams of our country dirty. He killed the buffalo. He killed the antelope."

Chance was looking out across the prairie, not wanting to say anything, not being able to say anything.

"The white man," said Old Bear, "does not love this land."

Chance turned to look at the old man, so thin, his white braids tied with string, his back straight, his head high, held with pride and anger.

"I love this land," said Old Bear.

"I know," said Chance.

"Tonight," said Old Bear, "is the birthnight of the Son of Wakan-Tonka."

"Christmas Eve," said Chance.

Old Bear turned and looked at Chance. "The Son of Wakan-Tonka," said Old Bear, "said that all men are brothers, that they should love one another, that the warrior should bless and love his enemy."

"Yes," said Chance, "I have read that."

"Why does the white man not do as the Son of Wakan-Tonka has asked?"

"I don't know," said Chance.

"The soldiers will come and kill us," said Old Bear, "but it will not be easy for them." The old man spoke almost as if thinking aloud. He looked again across the prairie. "Many soldiers will die, but in the end, the people will die." Old Bear turned to Chance. "I am ready to die," he said. "I am old. I have fought many times. I have worn the eagle feather." Then the old man's eyes seemed infinitely sad as they rested on Chance. "But," said he, "I do not want the people to die—I do not want the Dakota to die."

"Maybe," said Chance, "there will be peace."

"Do you think so, Medicine Gun?" asked Old Bear.

"No," said Chance.

"I would like to make a last feast," said Old Bear, "a feast on the night that the Son of Wakan-Tonka is born." He smiled. "Long ago on such a night I might have given horses and buffalo robes and bullets but tonight, on the night the Son of Wakan-Tonka is born, I have nothing."

Chance noticed something on the prairie that made him lean forward in the saddle, straining his eyes. He wished Running Horse were here, for the young Indian's eyesight was unusually keen. There was a light in the distance, like a small star on the prairie.

"What is it?" asked Old Bear.

"I think there is a light down there," said Chance.

"Soldiers?" asked Old Bear.

"I don't think so," said Chance. "Probably a soddy. It's steady and small, not like a campfire. Probably a kerosene lamp."

Chance remembered the money he had, folded in a piece of oilcloth thrust in his boot, probably more than a hundred dollars.

If that were a house maybe he could buy some food.

"Yes," said Old Bear, "it is a lodge made from the dirt of the land; my young men have told me; there is a man there and his woman, and two children."

"The light," said Chance, "looks a bit like a star—out there on the grass of the prairie."

"A star?" asked Old Bear.

"On this night," said Chance, "the Son of Wakan-Tonka is born."

"Huh!" said Old Bear. "Let us ride!"

So the two men, leaning back on their horses, urged the mounts down the alkaline declivity to the prairie, the dust like white clouds rising behind them, and began to ride slowly toward the light in the distance.

Call it a star, said Chance to himself, call it a star.

For a quarter of an hour they rode, not speaking, through frosted brown grass until they had approached the light, which came from a kerosene lamp that burned in the thick window of a homesteader's soddy.

"He does not know we are here," said Old Bear, "or he would put out the light."

Chance dismounted and went to the door of the soddy.

Old Bear, still mounted, holding the reins of Chance's horse, waited a few yards from the door, out of the range of light that would fall when the door was opened.

Chance knocked on the pine door of the soddy.

There was a sudden scuffling of chairs thrust back, and the lamp went out.

Chance stood there, then decided to move to one side of the door, in case anyone fired through it.

He heard the breaking open of a shotgun, and after a second, its snapping shut, and was pleased that he had stepped aside.

Then there came a voice from inside, from somewhere behind the door, but not straight behind it, calling out, "Who's out there?"

"My name is Edward Smith," said Chance. "I'm a friend. I'm a stranger. I'm passing through." He stood there for a time, listening. Then he added, for good measure, paying his respects to the holiday, "Merry Christmas."

The door swung open a bit, moved by someone he couldn't see.

"Step into the door, Mister," said a voice.

"I don't aim to get shot," said Chance.

"I don't either," said the voice.

"All right," said Chance. And he stepped to the threshold of the soddy.

He found himself looking down the two barrels of a
shotgun.

"Merry Christmas," said a voice.

"Right," said Chance. "Merry Christmas."

For a time he was studied in the half darkness, and then
the voice, speaking to someone he couldn't see, said, "Light
the lamp."

Chance heard the globe of the lamp being lifted off, and
the tiny sound of the knob on its side being turned, thrusting
up an inch of wick, and then heard the scratching of a
match, and saw briefly the interior of the soddy, the chairs
and shelves, a clock on a table against one wall, then lost it
as the match went out, then regained it as the wick took the
fire and the globe was replaced.

A thin woman, angular with prematurely gray hair, held
the lamp up.

She had thin lips, gray eyes, strong, chapped hands. She
wore a cotton dress, plaid with large pockets on the sides, a
man's shoes.

The man himself had a round, grizzled face, not unfriendly, but wary and curious. The bottom half of his face
was as bristly as a hog's back. His head and neck protruded
from the collar, a bit too large, of a red, wool shirt, most
probably a present.

"Howdy," he said.

"Howdy," said Chance.

"You hungry?" he asked, lowering the barrel of the
shotgun.

"Yes," said Chance.

"My name is Sam Carter," said the man, but looking beyond Chance to Old Bear.

"Pleased to meet you," said Chance.

"That's an Injun," said Sam Carter, jerking his head toward
Old Bear.

"He's my friend," said Chance.

Sam Carter looked Chance over more carefully, not seeing
any hat, noticing the folded blanket Chance carried over his
left shoulder, an Indian blanket.

"You hungry?" asked Carter.

"Sure am," said Chance. "My friend, too."

"If you want," said Carter, slowly, "you can eat with us."

"Thanks," said Chance.

"Not him," said Carter.

"Why not?" asked Chance.

"He's Injun," said Carter.

"I'm only passing through," said Chance, "with my friend." He looked at Carter, not angrily, more depressed than anything. "I can't stop. I can buy food."

Chance saw two boys now, standing behind their mother. One might have been five, the other seven. Both had bushy brown hair, cut straight around their head with a bowl and shears. Both wore bib overalls, heavy shirts and socks. Behind their shirt collars, which were open, Chance could see the soiled collars of long underwear, buttoned shut, but beyond this stitched closed for the winter.

"What kind of food you want?" asked Carter. "We ain't got much."

"What do you have?" asked Chance.

"I'm not selling any cattle," said Carter.

"What do you have?" asked Chance.

"In a coop out back," said Carter, "I got some chickens, a couple of turkeys."

"I'll buy all you have to sell," said Chance.

One of the boys, the older, had slipped past his father and went to look at Old Bear, who looked down at him impassively.

"What you doing on our land, Injun?" asked the boy.

Old Bear looked down at him. "My horse brought me," he said. "My horse did not know it was your land."

"All right," said the boy, "you can stay."

"Thank you," said Old Bear.

"Come in here!" said his mother sharply.

The boy came back to the soddy, fast.

"How in hell much you want?" asked Carter. "Enough for two?"

"About all you have I want," said Chance.

Carter looked at him suspiciously, and then at Old Bear behind him.

"I heard Sitting Bull got killed up at Standing Rock," he said.

"I heard that, too," said Chance.

"Plenty of Injuns, whole packs of 'em, pulled off the reservations right afterwards, I heard," said Carter. "Some jumped from way down in Pine Ridge. From what I hear, some of the Cheyenne even bolted the Cheyenne River Reservation."

"I didn't know that," said Chance.

"I ain't seen no Injuns come past here," said Carter.

Chance was quiet.

"But I did see a parcel of soldier fellers," said Carter.

"Oh?" said Chance.

"Yeh," said Carter, "and one of 'em rode over here and asked me about Injuns, but I hadn't seen 'em, and he said that all the Injuns what come in peaceful will get a pardon for going off the reservation. There's going to be a powwow at Pine Ridge Agency. You know where that is?"

"No," said Chance.

"I know the place," said Old Bear, speaking in Sioux. "It is past the hunting ground of Wounded Knee, where buffalo used to come to drink." The old man seemed lost in thought. Then he raised his head and looked at Chance. "Do you think the soldiers tell the truth?" he asked.

"What's he want to know?" asked Carter.

Chance, paying no attention to Carter, turned and addressed Old Bear in the language the old man had chosen to speak. "I do not know," he said, "but it would be good if it were true."

"Yes," said Old Bear, "it would be good."

"The soldier feller," said Carter, "said Big Foot's bunch is already on its way back to surrender."

"Did you hear?" asked Chance of Old Bear.

"Big Foot is a good chief," said Old Bear, in Sioux, "he is wise. If he thinks the soldiers tell the truth, he may be right."

Chance went to stand beside Old Bear's horse and together they spoke in Sioux.

"Will the Hunkpapa fight?" asked Chance.

Old Bear grunted. "Some will fight, I think," he said. "Drum will fight."

"But the Hunkpapa?" pressed Chance.

"The Hunkpapa," said Old Bear, "are men—not boys—men do not fight just to die."

"What about the Holy War?" asked Chance. "What about Sitting Bull?"

"I think," said Old Bear, "there should be no Holy War. Kicking Bear said that the Messiah told us He would come in the spring. He did not tell us to fight in the winter. He wanted us to dance and wait for Him."

Old Bear looked down at the ground.

"And we cannot make Sitting Bull be alive by killing all the Hunkpapa. Sitting Bull would not kill his people. I will not kill them. The buffalo are gone. There will be snow. If we do not go back the people will die of hunger, or the horse soldiers will find them and kill them."

"You are a wise man," said Chance.

Old Bear looked at him. "If I were young," he said, "and if I were not chief, I do not think I would go back."

"But," said Chance, "you are a father of the Hunkpapa, wise with many winters, and you are a chief."

"The Hunkpapa will go back," said Old Bear.

Chance without thinking grasped the old man's arm and squeezed it. "Good," said Chance. "Good!"

Old Bear smiled.

"I hope so," he said. "I hope so, Medicine Gun."

Chance turned to Carter. "We are going to make a feast," he said. "I will buy your chickens and turkeys."

"All of 'em?" asked Carter.

"I guess so," said Chance. "How many do you have?"

"Twenty chickens," said Carter, "two turkeys."

"I'll buy them," said Chance, reaching inside his right boot for the oilcloth wrapper.

"There's Injuns around here, ain't there, Mister?" said Carter.

"It's hard to tell," said Chance.

"How come you talk Injun?" asked Carter.

"Learned some," said Chance. "I really speak it very poorly."

"Who are you?"

"I call myself Edward Smith," said Chance.

Chance took ten dollars out of the oilcloth wrapper, thrust the wrapper back in his boot, smoothed out the bill and handed it to Carter.

Carter looked at it. "Thet's too much money," he said.

Chance shrugged.

"Git the coffee can," said Carter to his wife.

She brought the can and Carter, fishing about in some bills, and more change, put together about five dollars and gave it to Chance, who poured it in his pocket.

The transaction completed, Carter said to Chance, "You can come in if you want and eat with us, iffen you want. We'd be pleased to have you."

"What about my friend?" asked Chance.

"He's Injun," said Carter.

"I'll get the chickens and turkeys," said Chance.

"Want any help?" asked Carter.

"Thanks, no," said Chance.

"Merry Christmas," said Carter.

"Merry Christmas," said his wife.

"Merry Christmas, Mister," said the two children.

"Merry Christmas," said Chance and turned away as the door shut.

Chance walked over to Old Bear. "Tonight," he said, "we will have a feast."

"Your feast," said Old Bear.

"No," said Chance. "Our feast—the feast of Old Bear and Medicine Gun, his friend."

"It will be a good feast," said Old Bear.

"It will be a good feast," agreed Chance.

Chance then turned and walked around the corner of the soddy, heading for the back where the coop was.

As he turned about the back corner of the soddy an Indian leaped out of the darkness swinging at him with a long-handled hatchet.

With a startled cry Chance's hand flung up to catch Drum's hatchet arm and the two men grappled fiercely for an instant in the darkness.

"Medicine Gun!" said Drum.

"Goddam," said Chance, "where in hell have you been?"

Drum dropped his hatchet arm and Chance pulled his sleeves down again over his wrists.

"Many soldiers," said Drum, by way of explanation.

Nearby Chance saw six braves, painted and geared for war. He was covered by their rifles, but they were lowering them one by one.

"It is Medicine Gun," whispered one of them to the others.

Drum saw Old Bear and went to him. "We have come to join you, my Chief," he said.

"I welcome Drum," said Old Bear, "the son of Kills-His-Horse."

Chance saw that erect in the hair of Drum was a single feather, white with a black tip, the feather of an eagle.

"We will kill the white people in the lodge of dirt," said Drum to Old Bear, "and then we will bring the big birds with us to your camp."

Out of the corner of his eye Chance saw Sam Carter coming around the corner of the soddy with his shotgun.

At the same time he was aware of Drum's braves fanning out and lifting their weapons.

Carter would have six bullets in his chest before he could find a target, or jerk a trigger.

Chance waved his arm cheerily to Carter. "Just some of the boys," he said. "Merry Christmas!"

"Just some of the boys, eh?" said Carter, not altogether convinced. Chance wondered if he thought he was just going to wave his shotgun and watch the Indians run.

"That's it," said Chance. "No trouble. Just some of the boys."

Carter looked at the war paint.

Speaking in Sioux, Drum addressed Old Bear. "Let us kill this man," he said.

Old Bear then spoke loudly, and to Chance's astonishment, he spoke in English. "This man is my friend," he said.

Drum scowled, and the other braves once more lowered their weapons.

"Well," said Carter skeptically, "Merry Christmas."

"Merry Christmas," said Old Bear, slowly, speaking each syllable.

"Let us kill him," urged Drum, in Sioux.

"Drum," said Chance, speaking in Sioux, "on this night the Son of Wakan-Tonka is born. On this night, of all nights, it is bad medicine to take the warpath."

Drum now scowled at Chance but Drum's braves grunted in agreement, almost enthusiastic agreement.

Chance gathered there had been some theological discord on this point earlier in the evening.

"Then," said Drum to Chance, in Sioux, "as the Son of Wakan-Tonka has asked, I will love this man tonight—but tomorrow I will kill him."

"No," said Old Bear, "tomorrow we ride to Pine Ridge. There will be no war."

"I will fight," said Drum.

"Well," called Carter, backing away, "Good-night."

"Good-night," called Chance pleasantly, waving.

"Merry Christmas," said Carter, disappearing around the corner of the soddy.

"Merry Christmas," called Chance.

"Merry Christmas," said Old Bear.

And then the old Indian, sitting on his pony, lifted his arms and looked up at the stars. In Sioux he said, "Wakan-Tonka, I am glad for You that on this night Your Son is born. It makes my heart happy that on this night a Son is born to You." And then he cried out to the stars, in English, "Merry Christmas, Son of Wakan-Tonka!"

Yes, Chance thought to himself, Merry Chrismas, Son of Wakan-Tonka, on this night You are born, and on this night

You begin Your journey to Calvary. Somewhere on this night a dark tree is growing and nails are being forged.

"We will make a feast," said Old Bear.

"Yes," said Chance, smiling up at the old Indian, "we will make a feast."

The braves began to gather the birds, whose frightened clucks and squawks startled the December air. The noises ended quickly, one by one.

Old Bear, Chance and Drum walked back to bring the horses of the war party to the soddy. They were tied in a clump of trees about two hundred yards downwind from the soddy. It had been an unnecessary precaution. The Carters, for some reason, had no dog.

In the trees Chance stopped abruptly, straining his eyes into the darkness. He bent forward, approaching a slumped object among the horses. In the trees, almost under the hoofs of the horses, kneeling barefoot in the brush, slumped over, her hands tied behind her back and her neck roped to a sapling, was a woman.

Chance crouched beside the figure, taking her face in his hands, lifting it to his own.

"Good God," he whispered. "Lucia—Lucia!"

She opened her eyes, which were numb with shock and cold.

"No," she said. "No, please don't."

Chance shook her.

The eyes, glazed, stared at his face. "I never hurt you," she said. "Please don't."

Chance slapped her twice, hard, trying to jar life and recognition into her.

"I will," she said weakly. "I will."

"Lucia!" he yelled. "Lucia!"

She looked at him, slowly, as if she couldn't see him or understand him.

Then she said, "Edward?"

"Yes," wept Chance, "yes!"

"I can't feel my feet," she said.

Angrily Chance whipped out his knife and with it slashed apart the rope knotted about her neck, then carefully, prying with the tip of the blade, cut the rawhide thongs, one by one, that had sunk in even with her flesh. Chance picked the girl up in his arms and carried her from the trees, heading for the Carter soddy.

Drum barred his path.

"Get out of my way," said Chance.

For no reason he clearly understood Drum stepped to the side, and Chance carried Lucia, who had fallen unconscious, to the homesteader's soddy.

The kerosene lamp still burned in the window, like a star on the prairie.

Chance kicked at the door.

The girl stirred in his arms. "Edward?" she asked.

"Yes," said Chance, "it is." He kissed her on the forehead. "Merry Christmas," he whispered softly, almost crying.

"I'm so cold," she said. And then she said, "I love you."

"I love you," said Chance. "I love you."

The girl closed her eyes, falling asleep against his shoulder.

Sam Carter opened the door and Chance pressed past him, carrying Lucia gently into the soddy.

Chapter Sixteen

The Indian troubles were over.

Chance was glad.

On a butte at the edge of the Bad Lands, Chance, with Running Horse, watched two bands of Sioux begin the long, cold journey to the Pine Ridge Agency.

It was two days after Christmas.

Last night, Big Foot's band of Minneconjou Sioux had camped with Old Bear in the Bad Lands on their way to Pine Ridge. The Minneconjou had come all the way from Cherry Creek, which lay in the Cheyenne River country.

A few days before, several companies of soldiers had suddenly appeared at Big Foot's reservation, tenting in loose bivouac rather than the orderly formation of a more permanent camp. Apparently these men had meant business and whatever business they had in mind they did not expect to last very long. Big Foot, fearing his people were to be massacred, had led his Minneconjou by night from the reservation, while their campfires still burned, eluding the troops and making his way to the temporary safety of the open prairie, but it was a winter prairie and in time, not much time, with no food and almost no shelter, his band would starve or die of exposure.

Big Foot, who himself was dying of pneumonia, had decided to surrender at Pine Ridge, taking his chances with the soldiers there.

Last night he had ridden into the Bad Lands, tied upright on his horse, a shape in blankets, eyes glazed with fever, every breath like a knife twisting in his lungs, and had found Old Bear and with him had smoked and held council.

This morning, as Big Foot's band left the Bad Lands, Old Bear's Hunkpapa silently joined their ranks.

Chance had decided to ride with the Hunkpapa as far as Wounded Knee Creek on the way to Pine Ridge. There, he would cut southwest across country to Chadron, Nebraska.

After buying supplies at Chadron, he planned to cross over-
land to California. If Grawson followed him, he would turn
to meet him, but he would not deliberately seek him out. Perhaps, with the Indian troubles and the confusions of the past
days, Grawson had lost the trail, and would never recover it.
If this were true, Chance would let it go at that. If it were
not true, at some point he would confront Grawson.

The ride to California would be long, and hard, lasting
several weeks. Chance was glad to have the company of Running Horse and Old Bear for a portion of the journey. Also
he anticipated with regret the moment in which he must say
good-bye to these men, Old Bear, who was his friend, and
Running Horse, who was his brother.

Wounded Knee seemed to Chance a good place to break
away from the march. The Indians would camp there, so he
could spend the night with them, and Wounded Knee was
about fifteen or sixteen miles northeast of the Pine Ridge Reservation, and accordingly was about as close to civilization,
to white men with their law and their curiosity and questions,
as Chance cared in these days to come.

The Indians, leaving the Bad Lands, passed within a few
hundred yards of the Carter soddy, and Sam Carter, in front
of the soddy, still in his red wool Christmas shirt, with his
family behind him, watched the long, slow, quiet lines of
Sioux, both Minneconjou and Hunkpapa, begin their journey
to the Pine Ridge Agency, a journey which for many of them
would be their last, a journey which in its way was also to be
fateful for the Carters.

Hunched in their blankets, mounted on their scraggy ponies, the ribs of which were prominent jutting against the
brush of their winter coats, the Sioux rode.

Some of the warriors clutched their rusty firearms beneath
their blankets, to keep the guns warm and prevent their
hands from sticking to the cold metal. Others held the rifles
by the stocks, letting the barrels ride the ponies' backs. Many
of the Sioux, particularly the women, were on foot. Some of
the squaws dragged travois behind them, leaning against the
traces like beasts of burden. The Indian children, most of
whom had known nothing of the old life and were bewildered
by the cold and the loss of rations, were quiet, their eyes dull
with the depression of hunger, their lips pressed against the
ragged swiftness of the wind, the sharpness of the December
cold.

Chance, on horseback, Running Horse near him, watched

the loose grim lines of Sioux pass from the cruel shelter of the Bad Lands to the shelterless cruelty of the prairie.

These, he thought, are the mighty Sioux, who once ruled a country bigger than Texas. Now they are old men, like Old Bear or Big Foot, who was dying; or they were rebellious braves, like Drum, who scowled as he rode, men whose blood and whose culture had prepared them to take a place in a world that no longer existed; or exhausted women, or frightened, hungry children.

Chance and Running Horse urged their horses down the steep, white side of the butte.

When Chance and Running Horse reached the lines of Sioux, Chance cut north to make one last visit to the Carter soddy, telling Running Horse that he would join the march later.

For the last two days Chance had spent most of his time at the soddy, treating Lucia's frostbite, gradually helping her regain her strength, mostly just seeing her. Mrs. Carter's hot broths and fresh hot bread had burned some warmth and substance back into Lucia. The frostbite had not been as serious as Chance had feared and the first night, soaking her feet in cold water, he had managed to restore circulation and feeling. He had not massaged the frozen areas to avoid bruising the tissues, with the result of perhaps predisposing the extremities to gangrene. He had, however, near the frozen areas, rubbed with a dry, coarse towel, working toward but avoiding the frozen parts. At last he could gently move the joints, and then, though it might have seemed cruel, he forced Lucia herself to move about as she could. Perhaps even beyond the effective simplicities of his treatment, matters almost of physiology alone, Chance was most satisfied to feel that his presence, his own presence, had helped to revive the girl from the horror of her capture, helped to thaw at last from her soul the most terrible ice of all, the hidden, invisible ice of numbness and shock, ice that formed a last brittle, frozen barrier behind which she, for days a delicate, brutalized creature on the tether of Indian warriors, had sheltered her sanity.

Now as this girl sat across from him, propped up in the Carters' bed, wrapped in blankets, she was smiling.

Chance wondered how it was that this girl could be happy.

Mrs. Carter had had a knowing look about the house the last two days, and Sam Carter, Chance thought, had whistled a great deal, and both of them had found numerous chores to attend to outside the soddy. More than once both Carter boys, one by each ear, had been escorted from the soddy by one parent or the other.

Had Chance been of a more suspicious nature he might have suspected that he was the object of a benevolent conspiracy, but as it was, trained in medicine and tending on the whole to think well of his fellow man, he did not quite put all of two and two together. He was, however, vaguely grateful that he had had as much time to spend with Lucia alone as he had.

"I'm riding out with Running Horse," said Chance to Lucia. "I'm going to California."

"I'll like California," said Lucia.

Chance stared down at the dirt floor of the soddy, past the colored patchwork quilt on the bed.

Lucia began to kick under the covers and blankets, and finally kicked them off, sitting on the bed, quickly tucking her nightgown, from Mrs. Carter, about her ankles. She wiggled her feet and toes.

Chance could see there would be rope scars where her ankles had been bound. The same sort of mark would be carried on her wrists.

"Two days ago," said Lucia, "I couldn't even do that."

"That's right," said Chance.

"You might check the joints or something," suggested Lucia.

"They're all right," said Chance, "or you couldn't move like that."

"Oh," said Lucia.

She paused for a moment, and drew up her feet and put her head on her knees, looking at Chance.

"I didn't know that," she said.

"It's true," said Chance. He added, "You should be able to walk all right by now, too, but I wouldn't walk too far at first."

"That's a good idea," said Lucia, and she swung her feet off the bed and stood a bit too unsteadily beside it.

She walked a step or two from Chance, and turned to look over her shoulder. "I'm actually pretty good," she said.

"In a day or two," said Chance.

She took two or three more steps, and then turned to make it back to the bed.

She started to walk back toward Chance, tottering but brave, and then suddenly squeaked and had it not been for the fact that Chance swiftly, alertly, sprang to his feet, she might have fallen. Fortunately he managed to catch her.

"Oh," she said.

Chance held her softly beside the bed, and stood her on her feet, lifting her by the arms, and then with his hands touched her hair and as she looked at him, he gently, very gently, kissed her forehead.

"I guess," said Lucia, "I'm not as ready to walk as I thought."

"I guess not," said Chance.

Lucia was looking up at him and very slowly she lifted her lips to his and touched them. The sound of the kiss was very delicate.

"When you brought me inside two nights ago," said Lucia, "you said something to me."

"Merry Christmas," said Chance.

"Not that," said Lucia.

"Oh?" said Chance.

"I said something to you, too," she said.

"Did you?" asked Chance.

"Yes," said Lucia, kissing him again on the lips, a delicate thing, like the touch of a bird.

"You probably didn't know what you were saying," said Chance.

"I did," said Lucia.

"What did you say?" asked Chance.

"My feet are cold," said Lucia.

"Oh," said Chance.

"I don't have any money, you know," said Lucia, looking up at him.

"I know," said Chance.

Lucia pushed back from him a bit, careful not to let him go. "That's not a very proper thing for a doctor to say," she said.

"Sorry," said Chance.

"So I don't know what to do about your fee," she said.

"I'd forget it," said Chance.

"Not me," said Lucia.

"There's no fee," said Chance.

"If I were a hussy," said Lucia, "I'd know how to pay you."

Chance smiled.

"I'm a hussy," said Lucia.

Chance's laugh was cut short when she seized him by the

back of the head and pulled his face down to hers, kissing him so fiercely that he felt the imprint of her teeth on his lip. She then pulled back, and laughed. "There," she said, "you see!"

"Oh," she cried as he drew her into his arms, and then she was frightened, feeling herself by his arms bound against his hardness, unable to move, and his mouth covered hers and through her teeth as she struggled she felt his remorseless tongue thrust through touch hers, turning it back and her body, she felt as if it were flying as he lifted her from the floor and placed her on the bed, half across it, and his tongue never left hers and she felt on her ankle, gently controlling her, his warm hand moving thighward and she swam not caring in pleasure wanting only his closeness and the immersion like joy and fainting and wine and not being able to move and not wanting to and then, he threw back his head and shook it crying aloud and she too cried out with joy loving him and reached for him loving him, loving him.

Chance, recalling the matter later, remembered that she had said at one point that she would like California.

Chance never quite understood how things had been decided but he knew that they had been, and that he was glad, and that he, as a male, and a rational one, would probably never by himself have been responsible for a decision so foolish, and so incontrovertibly glorious, as the one to which he discovered, to his amazement, he had been party.

His life was one of danger, he himself was hunted. He had nothing to offer a woman, neither security nor prospects. He had no home, no practice, no future. He had little to give her but himself and his love, and to his astonishment, he had learned that this was all she wanted.

Chance did not bother comprehending love, but was thankful to move within it, as one might move in the air he breathed, in the sunlight that showed him the world.

And Lucia, too, was unutterably other than she had been; and so too was her world, even to the shine on the walnut chest in the Carter soddy, the gleam on the brass kettle on the shelf near the stove, the tiny drops of grease on the kindling bucket, the grains of dust in the floor of the soddy, the weaving of the blanket, the careful stitching in the quilt on the bed; all things were different and beautiful to her and objects which she had hitherto thought prosaic, like a glass jar, a metal spoon, a piece of string, a kitchen match, the wood

of a slat on a kitchen chair, now seemed to gather into themselves and radiate a startling, incredible perfection.

Chance replaced the blankets about Lucia.

"I've got to go now," said Chance.

Lucia nodded.

Chance looked on the luster of her eyes, the new softness
of her face. He held her wrist, noting the deep rhythm of the
blood moving through her body. When she spoke her voice
for an hour or so would be a bit lower than normal.

Chance smiled and kissed her.

He rose and slung the Indian blanket that was his only
wrap over his left shoulder.

He would write to her from California. She would join him
there.

Then suddenly as he stood there, looking down upon her,
seeing her as beautiful and as his love, he felt as though the
room suddenly darkened and as if his heart stopped beating
for that instant.

It seemed then as though the walls of his hope trembled,
and the towers of the future which had seemed so shining, so
bright with promise, crumbled.

Suddenly it seemed as though the air was gone, as if the
sun had vanished, leaving the pelt of night behind, the
darkness of which was marked by not a star.

"Edward?" she asked.

"It's nothing," he said.

It would be wisest, of course, not to write, but to try to
forget, best for her probably, maybe best for him.

"Edward?" she asked.

"It's nothing," he said, "nothing."

What sort of life would it be for her? What sort of life
could it be for her?

"You love me?" she asked.

"Yes," he said.

"You frightened me," she said, "—how you looked."

"I'm sorry," he said. "I'm sorry."

He turned and went to the door of the soddy, fumbled
with the latch, pushed it up.

At the door he turned to look on her once again, and as he
looked, tears formed in his eyes, because he knew that he
should not send for her, that if he loved her he could not do
so.

"Good-bye, Lucia," said Chance.

"Edward!" she cried.

But he was gone, and in a bound he had mounted his horse and the soddy was behind him.

"We'll take good care of her for you," Mrs. Carter had called after him.

He thought he heard Lucia's voice cry his name again, perhaps from outside the soddy, but the sound was indistinct in the wind and covered by the hoofbeats of his horse.

In a few seconds Chance, crying, reined his horse sharply to the left, turning it to follow the travois tracks and the pressed grass that marked the trail of the Sioux.

In an hour he had rejoined the band.

Chapter Seventeen

The winter morning was crisp, the air as brittle and clear as thin ice. It was the 29th of December, 1890, at the banks of Wounded Knee Creek.

The lodges of the Minneconjou, also on the whole sheltering the Hunkpapa of Old Bear, irregularly dotted the still prairie, like some silent, natural formation, not the habitats of men. The barkless tepee poles showed like bones through the weathered hide of the old skins that clung to them.

The camp was quiet.

Not even a cooking fire rippled the still December air above the lodges. None of the dogs crept through the camp to smell for food. They lay curled in the ashes of last night's fires, their eyes open, not willing to move.

Outside the perimeter of the camp, soldiers walked in pairs, calling the signals of their post. The sentries walked in short, shuffling steps to keep their feet warm. They carried their weapons at right shoulder arms, their free hands unmilitarily buried in the refuge of their blue greatcoats, except when officers checked the watch. The breath of the sentries hung about their rifles like gunsmoke, eventually drifting upward and behind them.

Yesterday afternoon the soldiers had appeared.

The Sioux had been on their second day of the march when the shout, "Long Knives!" hurtled like a volley of shots the length of the long, ragged line.

Chance had not counted on soldiers surprising the Sioux on the prairie, coming to escort them to Pine Ridge.

Chance supposed there were about five hundred of them.

On the left and the right they had appeared, dust moving into the sky about twelve hundred yards away, on both sides.

Old Bear had ridden the line of the Sioux, crying out, "Do not fire! Do not fight!"

About two hundred yards away, the two converging forces

of cavalry reined in, their sabers out of the sheath, their colors flying.

Chance had strained his eyes to make out the small triangular flag in the distance.

Running Horse had read it easily. "Seven," he said. And he had added to Chance. "That is bad."

Chance nodded. He, like everyone else, had heard of the Custer Massacre, but it had only been a thing in newspapers when he had been fourteen or fifteen years old; then he had read about it in a book or two. It had always been distant, remote, something that had happened to someone else on the other side of the world, meaning nothing much to him, nothing that wasn't abstract.

But somehow Chance felt that that event, that had been to him only a few lines of newsprint, a paragraph or two in a book, had not yet finished.

Not all of the Seventh Cavalry of course had been wiped out with Custer, only the detachments which he had personally led. There would be large numbers of career men left who would remember Custer, and their comrades, from fourteen years before. Chance could well suppose that these men might instill as a matter of course newer recruits with their own anger, their own vehemence. The Seventh might, for all Chance knew, suppose itself to have a score to settle; they might suppose, for all he knew, that there was a blot on that small, defiant triangular flag whipping in the wind some two hundred yards away, a blot to be rubbed out, a blot that had waited fourteen years for its cleansing.

Chance watched while Old Bear and Big Foot rode slowly out to meet the commander of the cavalry forces.

When the chiefs returned they told the braves to put away their weapons. The white man had come to go with them to Pine Ridge. There was to be no fighting. This pleased most of the warriors, who had little inclination to fight with an enemy four times as strong, particularly with one's starving women and children at one's back. Some of the men, the younger ones, like Drum, urged fighting, but they received for their show of bravery only the passive stares of the older men.

Chance melted in with the Indians, pulling the blanket more about his shoulders. He had wanted to go only as far as Wounded Knee and pull out before any soldiers arrived.

Old Bear rode through the ranks to Chance. He paused before him, his eyes sad. "There are men with the Long Knives who want to know if a white man is with us," he said. "They want to find such a man."

"What did you tell them?" asked Chance.

"I told them," said Old Bear, "that we are going to Pine Ridge and that white men are the business of white men."

"What did they say to that?" asked Chance.

"They want to look for you," said Old Bear. "But I told them it would not be good. There are young men too ready to fight."

"Thanks," said Chance.

Old Bear looked at him, the trace of a smile cracking the leather of his face. "I did not lie, Medicine Gun," he said.

Chance nodded, looking to where Drum and his braves were shifting on their horses, an angry knot of young warriors, glaring and shaking their rifles at the soldiers.

Drum rode a way into the prairie toward the soldiers, and then rode back. He did this twice, holding his rifle over his head, taunting them in Sioux. Then he returned to his young men. Chance guessed that Drum and his braves would not accompany the march to Pine Ridge, not if they could help it.

"Tonight," said Old Bear to Chance, "it will be hard to leave camp because the guard will be heavy. Tomorrow night, near Pine Ridge, maybe the Long Knives will not watch so close."

"All right," said Chance. "I'll wait, and move out when I can."

He hoped there would be an opportunity.

Chance looked out toward the encircling cavalry.

Suddenly among them he spotted the brown coat of a civilian. Something about the shape of the man and his carriage in the saddle told Chance it was Grawson. The man was putting something back in his saddlebags, possibly a pair of binoculars.

"He has seen you," said Running Horse.

After a while, the long lines of Sioux began to move again, and Chance, wrapped in his blanket against the cold, rubbing and blowing on his hands to keep the fingers flexible, rode with them.

"Where do we camp tonight?" asked Chance.

"Wounded Knee," said Running Horse.

In the camp of the soldiers, corporals went from bundle to bundle, shaking them awake.

This morning, even before reveille, they would be awake and ready for action.

The soldiers stirred, grumbling out of their damp blankets, cursing between chattering teeth, pulling the stiff cold leather of their boots over their wool stockings. When the last buckles were fixed and the last greatcoat was buttoned, the troops massed for formation.

Then reveille cut the morning like a saber.

The announcement of the bugle was not lost on the Sioux, most of whom had been lying awake, their weapons wrapped inside their blankets to keep the trigger housings from stiffening. The white men had oil for their guns, but the Sioux used marrow and grease, and the warmth of their own flesh.

Chance parted the flaps of the crowded lodge he had shared with Running Horse, Winona, and a Minneconjou family. He stared out across the brown grass at the blue dots that formed rectangles in the distance. The bugle sounded again, spearing its notes clearly and quickly to his ear. "Roll call," he thought. Next it would be mess call. Chance wished he had some of that black coffee that Running Horse called black medicine. He could go for some now. The last coffee he had had was at the Carters', where Lucia was sleeping now, warm in her blankets, with her hair soft over her cottoned shoulders.

Chance had dreamed of her last night but the dream had not been a good one.

His stomach still felt cold this morning.

In this dream he had gone to California as he and Lucia had planned, and then he had sent for her, but she had not responded to his letter, she had not come to join him.

He had returned for her for some reason to the Carter soddy but it had been gone.

The prairie had been empty of everything but the wind and the loneliness.

He remembered how she had called to him when he had left the soddy, and how frightened her voice had been, as though she might never see him again.

"Lucia!" he had called, starting out of his sleep.

Running Horse had been sitting cross-legged near the side of the lodge, softly clicking the trigger on his rifle to keep it pliant in the cold.

"It was only a dream," Chance had said.

Running Horse had said nothing but had continued to work the trigger of the weapon.

Chance, wanting to, had told Running Horse the dream.

Running Horse moved the bolt of his rifle back and forth twice. "My heart is heavy for you," he said.

"It's only a dream," Chance said.

Running Horse loaded his weapon. "It is not a good dream," he said.

"It's only a dream," Chance repeated.

Running Horse looked down at the bolt of his rifle, not meeting his eyes.

Damn, thought Chance, damn these damn Indians and their medicine, and their dances, and their superstitions.

"It's only a dream," said Chance.

Without looking at him, Running Horse had placed his rifle inside his blanket, holding it against his body. Chance could see the steel barrel in the light of the dawn that touched the interior of the tepee, falling through the tattered smoke hole at the juncture of the poles over their head. Winona had stirred in her blanket beside Running Horse and his hand had gently folded a corner of the blanket about her shoulders. The other Indians in the lodge, an old man, his two wives and a grandson, in that early hour, had been asleep, or lying quietly, their eyes closed, giving no sign they might be awake. Chance had judged from their breathing they were asleep.

He had looked again at Running Horse.

Running Horse had then lifted his head and looked at him, regarding him sadly. "My heart is heavy for you," he had said.

Shortly after reveille had sounded the Indians had emerged from their lodges and had begun the routines of the camp, urinating, building their fires, starting to prepare their food, as though the nearest soldier might be miles away in bivouac at Pine Ridge.

But for all the apparent unconcern of the Indians nothing the soldiers did escaped their notice, least of all the placement of four rapid-firing Hotchkiss machine guns that had been wheeled into position on a small ridge overlooking the camp. They were pointed downward into the midst of the lodges. If their spraying, sweeping fire were initiated, Chance surmised, it would take only a matter of a minute or so to lay bullets into almost every square yard of the camp.

Had it not been for the fact that the guns were manned by disciplined troops, undoubtedly serving under experienced officers, Chance would have been decidedly uneasy. As it was he supposed the weapons might have been placed as they were almost as a matter of customary field procedure. Beyond this Chance recognized that the commander of the troops, if an intelligent officer, could not be expected to refuse to take serious precautions when dealing with a large number of Indians, many of whom were armed and some of whom might still be hostile. He supposed that he himself in a similar situation, if he had had the weaponry, might have been tempted to deploy it similarly. On the other hand, he, had he commanded the troops, would have been worried somewhat about the effect the sight of the guns might have on the Indians. They might, for example, not understanding the motives of the military, assume, rather like Big Foot's band had assumed several days ago, that they were in danger of being attacked. Big Foot, of course, had fled, because he could; but here there seemed to be no place to which one might flee; there wasn't even sufficient cover; so the likely alternative here might seem to be to fight, perhaps, tragically, even to attack first.

But Chance supposed that one, in such situations, must rely on the good judgment of the military, and trust it, and so he did.

After all this sort of thing was their business, not his.

Chance was aware of Running Horse beside him. He, too, was watching the guns, their crews.

"Don't worry," said Chance. "It's simply a matter of military precaution."

Running Horse said nothing.

"They do that sort of thing," said Chance, "almost without thinking about it. It's just what soldiers do. Put up guns, have drills. It's like a parade."

Running Horse looked at him.

"The United States Army," said Chance, a bit irritably, "doesn't go about shooting down innocent people."

"Look," said Running Horse, pointing into the distance.

Chance looked closely. He could see horses, in dozens of groups of five or six, being led away from the soldiers' camp, out into the prairie. Chance was puzzled. If the soldiers were going to ride those horses to escort the Indians to the agency what was the point of leading them out into the prairie, taking them several hundred yards away?

"Why are they taking the horses away?" asked Running Horse.

"I don't know," said Chance.

"Why would you take horses away?" asked Running Horse.

"I don't know," said Chance.

"I would take them away," said Running Horse, "so they would not be killed, so they would not be in the way when people shoot."

"Those men," said Chance, "are United States soldiers." Even to Chance what he said sounded a bit naive, in the face of the movement of the horses. "United States soldiers," he said, asserting it as if it might almost be on act of faith, "do not attack without reason."

Running Horse watched for a bit longer. Then he turned to Chance and said, "Maybe they will find a reason."

Drum, an eagle feather high in his hair, stepped up to Running Horse and Chance. "I have come to Wounded Knee," he said, "for this morning." He pointed to the guns on the ridge. "Those are guns of many rifles," he said. "Now we must fight or we will all be killed." Then he added, "Old Bear was a fool to trust Long Knives."

Drum turned abruptly and left, beginning to move about the camp, urging the warriors to be ready to fight.

Already in the camp several of the warriors had begun to chant their death song.

The squaws gathered the children together, holding them closely.

The children watched the distant soldiers and the guns with curiosity.

Running Horse turned to Chance. "You are my brother," he said simply. "It has made my heart glad."

Chance looked at the young Indian. "You, too, are my brother," he said. "And, too, it has made my heart glad."

Running Horse and Chance now watched four riders approach the camp. Instinctively, Chance drew the Indian blanket more about his shoulders.

The first man was an army officer, of a rank that Chance could not make out at the distance. He was followed by two troopers, one of whom held a flag of truce. The fourth man, a large man, wore a heavy, brown, fur-collared mackinaw coat; leather gloves; and a fur cap with its earflaps turned down and tied under the chin. It was Grawson.

At the edge of the camp these men met Big Foot and Old Bear.

Chance could watch them talk, and he could see that the officer was impatient, judging from the way his white-gloved hands jerked as he talked. He pointed several times to the guns on the ridge.

Behind the officer, Grawson casually surveyed the camp until, from a distance of about seventy-five yards, he made out Chance. Then the big body in the brown coat, like a satisfied bear, seemed to relax on the horse, almost somnolently.

Meanwhile the soldiers of the Seventh, afoot, were rapidly deploying in a hollow square about the camp, taking advantage of the flag of truce,

Chance was not a military man, but even to him it looked a bit stupid, what was going on. The soldiers were extending their lines very thinly and, if fighting started, they would catch each other in their own cross fire. Nonetheless, whatever happened, of course, the Indians would be caught in the middle. Chance supposed that the officer in charge of the troops was not counting on any trouble. Chance found that reassuring, at any rate. He wondered if the officer understood the presence of men in the Indian camp like Drum, who could never forget that they were the sons of men such as Kills-His-Horse and in whose hair had been fixed, as of only days, the feathers of eagles.

Naturally the Indians were well aware that while the parley was taking place the Long Knives had moved into position.

The soldiers had removed their cumbersome greatcoats and stood shivering in their blue campaign uniforms, their rifles at the ready.

Chance looked at the officer again, the man talking to Big Foot and Old Bear. The carriage of his body, the motions of his hands, suggested the mien of a conqueror addressing the servile vanquished.

Chance looked at the surrounding soldiers, seeing here and there faces of hate, of anticipation, of fear, of distrust, but mostly they looked like simple men anywhere look, like the faces of men on any street in any town, clerks, carpenters, farmers, teamsters, coopers, smiths, cartwrights, merchants, barbers, just men.

They all looked cold.

Here and there one of them tucked his rifle under his arm and blew on his hands, stamping his feet and cursing to himself. "Goddam it's cold," Chance heard one of them mutter, and Chance agreed with him.

A Sioux child, a small boy with unbraided hair that hung to his waist, walked timidly over to one of the soldiers, his eyes fastened on one of the brass buttons on the man's jacket.

Slowly the boy put out his finger and touched the button. The trooper gently shooed him away. The little boy turned to go, looked at the trooper again, then smiled and ran back to his mother.

Big Foot and Old Bear now turned to face the Sioux.

As they did so, the officer and his party, the parley ended, withdrew rapidly, the hoofs of their horses sounding on the frozen prairie.

The message which Big Foot and Old Bear communicated to their people was simple.

The leader of the Long Knives had ordered the Sioux to turn in their weapons. They must give up their guns, after which the march to Pine Ridge would resume.

A wave of protest swept through the Indians. They supposed that it had been intended simply that they were to go directly to Pine Ridge. They were supposed to see, as they had understood, the agent at Pine Ridge, who was not a Long Knife, and get rations for their families, and be at peace with the Great White Father. Now the Long Knives, out on the open prairie, where the men of the Great White Father in Washington could not see, were going to take away their guns. After this, what would they do, these Long Knives of the Seventh Cavalry, some of whom had lost friends with Long Hair in the unavenged defeat on the Little Big Horn many snows ago?

The Indians looked at the four guns on the ridge.

Some of the squaws began to keen, as if wailing for their dead.

"Do not give up your guns," called Drum, his fierce eyes blazing with excitement.

"Be quiet," said Old Bear.

There shortly appeared in the camp a detail of twelve men, led by a sergeant, a heavy, swaggering man, authoritative, not well shaven, with an open holster, who stumbled a bit as he walked, glaring about himself to the left and the right at the silent Indians.

He stopped and, with the heel of a boot, scratched a large, irregular circle in the dirt.

"Bring out yer weapons and put 'em in a pile," called the sergeant, pointing to the center of the circle he had drawn on the ground.

Drum turned to the Sioux. "They will kill us when we have no guns," he said.

Old Bear called out to the Sioux. "Give up your rifles," he said.

Several of the Minneconjou clustered there looked past Old Bear to Big Foot, who stood nearby leaning on one of his wives. The chief could hardly breathe. His eyes were half shut, marked with fever. Weakly he nodded his assent to the command of Old Bear.

Drum, with two of his young men, went into a nearby lodge, and came out with two rusty rifles, which they contemptuously threw into the dirt circle. The gesture was not hard to understand. The Sioux were forcing no issue, but did not intend to disarm themselves. If the white men were intelligent they would accept this token.

The sergeant in charge of the detail blinked and glowered at the Indians. "You goddam Injuns," he yelled, "had better turn in your guns goddam quick or you're going to be all goddam dead!"

Chance's heart sunk.

He was not close but he guessed the sergeant might be drunk, literally. It was not an easy thing to do, to walk into a camp of frightened, angry Indians, and ask them to give up their only means of defending themselves in the presence of armed, blood foes. The sergeant, Chance guessed, might well be drunk. How else would they have gotten a volunteer to walk into the Sioux camp and make that demand? That was the officer's job, wasn't it? No, Chance decided, officers, at least those with sufficient seniority, were for looking through binoculars. Commanding from interior lines, it was called. But, drunk or not, the sergeant was foul and incoherent. The Indians were staring back at him as he shouted at them, and stopped to wipe his mouth on his sleeve, and then shouted some more, making his demand, insulting them.

Several of the Indians, of course, could understand English. And all of them, whether or not they could have been said in any meaningful sense to understand the language or not, were clear that this white man was cursing them, abusing them, and that he was doing this before their wives and children.

Old Bear was listening, apparently impassively, but Chance sensed that the old man was enraged.

The blue square of surrounding soldiers, nearly five hundred strong, shifted uneasily.

Old Bear shut his eyes for a moment and seemed almost to waver with fury, but then he opened his eyes, and lifted his hands to his people. His voice almost broke. "Give up your rifles," he called out, as loudly, as calmly, as he could.

"You there!" bawled the sergeant, jabbing his short finger at Drum, who was standing conspicuously a bit in front of the other Indians. "You gotta gun under that blanket! Give it to me!"

"Come and take it," said Drum.

"Do not take the gun," said Old Bear.

The sergeant hesitated an instant but then, sensible of the eyes of his men behind him, the troops beyond, the Indians gathered about, and the young man challenging him, stalked over to Drum and with both hands he tore open Drum's blanket, to find the muzzle of Drum's rifle, at a high angle, suddenly under his chin. Drum's hand, which was low, was on the trigger.

The sergeant's face went white and if he had been drunk before it was now a sober man that was looking down the barrel of Drum's weapon.

"Take the gun," said Drum.

"Do not take the gun," said Old Bear.

Desperately the sergeant made a sudden move to knock the rifle aside, and Drum simultaneously pulled the trigger and the sergeant stood there for a second oddly leaning backward in a noise his hat blown off with the top of his skull, and then fell backward, sprawling in the dust, and the four lines of the blue square almost at the same time opened fire.

Warriors threw off their blankets blazing away with hidden rifles. Some of them used bows and arrows. Several charged the soldiers across the open ground with knives and hatchets. The quiet, cold December morning suddenly shattered in the staccato cough of gunfire and the shrieks of human beings who had not expected to die.

Chance threw himself to the ground about the same time the cross fire from the lines of soldiers cut through the camp. He discovered, not remembering drawing it, his weapon in his hand. He saw soldiers to his left falling, struck by the bullets of their comrades across the camp. Fighting bodies broiled about him. A Minneconjou, about forty years old, fell near him, a groping hand caught in his own intestines, loosed by the slash of a bayonet. Chance saw Big Foot, blankets wet with blood, tottering and stumbling and then falling, and saw one of his wives, caught in the same burst of fire, fall across his body. He heard the frightened scream of a child pierce the shouts and cries for a second. One Hunkpapa brave was mounted and, hanging low on the neck of his pony, galloped through the fighting. He made it past the camp when the four Hotchkiss machine guns opened up, leaving both the horse and its rider rolling tattered in the grass.

Thank God, thought Chance, they don't dare fire the guns into the camp. Everywhere soldiers and Indians struggled, rolling in the dirt, slashing at each other, grappling, firing when they could, cursing. There were probably twice as many soldiers as Indians altogether, and the soldiers outnumbered the warriors, Chance guessed, about four to one.

Chance saw a frenzied Minneconjou drawing a bead on him, and would never forget the wild eye glinting down the carbine sight, and Chance raised his arm to fire at the man, but before he could fire saw the man move as though knocked to one side by an invisible assailant, struck in the side of the head by a soldier's bullet.

The soldier grinned at Chance, shoving another bullet into his gun. He held up three fingers. You sonofabitch, thought Chance, of the man who had saved his life. Then the man was looking for another target.

A woman's shriek rang out near him.

A dozen feet to his right, soldiers were holding squaws and children while a private, one after the other, was thrusting his bayonet through their bodies.

Chance leaped to his feet and raced through the fierce tangle of fighting bodies, just as the child, the small boy, who had smiled at the brass button of a soldier a few minutes before, was kicked from the wet end of the bayonet.

Chance seized the soldier by the collar and spun him around smashing the butt of his Colt in the man's teeth, and the fellow, stunned, stood there and whimpered, and Chance tore away his rifle and threw it down, and then with his weapon covered the other soldiers.

"Turn them loose," said Chance, "all of them, or I'll kill you."

The soldiers, puzzled, not understanding, hesitated.

Suddenly he noticed that one of the men held Winona. He swung his gun on the man. "All right," he said, "you die first."

The man pushed Winona away from him and she scurried away.

One by one, under the barrel of Chance's gun, the soldiers released their prizes.

The squaws and children ran, some of them falling only a moment later in the fighting.

"What in hell do you think you're doing?" asked one of the soldiers.

"Who are you?" asked another.

"You're crazy, Mister," said another.

"You're a white man, ain't you," said another.

The man whom Chance had struck in the teeth was shaking his head and feeling his mouth with his right hand, running his finger over the broken teeth in his face. "Why'd you hit me?" he asked, and Chance, to his horror, knew that the man did not know.

Chance turned away, looking for Running Horse.

Instead he caught sight of Drum, his hatchet gone, himself red with blood and exultant, leaping on the back of a trooper, plunging his knife into the man's face and neck. Chance shook his head to get rid of the sight. Then he saw, to one side, Running Horse, who fired his weapon through the smoke and the moving bodies, bringing down a trooper who was aiming after a running squaw. As some of the Indians, mostly women and children, made it to the open prairie, the Hotchkiss guns opened up again, leaving them like flowers scattered on the grass.

The battle had broken up into a stew of small, fierce knots. It was only a matter of time now. Again the machine guns opened up, this time on the near end of the camp, the bullets falling like metal rain into a group of women and children who huddled there. In another part of the camp soldiers had begun to set fire to the lodges. The heavy tide of numbers and equipment had never left the ultimate issue of the battle in doubt, and the inevitabilities of the situation were even now moving swiftly to their relentless conclusion. Where they could the Sioux fled, some warriors standing their ground to cover the retreat of their comrades, then even these began to turn and run, if they had not already fallen. As if angered that anything might escape the closely woven net of death the Hotchkiss guns kept up alternating bursts of fire, pouring shells here and there about the camp and near it where Indians attempted to escape. At the rear of the camp Chance saw several warriors, led by Drum and Old Bear, fighting side by side, trying to shield the flight of women and children, some of the children in arms, from the camp. Most of these it seemed, once they cleared the camp, fell under the sharp, irregular rhythms of the guns on the ridge.

Some of the women would not leave and desperately, under fire, they brought screaming, pawing horses to their warriors, some of the women pulling as many as three or four of the frightened, snorting animals. Chance saw a horse hit in the flank with a bullet sink to its rear legs, as if comically sitting, then regain its legs and break away from the squaw with a shake of his head and gallop squeaking out into the prairie, starting to turn in circles. Together in the confusion the braves and squaws mounted as best they could, a wild scattering of riders, and thundered from the camp, some sprawling from the horses in the fire of the guns on the ridge, others somehow making it away.

Chance saw Drum and Old Bear among the escaping Indians. Chance was glad.

He looked wildly about for Running Horse or Winona.

Most of the Indians left now were wounded or fighting savagely, individuals not free to run, locked in place by the constraints of immediate combat.

Chance ran to Running Horse, who suddenly swung his rifle on him to fire. Chance knocked the weapon aside. "Get out of here!" yelled Chance.

Running Horse nodded.

He began to back away after Chance, spitting cartridges from his mouth one by one into his hand, shoving them in his rifle and firing.

They moved slowly back through men fighting, each man intent on his own world, containing a single antagonist, red or white, a world that would not be divided between them, a tiny, sweating, horrifying world in which one of them must die and one live.

They fought with hands, knives, hatchets, gouging, kicking, slashing.

But of all these incidents Chance remembered one more clearly than any other.

Running Horse actually backed into a trooper and when the man turned to fire, Chance had held his arm and said very quietly, "No, don't shoot," and the man had said, "All right," and hadn't. Chance wondered afterwards about the strangeness of that. The man had obeyed him, he supposed, simply because he was white, and had sounded like he knew what he was talking about. Perhaps the man had supposed Running Horse was a scout or somehow attached to the command. But there hadn't been any Indians attached to the command. At any rate he hadn't shot, but had said "All right," and had turned elsewhere. Running Horse, too, hadn't attempted to fight with the man, when he saw Chance speak to him. Perhaps he assumed Chance knew him; perhaps he simply saw that the man was not going to fight him.

Chance and Running Horse continued to work their way backward through the jostling, fierce tangles of hand-to-hand combat. The crack of gunfire made their ears numb; the acrid smoke of expended cartridges stung their nose and eyes. Once a trooper turned and stumbled, falling into Chance's arms, and Chance put him down, seeing the man was dead. Another time a brave crumpled almost at his side, twisting, the cotton of his blue plaid shirt dark with powder burn, a wound in his side that had not yet begun to bleed.

Together Running Horse and Chance kept moving, working their way step by step back toward the rear of the camp.

We might make it, thought Chance wildly, we might make it.

Some had escaped, Drum, Old Bear, others.

We can make it, coursed through Chance's mind, we will make it.

A pistol jabbed into Chance's ribs.

"Drop your gun," said Lester Grawson.

It seemed in that instant to Edward Chance that he had died.

Numbly he dropped his weapon and Grawson, hatless and coatless, with his right boot, his eyes on Chance, not watching the ground, grinning, swept it a dozen feet away.

Grawson's face was cut and his ear torn but Chance could see that he was pleased, mighty pleased. "God how I've waited," said Grawson.

Chance lifted his hands.

"Totter should be here," said Grawson, "but he's having too much fun over there." Grawson nodded to his right, toward the edge of camp where there were burning lodges. The screams of women carried through the smoky air.

Grawson and Chance looked at one another, in their own world, lost by light years from the burning worlds about them.

"I'm not waiting any longer," said Grawson.

Chance saw Grawson's thumb click the hammer back on his weapon.

Then Grawson's hand seemed to tighten.

Running Horse, spinning around to look for Chance, saw Grawson covering him. Running Horse thrust his rifle into the back of Grawson's neck and pulled the trigger, but the cartridge, shoved in crookedly, jammed. Grawson grunted, startled, went white, turned to fire, but as he did so, Chance's hand caught his wrist. Running Horse smashed the stock of his rifle into the side of Grawson's head. The big man slumped to the ground. The young Indian put the rifle to Grawson's temple and pulled the trigger again, but the weapon still failed to fire.

Chance grabbed the rifle from Running Horse and with the palm of his hand slapped free the jammed cartridge.

A line of bullets, like a pattern of buttonholes, opened up the ground to the right of them. Somewhere some squaws and children were screaming. Near Chance's feet, he almost stumbled over him, lay an old man, his eyes opened, praying, his hands cupped over a bleeding chest. In the confusion the significance of the line of bullets suddenly became, like a flash of lightning, evident to Chance. The guns were firing directly into the camp, trying to pick out individual targets. The soldiers nearby, as startled as Chance, started yelling and cursing, and moving back.

"Come on!" yelled Chance, and he, with Running Horse, turned and ran toward the back of the camp, where Drum and Old Bear and others had made good their escape.

Suddenly it seemed to Chance that hell exploded under his feet and a hedge of dirt jumped up around him, marking the tracery of a burst from one of the Hotchkiss guns. A little girl, running to the left of them, threw out her hands and fell forward, two red dots on her back, one near the right shoulder and another near the small of her back. Chance seized Running Horse by the arm and dragged him to the ground, both of them falling behind the bodies of some three women who had fallen earlier to the guns. The bodies behind which they lay shook like bags of sand with the impact of the bullets splattering into them.

Suddenly the firing of the guns stopped. "Soldiers in the line of fire!" yelled Chance. "Come on!"

As one man he and Running Horse fled.

A short burst of Hotchkiss fire ripped the ground behind them. They heard some startled shouts and curses.

Chance and Running Horse were not more than fifty yards from the perimeter of the camp when they saw Winona running towards them, rifle shots kicking up the dust at her feet, holding the reins of three horses, Chance's, Running Horse's, and a third animal, frightened and riderless, which she had captured for herself in the confusion. In an instant Chance and Running Horse and Winona had mounted and had kicked their animals into a terrified gallop.

Some shots followed them, sliding through the air over their heads with a distant crack and a sound like the passing of an insect.

Here and there they saw other riders fleeing, all heading as if by instinct toward the Bad Lands.

Most of the Indians who had fled on foot had run to Wounded Knee Creek, to hide in the brush and the icy water. They would be found there, most of them, and slain.

In the distance, Chance heard the bugle's brave notes, sounding Boots and Saddles. The troopers were being recalled from the camp, to mount and follow. There was a sharp, in its way beautiful, sound in the notes of the bugle. It was a stirring call, thought Chance, that call Boots and Saddles, stirring.

Chance, Running Horse and Winona urged their mounts from Wounded Knee, racing for the Bad Lands.

Chapter Eighteen

The troopers of the Seventh Cavalry, hot with the blood of massacre, methodically burned the camp and hunted survivors. Some of the troopers turned to pillaging, hiding souvenirs of the battle inside their jackets or boots. These they could sell later as mementos of the battle which they now realized had occurred, somewhat after the shooting was over, a battle to be known by the place where it had taken place, Wounded Knee, called for the creek nearby. Several of the soldiers jerked the clothing from fallen Indians, in particular the Ghost Shirts which would bring the highest prices. Some of these would eventually be purchased by museums. There seemed no point in leaving the loot to civilians who would most assuredly, sooner or later, like vultures, come to pick over the field. The spoils, such as they were, belonged, if to anyone, to the victors.

As Chance, Winona and Running Horse urged their mounts over the prairie, they could look back and see columns of smoke ascending from the burning camp. The cold air kept the smoke pretty much together so it seemed the sky was stained with dark parallel bars. In the clear air they could hear the occasional gunshots that marked places and times where wounded Indians were found in the brush or among the bodies. There were no prisoners taken at Wounded Knee. It would take some time before complete discipline could be restored. By the time the troopers could be gathered from the massacre, reunited with their mounts and organized to follow up their victory, those Indians fortunate enough to be mounted would be scattered for miles over the prairie. Those on foot were less fortunate, of course, and several were killed, some as much as three miles from Wounded Knee.

"We are safe now," said Running Horse, reining in his pony.

The three riders slowed their mounts and turned to look back at the bars of smoke rising in the sky.

"My people will not forget this place," said Running Horse.

Chance saw that there were tears in the eyes of Winona.

After a time Running Horse turned his pony north again, and Chance and Winona followed him.

That night the first snow of the year fell, cutting off, for a time, any threat of pursuit. In the afternoon, as Chance, Running Horse and Winona made their way north toward the Bad Lands, the wind had gathered its strength and rushed to meet them, howling, cutting their faces, hurling itself like a lonely, whistling saber across the brown prairie. By dusk the wind carried in its train sleet, that forced the horses and their riders to shut their eyes, and when dark came, the white shrapnel of a blizzard pitted the night, screaming from the north, blurring the air with ice, numbing their hands and stiffening the leather of Chance's reins, the nose ropes of the Indian ponies. Chance had lost somewhere the blanket he had had at Wounded Knee; similarly neither Running Horse nor Winona had covering from the storm other than what they had worn that morning. Chance tried to consider how long they might live thus exposed in the storm. He could not consider the matter rationally for the buzzing of the white hornets about his ears, the jabbing of thousands of delicate snowflakes, each a frozen architecture of icy crystal, driven at high speed against his face and hands, pelting his body. The horses put down their heads, continually shifting to the left, trying to face away from the storm. The riders dismounted and, in single file, pulled the stumbling animals behind them, wading through snow already drifting high enough to cover the tops of Chance's boots.

For an hour they continued to move north, into the blizzard, fighting it.

"We'll freeze!" yelled Chance at the top of his voice, hoping Running Horse could hear him.

"No," shouted Running Horse. "Keep moving! Do not stop!"

Chance felt as though his boots were filled with frozen wood.

They trudged on, dragging the ponies, Running Horse first, then Chance, then Winona.

It was maybe an hour or so later when Chance looked

back, perhaps because he suddenly became aware that he no longer heard the noises of Winona's pony, indistinct in the whipping snow, behind him.

He could not see the girl.

"Running Horse!" he yelled. "Winona!"

Running Horse turned and squinted back through the snow, and then, together, dragging their horses, the two men began to retrace their steps. The trough they had cut with their feet and the hoofs of the horses was already invisible. They had gone about a hundred yards when, some twenty yards to their left, they heard the snort of a pony, and, a minute or two later, they found the animal, and Winona slumped in the snow beside it, her fist still holding the nose rope.

Thank God, thought Chance.

Running Horse gave Chance the nose rope of his pony and bent to the slumped figure of the girl.

The two horses and Chance stood together for warmth.

Chance watched Running Horse lift Winona to her knees and shake her, two blurred shapes in the whirling snow.

"I am tired," Winona was shouting at him, "I am tired!"

"Get up!" yelled Running Horse.

"I am warm now!" shouted Winona. "Go on! I am tired! I will find you later."

Running Horse then began to strike her with his open hand, again and again, savagely.

Winona looked at him blankly, almost increduously, then her eyes betrayed bewilderment, incomprehension at his cruelty, then pain, and then her face and body burned with feeling, with shame, under his blows. Her mouth bled, a red trickle across her snow-encrusted lips.

"Get up," said Running Horse.

"Yes, Husband," said Winona, struggling unsteadily to her feet.

Then together the three of them, Winona now in the center, single file, pulling their ponies, leaning into the wind, continued to force their way northward through the snow.

The next day the wind died and, although more snow fell, the cold relaxed, and a deep, gentle white covered the prairie.

Sheltering themselves in a grove of cottonwood trees, Chance and Running Horse at last built a fire, taking the risk that even Running Horse now granted was permissible. The horses, tied by their reins to cottonwoods, knocked the snow from these trees as far up the trunks as they could reach and peeled the bark in long strips with their front teeth. The sound of their feeding made Chance feel even more hungry.

Winona stood up near the fire and listened. Then her face beamed. "Spotted Buffalo," she said to Running Horse. "Listen."

Both men listened.

In the near distance, possibly no more than seventy-five yards through the trees, they heard a plaintive, soft lowing. Three or four cattle had taken refuge in the trees last night, trying to escape the blizzard.

"Wakan-Tonka is kind at last," said Running Horse, wading with his knife through the snow toward the sound.

Winona, Chance and Running Horse remained in the grove for a day before moving on, waiting for the snow to stop falling. The next morning, the first of January, New Year's Day, 1891, they led their horses from the trees and continued their journey north to the Bad Lands.

A few hours later, two men, on large-boned army horses, rode into the cottonwood grove. Their big horses stepped through the snow with comparative ease. The men wore greatcoats and fur caps, carried rifles and led a provisioned pack horse.

"This is where the rancher saw the smoke," said Corporal Jake Totter, dismounting and kicking at the embers of the dead fire. He scratched his ear carefully under his fur cap. His squarish face looked satisfied.

"They aren't far ahead now," said Grawson. There was victory in his heavy voice.

"I think you're like to crazy to go after that feller so goddam quick," said Totter. "I near froze last night."

"You had a tent and fire," said Grawson.

Totter looked around himself uneasily. "There's probably Injuns around," he said.

"They're running," said Grawson. "Running."

"They might stop," pointed out Totter.

"You want to get the man that shot you, don't you?" jabbed Grawson.

"I don't aim to get myself shot gettin' him," said Totter.

Corporal Jake Totter wasn't too happy with law officer Grawson. There was something strange about the big fellow, and the side of his face, the way it moved sometimes. It made Totter nervous. And the big fellow didn't seem to have much common sense. Totter was not the brightest man in his unit but he'd been on the prairie long enough to know how to be careful. Grawson wasn't. Totter had no particular hankering to meet up with Sioux stragglers after Wounded Knee. For his money, he'd prefer to be back in Good Promise, on leave, to go to the saloon, to see Nancy upstairs, who'd said she liked him. I might marry that gal, someday, thought Totter. But there wouldn't be any leave, or any drinks, or any Nancy, if Grawson got them both scalped. Vaguely Totter wondered about putting a bullet in Grawson. They'd probably never bother digging it out. They could take it for a Sioux bullet anyway. He could say Indians did it. What was Chance to him? He wouldn't mind shooting him, or getting him and giving him to Grawson, but it didn't really make that much difference to Totter. Totter made more difference to Totter. If he never saw Edward Chance again Totter would not have much minded. Live and let live, said Totter to himself.

"Mount up," said Grawson.

"Yes, Sir," said Grawson, climbing into the saddle.

"If we get Chance by sundown," said Grawson, "I'll give you a month's liquor as a bonus."

Totter grinned. "That's a lot of likker for me, Mister," said Totter.

"After I get through with our friend Chance," said Grawson, "you might feel like getting drunk for a month."

"Hell, I'd celebrate," said Totter.

Totter pulled his horse back beside Grawson's.

"No," said Grawson, "you first," gesturing ahead.

Totter shrugged and led the way, the two men riding from the cottonwood grove, following the tracks in the snow, the tracks of two ponies and one shod horse.

Late in the afternoon, Chance, Winona and Running Horse could see the jagged rim of the Bad Lands rearing in the distance. In the snow it looked like the teeth of broken jaws.

"I'll meet you later at the old camp," said Chance. "I want to see Lucia first, down at the Carters'."

Chance had thought that he would not see the girl again, but now, being so close, he knew that he would not resist, foolish though it might be. He must see her again, if only once more.

But Running Horse was looking at him, his eyes sad. "My heart is heavy for you," he said.

Suddenly Chance's heart seemed to stop beating, went cold.

He forced his horse through the snow, wildly, up to the top of a slope, from which he judged he would be able to see the Carter homestead.

Gasping, its flanks sore from the blows of Chance's boots, the horse stopped bewildered turning on the top of the slope, trampling the snow, snorting, and Chance jerked it around and searched the valley, seeing back in the trampled snow some quarter of a mile away the black shell of the Carter soddy. The roof had been burned; there were no livestock in sight; a wagon was overturned in the yard.

"Lucia!" cried Chance at the top of his voice, and kicked the horse, driving it down the slope toward the soddy.

Running Horse and Winona followed him, slowly, not wanting to be there when he first reached the ruin.

At the door of the soddy Chance leapt from the back of his horse and stood in the threshold. The door of the soddy, marked with the blows of rifle stocks and hatchet scars, hung broken on its leather hinges.

Inside the wind had blown some soft snow over the ashes of the fallen roof, making the place seem calm and white. Under a charred beam, dusted with snow, lay the scalped body of Sam Carter, his little shape crumpled into a crooked heap, still wearing its Christmas shirt, a red wool shirt, the collar of which was too large.

"Lucia!" yelled Chance.

She was not in the soddy.

Running Horse looked through the opening where, perhaps yesterday, the door had been locked.

"Lucia!" yelled Chance at him.

Running Horse shook his head.

"Did you find her?" yelled Chance.

"No," said Running Horse.

"Is she outside?" yelled Chance, irrationally.

"No," said Running Horse.

"Where is she?" demanded Chance.

"She is alive," said Running Horse.

Chance drew a deep breath, the deepest it seemed to him he had ever drawn. His hands and arms trembled.

"How do you know?" he asked.

"She is not here," said Running Horse simply.

"Weve got to find her," said Chance.

"It will not be hard," said Running Horse, something strange in his voice.

The young Indian turned, and Chance, stumbling, followed him from the grisly soddy.

Outside, Running Horse pointed in the snow. There, a few feet from the overturned wagon, a sign was drawn, like a diagram in sand. It was a crude angle, and inside the angle were two circles, connected by small lines.

"It is the sign of Drum," said Running Horse, speaking slowly, watching Chance's face. "The pointed lines show which way the war party went. The sign is left to guide any of the Minneconjou or Hunkpapa who come this way."

The angle of the sign pointed to the Bad Lands.

"All right," said Chance, gathering himself together, trying to regulate his breathing. "Let's get the horses."

Running Horse put his hand gently on his arm. "If you want your woman," he said, "you must not rush to the camp. You must not try to fight. They are ready to kill anyone. If you try to take her away from them, you will be killed, maybe her too."

"I'm going to get her out," said Chance.

"There are braves, maybe twenty," said Running Horse. "You do not even have your gun."

Chance remembered he had dropped the Colt at Grawson's command and Grawson had kicked it away. The Hotchkiss guns had opened up on the camp about that time and he and Running Horse had fled. He hadn't had time to pick up the weapon. Between them they had one carbine, which belonged to Running Horse, and a handful of bullets, also belonging to Running Horse. Chance's bullets, contained in the tiny loops on his gun belt, were useless unless he could find a .45 caliber pistol.

"I do not think they will kill her," said Running Horse, "at least not until after the Scalp Dance."

"Scalp Dance?" asked Chance.

"Tonight," said Running Horse.

"I've got to get her out," said Chance.

"You must be wise as well as brave, my Brother," said Running Horse.

Chance nodded. There was no question of bravery. Indeed, he was ready to act like a damn fool, do anything. It would be hard though, to be wise, even to be patient, even to wait an hour.

Chance shook himself, looking at the soddy. There was work to be done here. The Scalp Dance, whatever that was, would not take place until tonight. There was time. Chance would force himself to wait. And there was work, there was work to be done here.

Chance found an ax and a shovel, and kicked the snow away from a small area about the size of the wagon box. Then he began to chop and cut at the frozen ground. Winona and Running Horse carried the bodies from the soddy and laid them in the snow. Soon Chance had cut and scooped out a shallow grave. He put the four bodies in the grave, composing their limbs as well as he could, and covered them, laying chunks of frozen earth on by hand.

"The spring rains," said Running Horse, "will make the dirt soft."

Chance went back into the soddy and took the back of a broken, burned chair. He carved: "Samuel Carter, Wife and Two Sons. Died Maybe New Year's Day, 1891." He didn't know the names of the woman and the two boys. Someone probably knew. Someone would come sometime, and they could do things better. Chance, using the ax, sharpened the side slats of the chair and then, tapping with the ax head, drove his simple marker into the soil.

Finished, he stood up.

Running Horse and Winona, who had stood by not speaking, regarded him.

"I suppose I ought to say something," said Chance.

Neither of the Indians spoke.

"I can't say anything," said Chance.

Running Horse shrugged.

Chance looked up into the blue, cold sky, watched a white cloud move past, some thousands of feet above, moved by the wind, the pressures and volumes of the air. Then the cloud was gone and the sky seemed empty to Chance, very beautiful, but not much concerned, and empty.

He looked down at the chopped clods of frozen soil, brown, black chunks; at the snow muddied by his boots; at the shovel he had dropped to one side; at the bit of a piece of chair that he had pounded into the hard soil at the head of the grave.

"I don't think the coyotes will get them," said Chance.

"No," said Running Horse.

Together the three of them, the two men and the woman,

went to their horses, mounted and rode slowly through the snow toward the looming Bad Lands, leaving behind them the burned soddy and the turned soil nearby, a patch about the size of a wagon box.

Chapter Nineteen

"God," said Jake Totter, steadying his horse near the Carter soddy. "I thought you said the Injuns was scared." His eyes took in the desolate, calm scene, ending on the simple grave.

His horse shied, backing away, stamping the snow.

"What's wrong with your horse?" asked Grawson.

"He don't like the smell of killing," said Totter. "I don't either, leastways around here."

Grawson pointed to the marker on the grave. "A white man did that," he said. "Chance came this way."

Grawson dismounted and went to some tracks in the snow. "Three horses," he said, "two unshod, one shod." He crouched down, looking at the sides of the prints, their relative sharpness. "Not over three hours old," said Grawson. He stood up. "We got him," he said.

Totter looked off where the tracks led. "I ain't riding into the Bad Lands," he said.

Grawson mounted, loosening the carbine in his saddle boot. "A month's liquor is a lot of liquor," he said.

"Not if you ain't alive to drink it," said Totter.

Grawson drew the carbine from the boot. "There's only three of them now," he said.

"Where they're going," said Totter, "there may be fifty of 'em. I ain't going into the Bad Lands."

Grawson checked his weapon, released the safety. "You're on special orders to me, Corporal," he said.

"I ain't going there," said Totter.

The carbine rested across the saddle, casual. "Yes, you are," said Grawson.

"Not me," said Totter.

"I guess you don't understand, Corporal," said Grawson, "that's one of those special orders."

"Go to hell," said Totter. "I ain't going."

Totter saw he was looking down the barrel of Grawson's

carbine. When Grawson pulled the trigger it would hit him about two inches over the belt buckle.

"If you ain't going, Corporal," said Grawson, "I'm going to leave you right here."

"You can't go shooting a white man," said Totter, his voice stumbling, his eyes not leaving the penny-sized hole at the end of the carbine.

"I wouldn't," said Grawson, "but Indians might—right here."

"I'm coming," said Totter.

"Ride ahead, Corporal," said Grawson.

Cursing under his breath, Totter turned his mount toward the Bad Lands.

"You're crazy, Mister," he said over his shoulder.

Totter heard the hammer snap back on the carbine, as though it was jerked, the way Grawson's face moved sometimes. The hair lifted on the back of Totter's neck. Then no bullet came and he rode on, his hands shaking on the reins.

As the two men rode from the Carter soddy they passed, not noticing it, a sign drawn in the snow, two circles connected with short lines, and an angle pointing toward the white ridges in the distance.

In about a half hour Totter and Grawson were making their way through the first arroyos of the Bad Lands. They had ridden a few minutes, down the bottom of one arroyo, when Totter stopped.

"I thought I heard something," he said.

"Keep going," said Grawson.

Totter kept going.

Then in about a minute he stopped again. "There it is again," he said. He looked around. Everything seemed still. "Snow," said Totter, "snow slipping into the arroyo."

"The wind pushed it off," said Grawson.

Totter looked at him, and at the carbine which had not been returned to the saddle boot.

"Let's go, Corporal," said Grawson.

"There ain't no wind," said Totter.

Grawson gestured with the barrel of the carbine.

Totter, his face white, trembling, watching, moved his horse slowly ahead.

It was dusk in the Bad Lands when Chance, Winona and Running Horse reached the camp.

For the past few minutes they had heard the light tap of a tom-tom, getting louder as they approached it.

"It'll give their position away," Chance had said.

"No one will hear," Running Horse had responded.

Chance realized then that the young Indian was right. There were no soldiers within miles. The Carters, even if they might have heard, were dead.

A woman's scream carried over the snow, through the cold air.

"Lucia!" said Chance, kicking his horse forward.

Running Horse turned his pony into Chance's path and the two animals struck shoulders, snorting. "No!" said Running Horse, sternly. "No!"

Chance's face contorted with agony.

"No," said Running Horse gently, putting his hand on Chance's arm.

Together then he, with Winona, following Running Horse, continued down the arroyo, following the sound of the tom-tom. At last, turning a final bend, they passed two grim Hunkpapa guards, and came to the camp.

It was in a small canyon, something like a box canyon except that at the far end there was a cut, giving access to another arroyo beyond. The walls of the tiny canyon were pretty steep, and the place, like the arroyos, was sheltered from the wind. Finding such a retreat in the Bad Lands, had Chance and Running Horse not known where it was, might have taken days.

In the canyon the snow had been trampled down over a space about twenty-five yards wide, circling out from the leeward wall of the canyon. That wall was fringed with makeshift shelters, mostly contrived from blankets, sticks and brush.

Toward the center of the canyon was a large fire, lighting the walls of the canyon. It had already melted the snow back in a wide, damp circle. It was muddy near the fire. It was too large a fire for the uses of the camp. Chance judged, correctly, that it was a council or ceremonial fire, and the wood it fed on might have been carried, some of it, from as far as the Carter soddy.

About thirty-five Indians, few of them women and children, were gathered about the fire. The men were sitting on brush and blankets. The women and children stood behind them.

Most of the women wore the signs of mourning. They had

cut their hair; their faces were smeared with dirt and their clothing had been torn. Some had cut open their cheeks and arms, and heavy blood clots marked the wounds that would become scars.

The children, Chance noticed, did not run about as Indian children normally did, busying themselves here and there, getting into whatever trouble they might find. Instead they stood by the women, clinging to them, afraid to let go.

He did not see Lucia; but he had heard her cry; she was somewhere here.

He must wait.

Chance hoped that more of the Indians might find their way across the prairie to this retreat, or others like it; he did not understand at that time how few Indians had escaped Wounded Knee.

At least there would be food in the camp, meat; Chance remembered that the Carter livestock had not been in evidence, what there had been of it.

Lucia was nowhere to be seen, but he had heard her cry; she was somewhere here.

He did not like to look at the eyes of the children.

He must wait.

Old Bear sat a little forward of most of the warriors, his eyes staring into the fire, not really seeing it.

Chance noted that Drum, too, was not present, nor any of the young warriors who habitually followed him.

Perhaps Lucia was with Drum, and his men.

Chance's fists clenched.

Then he saw, suddenly, revoltingly, in a clear place near the fire, scalps, hair and skin, heaped on the ground. Lucia had screamed. It was a dark, loose pile, grisly, matted, stained with brownish reds, some of the hair stiff, the whole pile rather damp from the mud and snow, droplets glistening here and there on it, lying in the mud near the fire. Many scalps. More, Chance noted, than those of the Carters alone. Lucia. She had screamed. I heard her. No. None of the scalps blond. None blond. None. Not blond. And Chance took a deep breath, and let it out very slowly, his hands trembling. Lucia, he told himself, is still alive.

Old Bear stood to welcome Winona.

She went to him, standing before him, and Chance could see that the old man was happy beyond happiness, though hardly did his expression change. "Huh!" he said to her. Winona inclined her head to him, gently. "Huh!" said Old

Bear again, and motioned for her to go and stand with the other women, and the children, which she did.

Running Horse took his seat as a warrior, a bit behind Old Bear. The young Indian motioned for Chance to sit beside him. None of the braves objected to Chance taking that place. Drum was gone, and his young men, and the rest of the Hunkpapa, or most of them, had long ago come to accept Chance as a part of their camp; he was Medicine Gun; even the Minneconjou who were there did not protest his presence, remembering him from before, from the camp before the march, from the march, from Wounded Knee. Indeed, though Chance did not understand it at the time, the fact that he had been at Wounded Knee, with them, was important to these people. They would say to one another, in years afterward, when a child might ask, or a stranger, "Yes, Medicine Gun, he was with us at Wounded Knee."

"Welcome, Medicine Gun," said Old Bear.

Chance nodded, sitting cross-legged near the chief. "Where is Drum?" he asked, as casually as he could manage.

"You were followed by two men," said Old Bear. "Drum has gone to get them." The old man had spoken simply, as though what he had said had been a matter of course.

"Drum didn't pass us," said Chance.

"He passed you," said Old Bear.

Chance looked at Running Horse. The young Indian smiled. "Yes, my Brother," he said, "it is true."

"We led someone into a trap?" asked Chance.

"Yes," said Old Bear.

There was little doubt in Chance's mind who the two men who had followed would be.

The beat of the tom-tom, incessant, seemed to throb in his bones and flesh.

He felt a strange mixture of swift, unclear, irresistible emotions, pleasure, cruelty, pity, relief, apprehension, confusion, difficulty.

Somehow, in a moment, perhaps paradoxically, he found himself hoping that Totter and Grawson might escape; he knew they would not.

Chance did not envy a man the death which the Sioux might contrive.

Suddenly the tom-tom stopped.

The silence, save for the noise of the fire, startled Chance.

He followed the eyes of the Hunkpapa and Minneconjou

to the opening of a blanket shelter stretched between sticks at the foot of the rock wall to his right.

A thin Hunkpapa woman, with a sharp stick, her narrow face disfigured with four mourning wounds, prodded a wretched, stumbling figure from the shelter, a slim, blond girl who fell in the snow.

Chance felt the hand of Running Horse tight on his arm.

The thin woman jabbed the girl twice with the stick and then, using it as a club, struck her several times across the shoulders as she struggled to rise.

Lucia Turner now stood on her feet, but unsteadily, her hands reaching out, trying to keep from falling again.

Her feet had been bound, Chance surmised; it was hard for her to walk.

Lucia was looking at the fire.

Her eyes were wide with fear.

She stood still in the snow, trembling, rubbing with numb, stiff fingers the bruised flesh of her wrists. Chance could see, clearly visible against the white skin, the deep, red burns of rawhide strands.

She had been put in Indian clothing, moccasins and a dress of deerskin. Her hair had been braided behind her back, tied with two strings of cheap glass beads. Chance judged she wore nothing beneath the deerskin. She had not even a blanket to clutch about herself. There probably weren't enough blankets even for the Indians.

The girl shuddered, though whether from fear or cold, or both, Chance did not know.

He wondered if the girl had been brought out to be killed.

Neither of them knew.

They will have to kill both of us, thought Chance, both.

The thin woman struck Lucia again across the back with the stick, sharply, viciously, but Lucia did not cry out. Then the woman, thrusting with the stick, prodded her toward the fire before the men.

Lucia did not cry, and Chance felt proud of her for that.

He also felt helpless.

When Lucia stumbled into the circle of firelight, she saw Chance.

She seemed stunned; her lips moved as though to say his name; then she looked away; that she might not appear to know him; that she might not involve him in whatever might happen to her.

She is magnificent, thought Chance. I love her.

He regarded her, his face expressionless, giving no sign of recognition.

Old Bear addressed the girl. "White Woman," said he, "how did you come here?"

Lucia looked at him. Old Bear knew this as well as she. The thin woman jabbed Lucia sharply with the stick. "I was brought here," she said.

"How were you brought here?" asked Old Bear sternly.

Lucia looked at him, bewildered.

"Say it," said Old Bear.

"They came," said Lucia, trembling. "They killed my friends. They burned the house."

"How did you come here?" demanded Old Bear.

"I didn't want to come here!" cried Lucia.

"How did you come here?" demanded Old Bear.

"On foot," said Lucia. "My hands were tied behind my back. A rope was put on my throat."

"Huh!" said Old Bear, satisfied.

Chance then understood that Lucia was being made to understand, and acknowledge, the simple fact of her capture, and what this meant; that her life had been spared but that she was a prisoner; and that her life was in the hands of the Sioux, to whom she now belonged.

"On the rope of a warrior," said Old Bear.

"Yes," said Lucia.

"What warrior?" asked Old Bear.

Lucia dropped her head. "Drum," she said, "the son of Kills-His-Horse."

"You are the squaw of Drum," said Old Bear.

"That cannot be," said Chance simply.

A chorus of surprise greeted this announcement.

Old Bear looked at Chance, puzzled. "Why?" he asked.

"She is my woman," said Chance.

Old Bear was evidently startled. "I did not know this," he said.

He looked at Lucia.

"Yes," said Lucia softly. "I am his woman."

At that moment Chance stood ready to fight the entire Sioux nation.

Old Bear looked at Chance. "One blanket?" he asked.

Chance recalled the Carter soddy. "Yes," he said, "one blanket."

Lucia dropped her head.

Suddenly the thin woman with the stick screamed shrilly.

"She is the woman of Drum! I saw him bring her to the camp! Medicine Gun is white! He lies! They talk with the tongues of snakes to save each other!"

"My Brother, Medicine Gun," said Running Horse, "does not lie."

The thin woman recoiled, as if she had been stung with a whip. "Short Hair!" she hissed.

The voice of Running Horse did not rise, nor show emotion. He said, "I have danced the Sun Dance; I have smoked with Sitting Bull; I have fought at Grand River; I have fought at Wounded Knee." Then he looked at her and said, "Go take your place with the women."

The thin woman said nothing, but retreated sullenly to stand among the other women, and the children.

Old Bear looked at Chance. "It is not good," he said. "Drum wants the yellow-haired woman."

"He may not have her," said Chance. "She is mine."

"Drum," said Old Bear, "is the son of Kills-His-Horse. By birth and blood he is Hunkpapa."

"Not by birth," said Chance, "but by the blood of Running Horse, my Brother, I too am Hunkpapa."

"In the way of the Hunkpapa," said Old Bear, "the woman belongs to the warrior who takes her."

"That is true," said Chance, "but in the way of the Hunkpapa one warrior does not steal from another warrior."

Old Bear looked at him. "Drum will fight," he said.

"I too will fight," said Chance.

Old Bear looked into the fire, thoughtfully. "It is not good," he said.

"It must be, Father of the Hunkpapa," said Chance. "I am sorry."

Old Bear looked up at Lucia. "Squaw," said he.

Lucia's lower lip trembled. "Yes," she said.

"Warriors will fight for you," said Old Bear. "One will die."

Lucia looked at Chance, frightened. "No," she said.

"Be silent," said Chance.

Lucia was silent. She knew that if she were his woman, she must obey him. He, though he were white, was in his way Hunkpapa, and she knew herself, by capture, to be a squaw of that people, and they would expect her to obey him, as she must Drum, or any other whose squaw she might be.

Old Bear looked at Lucia steadily, closely, watching her

eyes. Then the old Indian pointed to Chance. "In the Hunkpapa this is Medicine Gun," he said.

"I know," said Lucia. Chance had told her of his Indian name when they had visited, for hours, in those precious days at the Carter soddy.

"If Medicine Gun is not killed," asked Old Bear, "will you be a good squaw to him?"

Lucia dropped her head. Perhaps in spite of her peril she smiled a bit, somewhere in her heart, she, Lucia Turner, who had held in the East the radical opinions of the most advanced women, extending even to the right to vote, she who had been in her way a heretical, militant outpost of feminism on Standing Rock, who had waged her one-woman war to raise the status of her sister, red or white. "Yes," she said, head down, "I will try to be a good squaw to him."

Chance, well aware of Lucia's unusual opinions and political convictions, smiled too, though the smile could not be read on his face. He recalled how he had enjoyed teasing Lucia on such matters, to see her flush and defend herself, and marshal her arguments.

This was lost of course on Old Bear. "Try?" asked Old Bear, sternly.

Lucia looked at Chance, shyly. "I will be a good squaw to you," she said.

Suddenly Lucia, for a moment, was afraid of Chance. He sat so quietly, giving no sign of his feelings. She asked herself suddenly what she knew of this man, with whom she had somehow desperately fallen in love. He stayed with the Sioux. He might be for all she knew more Indian than white. He was perhaps a renegade. It suddenly crossed her mind that this man might indeed keep her and use her as simply that, his squaw. Then even this alternative did not frighten her. Do with me what you please, Edward Chance, she thought. Yours. I am yours. However you choose to want me, I am yours.

Old Bear then addressed Lucia again. "If Drum wins," asked Old Bear, "will you be a good squaw to Drum?"

Lucia looked at him, frightened.

"She will," said Chance, his voice sounding strange and distant, harsh.

Old Bear did not drop his eyes from those of Lucia.

The girl nodded, shivering in the cold.

Still Old Bear did not drop his eyes from those of Lucia.

"Speak," said Chance.

"Yes," said Lucia, "if Drum wins I will be a good squaw to Drum."

A shout flared at the entrance of the camp.

Drum had returned!

Drum, lifting his rifle in triumph and singing, rode into the camp, astride a huge army horse.

Tied by ropes to Drum's saddle stumbled Lester Grawson and Corporal Jake Totter, their arms bound behind them.

After Drum came Drum's warriors, seven of them, grinning, their faces still damp with a sweat that seemed incongruous in the cold, all of them on foot except one, who brought up the rear on a second large-boned army horse, a "U.S." burned on its flank.

The women, the children hanging to them, pressed forward to see the prisoners.

Swelling under the eyes of his people Drum brought Totter and Grawson to where Old Bear sat near the fire; there Drum forced his two prisoners to the ground before the old chief.

The thin woman, she who had beaten Lucia with the stick, coming as close as she dared, shrieked with glee.

Chance felt sick.

One of the warriors dropped the captured rifles and pistols before Old Bear.

Grawson struggled in his bonds, his huge muscles straining against the ropes. "Renegade," he said to Chance.

Chance said nothing, not even knowing for certain how he felt. He was more worried about Lucia, and Drum, than anything else.

Totter caught his eye. The soldier's frame shook with terror. Chance did not judge him a coward. Totter knew the Sioux better than Grawson, in some ways perhaps better than Chance, who knew them only as friends; the Sioux were warmhearted friends, generous, loyal, among themselves good humored, fond of jokes; but as enemies, Chance did not know; he would not have cared to have them as enemies. Totter's eyes were pleading. "You're white," he whispered. "Help us, Chance."

"Shut up," said Grawson.

"Or kill us," whispered Totter, "or for God's sake kill us."

Chance shivered.

Then Totter saw Winona standing among the women. His face went chalky.

The girl was watching him, her face showing not the trace of an emotion.

Old Bear dipped into the weapons, taking Grawson's Colt, which he gave to Chance.

"Thank you," said Chance, checking over the weapon. Never had he meant an expression of gratitude as deeply as he did that. It not only meant that Old Bear still regarded him as Medicine Gun, and of the Hunkpapa, that he trusted him, but that now in his own eyes and in the eyes of all he was once again a warrior among warriors, for he held a weapon among armed men. The Colt was in good order. Chance slipped it into the holster; too long had the holster been empty.

Old Bear then lifted the two rifles, one by one, examining them. He gave the best one to Drum; the other he kept for himself, handing his old weapon to another Indian. The remaining pistol Old Bear held up by the barrel. The pistol was a weapon for which Sioux had never much cared. It was thought, correctly, to be inaccurate, except at relatively short ranges; it could be beaten in accuracy and distance, of course, by a rifle; it was hard even to hold steady in firing and when it fired the barrel threw the hand up, requiring a separate adjustment for the next shot; it did fire rapidly, but now that shoulder weapons universally used cartridges instead of powder and ball the differential was not that significant. Moreover, some of the Sioux felt that the revolver was somehow a uniquely white man's weapon, and that only they could use it properly; only they knew the medicine of its steel. Nonetheless Drum reached out and took the pistol, handing it immediately to one of his braves. He was in a good mood but he saw no reason at all in giving Chance two of the weapons.

Chance decided this was the moment, if any, when Drum was in high spirits, basking in the glory of his people, to speak to him, hopefully to avert bloodshed between them if it were possible.

"Drum," said Chance, "you are a great warrior."

Drum looked at him, surprised.

"Yes," said Chance, pointing to Grawson and Totter, who squirmed in their ropes, the one defiant, the other terrified. "These are strong, dangerous men," he said, "but to you they are nothing—you bring them like horses to your people."

The ropes which had been tied about the necks of Grawson and Totter were held by one of Drum's braves.

Drum laughed. "It is true," he said.

"I watched you fight at Wounded Knee," Chance continued, watching Drum's face. "You made the Long Knives pay much for their treachery."

"Yes," said Drum, grinning and kicking Totter with his foot. "And here," he laughed, "is another Long Knife."

"Even more than all this," said Chance, "you have saved my woman and brought her to the camp of the Hunkpapa. My heart is grateful to you."

Drum looked puzzled.

Chance pointed at Lucia. "This yellow-haired woman," said Chance, "is my woman."

"No!" shouted Drum. "She is my woman! If I want, she will keep my lodge! If I want, I will kill her!"

"No," said Chance. "She is my woman."

"If she was your woman," said Drum, "she would have come willingly to the camp of the Hunkpapa."

"She did not know I was still with the Hunkpapa," said Chance.

"Are the Hunkpapa not your people?" challenged Drum.

"They are the only people I have," said Chance.

"Then," said Drum, triumphantly, "she is not your woman or she would know you would be always with your people. She would have come with us, singing and happy."

"Drum is a warrior who is wise as well as brave," said Chance, "but how could you expect her to come with you when you had killed her friends?"

"I will not give her up," said Drum.

"I will pay you horses and bullets," said Chance, "even though she is my own woman, I will pay you horses and bullets, because I do not want to fight you."

Drum looked at Chance.

"Though she is my own woman," said Chance, "I will buy her."

"I will not sell her," said Drum, "not for twenty horses or a thousand bullets."

"I will give you forty horses," said Chance, "a hundred boxes of bullets." He did not consider at the moment where he might obtain such riches. Somehow he could; somehow he would.

"I will not sell her," said Drum.

"Please," said Lucia.

Drum regarded her contemptuously.

"Please—" said Lucia, begging him, "—sell me."

"Do you want to be my squaw?" asked Drum.

"No!" cried Lucia, "no, no!"

Drum threw back his head and laughed, and then he slapped his leg with pleasure. "If you wanted to be my squaw," he said, "then maybe I would sell you."

Chance's fists closed. Lucia subsided into crushed, helpless silence.

"Why will you not give up the woman?" asked Chance.

Drum looked at him. "I want her," he said.

"Tomorrow morning," said Old Bear, speaking to both men, "you will fight."

About the campfire there was a murmur of assent to Old Bear's words.

"No," said Lucia to Chance. "I will be his woman."

"I will not permit it," said Chance.

"Please," said Lucia.

"No," said Chance. "I will not permit it."

Drum looked at Lucia, puzzled.

Then the two men regarded one another.

"For a long time, Medicine Gun," said Drum, "there has been bad blood between us. Tomorrow we will end the blood that is bad between us."

Chance nodded.

Drum looked down at him. "I am not angry with you, Medicine Gun," he said.

Chance looked up, surprised. He regarded the swift, lithe young brave. Somehow, now that the matter was settled, he, too, felt no anger. "And I," said Chance, "am not angry with the son of Kills-His-Horse."

"Good," said Drum.

Chance nodded, looking down at the dirt.

"Give up the woman," said Drum.

Chance looked up again, more surprised than before. "I will not give her up," he said.

"Then," said Drum, "we will fight."

"Yes," said Chance, "we will fight."

Tomorrow one of them would be dead.

"Take the coats of these men," said Old Bear, gesturing to Grawson and Totter, "and give them to the women and children."

Two braves tied the feet of Grawson and Totter. Then, they untied their arms and removed the warm greatcoats, afterwards rebinding their arms.

When Totter's greatcoat was pulled off, Drum's eye was

taken of a sudden by the soldier's sleeve. He went to Totter and held the bound arm. Then Drum's sudden cry of joy rang through the camp, like sun off the blade of a lifted knife. Chance looked more closely. In the light of the fire he could see Drum's hand on Totter's arm, and the blue sleeve, where two chevrons had been torn off.

As the Indians bent forward to see more closely, and the women and children pressed in, Drum released Totter's arm and from the recesses of his medicine bag withdrew one stained, wrinkled yellow chevron. This he held against Totter's sleeve, his face evil with delight.

"Winona!" cried Drum. "Winona!"

Winona came forward, facing Totter, who knelt frozen with fear bound before her.

At the side of Winona stood Running Horse.

Totter numbly shook his head, back and forth, denying a charge that had not yet been made.

"It wasn't me," said Totter. "Not me." Totter began to whimper. "You got the wrong feller," he said. "It wasn't me."

Without speaking Running Horse withdrew from his own medicine bag a second wrinkled, yellow chevron. This he too held to Totter's sleeve. It too, of course, matched.

Totter shook his head again. "No," he said, his voice only a whisper, terrified. "No," he said, "it wasn't me." His eyes screamed, looked to Winona, imploring.

The girl's face bore no trace of emotion; then without speaking she turned and made her way back through the Indians, leaving him.

Totter looked from Drum to Running Horse, to Old Bear, puzzled, not understanding.

"Give him to the women," said Old Bear.

Totter screamed like a girl, struggling and biting as he was staked out near the fire. Now he was sobbing, his body stripped and his legs and arms tied widely apart. Several of the women, led by the thin woman with mourning wounds, crowded about his helpless figure.

"Let us dance," said Old Bear, unpacking his pipe, putting his tobacco pouch in his lap. He gestured to one of the children to bring him a twig from the fire which he could use in lighting the pipe.

The Indians began, with the exception of Old Bear and two or three rather old men, to get to their feet.

Two of Drum's young men carried Grawson, bound hand

and foot, from the fire to one of the blanket shelters against the lee wall of the camp. His fate would be decided later.

The tom-tom resumed its beat.

Chance, still sitting by Old Bear, watched the Indian men form a large circle about the fire. This dance, he knew, was a dance of men. It was not a dance in which the women might participate. But this time the women would not stand outside the circle, stamping the time with their feet. They were within the circle, crouching over the body of Totter, arguing, planning.

"Where is the Scalp Pole?" laughed Drum.

He seized Lucia by the arm and dragged her inside the circle of warriors.

Old Bear put his hand on Chance's knee, keeping him from interfering. "No," said the old man. He drew a slow puff on his pipe. "It is an old custom of the Sioux," he said, "that the captive female will hold over her head the scalps of her people while the victorious warriors dance about her."

"Edward!" cried Lucia from inside the circle.

Drum's hand was in her hair and he had forced her to her knees over the grisly bundle of scalps, but she would not put her hands in them.

He bent her face closer and closer to the scalps as she, fighting the agony of her hair, tried to pull away.

Then for some reason Drum, though he did not permit her to rise, nor did he remove his hand from her hair, allowed her to lift her head and then he twisted it suddenly to face Chance.

The tom-tom stopped.

Drum, holding Lucia, watched Chance.

Lucia's eyes were half crazed with pain, and Chance, by an effort of will, restrained himself from leaping to his feet and attacking Drum with his bare hands.

Chance looked at Lucia, trying to show no emotion.

"Edward!" she cried piteously. "What will I do? What will I do?"

For a moment the only sound in the camp was the crackle of the large fire.

Then Chance said, "Pick them up."

Lucia looked at him with disbelief; then she shook with revulsion.

The Indians, not simply Drum, were watching. If she were his woman, she would obey him.

"Pick them up," repeated Chance, quietly, matter of factly

issuing the girl her imperative; his tone of voice expressed no doubt whatsoever of her compliance, in its gentle way permitted her no alternative save obedience.

Lucia looked at him with horror.

Then, shutting her eyes, she thrust her hands in the scalps, clutching them.

The tom-tom suddenly resumed its beat.

Drum jerked Lucia to her feet and dragged her near the fire, and then, holding her wrists, lifted her hands and their grisly burden over her head, as she must hold them for the duration of the dance, even though it might take hours. Drum stepped back and laughed with pleasure, seeing her standing thus, captive female, dressed to the pleasure of her captors, holding over her head the scalps of her kind, a living Scalp Pole, about which men might dance.

Then Drum took his place in the circle of warriors and terrible in the light of the ceremonial fire the contorted shapes of the dancing, shouting, fighting men of the Hunkpapa and Minneconjou began to turn and shuffle and stamp about her in a ritual that antedated in the lives of the Indians the horse, the firearm, even the steel knife; a ritual that was ancient even before the first ships of the white men, their sails like the wings of birds, had come to the New World.

As the dance went on it seemed to become even wilder and one brave or another would leap into the air, drunk on the frenzy of the dance, and cry out and strike to the left or the right with a knife or hatchet.

As they danced they acted out wars and victories, their triumphs and the triumphs of their people.

Shuddering, Lucia watched the men dance, knowing that they danced not only about the scalps, but about her as well, and that she herself, like the scalps, was trophy, prize.

Sudden screams from Totter began to pierce the noise of the dance, each scream seeming to spur the warriors to a new frenzy of joy.

Chance couldn't see much of Totter, because of the women kneeling about him, working; he had some idea of what they were doing, with their awls and scrapers; in spite of his experience in medicine and surgery he did not expect he could have observed their performance with equanimity; he was familiar with the patient bead and needle work of Indian women, the intricate patterns, the delicacy, the care with which the work was done.

Old Bear was smoking, watching the dance.

Running Horse, Chance noticed, did not dance, undoubtedly because of Chance, and his respect for the wishes of his brother. Winona was with the women, near Totter, but not working on the body, rather watching. She did not, as far as Chance could see, show any emotion.

Some of the work done on Totter involved pine needles, shavings, tiny beads of pine resin and fire, but the women, too, had taken a handful of bullets from his saddlebags, in spite of how precious these things were, and had patiently, for this occasion, pried the bullets open, making two rows of tiny brass cups filled with gunpowder, like so many miniature thimbles; then, with their knives and awls, they had opened pockets in his flesh which they filled with the powder from the cartridges. Then, from time to time, they would touch fire to one of these pockets and there would be a sudden start of smoke and a terrible scream from Totter. When he lost consciousness as happened frequently, they would rub his face and body with snow, reviving him. Because of the careful nature of their work, Chance supposed Totter might last several hours, or indefinitely; he would last, Chance supposed, until the women tired.

Chance found Totter's screams like nails driven into his head. He, Chance, a white man, was sitting there, doing nothing, while Totter, another white man, was being tortured. Yet what could he do? He was armed. It wouldn't make any difference. He might try to rescue him, but would probably get them both killed. It would be foolish. And there was Lucia, who must come first.

In the morning, said Chance to himself, I must meet Drum.

He watched Lucia, her arms holding the grotesque, matted bundle over her head. Her eyes were shut. Chance knew by now her arms would be aching. Yet she would stand thus, alive, shamed, a trophy, for as long as the Indians wished, until the dance was ended.

The circle of warriors turned ever more fiercely about the fire and the girl; the cries of Totter became ever more hysterical; the fire seemed to burn hotter and fiercer until the world seemed shadows and cries and turning bodies and the fire.

Chance looked on Lucia.

Opening her eyes she saw him, watching her, quietly sitting cross-legged near Old Bear and Running Horse, like an Indian, watching the dance, not showing feelings.

Then for the second time was she afraid of him.

What are you, she asked herself, that I cannot help loving you; what are you that I must love you; I belong to you, Edward Chance, man, but I do not know you; what are you that I belong to; you sit so quietly, you watch; what are you thinking; what are your feelings; are you civilized, my love, and kind, or are you in your heart like these, a savage; in your heart are you among these others, dancing about me, a cry on your lips, in your hand a knife; are you tender, Edward Chance; will you be gentle; or will you lead me, like Drum, bound, to your lodge; why did you tell me to do this; why did I obey you; why did I know that I must obey you; you are strange, Edward Chance; I do not know you; I know little of you except that I am yours, that I belong to you; I am frightened; you frighten me, you sit so quietly; you watch; my arms hurt; so much my arms hurt; but I will not put them down; I cannot, because you have not told me; when will you let me put them down; when will you say to me, "Put them down"; I am tired, my love; when may I rest; when will you say to me, "Put them down"; what is this love that so gives me to you; why is it that I, softness, must yield to your hardness; my flower to your steel; that I, woman, must be yours, my Edward Chance, beloved stranger?

She looked at him, and he, with his eyes, answered her.

I am no longer afraid, she said to herself, no longer. I am with my love. I am not afraid.

Chance, torn, watched the dance, waiting for it to end, but it did not seem it would. How brave she is, he thought; how fine and strong; even the Hunkpapa and the Minneconjou must acknowledge this woman, who is a strong person, who has good heart; she is superb, this woman, my love; my tender, gentle, sweet love.

The sudden yelps of the dance startled the night and the burning of the huge fire of the Scalp Dance continued unabated. The stamping of the feet and the twisting of the bodies and the cries and the beat of the tom-tom swirled like clouds and flaming wind in the stone cup of the canyon, madness and natural forces whirling mixed with man and cruelty and victory in that distant, isolated place called the Bad Lands, where so little grew, where the bones of ancient predators lay strewn in the white dust, where the outside worlds that Chance remembered and knew, the worlds that had formed him, seemed unknown, remote, forgotten, nonexistent.

Totter was screaming again, incoherently. "Nancy, Nancy!" he cried. "Don't let them hurt me!"

Chance saw Winona rise from among the women and stand over Totter, looking down on him.

Still he saw no trace of emotion on the face of the Indian girl.

"Nancy!" cried Totter. "Don't let them hurt me!"

He never understood what the girl replied, for she spoke in Sioux. "I am Winona," she said, "the daughter of Old Bear, chief of the Hunkpapa, and the woman of Running Horse, who is a warrior, and wears the feather of an eagle." Then Winona turned away from him, leaving him to the others.

Totter gave one last, long wavering scream and then Chance heard no more. He didn't know if the man had died then, or if only from that time on he had been unable to scream. Chance judged the latter, as the women did not leave him. On the other hand it was possible they were simply mutilating a corpse, blinding it, castrating it, making it unfit for the next world.

But the dance continued and in his concern for Lucia the fate of Totter was forced from his mind. He hoped for Totter's sake the man was dead. But Lucia was alive.

He looked on the girl, in the midst of the dancing bodies, the scalps held over her head. He saw the blond hair, braided, knowing it bound with glass beads; he saw the reflection of the fire in her eyes; he sensed from the lines of her face the pain she felt; how cruel must be the protest of the muscles in her arms now; how tired she must be to stand thus for so long; and yet to Chance in that moment she seemed barbaric and beautiful, the proudness and fineness of her face and head, the carriage of her slender, courageous body, its delicate, subtle lineaments unmistakable beneath the single, thin garment permitted her, accentuated with cruel frankness by the dictated posture of the Scalp Dance.

This woman, said Chance to himself, looking on the girl in the light of the fire, seeing her through the dancing ring of howling warriors, is indeed trophy.

The incessant beat of the tom-tom seemed to pound in Chance's blood.

Never before, thought Chance, have I seen her thus, as pure woman, as prize.

And Chance sensed then, as he had never sensed before, the ritualization of courtship, the meanings of the stylized amenities he had found so much a nuisance so many years ago, the teas, the suppers, the dances, the visits here and there, the formal calls on Sunday afternoons; all of it, said

Chance, is this; pursuit and capture, dignified, made acceptable; no longer do they flee from us like deer through the
forest, to be driven into brush or backed against rocks, to be
cornered and bound, and led back as brides; no longer; but
only the nature of her flight is changed and the nature of the
bonds determining to whom it is she belongs; in the end it is
the same, the flight and the capture; and here, in this place,
her meaning as woman is clear; here, apart from symbols and
disguises and distortions and frivolities, she stands as a
woman, the prize of man; does she, this woman, now know
her femaleness; does she understand; is the meaning of her
excruciatingly desirable body now brought home to her; does
she now understand the significance of her sex, that she is female, that nature has destined her for man?

Yes, thought Chance, she is very beautiful, marvelously, incredibly beautiful—Miss Lucia Turner, educated Eastern
gentlewoman, sophisticated and refined graduate of a finishing academy for young ladies, holder of advanced opinions,
reader of French literature, intellectual, reformer, feminist—
captive female—suddenly unexpectedly astoundingly shame-
fully simply captive female—reduced utterly, she, Miss Lucia
Turner, gifted and beautiful, to ancient, primitive essentiali-
ties—owned, literally owned.

The tom-tom's beat raged on, drunken, intoxicating.

I want to own that woman, thought Chance.

No, thought Chance, no.

He tried to shake the wildness from his thoughts, his
wanting to possess the woman, tried not to respond to the
heady, fiery rhythms of the tom-tom, the stamping feet, the
twisting bodies, the cries, the Scalp Dance of the Hunkpapa
and Minneconjou. He was a civilized man, a gentleman, bred
to courtesy and regard, the product of a silken, chivalrous
tradition, a gracious tradition of white linen and polished silver, candlelight and imported wines, a man whose first
thought would once have been always to favor and respect
the fair, gentler sex; and yet Chance had realized in the past
years that the implicit condescension of his familial, Southern
tradition, with its indulgence and courtesy towards the fair
had been in its own way an imprisonment of the very creatures it purported to shelter and honor; and then he had been
convinced, partly by Lucia Turner herself, that a woman
must be accepted and esteemed for what she might be in herself. as a person, and not for her sex, no more than a man,
and this had seemed decent to him and probably right; but

this night he had seen that woman, whatever might be her ca-
pacities, her glories, her rights, was yet woman; and his blood
told him older secrets than he had imbibed during evening
suppers in South Carolina, undiscussed, unremarked secrets
beyond the tutorings of liberals and radicals with their insane
myopia to the subtle chemistries of human conquest and surrender, to the genetic tenacity of the instincts of the female
to belong, of the male to possess. Beautiful as they are, intelligent as they are, they are weaker than we, thought Chance,
and they are our mates, ours forever, in their hearts and in
our blood, victorious only in surrender, whole only in annihi-
lation, fulfilled only by the incontestable delight of complete,
unconditional submission, wanting it, desperate for it, ancient
as the caves, knowing it or not.

Lucia Turner, standing before him, captive female, woman
of the enemy, he by the blood of his Indian brother
Hunkpapa, was woman, so designated by a handful of cheap
glass beads that bound her hair, woman alone, female, all
else, education, accomplishments, stripped away from her,
meaningless, save the worn dress of an Indian squaw, the thin
hide of an animal given to her that her nakedness might be
clothed.

The madness of the drum swept through Chance.

As the dance swirled about Lucia and the tom-tom's beat
infused her blood, making her senses reel, and the imperious
demand of the drum, the wild turning circle of men who
shouted and stamped about her, spoke words to her without
speech, she felt for a wild moment that yet another dancer
had suddenly entered the circle, that about her, knife in hand,
howled and reeled and stamped yet another warrior of the
Hunkpapa.

No, he was sitting quietly beside Old Bear, watching, not
stirring, the reflection of the flames on his impassive
countenance.

Yet still Lucia could not rid herself of the wild feeling that
had swept her, that yet another presence now shared the savage circle, one claiming her more than any other, one more
fierce and terrible than any other, one who would not yield
her to another, not for horses or gold or life itself.

Yes, she said, half drunk with the fire, the madness, the
pain, the howling dance, the tom-tom, join them, my love.
Thou, too, my love, join them and dance about me; dance
your victory and your desire and your pride; dance your

manhood, your claim on this she, whom I am. Dance, Edward Chance, Medicine Gun of the Hunkpapa, dance about me; thou more than any other.

Edward Chance leaped to his feet.

Chapter Twenty

The morning after the Scalp Dance Chance awoke thinking maybe it was strange he should have slept those few hours between the ending of the dance and dawn. Quite possibly it had been his last night. Yet he had slept. He did not object. If he had to die in an hour or so he preferred to do so with his senses alive and keen.

He lay wrapped in a saddle blanket which had been taken from Totter's horse.

He recalled the ending of the dance, how he had gone to Lucia and helped her to lower her arms, taking the scalps from her, moving her arms for her.

Old Bear had not permitted her that night to go to the shelter of Drum, nor had he permitted her to sleep beside him. Such matters were contingent on the outcome of the morning's business.

It was dawn now.

Old Bear had been kind. He had designated Totter's greatcoat for Lucia's use. After the dance Lucia had been returned by Winona to the blanket shelter from which Chance had first seen her emerge, driven by the thin woman with the pointed stick. There, Winona made Lucia sit upon Totter's greatcoat, which she opened under her like a blanket. Then, as Winona ordered her, not resisting, Lucia crossed her ankles and placed her wrists, also crossed, behind her back; then, with rawhide straps, Winona bound her. She had not tied Lucia cruelly, as Drum might have done, but she tied her well; Lucia had hoped that the Indian girl might free her or, intentionally or through lack of skill, bind her loosely enough that she might, with effort, escape; but after an hour's piteous struggle in the lonely darkness of the crude shelter Lucia knew this hope was unfounded; that her former pupil had secured her perfectly; that she had been bound by a Hunkpapa woman, who did not intend her to escape; when the men came in the morning she would be, thanks to Winona, yet a bound captive in the blanket shelter, awaiting her fate. But before she had left Winona had gently placed Lucia on her side, wrapping Totter's greatcoat about her, buttoning it closed for warmth.

Chance sat up in the blanket, wiping his eyes.

The ashes of the huge fire formed a sloping mound, now covered with a light dust of snow that had fallen in the night. Near the fire, naked, still staked out, lay the corpse of Jake Totter, mutilated and eyeless, the snow on it not melting any more than on the rocks and brush.

Chance was waiting for the discovery to be made, that Grawson had made his escape.

He had not tried to free Lucia.

On the snowy prairie, had they been able to clear the Bad Lands, they might have been trailed easily, and the vengeance of Drum would have been terrible, falling on Lucia perhaps as well as himself; Chance did not wish to face the almost certain dilemma at the end of such a flight, whether to allow the girl to fall into the hands of Drum or to put his last bullet through her brain; if he stayed to fight he might win, and if he did, he was free to go, taking the girl with him; if he lost he did not know what would happen, other than the fact that he would be dead and the girl would be Drum's; perhaps she would live for a time as his squaw and sometime, perhaps, if he tired of her, he might sell her to another, and perhaps this other, or the next, might take ransom or trade her, perhaps for a pair of horses, or a rifle, or a handful of cattle, perhaps to homesteaders, perhaps to a patrol of soldiers; it was possible she might be carried as far as Canada, or after weeks, across the Rio Grande to Mexico, changing hands several times; if this sort of thing happened, eventually, somewhere, somehow, she would find her freedom; a greater danger was that soldiers might attack the Indians who owned her, and that she might fall in the fighting; or be slain by the Indians, whom she might otherwise impede in their retreat; perhaps she would be shot that she might not fall alive into the hands of the soldiers, not be rescued; Chance could imagine Drum killing her under such circumstances; all things considered Chance decided it was best for Lucia that he meet Drum; it was hard to judge the matter.

And something within him was not altogether dissatisfied with this decision.

Old Bear, Running Horse, the others, expected him to meet

Drum; he had said he would do so; he was expected to fight, as a warrior fights, not run.

Chance smiled to himself thinking of honor, and of a distant field many years ago.

How foolish that had been.

But, Chance realized, the foolishness of that act in which he had found himself involved, expected to assume a homicidal cultural role, had not been the consequence of the foolishness of honor, but rather of its perversion and distortion; that act, in its special circumstances, had been a misunderstanding of the obligations and significance of honor; a misrepresentation of its imperatives; it had been vanity, not honor.

Chance wondered on the thing honor, understanding it not much at all, wondering if it could much be understood.

It was a strange thing.

If he had run, he knew, astoundingly, that when Lucia was safe, he would then have turned his horse once more toward the Bad Lands, would have returned to meet angry Drum and his people.

Was that honor?

Or foolishness?

Or only the blood of Running Horse in his veins?

Hunkpapa pride?

How can we understand honor, Chance asked himself, or pride, or courage or loyalty; how can we understand what we are, man, ourselves?

What are these remarkable genetic dispositions to nobility, so easily betrayed, that will insist on stubbornly, doggedly filing their claims, whether they be acknowledged or not?

Yet Chance, partly from himself, partly from the bravery of a fine, beautiful girl, partly from the Hunkpapa, understood himself somehow, not quite knowing how, to have learned in the past few weeks something of the mysteries of honor and such matters, more than he had learned in all the preceding empty years of his past life, before he had known friendship, and love; perhaps he had learned most from the Indians, from savages, where honor's primitive rudiments were least concealed by the complex customs and hypocrisies of a civilization of bricks and dollars, that could preach love and brotherhood and on the banks of a creek in South Dakota bayonet women and children. Running Horse, his brother, had taught him something of honor; and so too had Old Bear, Sitting Bull, and Drum; and the Sun Dance had

taught him, and smoking, and Wounded Knee; he had
learned lessons of truth to oneself, of the keeping of pledges
and the being of a brother, and of the incomparable horror
of the dishonorable deed, performed because it may be accomplished with impunity.

And so it was that the physician, Edward Chance, in an
Indian camp in the Bad Lands of South Dakota discovered
himself incontrovertibly sensitive to certain kinds of claims,
those of honor among them, sensitive to the coercions of
codes of nobility; in this he was a man, not the sly animal
that denigrates honor and courage as stupidity and foolishness, the petty envious animal incapable of either, scurrying
about in its smugness, the intellectual rodent seeking its hole
when the wind blows or the cat prowls, content to be protected by the works and valor of others, men, whom he fears and
despises, to whom he owes his wretched existence.

Chance had gone to the brush shelter of Grawson.

He wondered if it had been honor that had sent him there,
cutting the big man free. He doubted it. He thought rather it
might have been, incredibly enough, pity, perhaps the
memory of the screams of Totter.

Pity?

Grawson would have hated that.

He had given Grawson his Colt, unloaded, and a handful
of bullets.

"You're a fool," the big man had said, taking the weapon,
the bullets.

Perhaps, thought Chance, perhaps I am a fool, but perhaps
there is some difference.

I saw, as you did not, what was done to Totter.

Edward Chance, though he rode with the Hunkpapa,
though he was used to the weight of a weapon at his thigh,
the precision steel of a device for killing, had seen enough,
had seen too much; never again, if he could help it, would a
man die as Totter had, no matter who the man might be,
Grawson or any other, stranger or mortal enemy.

And yet if this simply, this alone, was his motivation, he
found it hard to understand what he had said to Grawson.
He had said simply, knowing he would meet this man again,
"I do not let the Hunkpapa do my killing."

The big man had disappeared from the brush shelter.

Chance remained behind, to meet Drum, to fight for a
woman—whom he could not keep even should he win her.

There was the scream, announcing the discovery.

The thin woman, she with the scabs of mourning wounds crusted on her face, had crept to Grawson's brush shelter, to be the first to taunt the prisoner.

Her shriek awakened the camp.

She scrambled among the blanket shelters and the snowy figures of sleeping warriors curled like dogs in the snow, pulling at them with long fingers, jabbing them, shaking them, screaming. Then she stood in the center of the camp, almost over Totter's corpse, holding Grawson's severed bonds in her fists, shaking them like snakes, looking at the gray sky, howling in disappointment.

Warriors sprang up bewildered, some angry, some looking about as if to see soldiers on the cliffs or the horses gone. The startled shrill voices of the squaws pierced the bedlam, ringing from the stone walls of the canyon.

Then suddenly the camp fell quiet.

Chance, not looking or paying much attention, felt them turn toward him, then heard the movement of dozens of moccasined feet on the snow, coming towards him.

He stood up, getting himself out of the blanket. He picked it up by one corner, straightened it out and began to fold it into neat squares.

When the blanket was folded Chance dropped it to the ground and looked at the Indians.

Their eyes were not pleasant.

It suddenly occurred to Chance that they might expect him to take Grawson's place. He hadn't even thought of that. He did not much care to think of it now.

He met Old Bear's eyes. The old man's gaze was stern. "The red-haired man is gone," he said.

"I set him free," said Chance.

Anger swept through the Hunkpapa and Minneconjou clustered about him; it was almost like a wind shaking branches, or the sudden, surprising shock that can move between animal and animal in a herd or pack when a stranger is suddenly, unexpectedly confronted.

"I'm sorry," said Chance.

"Why did you do this?" asked Old Bear.

Chance thought about it. "I didn't want you to kill him," he said.

"There is still a white man," said the thin woman.

She meant Chance. Bless you, thought Chance, unkindly.

"Why did you let him go?" asked Old Bear, still not satisfied.

"There has been enough killing," said Chance.

Drum pushed forward. "We can still catch him," he said. "I have looked at the prints. He bit through a picket rope and took a horse, but the prints are fresh."

"Do not go after him," said Chance.

"Why not?" asked Drum.

"He is armed," said Chance. "I gave him my gun. By now he is on the prairie and you cannot surprise him. He is dangerous. He may kill someone."

Drum moved as though to leave.

"Wait," said Old Bear. "There is time." He was looking at Chance closely.

Drum chafed with impatience.

Chance looked at him. "Are we not to fight?" he asked.

Drum glared at him, angrily.

Old Bear, regarding Chance, shook his head. "I do not think it is a good thing you have done," he said.

"Old Bear," said Chance, "is wiser than I and he may be right, but I do not think so." Chance looked at the Indians. "There has been killing at Grand River," he said, "at Wounded Knee, and on the prairie." He pointed to the stiff, angular figure of Totter. "There has been killing here." He looked at Old Bear. "Has there not been enough of killing?"

"No," said Drum.

Chance looked at him.

Drum turned to the Indians. "What of Wounded Knee?" he asked. "Medicine Gun says there has been enough killing, but Drum says there has been enough killing of the Hunkpapa and Minneconjou, not enough of white men." Drum regarded the Indians. "Drum," he said, "does not forget Wounded Knee." He pointed to the thin woman with the scabbed mourning wounds on her narrow face. "Where is your brave and your son?" he asked. "Wounded Knee," she said, looking at Chance. Then Drum, over and over, jabbed the Indians with his words, reminding each of loved ones lost at Wounded Knee, men, wives, sons, daughters, children, infants. There was almost no one present who had not lost at least one member of his family at Wounded Knee. The Indians began to stamp with rage, awaiting Drum to address them individually. And as each in turn cried "Wounded Knee!" in answer to his question, the others repeated it, and soon in Chance's ears rang a violent, enraged chorus, "Wounded Knee! Wounded Knee! Wounded Knee!" Then Drum cried out, "All the blood of all the white men in the world will not make up for Wounded Knee!"

The Hunkpapa and the Minneconjou grunted their assent.

Then the Indians were silent, regarding Chance.

He would speak very quietly. "Drum," he said, "is right. All the blood of all the white men in the world cannot make up for Wounded Knee. The white men can never make up for Wounded Knee." Then Chance paused. "But the stain of blood," he said, "cannot be made clean with more blood."

The Indians looked at him.

"I think my Brother is right," said Running Horse, now speaking for the first time. "I think what he says is hard to hear but I think it is true."

Old Bear looked thoughtful.

"Are the Hunkpapa and the Minneconjou afraid to fight?" cried Drum.

"No," said Chance, looking at Drum, speaking very quietly. "They are not afraid. They have proved their courage to everyone, to me, to the Long Knives, to themselves. It is only Drum who asks if they are afraid. If anyone thinks they are afraid it is only Drum."

As one man the Indians regarded Drum.

"No," said Drum, looking down, "I do not think the Hunkpapa and the Minneconjou are afraid—they are warriors."

Chance turned to the Indians. "If you go on fighting and killing you will take more scalps, you will kill more white men, more Long Knives, but in the end you must lose—there are too many to fight. If your women are to bear children and live you must live in the world with the white men."

"In the spring," said one of the Indians, a Minneconjou, "the Messiah will come and kill all the white men."

"The Messiah, said Chance, "taught peace and forgiveness."

Old Bear looked at him. "The Messiah," he said, speaking as much to himself as to Chance or the others, "taught that all men should love one another." He regarded Chance. Then, to Chance's surprise, he said slowly, repeating them from memory, the words, "Blessed are the merciful for they shall obtain mercy. Blessed are the peacemakers for they shall find peace."

Chance stood, stunned.

"Those are good words," said one of the Indians.

"Who is to know if they are true words?" asked Old Bear.

No one spoke.

"I think," said Chance, "if you go back, you will find they are true words. I think the white man will have a heavy heart because of Wounded Knee. I do not think he really wants to fight the Hunkpapa, the Minneconjou."

"If you go back," said Drum, "you will be killed. The white man showed how he loved his Indian brothers at Wounded Knee."

"If we stay in the Bad Lands," said Old Bear, "we will starve or be killed by soldiers."

"If we are going to die," said Drum, "it is the way of the Hunkpapa and Minneconjou to die fighting." He did not speak arrogantly; he was reminding them of a fact.

"That is true," said Old Bear, "if we are going to die we will die in war. That is the way of the Hunkpapa and the Minneconjou—the way of the Oglala and the Brule—the way of all the Sioux, the seven council fires, the people—the way of the riders of painted horses, the way of men who wear the feathers of eagles."

The Indians grunted their assent.

"It is true," said Chance. "It is well known that the riders of painted horses and the men who wear the feathers of eagles can die with bravery, but I say to such men, whom I respect as my brothers, sometimes it takes more courage to remove the paint from your horses and take from your hair the feathers of eagles. Sometimes it takes more courage to live than to die. It is easy to fight, but your people will die; it is hard to go back, but your people will live."

"How do you know this thing, Medicine Gun?" asked one of the Sioux.

"I do not know it," said Chance, "but I think it is true—I think it is true that if you go back in peace you will be received in peace."

"I will never go back," said Drum. "I will never take from my hair the feather of an eagle."

Chance looked to the other Indians. "If you go back in peace," he said, "it is my belief you will be received in peace."

The Indians looked to one another, and then to Old Bear. They were quiet.

"It is a hard thing to know," said Old Bear.

The old Indian then left the group and went to stand near the ashes of the ceremonial fire. He looked up into the gray sky, and standing lifted his hands to the sky. Then, after so standing for perhaps a minute, he returned to the group. "Wakan-Tonka will decide," said Old Bear.

Lucia Turner was brought from the blanket shelter, led by one of Drum's warriors, accompanied by another. The strap which had bound her ankles had been removed and fastened, like a halter, about her neck. The girl's wrists were still lashed behind her back, as securely as they had been the night before. The two braves had removed Totter's greatcoat.

Lucia looked at Chance, frightened.

"I do not understand the meaning of Old Bear," said Chance.

Old Bear pointed to Lucia. "Whose is this woman?" he asked.

"She is my woman," said Chance.

"No," said Drum.

"As warriors of the Hunkpapa you will fight," said Old Bear, addressing both Drum and Chance. "But you will fight for more than this woman. If Drum wins, the woman is his, and the Hunkpapa and the Minneconjou will take the warpath. If Medicine Gun wins, the woman is his, and the Hunkpapa and the Minneconjou will go in peace to the reservation."

"Wakan-Tonka will decide," said Drum.

Drum took the rifle which he had taken from Grawson, and five cartridges. Old Bear gave Chance the rifle that had been Totter's, and five cartridges.

"I must kill you, Medicine Gun," said Drum, "for my people." He looked at Chance. "My heart is heavy," he said, placing a cartridge into the weapon.

"If I die," said Chance, loading his weapon, "I am proud that it will be by the hand of Drum, who is like Kills-His-Horse, his father, a great warrior."

Drum regarded Chance, no enmity or hostility in his face. "My heart is heavy," he said, impassively, and then turned and, rifle in hand, disappeared into the arroyo at the head of the camp.

Chance waited a few minutes, feeling cold.

He looked at Lucia.

At a sign from Old Bear the brave who held the strap knotted about her neck permitted her to approach Chance. She did so and, standing near to him, lifted her lips to his, kissing him lightly. Her lips felt cool. "I love you, Edward

Chance," she said. Chance kissed her and then, carrying Totter's rifle, began to walk slowly toward the long, winding arroyo. Somewhere ahead, down that path, Drum was waiting for him.

Chapter Twenty-one

Chance trudged down the arroyo, wading through the snow; in places it had drifted to his knees.

He saw Drum's tracks ahead of him, extending indefinitely.

If I were Drum, Chance asked himself, how would I fight this?

His eyes searched the top ledges of the arroyo. That's it, thought Chance, I'd make tracks for a way down the arroyo until I came to a bend; then I'd double back above the arroyo; when he passed under me, I'd shoot. Chance shivered a little. Drum might already be above and behind him. Chance paused, listened, heard nothing. Everything was still, white, rugged, calm, desolate.

He looked up the side of the arroyo. It was about nine feet above him on both sides. He began to climb, carefully, not wanting to kick loose much snow; even a soft sound would carry on the cold winter air.

Near the top Chance paused, wished he had a hat to lift over the top of the arroyo on his rifle barrel; then he thought it wouldn't work; Drum would probably suspect such a trick; even if he did not, he would not be likely to fire until he had a fair, clean shot; shivering, Chance lifted his head just over the top of the arroyo, clearing it only to the level of his eyes. He swept as much of the terrain as he could, which wasn't much from that level; he couldn't see anything but a few rocks, outcroppings, piles of drifted snow, the tops of ridges some hundred yards away or so.

Clutching his rifle, making certain his feet had solid footholds, Chance eased himself up out of the arroyo.

He was elated.

The snow at the top of the arroyo was clean, on both sides, as far as he could see; there were no tracks; the Indian was nowhere in sight.

He's still ahead of me, ran through Chance's head. He

hasn't come out to double back yet. I didn't think he had. It
was too soon.

Chance crawled behind some rocks that would shield him
from the direction that Drum would come.

Chance wondered if the young Indian had left the arroyo
yet, if he were now approaching him. It was possible, of
course, that Drum had left the arroyo ahead and was simply
waiting for him to trudge by underneath. Chance smiled.
Drum would have a long wait. When he tired, perhaps thinking Chance had fled or not entered the arroyo, and when he
came back to investigate, Chance would be waiting for him,
shielded by the rocks, commanding the top of the arroyo on
both sides.

Drum might, though, thought Chance, make a wide circle,
perhaps behind those ridges in the distance. Probably not.
That would take a long time, at least. He wouldn't figure
there was a point in it. And if he did he'd probably still close
his circle and come out ahead of me. At any rate, thought
Chance, I'll worry about that in an hour or so.

Chance found himself thinking about having a smoke. He
didn't have any more tobacco, of course, and if he had had,
he would not have smoked it at the time; a wisp of smoke,
the odor of burned tobacco, might have revealed his position.

The wind blew across the Bad Lands, moving driven snow
in strange patterns through the irregular formations; the air
was cold.

Chance had no taste for the killing of Drum, or any man,
but he had not made the choice; one or the other of them
must die.

Drum will not expect me here, said Chance to himself;
Drum will underestimate me, because I am white; he underestimated me on the prairie, and he will do so again, and
it will be his last mistake.

I am sorry, Drum, thought Chance, I am sorry to have to
kill you.

In Chance's mind there passed the fantasy of returning to
the Indian encampment, free, for Lucia, of holding her in his
arms, of cutting her loose, putting her behind him on his
horse and taking her from the captivity and the terrors of the
Bad Lands, ending the nightmare of the Scalp Dance and the
torture of Totter, the nightmare of the cold and the cruelty of
bonds, of the halter on her neck, of the not knowing if she
was to live or die, or to whom she would belong.

I am sorry, Drum, thought Chance, but I must kill you. I

must lie here and wait for you, as quiet as the steel of a trap, and when you come I must kill you.

A shot rang out. The bullet struck Chance in the back of his left shoulder, smashing him against the rocks behind which he lay, moving upward, emerging through his upper left arm and breaking rock like popping glass about his chin and mouth. Not trying to turn and fire Chance threw himself to the side rolling to the edge of the arroyo and pitching over, falling down the steep side in a slide of gravel and snow, scrambling behind an outcropping of rock.

He knelt behind the outcropping, trying to brush the snow from his eyes and rifle.

He was aware, somewhat now as if it might be someone else, that he was hit.

But the bullet had come from his left, from behind somehow. Drum could not have been there.

There were no tracks, the snow was clean.

Chance's shoulder and upper arm felt numb, as though a sledge hammer had struck him.

Gradually, as Chance knelt with his rifle high, scanning the rim of the arroyo across from him, the shoulder, someone's, began to ache; then it began to feel heavy; the back of the inside of his shirt and his left sleeve started to feel wet and warm; Chance decided it was hot in the arroyo; he was covered with sweat.

Then he saw the tracks.

They passed his own in the bottom of the arroyo.

Damn, thought Chance, damn.

Drum had realized what Chance would figure him to do. Instead of doubling back on the top of the arroyo, as Chance had expected, the young brave had doubled back along the bottom, first having waited a time, long enough for Chance to clear the passage; then, in retracing his steps, he had of course found the place where Chance had climbed out, thus in effect determining the approximate position of his enemy; he had then continued on for several yards, climbed out himself, well behind Chance, where Chance would not expect him—found his target, and fired.

Chance realized bitterly that Drum, once having under-estimated him on the prairie, was not going to do so again. Rather this time it had been he, Chance, arrogant Chance, who had underestimated the young Indian.

Lucia, he thought, Lucia.

Chance winced. The bullet, he knew, had it been placed

four inches differently in one direction, or six in another, would have been the finish for him.

Another shot whined over Chance, disappearing smoothly into the snow on the far side of the arroyo, then exploding back a handful of rock fragments that took a bucketful of snow with them. It was only in his memory, or maybe his imagination, a second or so afterwards, that Chance had realized there had been a sequence.

Chance nearly squeezed off a shot for no reason, with no target, just to fire back.

He cursed his irrationality. He tried to gather his thoughts, forget the ache, the heat and the sweat.

That shot, he told himself, was not directed at the outcropping.

He doesn't know for sure where I am.

Only that I'm somewhere here, somewhere here in the arroyo.

He wants to draw my fire.

He has three cartridges left.

Chance began to pull off his plaid cotton shirt. It was hell to get it off his left arm and shoulder but finally he teased it from his body.

He shoved his back against the snow on the arroyo wall; with his right hand he scooped up more snow and packed it against the wound in his upper arm.

Slow the flow of blood, thought Chance, slow it.

Clinically he watched the snow held against his left arm turn red, how fast it did so.

Too fast, thought Chance.

He was satisfied to see the wound was reasonably clean; Drum had not cut the heads of the bullets.

He shoved the shirt he had taken off against the wound on his upper arm.

The sweat on his body had frosted now. He no longer felt hot. He was no longer sweating. He began to feel cold.

Chance sat there in the snow for a couple of minutes, feeling stupid, the rifle across his lap.

Then he pulled the cotton shirt from the wound and the way it stuck pleased him, though it hurt to tear it off the wound. Good, thought Chance. The wound began to bleed again. Chance then thrust the cotton shirt behind the outcropping of rock, a spot of color in the bleak whiteness of the arroyo.

Then, gritting his teeth, carrying his rifle, his right hand on the trigger housing, finger on the trigger, the barrel cradled painfully in the crook of his left elbow, Chance began to back down the arroyo, keeping his eye on the ledges, sweeping from the left to the right, looking for Drum.

The young Indian was nowhere to be seen.

At last, about forty yards down the arroyo, Chance sat down in the snow, leaning back against one wall of the passage. He was numb with pain. He seemed tired now. He speculated on how much blood he had lost, how much more he could afford to lose before he became unconscious.

His eyes blurred for a frightened moment, and he was afraid he was going under, but they cleared.

If Drum was crawling along the ledge he might be overanxious, he might fire on the shirt, especially if he came abruptly on the sudden color.

Chance might get a shot at him then.

But Drum was no fool. He might look for something like that. So far Drum had been a jump ahead all the way. He was cunning, too damn cunning. He knew what he was expected to do; then he would do the opposite, catching his opponent unawares.

All right, said Chance to himself, what do I think Drum will do?

The shoulder ached like hell now. That was good. He wasn't going into shock.

He could take that kind of pain, plenty of it.

He would have to.

Chance leaned back against the wall of the arroyo, packed snow again against the wound he could reach.

Mostly he watched.

And thought.

Too wildly maybe.

He must be slow.

Leave out nothing.

Drum might expect the trick with the shirt, or something like it. Drum knew he'd been hit, that he wouldn't be far, that he'd be laying low, and waiting. Given that much, the trick with the shirt, or something like it, would make sense.

Drum would reason that if Chance had done something like this he would have gone down the arroyo some yards, waiting for a clear shot when the Indian jumped for the bait.

In fact he would be right about where he was now, right about where he was.

Chance felt sick.

Drum knew his position, at least within yards.

But, Chance reasoned, Drum may not count on my knowing that he's figured me out. He'll try to trick me into firing, or into showing myself.

He can't know exactly where I am.

A few yards could make a hell of a difference.

Suddenly Chance heard a sound from the arroyo, about a hundred feet from behind him. Chance swung the rifle around. He nearly stepped away from the wall to fire.

No, said Chance, don't.

He stayed close to the wall.

It could have been, Chance thought, a rock, a rock thrown behind me, to pull me into the open facing the wrong direction. But it might be Drum, said Chance. I'll wait, he decided, I'll wait.

Chance sat in the snow, leaning against the wall of the arroyo.

He closed his eyes for a moment against the pain, the damned whiteness of the arroyo, the glare. When he opened them again they had blurred again. He shook his head. He wondered if he had lost consciousness for a few minutes. His eyes cleared. The world seemed very quiet, very bright, very cold, very pure.

He felt stupid sitting there, naked from the waist up, losing blood.

Somewhere in that bright, quiet, cold, pure world a man was hunting him, a young man but a good man, one who knew his business.

I can wait, thought Chance. Then he smiled grimly. I guess I can wait, he thought.

He felt tired, weak.

He thrust more snow against his arm, pushed back further into the snowbank. The cold numbed the pain; it slowed the bleeding.

He closed his eyes again.

Suddenly he opened them, startled, fully awake.

The shadow of a figure, a man with a rifle, was falling on the arroyo side opposite where he sat.

He's on top, on the left, thought Chance, there!

Chance silently, painfully, gathered his legs under him, to spring to the center of the arroyo, turn and snap off the killing shot at the figure on the rim.

If I move fast, thought Chance, I'll have one clean shot before he can bring his gun around.

Chance's legs knotted under him like springs; he tensed to leap to the center of the arroyo, turn and fire; he stopped; he didn't move.

Why would Drum stand upright?

Why would he let his shadow fall into the arroyo?

With his thumb Chance clicked back the hammer on his rifle.

He wanted Drum to hear the noise.

Then, with his back to the ledge where Drum must be, he stepped to the center of the arroyo, facing toward the shadow, away from the object which cast it.

He held the rifle painfully high, steadied in the crook of his left arm.

Chance stood that way for an instant, waiting for the bullet in the back.

The bullet did not come.

Chance smiled.

I have won, he thought, I have won.

He crouched in the middle of the arroyo; with agony he struggled to keep the weapon steady; its weight seemed incredible to him; then the front sight, wavering only minutely, fastened on a patch of blue sky above the arroyo, over the place where the shadow fell.

"Yah!" yelled Chance, the sudden shout ringing in the still arroyo. Almost at the same instant, above the shadow, Drum's figure reared into view with incredible swiftness, his rifle pointed downward.

Chance squeezed the trigger and Drum caught the bullet in the chest. His eyes looked startled for an instant and then he toppled into the arroyo, falling in the snow at Chance's feet.

Drum wore no shirt and his body looked dark in the reddening snow. Chance kicked away Drum's rifle.

Drum's eyes were half shut; he was fighting for breath.

Chance stood up wearily, dropped his own rifle into the snow. It was too heavy to hold any longer.

Chance saw that the shadow, of course, still fell calmly on the arroyo wall. He turned, looking upward and behind him. There on the rim of the arroyo opposite, casting the shadow, was Drum's shirt, hooked on a stake of brush. One stick had even been thrust into the brush, looking in the shadow as if it might be a rifle.

Chance, his left arm hanging at his side, knelt beside Drum. He looked at the wound, its placement, considered the angle at which the bullet had entered.

I'm sorry, he thought, kneeling in the snow, I'm sorry.

Drum's eyes opened. In them there was no anger, no fear.

Chance, to do something, not because there was much point in it, scooped up some snow, trying to press it on the wound in Drum's chest.

Weakly Drum pushed his hand away. "No," he said.

Chance was silent.

There was nothing much to say or do. The handful of snow had been a gesture, nothing more. The heart would stop long before the body had lost much blood.

And so Chance knelt in the snow in the bottom of the arroyo, near the young Indian, watching him, listening to him breathe, with his physician's ear marking the change of breath from minute to minute, the alternation of its rhythm, its frequency, the change in the sound, parameters and gradients familiar to Chance; soon gases would no longer be exchanged; a certain natural process would terminate; a man would be dead.

Drum had turned his head toward him, was looking at him.

"My heart is heavy," said Chance. "You will ride the death trail." He looked at Drum. "Tonight," said Chance, "your pony will trample stars and among the stars a second rider waits for you, that you will hunt with him, and there will be antelope and buffalo, and together through the high sweet grass under the blue sky you will ride with him, and all the Indians will say these are the greatest of our hunters, they, Kills-His-Horse of the Hunkpapa, and Drum, who is his son."

Drum smiled at Chance weakly. "No," he said.

Chance said nothing, looking down at the snow.

"I am proud it was you," said Drum. "No Long Knife could kill Drum."

Chance looked at him. "No," he said.

Drum put his right hand over the wound in his chest. Then, weakly, he tried to lift his hand to Chance's wound. Chance took the hand in his own right hand and put it, bloody, to his shoulder.

"My Brother," said Drum.

"I am proud," said Chance, softly.

Drum closed his eyes, and Chance speculated that it was the end. But before he died he opened his eyes once more, and said, "The blood of the badger is true."

Chance never understood his last words. He was not even

sure he had heard them correctly. If he had, he guessed Drum was delirious.

He looked at the red body sprawled in the snow; now the wound had stopped flowing. Mechanically Chance listened for the heartbeat, felt the pulse. He saw the eagle feather in Drum's hair, lying in the snow, wet. He took it in his hands, wiped it a bit, and laid it over Drum's left shoulder.

Then Chance got up, went down the arroyo to get his shirt, tied it as well as he could around his shoulder, and then returned to where Drum lay and sat down beside him in the snow, waiting for the Indians to come.

Chapter Twenty-two

Chance, his left arm in a sling, and Lucia, in her squaw dress, dismounted before the remains of what had been her soddy on the reservation. She had ridden Totter's horse, with the cavalry saddle and the "U.S." branded on its flank.

"You shouldn't have come back with me," she said, touching her lips to his.

"You can reach the agency alone from here," said Chance. "You'll be safe."

Lucia looked at the burned-out shell of the soddy, now gentle with snow.

They had ridden northeast with the Hunkpapa and the Minneconjou from the Bad Lands to the Grand River country. There had been no incident. The ragged, proud file of Indians had made its way openly and with deliberate slowness through the snowy South Dakota prairie. They had passed without being challenged, sometimes riding under the binoculars of distant patrols, sometimes past the gun ports of squat soddy forts, bunkers of a sort, manned by armed homesteaders. It had been clear that the Indians had not been attempting to conceal their movements or position. It had been clear they were returning to Standing Rock. After Wounded Knee no one had made any attempt to interfere.

Lucia and Chance watched the Indians ride by the soddy, heading for the agency buildings on the Missouri, a few miles to the east.

Aside from their night camps and their pauses in the march to cook and eat, the Indians had made only one stop, that at the place of scaffolds. There, wrapped in a blanket and buffalo robe, tied with rope, fastened in the branches of a cottonwood, they had left the body of Drum. It would remain there until the wind and the rain, and the birds, maybe a century from now, had finished with it. To the bundle they had tied a gourd rattle, that would move when the wind blew, making its noise, and seven eagle feathers, that which Drum himself had worn, and one for each of the young men who had originally followed him from Grand River, two of whom survived.

Lucia and Chance lifted their hands, waving good-bye to Old Bear, to Winona and Running Horse, the others.

"You've got to go," said Lucia, standing close to him. "I know you've got to go."

"I'll write to you," said Chance. "Really I will." And he knew that he would. Come hell or high water, for her sake or his, he was not going to give up this woman. He had been through that. Now the morality of loving her and wanting her had triumphed. He had won her in an arroyo in the Bad Lands of South Dakota. They were one blanket. The Hunkpapa does not desert his woman; he does not abandon her.

"Will you come to California?" asked Chance.

"I'll run all the way," she said, nuzzling against him.

"When you get tired," he said, mumbling, pressing his lips to her throat, "take the train."

Her head was back. Her eyes were closed, her lips slightly open. "I'll never get tired," she said. "Never."

He kissed her on the shoulder, under the buckskin dress.

"It's too bad you can't carry me across the threshold," she whispered. "I always wanted to know what it feels like."

Chance looked skeptically at his left shoulder, at the sling improvised from a strip of blanket. Then suddenly he scooped her up with his right arm, tossing her over his shoulder like a sack of barley.

"No!" she shrieked, laughing.

He carried her, teasing and laughing, through the door of the soddy. Just as he dropped her to her feet the laugh stopped in his throat. Lucia, who was trying to regain her balance, turned, laughing. Her body stiffened at what she saw.

In the center of the room, at a scarred, blackened table, a six-gun laid heavily before him, sat Grawson.

Lucia screamed.

Grawson picked up the weapon.

Chance wore a pistol at his belt. It had been Totter's and given to him by one of Drum's braves, after Drum had died. The young man hadn't wanted it. It had been a gift to Medicine Gun, because of whom the Hunkpapa and Minneconjou were to return in peace to Standing Rock. But the pistol might as well have been back in the Bad Lands, or a thousand miles away, or on the dust of the moon.

"Unbuckle your gun belt," said Grawson.

"No," said Lucia. "No." She shook her head. "He saved your life," she said.

The side of Grawson's face twitched minutely, but then it was again heavy and calm.

Chance's gun belt fell to the dirt floor.

Lucia looked at it wildly.

"Tell her not to interfere," said Grawson, "or I will shoot her dead."

"Stay out of it," said Chance to the girl.

"Back up and put your hands up," said Grawson, getting out of the chair at the table.

Chance did so and Grawson removed the pistol from Chance's fallen holster, thrusting it in his own belt.

He doesn't want to shoot me in front of the woman, thought Chance.

Grawson looked at Lucia, and his face jerked ugly with annoyance.

But the pistol was steady in the strong hand, covering Chance.

Grawson seemed to be too conscious of Lucia; the side of his face moved twice.

Good God, thought Chance, he's thinking about killing us both.

"Let's go," said Chance, brusquely. "Lucia," he ordered, "stay here—don't follow."

"No," she said.

"Do it," said Chance, savagely.

"No," she said. "I won't leave you."

"Do it," yelled Chance, "you dumb bitch! He'll kill us both!"

Grawson shook his head violently. "No," he said. "You're the killer, not me!"

Chance looked at him puzzled. Lucia was crying. "I'm sorry, Lucia," he said. "I'm sorry."

"He'll kill you," she said.

"I am the law," said Grawson. "I do not swerve. I do not yield. I am an eagle with arrows in my claws."

The side of his face moved, spasmlike.

Suddenly Lucia looked at him, and said, very clearly. "No, you are not."

The pistol swung between Chance and Lucia, then back to Chance.

"I know all about you," said Lucia.

"For God's sake, shut up," said Chance.

"You don't know anything," said Grawson.

"I know it was a fair fight," said Lucia. "A duel."

Chance had spoken of these matters with her in the Carter soddy, and later at the camp of Old Bear. He had told her about Clare, the duel, the rest. She had wanted to know. She had had to know.

"No," said Grawson defensively. "It wasn't fair."

"Why not?" demanded Lucia.

"Frank didn't shoot," said Grawson. "He didn't fire."

"Why not?" demanded Lucia.

"Shut up!" screamed Grawson at her.

Chance was puzzled; it was true that Frank Grawson had not fired; he would have fired but he had not had the chance; he had been bringing up his arm to fire, bringing it up easily, as in target practice; he had lifted his arm easily; he had been in no hurry; Frank Grawson had not fired; he had not had a chance to fire; before his gun was level with his chest Chance had shot and killed him.

"Frank wasn't pushing," said Chance. "He never got a chance to fire." He looked steadily at Grawson. "Why not?" he asked.

Grawson looked at him, tears in his eyes, the gun suddenly wavering.

Good God, thought Chance to himself, I know.

"I told him you wouldn't fire," said Grawson, whispering.

Chance shivered. Lucia stood quietly.

"Why did you tell him that?" asked Chance.

"I loved my brother," said Grawson.

Suddenly it seemed to Chance that something had formed, coming whole from pieces the nature of which he had only barely suspected before.

There had been Clare Henderson, silken Clare, the broken engagement, the fiery suitor Frank, eager to avenge her honor, and in the background, always, cumbersome, conscientious Lester, the older brother. It had been a joke, that they had been brothers, supple, swift, witty, laughing Frank, and dull Lester, as imaginative as a clod of mud, but as dependable, as honest as a rock. How many times had Lester managed to win Frank's fights for him, to take the blame for him, to preserve him as the darling of his parents and neighbors; and then once, somehow, this clumsy, large man had, from afar, fallen in love with a beautiful woman; Chance could remember the laughter of Clare, and Frank, as they had spoken of Lester, made him the butt of their jokes; Chance could remember that in those days he had felt sorry for Lester Grawson, hopeless Lester; but it had been a long time since Chance had felt sorry for Lester Grawson, a long time.

"I loved my brother," mumbled Grawson. "I loved him."

"Why did you tell your brother that he wouldn't fire?" asked Lucia.

Grawson's face moved uncontrollably. "It was dishonorable for Chance to fire," he said. "Chance was in the wrong—he should have stood there—stood there—I thought he was honorable, that he would only stand there—he was in the wrong—he should not have fired!"

Chance laughed.

Grawson looked at him, enraged. The hammer moved back on the pistol.

"You're a lawman," said Chance. "You were then." He looked at Grawson. "You knew more about men and living and dying than Frank ever found out—you were smarter than Frank ever was—Frank was a fool."

Grawson looked at him strangely. "No," he said, "Frank was smarter—always smarter."

"You knew men," said Chance. "You knew I'd fire."

Grawson looked at him, tears streaming down his face.

"No," he said, "I believed it—I didn't think you'd fire."

"I don't believe you," said Lucia.

"Be quiet," said Chance. "For God's sake, be quiet."

"It's true," yelled Grawson, "it's true!"

"No," said Lucia, calmly, "it is not."

"Please shut up, Lucia," begged Chance. "For God's sake, shut up."

"Nonsense," said Lucia, and her voice was very clear and very calm, like knives of logic, and it sounded irritatingly prim, very schoolteacherish; Grawson had probably heard such a voice, as had Chance, a thousand times in his youth, in a dozen classrooms, from a dozen righteous women instructing him, correcting him, pointing out his errors. "It seems to me quite clear," said Lucia, "that you are confused on this matter." She paused. "It also seems to me unlikely that you really entertained a serious affection for your brother."

"I loved him!" yelled Grawson, sweating, his face jerking, the gun in his hand trembling.

"Shut up!" yelled Chance to the girl.

"Perhaps your parents wished you to do so," said Lucia, "or perhaps you felt it was your duty, but I regard it as quite unlikely that you actually did so."

"I loved him!" screamed Grawson.

"Is that why you killed him?" she asked.

There was an awful silence in the room, and in the world. It seemed not even the wind moved outside the soddy.

Slowly Grawson turned to face Lucia, numbly.

Chance, his hands up, tensed, wondering if he could reach the large man. The risk. Lucia.

"I didn't kill him," he said, like a little boy.

"You most certainly did," said Lucia crisply.

"No," said Grawson, shaking his head, the word indistinct, protesting.

"Most certainly you did," said Lucia. "You told him Mr. Chance would not fire. Obviously you knew this to be incorrect. Thus, knowingly, you sent your brother to his death and thus, clearly, it is you who killed him."

Suddenly Grawson screamed and swung the gun on Lucia eyes wild face hideous jerking she twisting screaming Chance leaping striking the weapon it firing four times three times into the wall of the soddy once into the air.

With his right hand Chance, weak from the loss of blood, tried desperately to hang onto the barrel. His left arm was all but useless. Lucia scrambled for a stick of wood near the wall for a club. Grawson tore the barrel from Chance's hand, cutting the palm of his hand, a bloody line, with the weapon's sight.

Grawson, breathing heavily, stood covering them both with the weapon, his back to the threshold of the soddy.

They had lost.

"I get it," said Grawson. "A trick," he said, "a good trick." He drew a long breath. "It didn't work," he said. He eyed them. "You're both killers," he said. "Both of you."

"Not the girl," said Chance, "not her."

"Her too," said Grawson, sweating. He looked at Lucia. "You'd kill me, wouldn't you, Lady, if you had the chance, wouldn't you?"

"Yes," said Lucia. "I would."

"Her too," said Grawson. "She's a killer, too. Both of you." He wiped his glistening face with the back of his left

hand. He looked at them. "I am the law," he said. "I am justice. I do not swerve. I do not yield. I am an eagle with arrows in my claws."

Chance looked at him, feeling sick.

Grawson pointed his gun at him. "You killed Frank, didn't
you?" he said.

Chance said nothing.

Grawson turned the gun toward Lucia.

Chance thought he heard the snort of a horse, some yards
away, outside.

"Yes," said Chance, "I killed him."

"Guilty," said Grawson. He looked at Lucia. "You," he
said. "Lady, you'd kill me if you could, wouldn't you?"

"No, she wouldn't," said Chance.

"Yes," said Lucia, "if I had the opportunity I would most
certainly kill you."

Grawson looked at her. "Guilty," he said.

"What are you going to do to her?" asked Chance.

"I am the law," said Grawson.

Then he looked at Chance and shook his head. "I'm not an
Indian," he said, "or a bad man—I won't do anything to
her—nothing like that—just kill her—only that."

Chance closed his eyes for a moment, then opened them.

"Believe me," said Grawson.

"I believe you," said Chance.

Suddenly Lucia gasped. Chance, too, saw it.

Then it seemed to Grawson that Chance was strangely
calm, for a man about to die.

"What are you going to do now?" asked Chance.

The side of Grawson's face moved, not pleasantly. "I am
the law," he said. He moved the pistol to cover Chance. The
barrel seemed to waver. His hand trembled. His face was
ugly to watch. He lifted the gun to Chance's chest.

"Do not fire," said Running Horse.

Grawson felt the barrel of a rifle push into the back of his
neck, at the base of the skull.

"I saw the tracks of a horse," said Running Horse. "I came
back."

Lucia fainted.

Chance stumbled forward, took Grawson's gun, tried to
catch his breath.

Chapter Twenty-three

Chance looked at the bloody line on his right hand where the gun sight had cut him. He moved his fingers. He placed his own gun, taken from Grawson's belt, and Grawson's gun on the scarred, blackened kitchen table, checked them both over.

Grawson, for some reason, seemed calm, standing there with his hands up; his face was utterly calm, almost strong and handsome.

"I will kill him now," said Running Horse.

"Shoot," said Grawson.

"No," said Chance.

Then only did Grawson's face move, once, angrily.

"I do my own killing," said Chance, dropping his pistol into his holster, lifting it out, dropping it again. Then he approached Grawson and placed the man's weapon in his holster.

"You're a killer," said Grawson.

"That's right," said Chance.

"Let me kill him now," asked Running Horse.

Chance regarded the young Indian. "No," he said, kindly, "twice, my Brother, you have saved me from this man." He smiled at Running Horse. Then he said, "Now Medicine Gun fights."

Chance went to Lucia, who lay near the back wall of the soddy, still unconscious. He lifted her in his arms and kissed her, then laid her back on the snowy floor. It was better that she did not see what must be done.

Under the gun of Running Horse, Lester Grawson, his hands up, left the soddy.

Chance, and Grawson, followed by Running Horse, went some forty yards from the soddy, in front of it. "Stand here," said Chance to Grawson. Then he paced off some twenty yards through the snow and turned to face Grawson. The line of fire would be parallel to the soddy, so that no stray bullet might strike the building. Running Horse, still covering Grawson, withdrew.

Grawson looked about wildly. He jerked his thumb at Running Horse. "How do I know that Indian won't shoot me?" he asked.

"You don't," said Chance.

Grawson turned to Running Horse, and pointed at Chance. "That man killed my brother," he said.

"Yes," said Running Horse.

"So I have a right!" said Grawson.

"Yes," said Running Horse.

"So if I kill him you won't shoot me," said Grawson.

"If you kill my Brother," said Running Horse, "I will kill you."

"He isn't your brother," shouted Grawson.

"He is my Brother," said Running Horse.

"But you won't shoot me," said Grawson.

"If you kill my Brother," said Running Horse, "I will kill you."

"Why?" asked Grawson.

"It is my right," said Running Horse.

Grawson looked at Chance.

"If I am killed," said Chance, "do not hurt him."

"No," said Running Horse quietly.

"I ask it," said Chance.

Running Horse looked at him, stricken.

"Please," said Chance.

"I am Hunkpapa," said Running Horse.

"Please," said Chance.

Running Horse lowered his rifle. "If it is the wish of my Brother," he said.

"It is my wish," said Chance. Chance looked at Grawson. "If you win," he said, "you'll be safe." Then he said, "But my Brother will protect the woman. If you try to hurt her he will kill you."

"I don't want the woman," said Grawson.

"Edward," Chance heard, Lucia's voice, from the threshold of the soddy. He didn't take his eyes off Grawson. "Stand clear," he said. Out of the corner of his eye he could see her standing, in the buckskin dress, in front of the soddy, Running Horse now standing beside her.

Chance stood across the snow, some twenty yards from Grawson. The burned soddy, the woman and the Indian, were in the background. There wasn't much wind. The sky was clear. It wouldn't snow for a day or two most likely.

"All right," said Chance.

Grawson was watching him, but he made no move to draw his weapon.

The two men stood facing one another.

"Draw," said Chance.

Grawson would not move for his gun, but stood in the snow, almost to his knees, like a rock or a tree.

"I will fire one shot," said Running Horse. "Then fight."

"You hear that?" called Chance to Grawson.

Grawson, some twenty yards away, nodded.

Running Horse held the barrel of his rifle up, waited a moment and then fired a single shot.

The Colt moved cleanly, swiftly, from Chance's holster, a draw as swift as red silk in the hands of a magician, emerging from nowhere to astonish and delight.

The bullet would have taken Grawson in the center of the chest.

But it was not fired.

At the last instant Chance saw, and managed to react; Grawson had not reached for his weapon; Chance nearly lost his balance; he caught himself in the snow, brought the gun up again; bringing the sight to bear between Grawson's eyes, the center of his forehead.

"Shoot!" yelled Grawson.

Chance shivered.

Grawson had not reached for his gun.

"Shoot!" screamed Grawson, crouching down, clenching his fists.

"Shoot!" cried Lucia.

"He is yours," said Running Horse. "Kill him."

"Shoot!" screamed Grawson.

Chance wavered. He was bewildered, startled, frightened. Grawson was out to prove something, not to Chance, or to the woman, or the Indian, but to himself, something that was more important to him than his life, something against which he held his life worthless.

Why had Grawson been calm when Chance could have killed him, or Running Horse; why had he been unafraid in the alley in New York, in the soddy when Running Horse was ready to blow a hole through the back of his neck?

Chance lowered the weapon, letting it hang at his side.

"Shoot, damn you!" yelled Grawson. "Shoot!"

"No," said Chance. He looked across the snow toward Grawson. Then he was no longer confused, or frightened, or bewildered. It was then only that he clearly understood.

"Shoot!" yelled Grawson, pleading.

Chance looked at him, angrily. "I did your goddam killing once," he yelled, "no more—no more!"

Grawson seemed to tremble in the snow. He had given Chance the opportunity to fire, to prove that it was he, and not Grawson, who was the killer; but Chance had not fired, he had not killed.

Why did I tell Frank he wouldn't fire, Grawson agonized, why?

Because I didn't think he would, Grawson screamed to himself. He shouldn't have. He shouldn't have.

Why not?

Where is Frank, his mother had asked.

Frank is dead, he had said, his voice crushed, but his heart, he had not forgotten, had then leaped with ugly pleasure, the bounding thrill of the joy of it, the pleasure, Frank dead, at last, Frank dead, Frank dead, dead, dead!

I will bring the man to justice who did this.

"Shoot!" screamed Grawson.

But the thin, pale man in the snow some yards away was only watching him. Then the man had returned his weapon to his holster, and started to trudge through the snow toward the soddy, leaving Grawson alone in the snow.

"Shoot!" screamed Grawson.

The man was walking away, not watching him. Grawson fumbled with his pistol, his hands shaking. He drew the weapon. The man had turned now. The Indian was leveling the rifle. The man pushed aside the barrel of the Indian's weapon, and was now facing him, standing near the soddy.

Grawson tried to lift the weapon. With both hands he held it, shaking, pointing it toward Chance. The barrel moved wildly. The three of them were standing there, watching him. Tears streamed down Grawson's face.

Then Chance, Lucia and Running Horse saw the big man turn in the snow and stand there, shaking, his head thrown back, the pistol clutched in his right hand.

Lester Grawson howled to the sky of Standing Rock, "I didn't kill him, Mother!"

Then, sobbing, the big man fell to his knees in the snow.

The gunshot was loud.

Lucia screamed.

Chance and Running Horse ran to the body; it lay sprawled in the snow; the right side of its head was black from the powder; the bullet had entered slightly below and forward of the right temple; part of the skull was visible, the rest was red hair, blood, skin.

Chance turned to tell Lucia not to approach, but she was there, with them, looking down.

The girl looked at Chance. "Why?" she asked. "Why?"

"He was the law," said Chance, "and he did not swerve— he did not yield." Chance knelt beside the body, turning it on its back, closing the eyes gently with his thumb. "He was an eagle," said Chance, "with arrows in his claws."

Chapter Twenty-four

Running Horse had wanted to scalp the body, cut it up a bit, take the boots and weapon, and leave it somewhere on the prairie, moving at night, not stopping until well off the reservation.

"No," Chance had said, "I'll take it to Fort Yates."

Fort Yates lay on the Missouri River, commanding the Standing Rock Indian Reservation.

The colonel, a mild, strong man, shuffled clumsily through the papers on his desk. He had big hands, rough from wind and riding, hands more for the hilt of a saber than the impedimenta of an office. Chance sat across from him in the small room, thinking what a difference there was between this gentle, strong man and the impatient, antagonistic martinet he had seen at Wounded Knee.

"Mr. Chance," the colonel was saying, "some weeks ago I put one of my men, Corporal Jacob Totter, on special orders to a Mr. Lester Grawson, who presented the credentials of a Charleston law officer, in order to assist in the apprehension and arrest of an alleged murderer believed to be in hiding on Standing Rock—a Mr. Edward Chance." The colonel looked up. "You admit that you are he?" he asked.

Chance nodded, stared at the papers.

"For my own satisfaction, however," the colonel went on, "and because I deemed it of possible importance for our records, should the arrest actually take place on the reservation, I wrote to Charleston for certain information, the dating of the charge, its specifics, the records relating to the case." A half smile played at the corners of his mouth. "I learned to my surprise," he said, "that no formal charges whatsoever had ever been filed in Charleston against a Mr. Edward Chance, neither those of murder nor any lesser crime. I further learned that Mr. Lester Grawson, though he had once been a detective with the Charleston police force, had resigned that position several months ago and no longer held any official post or appointment with that city."

Chance nodded. "I thought it was that way," he said.

The colonel held up a letter. "This is the commissioner's letter," he said, "should you care to read it."

Chance shook his head. "No," he said.

"What was he after?" asked the colonel.

"Me," said Chance.

"A vendetta of some sort?"

"Yes," said Chance.

"But the act, as I understand it," said the colonel, "took place in a duel of some sort?"

"Yes," said Chance, "—in a stupid duel."

"That made no difference to Grawson?"

"No," said Chance.

The colonel leaned back in his chair, looked across the room at a map. Chance had seen it when he had come in; it was a map of North and South Dakota, with elevations marked; the Missouri divided the map, tributaries feeding into it, the Cannonball, the Porcupine, the Grand; the reservations were clearly indicated, and military installations; in the lower left-hand corner of the map Chance had seen the Bad Lands, Pine Ridge, Wounded Knee Creek.

"I cannot approve of duels," said the colonel.

"I'm surprised," said Chance.

"Why?" asked the colonel, himself surprised.

"You're a soldier," said Chance.

"I don't understand," said the colonel.

"A duel," said Chance, "seems much to me like a war—between men."

The colonel regarded him. "Sometimes," he said, "one must fight."

"Yes," said Chance. "I think so."

"And a war, I suppose," said the colonel, "is a duel—between nations."

"It seems so," said Chance. "Pretty much."

"It is permissible for nations to fight," said the colonel, "but not for men."

"I'll believe that," said Chance, smiling, "the first time I see nations fight—and men stay home."

"War," said the colonel, "is an institution developed by civilization for the adjudication of differences by the arbitration of arms."

"So is a duel," said Chance.

"We can outlaw duels," said the colonel.

"That's the difference," said Chance.

"Ah," said the colonel.

"I don't much approve of duels either," said Chance.

The colonel smiled, and looked up at the ceiling, at the kerosene lamp that hung on a chain there. Then he looked back at Chance. He wasn't angry. "Sometime though," said the colonel, "one must fight."

"Yes," said Chance, "I think so."

The colonel scratched one ear, looked out the small window in the office, past the porch outside, to the parade ground. "I understand you're going to be married," he said.

"Yes," said Chance.

"Fine institution—marriage," said the colonel.

"Yes," said Chance. "I hope so." He smiled to himself. They had just been discussing wars and duels as institutions.

The colonel was looking up at the lamp again, and then he suddenly looked down at Chance.

"Did you know," he asked, "that most of the other bands of Sioux and Cheyenne came in because they heard the Hunkpapa and Minneconjou got through safely?"

"No," said Chance, "but I'm glad."

"Hundreds of lives were saved," said the colonel.

"I'm glad," said Chance.

"I understand you were in the Bad Lands with the Hunkpapa and Minneconjou," said the colonel.

"For a time," said Chance.

The colonel was looking off through the window again, lost in thought. "They seem to respect you," he said. "They seem to trust you."

Chance said nothing.

The colonel turned to face him. "How's your shoulder?" he inquired.

Chance looked down at his arm, the white sling. "Fair," he said.

Chance was a bit puzzled. He wondered what the colonel was driving at.

"How soon before you'll be able to assume your duties?" asked the colonel.

Chance sat upright. "What duties?" he asked.

"She hasn't told you?" inquired the colonel.

"No," said Chance.

"Oh," said the colonel.

"My wife and I are going to California," said Chance.

"Of course," said the colonel. "California."

"I'm free to go, am I not?" asked Chance.

The colonel picked up a wooden, steel-pointed pen on the desk, fiddled with it a moment, tapped it twice on the desk and laid it back in its tray, between the two brass inkwells. He looked at it for a minute or so, then picked it up again.

He dipped it into the inkwell on the right side and scratched his signature on a slip of paper beneath two lines of writing.

He pushed the paper over to Chance and Chance picked it up and read it.

It was an authorization, giving him permission to travel across Standing Rock.

In effect, it said to him, You are Free.

"Thank you," said Chance, standing up. He placed the paper, folded carefully by his right hand on the desk, in his jacket pocket.

"That is, of course," the colonel said, "to be used only in case of need."

"I'm free to go, am I not?" asked Chance, wanting to check out this matter very carefully. Something in the colonel's attitude didn't strike him exactly right.

"Certainly," said the colonel. "You're going to California, that's it, isn't it?"

There was a kind of chuckle in the colonel's voice, which Chance did not quite care for.

"Yes," said Chance, regarding him somewhat narrowly, "that's right."

The colonel stood up and extended his hand. "We shall miss you at Standing Rock," he said.

Chance, puzzled, smiled. Over the desk the soldier and the physician shook hands.

"Well," said the colonel, brusquely, "before you leave, you'll want to say good-bye to your friends."

"Yes," said Chance, "I'd like that."

Now the colonel was straightening his neckerchief. He took his saber and revolver from a peg and belted them about himself. He put on his hat.

Chance followed the colonel from the small office.

They emerged on the roofed, wooden porch that fronted the building.

There Lucia, her yellow hair bright against a blue shawl, was waiting. With her was a white-haired, ruddy, handsome, well-built gentleman.

Lucia entered Chance's arms, lifting her face to him. She was happy.

He kissed her, gently holding her.

"It's all right," he whispered to her. "It's all right."

"I know," she said, "Mr. McLaughlin told me."

"I'm agent at Standing Rock," said the white-haired man, extending his hand. "My name is McLaughlin."

"My name is Edward Chance," said Chance. "I'm pleased to meet you." The two men shook hands.

"I'm only sorry," said McLaughlin, "that we can't afford to pay more."

"I don't understand," said Chance.

"But," said McLaughlin, "you'll have a free hand—no interference from me—you order what you need and we'll get it."

"I don't understand," said Chance.

"She hasn't told him yet," said the colonel to McLaughlin.

Lucia looked down, confused.

"What's this all about?" asked Chance.

"You're the new doctor at Standing Rock," said Lucia.

"The hell I am," said Chance.

McLaughlin looked puzzled. "The papers have already been processed," he said.

"I'm going to California," said Chance, firmly.

Lucia looked up at him. "Mr. McLaughlin is going to rebuild the school."

Chance looked down at her.

"Standing Rock needs a teacher," she said.

"Standing Rock," said Chance, "is no place for a woman."

"Certainly no place for a single woman," admitted Lucia.

"This is no place for you, Lucia," said Chance.

"It's actually rather nice," said Lucia. "There are large numbers of rattlesnakes; it never rains; there is a great deal of dust; the wind is always blowing; and this is where Edward Chance lives."

"I'm going to California," said Chance.

"Well," said Lucia, stoically, "if you insist on running off to California I shall certainly insist on running off after you."

Damn right, thought Chance. He wondered if it would be indecent to spank a fully grown woman.

"Before you leave," said Lucia, tipping her head up and kissing him, "you must of course say good-bye to your friends."

It would be hard, Chance thought, but I want to do it; I cannot leave otherwise.

Smiling, not letting go of his arm, Lucia guided Chance down the three wooden stairs from the porch and across the small dusty parade ground, toward the wooden gates of the fort. The colonel and McLaughlin followed.

Outside the gate Chance saw the Hunkpapa Sioux. With them were many other Indians he didn't know, except for a few of the Minneconjou who had fled to the Bad Lands with the Hunkpapa after Wounded Knee.

"Most of these Indians," McLaughlin was saying, "are Sioux—Hunkpapa, Minneconjou, Brule, Oglala—but there's Cheyenne in there, too, plenty of them."

"They want you to stay," said Lucia.

"You could make things easier for all of us," said the colonel.

"Well, Chance?" asked McLaughlin.

A boy pushed forward from the throng; it was William Buckhorn.

With his parents he had been at Fort Yates at the time of Sitting Bull's death; they had remained there, not fleeing; they had not been at Wounded Knee.

The boy came and stood before Chance and Chance asked him how he was feeling now, and the boy said all right.

Then the boy went to Lucia and tugged at her sleeve. He looked up at her, shyly. "I am well now," he said. "I will kill more rattlesnakes for you."

~~Lucia thought for a moment.~~

"Nonsense," she said, "from now on I will kill my own rattlesnakes—left and right."

Chance smiled.

William was looking up at her, puzzled.

"Yes," said Lucia grimly, "let them watch out for Lucia—let them watch out for Lucia Turner—" She looked at Chance, "—for Lucia Chance," she amended.

"You're crazy to hunt rattlesnakes," said William.

"Oh," said Lucia.

"You might get bit," said William.

"All right," said Lucia, confused, "then I won't hunt them."

"Good," said William Buckhorn. Then he added, "I won't either."

"Good," said Lucia.

"But can I have the rattles back?" asked William.

"Yes," said Lucia. She recalled that the baking-powder can behind the soddy had still been there.

"Thank you," said William, and then turned and went back to his parents.

"Well," said McLaughlin, "what about it, Chance?"

Chance regarded the Indians; naturally his eyes sought out the Hunkpapa among them; with them he had ridden; he had been with them when they had fought; he had, in his way, shared their struggle, their defeat; with them he had found food, shelter and friendship; among them he had won the woman he loved.

Near the front of the Indians, astride their ponies, were Old Bear, Running Horse and Winona.

"Medicine Gun!" shouted Old Bear proudly, lifting his right hand in greeting.

"Old Bear," said Chance, returning the sign.

Running Horse walked his pony to Chance. He pointed back to Winona, happily, who shyly dropped her head. "The Hunkpapa do not die," he said.

"No," said Chance, "the Hunkpapa do not die."

He wondered if the child would be Totter's or Running Horse's; somehow it did not matter all that much; the important thing was the child, that the woman was bearing within her promise and life. About Lucia he did not yet know. It was possible, of course, that his first child would be Drum's. He could imagine speaking to the boy one day, "Yes, I knew your father; he was by the mixings of blood my brother; I killed him." "No," said Chance to Running Horse, "the Hunkpapa—the people of Sitting Bull and Old Bear and Running Horse and Drum—do not die."

He put his arm about Lucia, happy and strong in her love and nearness.

"You know you must stay," she said.

"You might have told me," said Chance.

"It wouldn't have been a surprise," she said.

"You promised to be a good squaw," Chance reminded her.

"I shall make an excellent squaw," insisted Lucia. "It is also my intention," she said, "when you get around to asking me—to make an excellent wife."

"Marry me," said Chance.

"Say please," said Lucia.

"Please," said Chance.

"Pretty please," teased Lucia.

Chance decided, definitely, it would not be indecent, not at all, to spank a fully grown woman, especially a wench that deserved it like Lucia Turner, especially not if she were your wife, especially not if you could finish it up by removing her clothes and dropping her on the nearest bed.

"Nonsense," said Chance.

"All right," said Lucia, "I'll marry you anyway."

"Good," said Chance.

"Not that I have any choice," she said.

"Why not?" asked Chance.

"You didn't ask me like a true gentleman," she said, "you just said 'Marry me.'"

"So?" asked Chance.

"I must do what I'm told," said Lucia.

"Why is that?" asked Chance.

"Because," responded Lucia loftily, "I am an excellent squaw." She looked at him archly. "You have not forgotten, have you?"

Chance looked about, confused. The Indians were watching him. McLaughlin seemed puzzled. The colonel was looking off somewhere, studying cloud formations.

"Please, Lucia," whispered Chance.

"Have you forgotten?" demanded Lucia, one eyebrow quite high.

He kissed her to silence. "No," he mumbled, "excellent— excellent."

"Good rifle, good horse, good woman," Lucia was mumbling into his teeth.

"Please shut up," said Chance.

"Later," said Lucia breathlessly. "Please later."

"Pretty please," mumbled Chance.

"Pretty pretty pretty pretty please," said Lucia.

Mr. McLaughlin coughed rather loudly, twice, the second cough somewhat louder than even the first.

Chance disengaged Lucia's arms from his neck, which he had to do again.

"Well, Chance?" asked McLaughlin. "The proposition stands. What about it?"

Lucia was looking up at him.

"We want you here," said the colonel. He gestured to the gathered Indians. "They want you here—Medicine Gun."

Chance smiled.

"My fiancé," Lucia was saying, "is leaving immediately for California."

"Lucia, will you please shut up," said Chance.

"Certainly," said Lucia.

"You will stay with us, won't you?" asked McLaughlin.

"My Brother," said Running Horse, "you will not leave us?"

Chance looked at the young Indian.

"No," said Chance. "I will stay. You are my people."

McLaughlin was shaking his hand, and the colonel, and Lucia kissed him; the Indians were shouting; they stamped their feet and crowded about him, to touch and hold him.

Chance felt Lucia's lips against his cheek; she was crying; her warmth was marvelous in his arms; her happiness.

It was good, Chance decided, it was good.

Chapter Twenty-five

In the spring the grass came as usual to Standing Rock, thrusting itself up green between the melting snow and the black earth. The prairie became sweet and flowed with grass and wind. The Grand River, swollen in its banks, rushed its cold, muddy waters downstream to the wide Missouri.

The Messiah had not come and the Ghost Dance was only a memory of the Sioux.

On an April Sunday, a day the white men called Easter, Old Bear, a chief of the Hunkpapa, rode his pony across the sweet-smelling spring prairies.

He had not ridden very far when he stopped his pony and dismounted. Heavy and sharp in the damp earth was the print of a hoof, wide, deep and fresh. Old Bear knelt beside the print and bent close, inhaling even the smell of the earth in which the print lay. His heart leaped. In many years he had not seen such a print. It was the print of a buffalo. Most likely the animal had drifted south from Canada, separated or driven from its herd; probably for days it had been browsing southward across the North Dakota prairie; at last it had come to Standing Rock.

Old Bear began to follow the sign. He sang softly to himself as he rode, an old buffalo hunting song. His right hand carried his unstrung bow. The quiver at his side held four hawk-feathered arrows and one long, fine arrow, an eagle-feathered buffalo arrow which Old Bear had been saving for many years.

Toward noon his eye found a place where the buffalo had rubbed its back on an outcropping of stone. Old Bear trembled as he looked at the stone. Caught in the chinks of rock and fallen to the grass, here and there, were coarse hairs from the animal. These hairs were white. Old Bear had found, at last, the trail of the white buffalo, the Medicine Buffalo. He had seen the old robes that proved such animals

existed, but he had never spoken to a man who had seen one
alive.

Without stopping to eat or drink, Old Bear urged his pony
ahead in the hunt. At last, near dusk, he saw the animal
shambling along in front of him. It was a thin, shaggy buffalo, an old animal, a bull, one ready to die. It didn't hear
him nor did it smell him.

Old Bear, heart pounding, strung his bow quickly; he fitted
the long buffalo arrow to the string.

Trembling, Old Bear edged his pony close to the old animal, until they were side by side.

The old bull, its wide, pale eyes understanding nothing,
watched Old Bear draw his bow taut. For a long time Old
Bear held the bow taut, the arrow poised over the heart of
the bull. He watched the shaggy white hair lift and fall with
the beating of the heart; he listened to the buffalo's slow hard
breathing; he watched the muscles of its neck swell and fall.

At last Old Bear lowered his arm, slowly relaxing the bow.
"Old Warrior," he said, "do not be afraid. I will not kill
you."

Old Bear unstrung his bow and put the long buffalo arrow
back in his quiver. Then he turned his pony and began to
ride slowly away, leaving behind him the thin, shaggy bull.
The animal stood, its hoofs planted wide in the dust,
watching him go. There would be no white robe in the lodge
of Old Bear. The time of the white robes was gone.

Gone too were the days of painted horses and the feathers
of eagles; the days of Kills-His-Horse and of Drum, his son;
Old Bear lifted his hands to the sky; the Messiah had not
come; the wire remained on the prairie; the buffalo had not
returned. Tears from the eyes of the old man fell in the mane
of his pony.

Weeping he rode from the place where he had found and
spared the white buffalo.

He would go home now, letting the white buffalo go where
it might, untroubled, eating what grass and drinking what
water it could.

He rode away, weeping.

He would go home now. The hunt was done.

Presenting MICHAEL MOORCOCK
in DAW editions